Dark Rhapsody

Also by Helaine Mario

The Lost Concerto

Firebird

Dark Rhapsody

A NOVEL

HELAINE MARIO

OCEANVIEW PUBLISHING
SARASOTA, FLORIDA

This book is a work of fiction. Names, characters, businesses, organizations, places, and incidents either are the products of the author's imagination or are used fictitiously. Any resemblance to actual events, businesses, locales, or persons living or dead, is entirely coincidental.

ISBN 978-1-60809-351-9

Published in the United States of America by Oceanview Publishing
Sarasota, Florida

www.oceanviewpub.com

10 9 8 7 6 5 4 3 2

PRINTED IN THE UNITED STATES OF AMERICA

For my parents, Helaine and Gerard Swarbrick, with love
This one's for you

For my five beautiful grands, who fill my world with joy—
Ellie and Tyler Danaceau
Clair Violet, Declan, and Ian Mario
Always remember where you came from
(And, Darlings, don't ever forget there's magic!)

And for RJ. More than you can imagine

"A musical composition of irregular form having an improvisatory character"

ACKNOWLEDGMENTS

Once again, I want to acknowledge—and express my heartfelt appreciation for—our service men and women, and their families, for their remarkable patriotism, bravery, strength, and sacrifice. Colonel Beckett and Simon Sugarman could not have "come to life" without their stories and inspiration.

I am most grateful to five people whose thoughtful comments, suggestions, and support made *Dark Rhapsody* so much better: William Rosner, MD, and Barbara Rosner; Deborah Schiff; Sue Kinsler; and, most especially, classical pianist Betty Bullock of Washington, DC, who so generously shared her knowledge, expertise, experiences, and emotions in the world of music. While any musical mistakes would be mine, Betty answered my countless questions with honesty and grace, enriching Maggie's world as, chord by chord, Rachmaninoff's Rhapsody became the heart of her story.

A special thank-you, also, to Stella—a beautiful three-legged rescue dog in Georgia who was the inspiration for Shiloh.

Finally, a very personal acknowledgement to Pat and Bob Gussin and their team at Oceanview Publishing for their remarkable publishing and writing skills, and love of books. Thank you for continuing to believe in Maggie's story.

Dark Rhapsody

OPENING CHORDS

MAY 1945
THE AUSTRIAN ALPS

THE REMOTE ALPINE lake framed in the loft window was long, narrow, and as still as black glass. Snow-topped mountains ringed the lake like guardians, their heavily wooded slopes rising steeply from the water's edge, their jagged peaks etched against the cobalt sky.

A slight, fair-haired girl gazed toward the lake, her cheek pressed against the cold glass of the barn's window. Just below her, the courtyard where she'd hidden her bicycle in the juniper bushes was in deep shadow. If she tilted her head, she could see the front porch of her aunt's steep-roofed home, nestled into the blackness of the forest. All the lights were off.

Her eyes found the rutted track that twisted down through the pines to the lake. She knew how deep the lake was. How cold. She shivered beneath her heavy loden coat, her breath misting on the icy window as she reached for a tattered woolen blanket left on the warped wooden floor.

Gathering the blanket around her shoulders, she looked down and saw that it had covered a pile of torn candy wrappers, a chipped mug, and a man's forgotten glove. She remembered the story of a Yank who had spent two nights hiding here in March, on his way north to Berlin. She had asked her aunt about him once, but her aunt had held up a warning hand.

Hush, Gisela, you must never speak of him again. It is too dangerous for all of us.

Then her aunt had turned back to the stove and continued to stir her *Rindsuppe.*

And now, just two months later, Berlin was burning. She'd heard it on her parents' radio.

Did the glove belong to the Yank? Something glinted beneath it, and she pushed the leather aside. A knife! Long, some fifteen centimeters, the span of her hand with her fingers spread. She held it up to the loft window. Sharp, and stained a dark, rusty red.

Had the Yank killed a Nazi with this knife?

Gisela tucked the blade into her belt and pulled the blanket more tightly around her. She would show it to Johann when he arrived.

Below her, past the shaky wooden ladder, she could hear the huff and snorting of the workhorses, restless in their stalls.

Almost eleven o'clock. Where was Johann?

She had pedaled from the village, just over the hill, an hour ago. Had he forgotten? But they always met here on Friday nights, to plan their weekend adventures. She would climb out her window after her parents were asleep—well, she was ten, after all, she could take care of herself. And it was such fun to have a secret with Johann, two years older, more like a big brother than a friend. Sometimes, he would bring paper and chalks, and sketch her face—her hair pulled back with a ribbon, large dark eyes gazing at him. Or her profile by the window, the lake icy and shining behind her. He made her look . . . older, beautiful. Different.

She gazed down at the silent, empty courtyard. *Where are you, Johann?*

A sound. A soft rumble. Not a bicycle. *Not Johann.*

She sat very still, chin raised, listening. The rumble grew louder.

Thunder?

No. Engines. Trucks.

She peered out the window. Darkness. No headlamps.

A sudden shaft of moonlight speared through the clouds, skimming across the black lake so that it shimmered like a silvered mirror. A convoy of three trucks pulled slowly into the courtyard.

The murmur of worn brakes, engines turning off. Silence.

Gisela pressed back against the wall, out of sight, fear welling in her throat.

Doors opening and closing. Guttural voices, the stamp of boots. She inched toward the window once more, peered cautiously over the sill. Flashlight beams probed the air. She counted nine men, most of them tall, with long dark coats and capped hats.

The light beams caught the trucks. She could see the fearsome letters, *SS*, and the double lightning strikes of the Nazis, emblazoned on the sides. What were they doing *here*, in this remote forest so high in the Alps?

One of the men climbed the porch steps, pounded on the door. Panic iced down her spine. *Don't answer the door, Ida,* she begged her cousin silently. *Hide!*

More pounding, harder. "*Aufwachen!* Wake up! Open the door immediately!"

A light came on upstairs.

The man turned toward the barn, lifting his face just as the porch light winked on. In that moment, Gisela glimpsed the shine of his eyes under the cap. Even from a distance, they glinted like chips of ice caught in the light of the lamp. Blue ice, she imagined, cold as the lake.

The front door of the house swung open and her cousin Ida, wrapped in her old pink robe, stepped into the light. Gisela held her breath. Questions, demands in German. Ida shaking her head, then nodding, pointing. Toward the barn!

A sharp command, her cousin disappearing behind the door, the porch lights suddenly out.

Gisela shrank back against the loft wall and closed her eyes.

The barn door squealing open, a curse, the gleam of flashlights. Light through the broken floorboards touched her face. She pressed her hands against her mouth to keep from crying out.

A scrape, a high whinny. The jingle of a bridle. The slow clip-clop of two horses being led from the barn.

The creak of ancient wheels.

The cart? They were taking the horse-drawn cart. For what?

She waited. When she was sure they'd left the barn, she dared to look out the window once more.

Two of the soldiers were hitching the horses to the wagon. Others had opened the rear doors of the trucks and were unloading boxes with swastikas and numbers painted on the sides. She squinted through the darkness. Most of the boxes looked to be metal—iron? A meter or more in length. Like small trunks. Or treasure chests. And heavy.

Gold? She'd heard the rumors in the village. Gold and silver, secrets and treasures being hidden high in the Austrian Alps while Berlin burned.

She watched the men load dozens of chests onto the cart. Then they pulled on the harness and the cart trundled down the winding track toward the lake.

The lake, she thought. *They are going to hide their gold in the lake.*

She watched as the cart turned the bend and disappeared into the forest. There were three old rowboats on the edge of the water, she remembered suddenly. The men would row out to the center of the lake, drop the boxes in the deepest water. Her aunt said it was over one hundred meters deep there. No one would ever find those chests.

Almost all of the soldiers had gone with the horse cart—only one had stayed behind to guard the trucks. His tall silhouette wandered to the far side of the courtyard, turning toward the lake. She saw the bright red ember of his cigarette, arcing through the shadows.

Hurry, she thought, *get your bike, be gone before he returns to the trucks.* She stood up, clambered down the ladder, and slipped quietly into the shadowed courtyard.

Dozens of boxes were still piled on the ground by the trucks, waiting to be brought down to the lake. Dodging behind the first truck, she stopped, looked around.

Gold.

She could not resist. Cloaked by the darkness, she touched the lid of the closest box. Sealed. She grasped the handle, pulled. Too big. Too heavy.

Another.

Another.

Then, behind them, she saw the smaller box, just over a meter in length. She reached for it. Not so heavy. She eased it toward her.

High above the alpine peaks, the clouds blew open like a curtain, and she gazed down at the metal box, glinting silver now in shafts of pale moonlight. The lock felt cold beneath her fingers. Her eyes widened as she realized that the lock had not fully caught.

And in that moment, she made a decision that would change the course of her life forever.

She did not think about her cousin, her aunt, Johann, or even the danger to herself. She grasped the box, clutched it to her chest, and ran into the barn, setting it down in the back corner of the farthest stall.

Very carefully, she eased off the lock.

She would take just one bar of gold, for her mother. The soldiers would never miss it. Then she would return the box to the truck, and no one would ever know.

Holding her breath, she raised the lid slowly, expecting the bright shine of precious metal. But the chest held only a long mahogany case and, beneath it, dozens of papers rolled up like her mother's best hand-sewn pillowcases. She shook her head in fierce disappointment. But perhaps the treasure was in the case?

Flicking the silver latch of the wooden case, she opened the lid and peered inside. A violin, nestled in soft gray velvet. Johann's father was a musician, as she wanted to be. He gave her piano lessons after school and played in the village band on Friday nights—three men, two violins, and a cello.

Where was the gold?

She snapped the case closed, shifted it aside, and reached for one of the paper rolls. It was a bit longer than her *Opa*'s cane, thick and grainy, rough beneath her fingertips. Not paper. Canvas. Like the canvases Johann used when he painted the mountains.

A shaft of moonlight fell through the stall's high window, and she saw words printed in Italian on the rolled canvas in her hand. *Proprieta di Felix Hoffman Galleria, Firenze* 1943. Firenze was . . . Florence?

Florence, she thought, picturing sunlight on golden spires. Her mother had told her stories about Italy. *Someday, I will visit Florence.* Very slowly, she began to unroll the canvas.

A tall window, filled with the shimmering dark blue of a night sky.

Something unfamiliar stirred in her chest, and she exposed more of the painting. A woman, seated by the window, her long black hair falling like a curtain down one side of her face. Her eyes were closed. She was playing a cello, just like the one Johann's father played in his band. A single candle flickered on the table beside the woman, casting golden light and deep shadow across her face.

Gisela stared down at the hauntingly beautiful face. Who was she? What music was she playing? Gisela closed her eyes and listened, half expecting to hear the deep cello notes . . .

The rumble of the empty cart. Coming back up the path!

Panic seized her. *Leave!* No time to replace the box. She rolled up the canvas, shoved it back into the chest with the violin case, and pushed the chest under an old horse blanket.

Then she ran outside. The moon was gone now, the courtyard in deep shadow. She wrenched her bike from the bushes.

A footstep behind her. A hand, gripping her shoulder.

She spun around and looked up into eyes of blue ice.

MOOD INDIGO

"Music is the art which is most nigh to tears and memory."

— Oscar Wilde

CHAPTER ONE

THE PRESENT
THE BLUE RIDGE MOUNTAINS, VIRGINIA
OCTOBER 15

THE CABIN PERCHED on the edge of the mountain, surrounded by tall whispering pines. A broad redwood deck cantilevered out over the steep hillside like the prow of a ship.

Maggie O'Shea stood still as a statue against the railing, watching the geese fly south, high overhead. The last sunlight of the day slanted over the mountain peak in bright rays, lighting the tips of the high firs like candles and turning the wings of the geese to flame as they vanished beyond the blue mountain.

Hurry, she told the wild birds. *Already I feel the cold coming. Hurry . . .*

A new wave of exhaustion washed over her as her eyes searched the lake.

Not far from the shore, an arched fishing pole flashed silver in the light. A man and a dog sat hunched in a gently rocking rowboat, stark silhouettes against the darkening sky.

A deep tenderness for the man welled inside Maggie and she smiled, knowing by heart the words on the old baseball cap pulled low over his forehead: *Fish Fear Me.*

Her eyes followed the steep wooden steps that wound down through the pines to the crescent of rocky beach. Her breath caught as she remembered the first time he'd led her up those stairs by the hand, just two weeks earlier, with his Golden Retriever ahead of them leading the way. A night as blue as this one, but softened by a curve of orange moonlight.

"We're home, Maggie," he'd whispered against her hair.

Despite his injuries, he had gathered her in his arms and carried her over the threshold like a bride. White lilacs had filled the room, their petals falling like snow on the carpet. They had made love for the first time on those petals, in front of the fire.

Michael had known Chopin was her favorite composer, and had surprised her that night with a CD of the *Piano Concerto No. 2.* She had watched him come toward her as the opening chords filled the room, the hard planes of his face catching the firelight. Now that indescribably beautiful, impassioned music would always be linked in her mind with that first night in the mountains.

She'd seen it in the silvery eyes, glinting down at her like stones. Heard it in his soft Virginian voice, felt it in his touch—the need to love her in a place that wouldn't remind her of her husband.

But the reminders still ambushed her. She looked down at the envelope in her hand. Her mail had been forwarded from her home in Boston and arrived an hour earlier. Bills, announcements, invitations to concerts, the Boston Symphony newsletter. And then—an envelope from a news organization addressed to her late husband, Johnny O'Shea. Almost one year after his death.

One year . . . I still love you, Johnny, I always will. But now . . .

Now, Colonel Michael Beckett was in her life. Alone on the high deck, Maggie looked out at the indistinct shapes floating on the dark water. The colonel's face was hidden, but she knew every plane and angle under the old cap. The battered, hard face. Spiky peppered brows drawn over storm-gray, distant eyes. He was like his mountains, she thought. Hard as granite, towering as the pines, with eyes like river stones.

These last two weeks, she'd lived with him here in the shadow of his beloved Blue Ridge Mountains—this proud, scarred man with the darkness always at the back of his eyes—learning about him and watching the September-green leaves turn slowly to russet and bright amber.

Now the mountain air was bitter-cold with the hint of first snow, and the last leaves were about to fall. She thought of the short story she'd read late into the night—"The Last Leaf"—when the dreams invaded and sleep once again eluded her.

I won't leave you until the last leaf falls, Michael.

That had been her silent promise. But the call from Carnegie Hall had come this afternoon. She needed to be in New York; she had to leave first thing in the morning. *How do I tell him?*

And what would he do when she left? She knew the answer, deep in her bones. *He would go after Dane.*

An image of Dane's cruel face spun into her head. He was always there, like a wolf watching her from a curtain of fog. Waiting.

Shivering with a sudden, cold foreboding, she raised her eyes. Above her, the huge vault of sky shimmered with the deep indigo blue of twilight. Without warning, the sky exploded with wild roaring and the light became a drowning, fearful blue, a blue that had flooded like spilled ink into her dreams since childhood.

Panic stirred in her chest, and she felt the first waves of pain behind her eyes. With an oath, she turned and ran back toward the sanctuary of the lamp-lit cabin.

The high-beamed room wavered with firelight. This was Michael's refuge, a beautiful room of glowing red woods, huge windows, and handmade bookcases—as dark and rough-hewn as the colonel himself. Tonight, the room smelled like autumn, spicy-sharp with the scent of chrysanthemums and apples piled high in a deep earthen bowl. Soft leather chairs were drawn close to the fireplace, and her eyes were drawn, as always, to the framed quote by John Muir above the mantle. *The Mountains are Calling and I Must Go.* Yes, they suited this man she was coming to love.

In the far corner of the room, a circular staircase disappeared into the bedroom loft. Just looking at those stairs brought a faint flush of heat to Maggie's skin.

Reaching unconsciously for the small pink rubber ball on the table, Maggie began to squeeze it in her right hand the way the physical therapist had taught her. Her eyes sought, as always, the old Baldwin grand piano set against the rear picture window. The dark-visaged colonel, whose musical taste ran to guitar, country, and blues, had bought the piano for her in a secondhand shop in Front Royal, surprising her that first night in the mountains.

The piano will help you heal, Maggie.

"Surely you haven't abandoned Otis and BB King, Michael?" she'd teased him, overwhelmed by his uncharacteristic tenderness.

"Mozart may not be the sharpest knife in my drawer, ma'am," he'd answered gruffly, "but he tends to grow on you."

She had tried to play that piano for hours every day, willing her weakened fingers to grow strong again, while Shiloh, the Golden, slept at her feet and the great picture window glowed like a painting as the sky spun from day to night. Twelve major scales, thirty-six minor scales, fingering, technique. Over and over. Maggie looked down at her slender fingers clutching the rubber ball and walked slowly toward the old piano, allowing the memories to flow like a sonata into her mind.

Only one year earlier, she'd believed her life was settled. She'd been happy and filled with purpose, a wife and mother of a married son, owner of The Piano Cat Music Shop in Boston, and an acclaimed concert pianist. Then her godson had disappeared. Her husband, Johnny, had flown to Europe to search for the child, and her life had changed in one shattering October night when Johnny's boat had exploded on a faraway sea. That night, with the horrific words of a stranger's phone call, grief had enveloped her in a numbing, haunted smoke.

Her husband's death had been the beginning of a terrifying journey that eventually led her to France—and to the dark, fierce-browed colonel. Angry and remote at first, more adversary than protector, still, somehow, he had understood her pain. And, in the end, had found a way to ease her sorrow.

But not before she crossed paths with Dane.

Maggie shuddered as she sat down on the piano bench and held out her hands toward the flames of the fire. The heat felt good on her fingers, taking away for just a moment the image of a brutal monster with a wolf's face and eyes the color of yellow ice.

Dane.

Months earlier he had attacked her on a beach in southern France, and she'd been fighting off the memories of those eyes ever since. And finally, as she forced her fingers to move again and again over the keys here in the refuge of the mountains, the music lost to her for so long began to return.

But still the nightmares came.

Maggie bowed her head. For a time, she'd even dared to believe that the always-hovering violence of the colonel's life was behind them.

We dared the gods, she thought. *I should have known.*

Because just last night, while searching for a pen, she had opened his nightstand drawer and seen the gun. Black, shining, deadly.

Pop! Pop! Pop!

She'd jerked back as the memory of quick loud shots crashed into her head.

I almost killed a man in France, she thought. *I wanted to.*

Was it any wonder she couldn't sleep? Any wonder the headaches were growing stronger? Maggie gazed into the red embers of the fire as if she could find the answers she sought. But all she saw was Dane's face, smiling at her through the flames. And then, rising from the hiss of the embers, she heard the last words Dane had spoken against her hair, the whispery, terrifying voice of her nightmares echoing like a Bach fugue in her head.

I will come for you, Magdalena. And I will break your fingers one by one.

God. No. That part of her life was over.

Wasn't it?

CHAPTER TWO

A VILLAGE IN TUSCANY, ITALY
LATE NIGHT, OCTOBER 15

THE MAN STOOD at the narrow-arched window, gazing out across the vineyards that fell away in undulating waves beneath him. The midnight moon was full tonight, spilling on the purple vines and hillsides in a river of silver light. He had been staring at these hills day and night for weeks. Waiting. Waiting.

He shook his head as he turned away from the window. "My home was a white cube on a cliff overlooking an azure sea," he murmured, "with the sun so bright it blinded me." Now, all he saw every morning were browns, faded yellows, dusty green.

But all the pain and loss would be worth it. Interpol had the photos of his old face. Not the new one.

He moved across the peaked attic room toward the single cracked mirror over the basin, his bare feet soundless on the tiles. The face staring back at him was a mummy's face, swathed in broad white bandages, with only holes for his nostrils and his right eye. The golden tiger-colored iris glittered back at him with a cold, angry light.

He needed at least two more surgeries, but that fool of a doctor had sealed both their fates when he threatened to go to the *Policia*. *Il Dottore's* funeral had been held just that morning, attended, he'd been told, by the whole village.

The local newspaper had run an unheard-of special edition—*Farewell, Il Dottore*. A terrible accident, they reported, describing in excruciating detail the late hour, the treacherous mountain road, the brakes in the old truck worn beyond repair.

Rest in peace, Il Dottore. You should never have threatened me.

"What's done is done," he murmured, turning away from the mirror. His face no longer mattered. Now, it was time to move on. Finding the art was his number-one priority. He had to have those paintings if he was to take control of the business. The opening act would begin in Rome, where he would make the first of the many moves in the intricate dance to take back his life.

He reached for the newspaper he'd tossed onto the table. It was a three-day-old edition of the *International Tribune*, folded to the arts page. He found the article he'd circled just hours earlier, and smiled. An invitation-only Old Masters auction at *La Galleria dalla Chiesa* in Rome on October 23.

Perfect. All the black-market art dealers would be there. He would plan his attack for October 23, in Rome. Send a message, loud and clear. Show the buggers who should be in charge now that Victor Orsini was dead.

The patient reached for his iPhone. He still needed the new identity papers. Then he could open bank accounts under his new name, get fitted for contact lenses, color his hair, arrange transportation to Rome.

His first call was to Angelo Farnese—"the Angel"—the Roman black market art dealer known to have the best connections with the wealthiest private collectors and clients. The man who wanted, at all costs, to maintain control of the stolen art market—and the enormous wealth and power that went with it. The man who had told Dane he was *not welcome* to attend the meeting of the art dealers.

And so, using an assumed name, Dane arranged a meeting on October 23 to discuss the private sale of a Botticelli, at the Angel's gallery in the Piazza Navona. *La Galleria dalla Chiesa*—The Art Gallery by the Church.

The cost may be higher than you thought, Angel.

Then, pressing a series of international numbers, he placed a call to his contact in the United States. "I have two jobs for you, Thanos." A nervous, murmured response. "I didn't kill you when I could have. I thought I might need you some day. Now that day has come. Go to New York and wait for my instructions."

Finally, his business done, he turned once more toward the casement window. By week's end, the bandages would come off. He would make his way to Rome, and his new life would begin. He would take back the power that was rightfully his; he would find the art that had been ripped from him. And the woman who destroyed his life—who took away his face, his future—would suffer before he took her life.

"A kiss long as my exile, sweet as my revenge," he quoted softly.

The moon's light fell in golden bars through the high window, sending wavering patterns of dark and bright across the tiles. He reached into his duffel bag, searching for the CDs he always carried with him. Beethoven's *Moonlight Sonata* would be perfect for tonight.

Finding his choice, he slipped the disc into the ancient player, careful to keep the volume low. The soft notes of the first movement flooded into the room. Evocative, surely. Nocturnal. But the pianist was brilliant. She understood that the music was not describing the romance of moonlight but a mood far more mournful. Ghostly. A lamentation.

He remained still, listening and remembering. He pictured a long, light-filled gallery, lined with the most beautiful paintings he had ever seen. A ballerina in green tulle tying her slipper. A busy Parisian square at twilight. A portrait of an Italian Renaissance youth. And, of course, the Klimt.

Degas, Pissarro, Raphael, Klimt. Just four of the dozens of paintings, looted from a Jewish art dealer named Hoffman in World War II, that his mentor Victor Orsini had found hidden in his mother's Italian villa. Where were all those exquisite paintings now? Orsini was dead, the villa long ago burned to the ground, the priceless Hoffman Collection hidden away once again—somewhere—just before Orsini's death.

The second movement of the sonata began. He leaned back on the narrow bed and let the memories flow. *A lavender field beyond an old abbey, a thunderstorm in the hills. A violent and brutal fight with an American colonel, a scorching lighter flame held to his hand.* The patient looked down at his hands. The burn scars, ridged like thick, bright red worms, would never heal. He would have to wear gloves when he left the village.

Now Beethoven's third movement began, the most powerful of the three. The storm of notes flung into the air, the unbridled arpeggios, the ferocity. The music as astonishing as the pianist who played the chaotic notes with such breathtaking intensity. He flexed his fingers, closed his eyes, and saw a woman's green eyes, looking into his with fear and loathing, her body struggling beneath him. *Saw the silver flash of his dagger . . .*

He lifted the CD case, held it beneath the light of the candle. The pianist's face gazed back at him, flickering in the shadows, almost alive. Beautiful, ethereal, with deep emerald eyes and hair that was black as a starless night. The woman responsible for his scars, his pain. His exile. For Interpol's freezing of his bank accounts and chasing him to ground for murder. She had taken away his life.

No more. Now he would watch her suffer.

"The past is prologue," whispered Dane. "I am coming for you, Magdalena O'Shea."

CHAPTER THREE

THE BLUE RIDGE MOUNTAINS, VIRGINIA
OCTOBER 15

"YOU'VE SCARED OFF all the damn trout again, Shiloh."

The Golden Retriever, a three-legged dog rescued from Afghanistan and still fearful of most humans, gazed at him with a sorrowful expression.

"Yeah, you're right, trout has too many bones anyway." Colonel Michael Jefferson Beckett scowled at the dog as he reeled in the line. He'd expected a look of satisfaction. Of "gotcha." The dog had been doing so well. Until now—he was losing weight, just wasn't himself these last few days. Beckett looked down at the sad eyes, the soft ears folded back. What was going on?

Depression comes and goes, he reminded himself. Even for animals.

The Golden struggled to his feet, his aging limbs stiff, and Beckett felt his heart twist in his chest. "We're just a couple of old dogs," he murmured, "going grayer by the day." It was getting late. Beckett turned to search the mountainside.

The deck was empty now. Nothing but blowing leaves, dark shapes in the dusky shadows. She'd gone inside.

But he'd watched her as she stood alone on the balcony, so still, with the maple leaves falling around her like scarlet rain and the setting sun burnishing her hair with fire. Hair the color of a mountain night sky. Gazing out over the water, like the oil painting of a woman he'd seen in the National Gallery—mysterious, complex, and very, very beautiful. A woman of haunting grace. What had she been thinking?

He grinned as he pictured her lifting her head to watch the geese. She loved watching the wild birds—but always worried that they were flying in the wrong direction.

"You are still a piece of work, Maggie O'Shea," he murmured.

He'd fallen for her the first moment he'd laid eyes on her, without knowing it, in an old Paris cemetery lit by the violet light of dawn. Slender as a birch tree, small and pale as winter sunlight, with a voice like a bass guitar that a man couldn't get out of his mind. And—the most remarkable eyes he'd ever seen. Shining with intelligence. Green as river moss.

Speaking eyes.

When he'd first met her, she'd been grief-stricken. And haunted. He'd watched as she'd come slowly, fiercely back to life, brave and strong as Persephone returning from a cold dark world.

And then he had betrayed her.

Beckett's breath came out in a harsh gasp. It was his fault she'd almost been killed in France. Now the killer was still out there, somewhere. And Dane was a man who sought vengeance. Beckett had followed him for weeks, coming close, but lost the trail in Greece. And then last week, the untraceable text appeared on his cell phone.

I am coming for her.

To take away the one thing a man fears losing . . . it was the ultimate revenge. What the devil should he do now? Because Dane *would* come for Maggie. There was no doubt in Michael Beckett's mind.

Unless I stop him first.

Beckett's fist hit against the old boat in frustration. He thought of the gun near the bedside, and reached for the oars. The familiar pain speared like hot pokers through his chest.

"I'm still putting her in harm's way," he said to the Golden. Shiloh turned to gaze thoughtfully up at the cabin in the woods.

Beckett clamped his teeth together and pulled on the oars, ignoring the fire that shot through his body. The air was blue with twilight as he turned the boat toward the shore. His eyes found the cabin windows through the pines. He thought he saw Maggie's shadow move across the lamp-lit glass.

I wish you were right here beside me now, Maggie.

But that would never happen, he knew. She was deathly afraid of water—he'd seen it for himself the day he'd tried to get her to board a Parisian houseboat moored in the Seine. Paralyzed with terror. And now—she steered well clear of the lake, wouldn't swim, or step a foot into his rowboat. He'd thought that it was caused by her husband's drowning. Well, maybe. *Or maybe not*. Something told him this fear ran deeper. One more piece of the intricate puzzle that was Maggie O'Shea.

All he knew now was that something was wrong with her. She was too pale, too damned skinny, skittish as a cat in a room full of hound dogs. Lately the huge eyes that looked into his seemed bright with pain and fever, like moons under green water.

He reached to ruffle the Golden's fur. "You and I, we're both vets. We know more than we want to about PTSD, don't we, boy? We've seen too much death," he murmured, trying not to think of the carnage they had witnessed together in Afghanistan. And the post-traumatic stress that had followed.

Like night follows day, he thought.

Maggie, too, had been through a horrific trauma. And she wasn't ready to talk.

First, he knew, she would pour her feelings into the piano . . .

The rowboat scraped against the stony beach. Now it was the only sound disturbing the quiet, the song of the geese only a memory. Shiloh lurched out, then stopped and waited for Beckett. The colonel gripped a heavy wooden cane and grunted with pain as he climbed slowly over the bow.

In the blue dusk, his eyes searched for the wooden steps that climbed the steep hillside through the pines up to the cabin. How the devil was he supposed to protect her when he still couldn't even run up a bloody flight of stairs?

He'd *built* those steps! And now . . . His three-legged dog climbed them faster than he did.

A storm of piano chords broke the stillness.

He stopped and raised his chin to listen. "Beethoven," he said to the Golden. "Damn if I'm not learning to recognize those crazy long-hairs."

Shiloh's intelligent eyes turned to Beckett and he gave a long, low woof.

"You're right," said the colonel. "She only plays Beethoven when she's troubled." *Or afraid . . .*

He felt suddenly hollow inside, sensing, somehow, that she'd be leaving him soon, that their time together here in the cabin was coming to an end. He wanted her to stay. But he knew deep in his bones he would have to let her go.

His cell phone buzzed in his pocket and he stiffened. Another text from Dane? He checked the number, squinting in the fading light. Not Dane. "The third call today from DC," he said. "Not good."

As if he knew what was coming, Shiloh's ears laid back and he growled low in his throat.

CHAPTER FOUR

THE BLUE RIDGE MOUNTAINS
OCTOBER 15

THE ONLY SOUND in the cabin was the music pulsing from the old Baldwin.

Beckett moved to stand behind her, setting his big hands on her shoulders. Her bones felt like sharp wings under his fingers. "Jazz? I've never heard you play jazz before. What is this piece?"

She kept playing, filling the room with a tumble of heartbreaking chords.

"I know you're hurting, darlin'." His hands tightened on her shoulders. "What's going on in that beautiful mind of yours?"

Maggie's fingers stilled. The notes hung in the air, unfinished. She spoke into the sudden silence. "It's Duke Ellington's 'Mood Indigo.' He played it every single night for years, always improvising, until he died."

The low resonant voice stirred him, as it always did. He raised a finger to her chin, gently turned her face toward him. "Talk to me."

A soft sigh escaped her lips as she raised her eyes to his. "For so long my life was ordered, logical. Like the notes of classical music. But since last year . . . it's all about improvising."

"Like 'Mood Indigo.'"

"I'm not good at improvising, Michael." She reached for the envelope she'd set on the edge of the piano and held it out. "This came with my forwarded mail."

He glanced at the address, felt himself go still. "It's addressed to your husband."

"It's been almost a year, and I still get ambushed. I don't know what I'm feeling . . ."

"Looks like grief to me."

She turned rain-filled eyes on him. "Maybe it's too soon to be happy again."

"No. We lose people, we find new ones. Your husband died, Maggie, but *you didn't.* I know you still love him, but if you keep loving a ghost, you can end up being a ghost yourself."

A flash, deep within the green eyes.

"Christ, Maggie, I didn't mean—"

"Yes, you did. And you're right." Very carefully, she set the envelope back on the piano. "I still get mail for my dead husband, my best friend was knifed in a chapel, my godson vanished, my music left me, I spent months talking to a ghost. You were shot, I almost drowned, and—oh, yes—I almost killed a man. Just an average day in the life of the woman you have fallen for. Why on earth would you want to be with me, Michael?"

"Because I've done worse, darlin'." He tucked a strand of hair behind her ear. "Grief doesn't make us noble, Maggie, just crazy. We've both lost people we love, lost our way. We've both been broken. But that's how the light gets in, right? In spite of everything, you make me feel optimistic about my life for the first time ever. I know this last year has been hell for you, Maggie, I see the chaos in your eyes. But Winston Churchill said, 'When you're going through hell, keep going.'"

Finally, she smiled. "The question is, go where?"

"For you, it's music. Just so long as you go with me. I know I'm not the best-looking tomato in the bunch, but . . ."

"But looking like Chopin is a *good* thing!"

"All these scars . . ."

"Just show where you've been. You're the best man I know, Michael." She gripped the edge of the piano. "Everything is swirling in my head. I just feel as if I've lost control of my life."

"For a while. But you're taking your life back, one note at a time. You're stronger than you realize. I've seen you fight the devil himself for a child you barely knew! What's really going on, Maggie?"

She shook her head mutely.

"I'm not married anymore, darlin'. Don't push me away."

Locking eyes with his, she took a deep breath and said, "I'm not the only one with secrets."

"My whole life is about things I can't say, Maggie. I told you that when we met."

"I found your gun. You're going after Dane again, aren't you?"

"I can't change who I am, dammit. Is that what you really want?"

"What I want is for you to not be in danger. Every intelligence agency in the world has been searching for Dane. It's been months, with no word. Dane is done with me. He's gone, Michael."

I am coming for her.

The words clicked into Beckett's brain, and he rubbed a hand across his jaw. "You don't know that, Maggie."

"I know *you*, Michael. I know that look. You have the same look on your face that you had the day I met you. You are off to fight the good fight once more and protect me. But I don't need protecting!"

"I've got to make some very tough calls in my work. I can't be worrying about how my choices make other people feel. I just need for you to be safe."

"But why would Dane go after me now? He would be crazy to come back, when everyone is looking for him."

"He *is* crazy, Maggie. He's a destroyer, a vicious sociopath with no conscience. You exposed him, you sent him into hiding, you've denied him all that stolen art. Hurt people hurt people. He wants vengeance. I'm not gonna let him get anywhere near you."

"Honorable but bone-headed," she murmured. "After everything he's done to me and the people I love, don't you think I want him to pay?"

"He will, Maggie, count on it."

"But not by your hands! I'm forty-eight, Michael. I've loved three men in my life. They all ended up in harm's way. You were shot. You almost died because of me. I *will not* lose you."

"You're not going to lose me, Maggie. Especially now." He smiled down at the Golden. "You heard her use the L-word, right?"

Maggie cupped his face in her hands. "After I lost Johnny, I thought I could never love again. Then I met you. My gruff, silver-eyed soldier." Her thumb rubbed across his lips. "All this—the cabin, the fire, the dog, the piano. The sound of your voice, these lips against my shoulder in our bed . . ."

"If only you could cook, ma'am, it would be perfect."

"Doesn't making toast count?" She boxed his arm gently. "I'm so damned happy when I'm with you. And that *terrifies* me. Because every time I've felt real love, it was the start of *losing* that person." Her breath caught. "Don't go after Dane," she whispered. "I don't want you to die for me, Michael. I want you to *live* for me."

"I will. Count on it."

"How did everything get so complicated?"

"You make boiling water look complicated," he said, taking her hands in his. "And it's okay. I'm scared, too. A man gets scared when he loves something enough to fear losing it. And the truth is, it's harder to love someone than to walk away from them." It was the closest he'd come to speaking his feelings in a very long time. "So we're different. I'm a distancer and you're a creator, that's just how life works. And maybe we'll blow it, but I want to try, Maggie."

He took a deep breath. *Just tell her.* "I know I'm not the first person you've loved," he said softly. "But I'd surely like to be the last."

She looked at him for a long moment. Finally, leaning closer, she touched her forehead to his. "Works for me. So what do we do now?"

"I just want to be with you. Watch the way you talk to the geese, the way your eyes shine in the morning light. Listen to your music. Take each day as it comes."

"I can't do that now," she whispered.

"You've got that bad-news look, ma'am."

"I'm going to have to leave you for a while, Michael."

He grew still. "You're going home to Boston?"

"New York. Carnegie Hall called."

He'd known she'd be leaving. But still the fear for her hit him like a punch in the chest. He wanted to say nothing, to let her go. "Call your Mr. Hall back," he said. "Tell him you're busy."

"If I can move on with my music, Michael, I can move on with my life."

"Dammit, woman, you'll be all alone in New York, and Dane is still out there." He exchanged a look with the Golden. "She's running in traffic again. With scissors!"

Refusing to smile, she turned to face him. "Look at these words. You bought this t-shirt for me, in France. *Je ne peux pas vivre sans musique*. I cannot live without music."

He frowned at the Golden, who sat protectively by Maggie's leg. "Life lesson, Shiloh. No good deed shall go unpunished." Then, with a slight smile, he turned his eyes on her. "The only thing I know about Carnegie Hall is that old Jack Benny joke—'How do you get to Carnegie Hall? Practice, practice, practice.'"

This time her smile was real. "Apparently one of the conductors said it after a very bad day."

Maggie walked away from him, out onto the balcony to stare across the darkening lake. He came up behind her and dropped a heavy woven blanket over her shoulders. Overhead, he heard the wings of the geese whispering against the purple sky.

She turned to look up at him. "Do you remember, Michael, one night in France? You told me, 'Sometimes we just have to do the right thing, like it or not.'"

"Why do I get the feelin', ma'am, that this is the part where I get hoisted on my own petard?"

"I happen to like your petard. And it won't be for long. Trust me, musician's honor."

"This trust business is new to me. Disorienting." He grinned. "But Shiloh and I will find a way to keep busy while you're gone, right, fella?" *I've got a bad feelin' we're going to DC.*

She touched his cheek. "I didn't know it would be so hard to leave you."

There was something in her voice, like the sound of rain on the lake.

He held her eyes for a long moment. Got lost in them. "Okay," he said gently. "No more talk of Dane. He's our past." He reached out, touched a finger to her mouth. "So let's concentrate on this moment. You said you don't have to leave until tomorrow morning?" He began to hum Bob Seger's song "We've Got Tonight."

She raised a feathery eyebrow, pulled the bright woven blanket closer around her, and smiled up at him.

"There is a Shenandoah Indian legend," he told her. "If a woman opens her blanket to a man, she wants to be with him."

Maggie kept her eyes locked on his as she opened the blanket like wings.

He stepped against her, and she wrapped her arms, and the blanket, around them both.

"Have you ever made love under the stars, Maggie O'Shea?"

"No," she told him. "Never outside, never like this."

"Come here, then." He led her to the double chaise and pulled her against him, kissing the inside of her wrist very slowly. Then, reaching for his phone, he pressed a button and suddenly the music of John Legend filled the night.

He eased her down onto the chaise. And then he was next to her, his hard mouth on hers, his hand slipping under her sweater to caress her rib cage.

He was falling into her. "Love your curves and edges . . ." he whispered against her skin.

Her eyes flew open. "You think I have edges?"

"Edges are *good*, Maggie. Being edgy makes you even more interesting . . ."

Somehow her sweater was gone. "I have only one question," he said against her bare shoulder. "How does a guy like me get to Carnegie Hall?"

She smiled into his eyes as she put her palm against his lips. Then she was lying on top of him, so that her hair fell like a dark curtain over his face.

His arms closed around her. He felt his blood singing. "You feel like home to me," he whispered.

And under the old blanket and the cold dark night, as the moon arced across the sky, he made love to her beneath the bare branches of ancient mountain oaks.

One last leaf fluttered down, until it was lost in the indigo shadows.

CHAPTER FIVE

NEW YORK CITY
FOUR DAYS LATER—SUNDAY, OCTOBER 19

MAGGIE O'SHEA RAN up the glass-walled staircase at Gansevoort Street, her Nikes hitting the steel steps with the quick steady beat of a metronome.

One step at a time. Just keep breathing.

Moments later, she emerged onto an aerial greenway, the High Line, a linear park elevated some thirty feet above Manhattan's streets. Built over a weedy, abandoned rail bed, the almost two-mile park ran north for some twenty blocks above New York's Tenth and Eleventh Avenues through Chelsea and the Meat-Packing District.

The soaring violins of Vivaldi's "Autumn," from his *Four Seasons* Concerti, spilled from her earphones. The Number 3 was her favorite of the four—and so appropriate on such a glorious fall day. She turned up the volume and ran on.

Only three more miles to 57th Street and Carnegie Hall. Or four? She smiled as she thought of Michael. How do you get to Carnegie Hall? She ran faster.

Today the hip-hop dancers and musicians were out in force along the narrow juniper-lined mall, their slouch hats and bright jackets catching the gleaming afternoon sun. She dodged around a mother with a wide stroller and ran on, past Chelsea Market, perched grandstands overlooking Tenth Avenue, and sundecks crowded with young New Yorkers. The architecture was modern, fanciful—zigzagging facades, abstract steel panels, glistening cylinders with angled glass panes catching the sun. And her favorite, Frank Gehry's curved glass schooner of a building near Eleventh Avenue.

Of course, running is good for the body, her doctor had told her. *But in your case, Maggie, it's good for the soul. It will help with the PTSD, the anxiety. The sleeplessness, the headaches. The nightmares.*

She'd been having the headaches and dreams since her husband had died, and they'd only grown worse after she'd been to France. Running hadn't stopped the recurring nightmares of a man with glittering wolf's eyes, holding a dagger to her breast. But she was able to hear a car backfire now without cringing into a fetal ball. She was taking back control. So why did she feel as if she was always just one deep breath away from panic?

As she ran, she squeezed the small pink rubber balls in her hands with rhythmic precision, keeping time with the beat of her Nikes. After so many months of disuse, her fingers were finally getting strong again. Inhaling deeply, Maggie filled her lungs with the sharp, clear scents of autumn. *Focus, Maggie. Concentrate on the good in your life.* Autumn in New York. Bright blue juniper berries crunching beneath her running shoes. Brilliant orange and gold leaves spinning in circles around her, as scattered and tossed as the images that swirled in her head.

Just don't think about today's date.

Think about the curved glass building shining gold in the sunlight.

Think about your son, his wife, and your sweet new baby grandson, enjoying the California sunshine.

Think of your friend Luze, back home in Boston running your Piano Cat Music Shop. And taking care of your crazy, music-loving cat, Gracie.

Think about your godson's visit, in just a few months. She hadn't seen TJ since France, and she missed him more than she could say.

Think about your music.

And Michael? Well, she hadn't heard from him since she'd arrived in New York three days ago, had no idea where he was. God. She couldn't shake the feeling that he'd gone after Dane.

Damn. Don't start thinking about Dane.

And don't think about today's date.

Just give yourself up to Vivaldi's violins. She ran on.

Breathe in. Breathe out.

Less than a mile now and she'd be turning onto 57th Street, toward Carnegie Hall and the practice room that waited for her. Why had she ever agreed to play Sergei Rachmaninoff's *Rhapsody*? Whatever had possessed her to choose Rachmaninoff's music for her comeback performance? At Carnegie Hall, no less. God, God. The twenty-fourth variation was so technically difficult that Rachmaninoff himself had broken his no-alcohol-before-a-performance rule and downed a full glass of crème de menthe to steady his hands.

Rubenstein, Ashkenazy, Van Cliburn . . . *they* all had taken on the Rhapsody. All men who had a much larger hand span than she did. Musical geniuses. Who did she think she was? She could just see the *Sunday Times* review now. "Following a personal tragedy, classical pianist Magdalena O'Shea returned to the stage for her first concert in over a year, a performance of Rachmaninoff's *Rhapsody on a Theme of Paganini*. But while wildly anticipated, her performance was vastly disappointing—a hollow and erratic hot mess of missed notes, chords, and phrases."

Would the *Times* ever dare to use the words "hot mess"? She grinned in spite of herself. Okay, so she wasn't *that* bad. Not quite "hot mess" bad. But she wasn't ready. Opening night was less than two months away. *I need insight from a professional*, she thought. *I need a miracle.*

She came to 57th Street. Jogging in place at the light, she turned off the Vivaldi. Now taxi horns, the clip of carriage horses' hooves, the rumble of busses, and the low murmur of conversation surrounded her. She waved to the pretzel vendor whose cart was parked every afternoon at the curb and—

Pop! Pop! Pop!

Gunfire! Maggie cried out, dropped to the sidewalk, and covered her face.

"Lady! Hey, lady! Are you okay?"

Maggie blinked and looked up into the face of the old vendor, bending close, his eyes full of concern. She shook her head in confusion and embarrassment. "I heard gunshots," she murmured. Her words echoed in her ears.

"It was just a car's backfire," said the vendor, helping her to her feet. "Can I get you some water?"

"No, I'm fine, thank you." *Right. So much for regaining control.*

No gunshots, she told herself. The Hall was just two blocks away. She would shower off the dust, practice for four or five hours, and still have time to make the benefit at the Morgan.

And buy a bottle of crème de menthe, she reminded herself, thinking of Rachmaninoff. A very *large* bottle. Or maybe a Barolo would be better.

Anything not to think about today's date. Just get through the day.

But how does a woman get through the one-year anniversary of her husband's death?

The light changed. She exhaled and sprinted across the street.

* * *

The stage door down the hall opened, clanged shut. Jimmy Cosantino heard the low murmur of the guard's voice, soft laughter, the quick, light footsteps.

The stage manager set his Starbucks coffee cup on the desk and gazed at his open office door, waiting, suddenly aware of a faint scent of roses drifting in the air. A moment passed, and then she was leaning against his doorframe, bent forward and trying to breathe, smiling wanly at him.

"Hey, Jimmy, have you got any water?"

"Anything for you, Mrs. O." He reached beneath his desk, tossed a Fiji water bottle toward her. She caught it with her left hand, and with a grateful nod, twisted the cap and drank. Every movement she made was fluid, graceful. He watched her, a slight-framed woman with dancers' legs and hair black as piano keys caught up in a careless bun. She was in her late forties, he'd heard, but you'd never know it. No way she was a granny. He tried not to stare at the words on the damp, clingy t-shirt, but the bright red letters were hard to miss. *The piano has been drinking, not me.*

He chuckled, and she turned those astonishing green eyes on him with a raised eyebrow.

The stage manager waved a hand at her, smiling. "Your shirt," he acknowledged. "Where the heck do you find those tees of yours?"

"Catalogs, Jimmy. Cheap catalogs." She returned his smile, but today it didn't reach her eyes. What was troubling her?

"Big practice scheduled?" he asked, tilting his chin toward the long hallway. Her rehearsal room was the last room on the left.

"Hope so. I'm going to shower first and then get started. Will you bang on my door around five?"

"Sure." He knew that she would lose all track of time when the music took over. "Headed to the benefit later today?"

This time the smile was real. "I love the Morgan Library. Are you going, too?"

"Wouldn't miss it."

"I'm meeting my godfather there, I'll introduce you."

"Great, see you later," he said, but the doorway already was empty.

The stage manager shook his head, too aware that he had just a bit of a crush on the beautiful pianist. What had that reviewer said? "Magdalena O'Shea looks like a nymph but plays like an angel."

Tell me something I don't know.

He was just reaching for his coffee when he heard her cry out.

His cup crashed to the floor as he lunged across his office and sprinted down the hallway.

She was standing outside her rehearsal room, very still, staring through the open doorway. He gazed over her shoulder. The air shimmered with an unsettling crimson light.

"Jesus H. Christ and all his little kittens."

The whole room was filled with vases of huge red roses. Roses that bloomed as brightly as blood.

CHAPTER SIX

NEW YORK CITY
SUNDAY

"I COUNT SEVENTEEN vases," said Jimmy. "At least two dozen roses in each one. Not to mention the ones scattered all over the floor."

Standing in the middle of the practice room, Maggie wrapped her arms around her body and shivered. "Four hundred roses? You're sure you didn't see anyone deliver them, Jimmy?"

He shook his head. "Maybe they were delivered while I was at the daily briefing. But I—wait a minute. There was a guy, early this morning, in a black uniform. And a backstage tour went through here about an hour ago. We'll check the security tapes." His eyes scanned the room. "We would never allow vases of flowers on the lids of our grand pianos. Any idea who would do this?"

She shook her head and wordlessly held out the folded note she'd found propped on the piano keyboard.

He took it from her, read the words inside, and whistled. "Happy Anniversary? Is this a special day for you?"

It's the anniversary of my husband's death.

"No," she said softly. "Not even close."

"Give me a break," muttered the stage manager. "A close friend, an admirer, a fan—maybe sends a dozen roses. At most. This has to be some sick joke."

Sick . . . and sinister. Maggie stared at the five bouquets crowded together on top of the Steinway. Under the ceiling lights, the beautiful polished wood glowed a deep red. The rest of the vases were scattered about the room, on every surface including the floor. "That was the only note," she acknowledged.

"Mind if I keep it?" Jimmy looked down at the thick, expensive parchment. The letters were printed in heavy jet-black marker. "I'll get someone to take these out of here. Room five is free today. Why don't you go practice there?"

"Okay. But don't toss the flowers, Jimmy. Send them to the hospital, or a nursing home, will you, please? *Someone* should get pleasure from them."

"Consider it done." He leaned toward her, touched her arm. "You're so pale, Maggie. Can I get you anything?"

"No, thank you, Jimmy. It's just been one of those days, you know?" She reached out, touched a velvet petal. "There's no good reason why I should be so upset by such beautiful roses."

Unless Dane had sent them.

She turned and walked down the hallway toward room five.

* * *

It was cold in the rehearsal room.

The new rehearsal rooms in the Carnegie education wing were bright, airy, state of the art, but this windowless room was basically bare, just the scarred Yamaha concert grand piano and a straight-backed chair in the corner next to a brass music stand. A long table on a side wall held several bottles of water and towering, precarious stacks of piano scores. That was it.

She adjusted the heat, sat down on the piano bench, closed her eyes and exhaled slowly, trying to clear her mind. The scent of the roses was still strong and sickening.

They weren't from Michael, she was certain of that. He had given her flowers just twice, once in France and then that first night at his cabin. White lilacs, both times. Because she had told him once that

Rachmaninoff had a secret fan who always sent white lilacs before a concert. Rachmaninoff had never found out who sent them.

The roses were beautiful, surely. But so many? She felt as if she were standing all alone on a stage in a darkened, empty theater—unsettled, anxious, enveloped by a sense of deep foreboding.

Happy Anniversary.

Before his death, her husband, Johnny, had always given her roses. *Red for passion, lass*, he would tell her. *Red for our love.*

She'd thought then that their love would last forever. Never for an instant had she imagined that he would die too soon, so horrifically, so far from home. So far from her . . .

A year after his death, the shattered white sailboat still spun into her nightmares.

Maggie closed her eyes. *Johnny?* she tried. For months after her husband died, she had felt him close, talked to him, heard the low whisper of his voice, glimpsed his bright eyes in the depths of her mirror. But no longer. The rehearsal room remained silent.

I want the roses to be from you, Johnny.

Maggie opened her eyes, straightened her shoulders, and shook her head, trying to banish the image of a small room filled with too many blood-colored roses. *Red is also the color of rage*, she thought.

No. They are just roses, *for God's sake. From someone who loves music. Get over yourself, damn you, get on with it. You have a concert in less than two months.* That's *what should be terrifying you.*

She checked her watch. Okay, practice here for the next four hours while the roses were removed from her rehearsal room. Then she could head home, shower, and be at the Morgan benefit by five.

She set her score on the stand, opened it to Variation #7. Rachmaninoff introduced the *Dies irae* here, the Latin funereal hymn, to create a disturbing, sinister melody. Perfect for the way she was feeling.

Slipping on her new tortoise glasses, she set the timer on her watch. Then she lifted her hands above the keys, counted to three, and, eyes on the score, began to play.

Four hours later, the tiny timer on her watch beeped. Already? Maggie finished a passage and let her trembling hands come to rest on the keys, reminding herself to breathe. God, Rachmaninoff was brilliant. He was the reason she had used her timer. She simply got lost in his music.

Fingers still cramping and slippery with perspiration, shoulders aching and stiff, she gathered her sheet music and made her way to the elevator at the end of the hallway. She loved wandering Carnegie's halls, as they were filled with framed, signed photographs of the great composers and musicians who had performed on its stage over the decades. Toscanini, Caruso, Isaac Stern. Midori, Rostropovich, Casals, Yo-Yo Ma. Zubin Mehta, Van Cliburn, and Horowitz. Leonard Bernstein. The Beatles, Billie Holiday, Isadora Duncan. Her mother, Lily Stewart, at the piano. And her father, Finn, his eyes closed and his baton held high . . .

The elevator doors slid open with a whir and, unable to resist, she pressed "S" for Stage.

The doors opened into the huge backstage area of the main auditorium. Tonight, the theater was dark, with no performance scheduled, and the backstage was quiet and deeply shadowed. Just the creak of her footsteps on the boards, the low hum of the theater's massive heating pipes, and the glow of the infamous "ghost light"—the single incandescent bulb set on a tall stand, always left burning in the center of an otherwise darkened stage.

It's called a ghost light, Maggiegirl.

Maggie stiffened, hearing her father's low voice thrum in her head. She had been—what? Eleven? Twelve? Standing with him on a dark stage just like this one. A time before her mother's death, when she and her father had been so close. She closed her eyes, let the memory come.

Many theaters have ghost lights, Maggie. The public is told that they are there to help navigate the stage, avoid accidents in the darkness. But performers know better. It's there for the ghosts who inhabit the theater, who come out to perform onstage late at night when no one is watching.

Every theater has its ghosts, sprite. That's why the theater is dark on Mondays. It's closed for the ghosts.

Somewhere behind her a metal door banged shut with finality, and the memories scattered.

Just one of the ghosts, she told herself, peering into the shadows.

Maggie walked slowly to the center of the stage and gazed out at the beautiful concert hall—"the house that music built"—now called the Isaac Stern Auditorium. The red velvet orchestra seats were barely visible in the shadows, the white and gold balconies set in an almost perfect semicircle around them, like enveloping arms. She counted the five levels, smiling as she remembered a long-ago breathless climb up the one hundred and thirty-seven steps to the top balcony.

Built in the late 1800s by Andrew Carnegie, the New York industrialist and music lover, the Italian Renaissance landmark building had been designed, she knew, by an amateur cellist named William Tuthill. The architect had been ahead of his time, forgoing the traditional heavy curtains and ornate chandeliers for an elliptical shape and a domed ceiling. Musicians and audiences alike, including herself, were in awe of the clarity and richness of the acoustics. Just yesterday, alone in the back of the theater, she had heard a musician onstage turning the pages of a score.

Maggie raised her eyes to the high dome, its circle of small lights like stars winking in the dimness.

She took a deep breath, enjoying the familiar scents of the theater. Old wood, paint, resin, perfume and perspiration, velvet. This was her world. God, she had missed it. A concert hall was what she knew. It was her safe place.

Maggie smiled, remembering a night in Paris during the summer when she and Michael had been standing on an empty stage, much like this one. The old Paris Opera House—the Palais Garnier. She closed her eyes, hearing his deep, low voice resonate in her head.

"How do you make something so beautiful out of thin air, Mrs. O'Shea? Where does the music come from inside you?"

"Music chose me. My body pulses with music. I wake up with rhythms singing in my head. Music is the last sound I hear before I sleep."

Now, standing alone on the dark stage, she felt close to Michael Beckett. That day on a shadowed Paris theater stage . . . was that the moment when their relationship had shifted? Become deeper?

There is just something about an empty theater, she thought now. Shadowed and mysterious, echoing with ghosts and the music of the great ones. A Steinway stood alone in the center of the stage, and Maggie ran her fingers over the keys. Yellowed now with age, they felt cool and worn beneath her fingertips. Who had played this piano? What music had they chosen? Why? *Music tells our stories*, she thought.

A noise backstage, behind her.

She turned.

A soft footfall. Then quiet.

She tensed. "Is anyone there?"

Silence.

A musician? A stagehand? Someone who had been on the backstage tour earlier? Maggie turned in a circle, peering into the darkness, the ropes and pulleys suddenly like a giant tangled forest casting long, distorted shadows. Fear fluttered like wings against her skin.

Breathing. Behind her!

She spun around.

The outline of a man, darker than the shadows. A pale face, featureless, appearing in the wings. Just for an instant. Then gone.

Quick footsteps in the blackness.

No. I will not be afraid here.

"This is *my* place, damn you!" shouted Maggie into the darkness. "You won't take it from me!"

Then she turned, gathered her music, and, with one last glance around the stage—*her* stage—she strode, fierce and angry as a Greek Fury, toward the wings.

* * *

In the Tuscan attic so far away, Dane held the cell phone to his ear, listening to the distant ring. Finally, a voice.

"Thanos. You did as I asked? You delivered all the roses? No one saw your face?"

A low, murmured response.

"Excellent. Ah, you followed her backstage as well?" He nodded, smiling. "Even better. I want her frightened, terrified. I am pleased with your work. And now—" he looked at his watch—"I have one more job for you to do. It's critical. I need to eliminate someone. Do not disappoint me."

CHAPTER SEVEN

THE MORGAN LIBRARY, NYC
SUNDAY

MADISON AVENUE WAS shimmering with dusky shadows when Maggie hurried up the wide marble stairs of the Morgan Library. As usual, she was running late.

The landing by the glass doors of the new, modern entrance was crowded with gala guests. She hesitated just for a moment before entering, her eyes on the streetlamps glinting on the young oaks that lined the sidewalk, her mind still whirling with questions about the roses left for her at Carnegie Hall. But those secrets would have to wait. She stepped through the glass doors into the grand foyer.

She saw herself reflected in the tall mirrors and polished marble, a slender dark-haired woman in a tube of deep forest-green velvet. Then she raised her eyes, once more marveling at the huge expanses of glass and the bright-colored panels that shifted and swayed above her, catching the very last glimmer of daylight and casting deep emerald, blue, and violet shadows across the upturned faces of the guests. Smiling, she accepted a glass of champagne from a tuxedoed waiter and moved into the glittering, buzzing crowd that ebbed and flowed beneath the soaring central court.

Even in her high-heeled sandals, most of the guests were taller than she was, and she felt surrounded by a murmuring sea of black. Jostled by the overflow crowd, she searched the guests for a friendly face. Her godfather had to be somewhere in the library. And Carnegie's stage manager, Jimmy, had said he was coming. She wanted to ask him about the security tapes, but he was not to be found. Where was he?

Stopping to speak with colleagues and friends, she slowly made her way up the small corner staircase into Mr. Morgan's East Room Library and stopped, as she always did, in the doorway to take in the space. The library was beautiful and intimate, with three tiers of centuries-old tooled leather volumes set on glowing walnut shelves that rose thirty feet into the air. The arched, ornate ceiling was decorated with murals and the signs of the Zodiac, which she'd been told had a personal meaning for J. P. Morgan and eleven of his colleagues. One more mystery.

"The preservation of art and ideas," murmured Maggie. It was what she always taught her music students. *History matters.*

"Hi, Lewis," she smiled at the room's aging guard standing in the doorway.

"Ms. O'Shea! It's been too long. Where've you been?"

She looked down at her hands. "It's a long story, Lewis."

He nodded as if he knew, then gestured toward the right bookcase near the door. "Well, you're back now, that's what counts. Remember when I showed you the secret staircase?"

She gazed at the wall of books, secure behind a locked metal grating. "You'd never know a staircase was concealed there. You promised you'd let me climb to the third balcony one day."

"Didn't forget," he whispered. "Come back early morning, just after we open, when it's quiet." He smiled and turned toward the long glass case behind her. "We've got Chopin this month. I remember he was a favorite of yours."

"Still is." She smiled as she turned toward the display case, set in front of a huge marble fireplace. She especially loved the Morgan because it highlighted and preserved rare, handwritten music manuscripts by the great composers. She leaned toward the case, and there it was. She caught her breath.

Chopin's *Etude for Piano in C major*, 1832. Autographed. Two whole pages, the pale blue ink faint, the notes tumbling one over the other. Her fingers skimmed the glass gently, aching to reach inside and touch the very same pages that the great Polish composer had touched.

A small dark portrait of Chopin, by Delacroix, was set beside the manuscript, and she leaned closer, drawn into the deep-set eyes. Eyes that had distance in them, eyes that reminded her of . . .

A French cemetery, four months earlier, just after dawn on a soft summer morning. A low voice in her ear. "Mrs. O'Shea? Magdalena O'Shea?"

She had been sitting on a bench in Père Lachaise Cimetière in Paris, before the tomb of Chopin. Staring at the high, carved granite headstone, where several cats slept in the sun. And then the shadow of a man had fallen across her, and she had looked up into the stone-silver eyes of Colonel Michael Beckett.

Beckett. A crusty, take-no-prisoners soldier who quoted Winston Churchill and lived in the Blue Ridge Mountains with a three-legged rescue Golden named Shiloh. Their chemistry had been immediate, tumultuous. She still heard the whispering in her bones when she thought of him. God.

The man was slowly bringing her back to life.

Maggie let out her breath. Where was he tonight? In his cabin with Shiloh? DC with old friends? Or maybe overseas?

God, don't let him be overseas. She closed her eyes, picturing his face. And without warning felt an icy chill slide across her skin.

Where are you, Colonel? And why do I suddenly feel as if something is wrong?

* * *

At that moment Colonel Michael Beckett was driving north, very fast, on the George Washington Parkway in northern Virginia. The blue BMW convertible he'd rented while his old jeep was in the shop responded immediately to his touch. *Oh yeah, baby, you were worth the splurge.*

He looked over at the Golden, curled in the passenger seat beside him, his sleek head down. Just a few months back, this dog would snarl and snap if anyone dared to come near him. But now . . . He was too quiet. It was more than old age. Something was wrong.

"It's okay to enjoy the wind, Shiloh, let it blow those ears of yours straight back from your head. C'mon, big guy, we're in a Beamer!"

The dog did not lift his head. The trees flew by in a dark blur, with an occasional silvery glimpse of the Potomac River just beyond the woods.

He'd be at the chief's McLean home in ten minutes. An after-hours call from the Number 2 at the agency had to be important. And he'd been wanting to make another trip to the cemetery . . .

"Killing two birds with one stone," he said to the Golden.

Shiloh gave a low growl in response, clearly not amused by the image.

"Okay, okay, so you missed the class where they said Retrievers aren't supposed to be bird lovers," muttered Beckett, his eyes once again checking the rearview mirror. And then, "Something's up."

The dark SUV was still there. Keeping up.

He accelerated into the curve.

The SUV pulled closer. Not good.

Someone sending a message? Trying to scare the bejesus out of him? *Not gonna happen.*

He glanced over at the dog. "Hold on, fella, it's gonna be a bumpy ride."

Beckett pushed hard on the accelerator, felt the Beamer leap forward. Good thing there wasn't too much traffic on this stretch tonight. He eyed the mirror.

The SUV was closing in on him.

Christ, it was too close. What the hell?

The sharp scream of metal against metal. The BMW shuddered beneath his fists as he gripped the wheel.

He reached out, pushed the Golden down onto the floor. "Down, Shiloh! Stay down, boy."

You're not going to hurt my dog, damn you!

His foot punched down, accelerating to eighty. Ninety.

Bright headlamps filled his mirror.

Eyes locked on the mirror, he reached for his cell.

The lights in the mirror came closer, filling the car, blinding him.

Sons of bitches.

The impact was sudden, hard.

He fought for control, cursing as the car headed toward the trees.

Shiloh's howl and the screech of tires filled his ears.

The sports car careened off the road.

Black tree trunks rushed at him.

Spinning down.

The silver flash of river . . .

Christ. Not the river!

He closed his eyes and hung on.

For a split second, he saw Maggie's face.

A splintering crash.

A blistering tower of fire, shooting high into the night.

Scorching heat.

Pain.

No way, dammit. Get out! Get the fuck out!

A high, agonized bark.

Where was his dog? "Shiloh!" he shouted.

Reaching. Lunging.

"Shiloh!"

The world exploded into a thousand stars of flame.

Blackness.

CHAPTER EIGHT

THE MORGAN LIBRARY, NYC
SUNDAY

LOUD LAUGHTER IN the crowded Morgan rotunda broke into Maggie's head, scattering her thoughts. Just as well.

She turned.

Several guests in cocktail dresses and tuxedoes stood in a circle behind her, deep in conversation.

"How do you get two lawyers to agree on a juror?" asked a voice that was deep and sonorous in timbre. "Shoot one."

She knew that baritone. *Alexander Karas.*

She stepped closer. "The delivery is good but perhaps not the most politically correct choice for a judge."

"Maggie!"

She smiled at the handsome judge. "Hello, Zander, I've been searching for you. It's so good to see you."

Karas walked toward her. Over six feet, eagle-faced, as charismatic as ever. He was built like a basketball player, but the Armani tuxedo and silk blue-gray tie fitted him perfectly. His silver hair, swept back from a high forehead as if by a strong wind, had grown longer since she'd seen him last, and now a salt and pepper shadow covered a strong jaw. A good look for him.

Karas clasped her hand, leaned down to kiss her cheek. Then he raised glowing hazel eyes to gaze at her. "I've been looking for you, also. It's been too long. I've missed you."

"You've just missed someone to laugh at your quirky legal jokes."

"Ah, go easy on your old godfather, will you, Maggie?" His eyes glittered at her as he held out a sparkling flute of champagne.

It had been almost a year since she'd seen her parents' closest friend, she realized, as she accepted the flute. After Johnny had died, she had shut herself away from everyone.

She raised her glass. "You look well," she told him truthfully. "To you. Congratulations, Zander. Or should I say Mr. Justice? It isn't every day someone I love is on the short list for nomination to the Supreme Court by the President of the United States."

"What was the President thinking?" Karas' smile flashed. "And 'Mr. Justice' is far too premature, Maggie. The operative words are *short list*. I'm afraid I could be the third choice, behind two very diverse and talented women. I expect the press coverage and hearings will be brutal."

"Well, clearly the President thinks highly of you. It takes courage to stand up to what should be supreme in a democracy—the popular will."

"Ah, but what side would I be on if I were king?"

"Just don't tell any jokes and they all will fall under your spell, Zander. As long as it's what you want."

"Heavy is the head that wears the crown," he said softly. "But yes, it's what I want." He raised his flute to her with a look of admiration. "And now to *you.* May we suffer as much sorrow as the drops of champagne we will leave in our glasses."

He kept his eyes on her as they clinked and drank. "I was so happy when you called. I know it's been a very rough year for you, but I have an idea I think you will like. Will you have a nightcap with me later tonight? Right now, I want to introduce you to my friends. New York's newest Cardinal. And Madame Giulietta Donati, the international pianist." He smiled. "I know you recognize her name."

Karas reached out to cup her elbow, guiding her toward a regal, stunning elderly woman in a long-sleeved velvet claret gown, seated in a wheelchair. Behind her, wearing the floor-length black cassock of the Catholic priesthood, stood a tall, slender man with soft gray eyes and light, wispy hair.

The woman lifted her face toward Maggie with a questioning smile. In her late seventies, perhaps, the woman looked much younger, with high, papery cheekbones and pure white hair braided in a coronet around her head. Huge ruby earrings sparkled and dangled from her ears.

"Madame Giulietta Donati," said Alexander Karas. "I want you to meet Magdalena O'Shea. Magdalena is—"

"Of course, I know who she is, Zander. Quite the pianist in her own right." Madame Donati leaned closer to Maggie, held out her hand. Jeweled bracelets shimmered on her wrist. "Please, call me Gigi. You are even more beautiful than your photographs, Mrs. O'Shea. I own most of your CDs, and heard you play Tchaikovsky's Piano Concerto in Boston several years ago. Gorgeous. It is a true pleasure to see you."

"For me as well." Maggie smiled into eyes of bright, glowing amethyst. "Call me Maggie, please."

"Come closer, my dear. I want us to—"

"God may be more willing to listen to you, Gigi, if you don't insist on monopolizing this beautiful woman." The Archbishop stepped forward, smiling, his ornate pectoral cross glittering against the black fabric of his gown.

Alexander Karas held out his hands. "And this, of course, is His Eminence, Robert Cardinal Brennan."

"How have you been, Maggs?" said the Archbishop in a low, warm voice as he bent to kiss her cheek.

"Hey, Robbie, it's so good to see you, too."

Karas and Giulietta Donati exchanged amused glances. "Maggs? Robbie? It seems you two already know each other quite well," said Gigi Donati.

The Cardinal chuckled. "I introduced myself to Maggie in Boston after a concert years ago. She has worked with me ever since, bringing music programs to many of our juvie kids in Brooklyn and the Bronx." He turned back to Maggie, smiling as he slipped the round red biretta on his head. "I must get back to the rectory. But I want to spend time with you. It's been too long. Will you stop by the church?"

"And you will just happen to have some kids there in need of piano lessons . . ."

"Same old Maggs." A smile lit the light eyes as the Cardinal turned to the older pianist. "I would be honored if you would come visit our church as well, Madame Donati," he said, taking her hand.

Gigi Donati shook her head with regret. "I'm afraid I don't go out much in the evenings anymore, Robert. But"—she raised her eyes to Maggie's—"perhaps Maggie would be willing to stop by my apartment for a cup of tea one day this week? We have so much personal history to catch up on, you and I."

Maggie raised an eyebrow. "Personal history? I'm sorry, Gigi. I'm not sure what you mean."

The lovely pianist reached out and took Maggie's hand. Her touch was light as a bird's wing. "Forgive me, my dear. The memory plays tricks. It seems like yesterday, but—of course you were too young to remember."

Maggie bent down to the older woman, intrigued, and found herself suddenly surrounded by the faint scent of Chanel. "Remember? We've met before, then?"

"Oh, yes, a very long time ago. You were just a young child—four, maybe five years old. And quite shy, always hiding beneath the Steinway. Your parents and I were very good friends. I was your mother Lily's piano teacher for many years, my dear. She was one of the very few people who knew that Giulietta was my middle name. She always insisted on calling me by my first name. Gisela."

* * *

"Hey, buddy!"

Pain.

"Buddy, can you hear me?"

Beckett tried to move. The ground was hard, cold beneath him.

"I hear you. Am I in heaven?"

A low chuckle. "I don't think they say 'buddy' in heaven."

Beckett felt the heat searing his eyelids. He forced his eyes open and struggled to turn his head. He saw a pulsing orange glow on the edge of the trees.

"Hell, then," he muttered. "Should have known . . ."

"You've been in a car accident. Thrown clear, you lucky bastard."

Thrown clear? He tried to focus. Some fifty feet away, the Beamer—his gorgeous baby—was engulfed in flames.

Christ! Shiloh!

Beckett tried to sit up. "My dog," he gasped.

"What dog?"

"A Golden . . ." He heard the string of curses spill from his dry, cracked lips—in English, in Pashto, in Arabic. He tried to sit up. Dizzy.

"Easy, bud, we've got to get you to the hospital," said the medic.

"Where's my dog, damn you? Shiloh! *Shiloh!*"

Silence.

Then a high, agonized bark, somewhere in the woods to his right.

Somehow, he was on his feet and staggering toward the trees.

CHAPTER NINE

NEW YORK CITY
SUNDAY, OCTOBER 19

THE ELEVATOR DOORS to The Top of the Strand Rooftop Bar opened, and Maggie stepped into the crowded, open space. White winking lights, candles, soft sofas, the deep blue dome of sky and, straight ahead, the iconic Empire State Building, lit tonight in bright orange lights in honor of the season. While Zander Karas stopped to speak with another guest, Maggie walked ahead toward the glassed railing.

The air was clear and cold, sharp with the scent of wood smoke and dry chrysanthemums. She gazed over the railing toward the street below, where streetlamps were blinking on and lines of cars and taxis crawled toward the East River. All around her, the East Side skyscrapers were tall graceful spires against the purpling sky.

It had been good to see Robbie again, and she'd enjoyed meeting Gigi Donati. She was looking forward to seeing Gigi again tomorrow, and asking for memories of her mother. She felt she didn't have nearly enough of her own—just photographs, the touch of a gentle hand on her forehead, a low musical voice, a trace of perfume in the air. A flash of bright green eyes.

So many of her memories were still shrouded in a dark blue fog.

A sudden coldness washed over her. Skin thrumming, she gathered her shawl around her shoulders and glanced behind her, half expecting—what?

Zander was walking toward her. "What is it, Maggie?"

"Just a feeling. Nothing. Imagination."

"Are you sure?"

She turned away with a shake of her head. "I can't believe I've never come up here before. It's a beautiful bar. And an even more beautiful view."

"I come here whenever I'm in town. I'm glad you like it." Karas moved to stand beside her, handing her a snifter of brandy and then leaning his arms on the railing. "Would you like my jacket?"

"I'm fine." She gazed at Karas with speculation. "You know the new Cardinal of New York City . . . *and* the world-renowned classical pianist Giulietta Donati?"

Karas grinned down at her. "Sounds like a bad joke, doesn't it? A musical legend, a Cardinal, and a Supreme Court wannabe walk into a museum . . ."

"You are full of surprises tonight."

"And more to come, Goddaughter." He raised his glass, touched hers with a soft clink. "I'm glad that you agreed to join me for a nightcap. I have a proposal for you. And"—he smiled down at her—"speaking as your godfather, it's an offer you can't refuse."

* * *

Alexander Karas looked down at the cap of upswept raven hair, shining in the light of the rooftop lamps. Maggie was a stunning woman. Smart as a whip and a brilliant musician. *You are your mother's daughter*, he thought. She could be very useful to him.

Tell as much of the truth as you can, he warned himself.

He smiled down at her. "I've been thinking about you since you called, Maggie. You went through such a terrible ordeal this last year. You said you've been having nightmares these last months?" He watched her skin turn translucent in the waning light.

She looked out over the city lights. "My doctor says it's post-traumatic stress. I keep seeing the face of the man who tried to kill me. Narrow and cruel, like a wolf." She shuddered. "And recently, for the first time in so long, I think dreams of my childhood have come back."

"Triggered by your father's death, I imagine. It shocked all of us."

At the mention of her father, her smile dimmed. "I thought I had put all that pain behind me, but—"

He bent toward her. "But the heart has a long memory. What do you dream about?"

"Just flashes, really. A haunting chord of music. A bare foot. Broken glass." She closed her eyes. "When I try to remember more, everything turns blue—a thick blue fog, and I can't see through it. It's called retrograde amnesia."

"Your mind is protecting you." He touched her shoulder. "Do you think the flashes are real memories?"

"I have no idea. They make no sense to me. I don't know what's real and what's not."

He nodded. "All these years . . . I still think of your parents every day. I miss them."

She turned to him. "Maybe the dreams are just because I'm . . . lonely." Confusion flickered deep in her eyes, and he realized that her words had taken her by surprise.

"I am lonely, also," he told her honestly. "Since my father died last year, I no longer have any family left. Other than you."

"Loss changes you," she said quietly. "In so many unexpected ways. My husband and parents are no longer in my life. My son and his family are in San Diego, visiting his wife's parents. My closest friends, and my godson, are in Boston and France. I miss them all. But we go on. I've found closure for Johnny's death—at least as much as is possible. Music is my anchor now."

"We all need an anchor, don't we? Mine is a place, now. I inherited the family estate from my father. Ocean House, in East Hampton, right on the edge of the Atlantic Ocean—do you remember it? Rolling dunes, tall sea grasses, endless sand, pine forests, wildflowers climbing shingled walls. The cry of the gulls, and always, the roar of the waves and that ghostly veil of fog. All very isolated and quite beautiful."

Her eyes were on the city lights. "I remember the fog," she said slowly. "And running on an endless beach, with the sound of the waves crashing all around me. My mother loved the ocean . . ." She closed her eyes for a moment against the memories, then tilted her head at him. "But I thought you were entrenched in Washington these days, Zander. US Court of Appeals, right?"

He shrugged. "Yes, I spend most of my time now in DC. And I admit, I like the rarified air of being 'inside the bubble.' I bought a condo on Pennsylvania Avenue. All glass and steel, with the Capitol building framed in my window. Quite the power view, but—even judges need some time off, Maggie. We need open spaces, the sea."

She flashed a smile at him. "Hence, East Hampton."

He returned her smile. "Hence. But Father spent his last year in assisted living, and the house has been closed up for a long time. It's huge, furniture covered in sheets, the grounds completely overgrown like Sleeping Beauty's castle. It needs . . ."

"If you say 'a woman's touch,' Zander, I'm leaving."

His laugh was deep and easy. "It needs restoration, family, laughter, music! I want to reopen the house, bring it back to its former glory. The contractors already are hard at work. Would you consider helping me?"

"Helping you do what, exactly?"

"A benefit."

"Good Lord, Zander, I'm a pianist. A *soloist*. Not a fund-raiser."

"Of course not. This would be a night of beautiful music. You, an orchestra, a gorgeous winter's night. The Yale Orchestra's fiftieth anniversary is coming up—they've asked me to organize a special alumni celebration. You know how much your parents loved Yale. You could play in their honor . . ." He saw her face change. "In your mother's honor, then."

Her gaze sharpened. "Same old Zander. Playing the parent card. And, of course, it wouldn't hurt your short-list portfolio . . ."

"Oh, come on, Maggie. Surely you haven't lost your sense of humor? It would be a good thing."

"It's a lovely idea," she relented. "But I don't know how much time I have. You've heard I'm working on the Rachmaninoff? Learning a great piece of music is grueling. It takes months of practice, so many hours every day that your fingers spasm . . ."

He gazed down at her, memory lighting his face. "Your mother always made it seem as if the music just flowed like moonlight from her fingers. My father was very fond of her, he loved to hear her play. We all used to have such wonderful Gatsby-like parties at Ocean House in the old days. Martinis in the garden, lanterns lining the great lawn down to the dunes. She and your father would play for our guests in the grand salon . . ."

He hesitated, caught up in memories. "Speaking of your father, how are you *really*? The announcement of his death was such a shock to all of us. I had no idea he was ill. Had Finn been in touch with you?"

Something in her eyes. "No. Why would he? He knew how I felt, knew that I—" She stiffened and stopped speaking, her gaze locked on something beyond his shoulder.

"Maggie? What is it?" He turned to follow her gaze.

A long moment of silence. Then her eyes found his, wary and unsettled. "Sorry. I thought I saw someone—a man—over by the bar.

His reflection, actually, in the mirror over the bar. He was tall, fair. Very still, dressed all in black. Just . . . watching us."

Karas spun around once more. Saw no one.

"Gone, now. Another guest, perhaps. Or a trick of the light?"

She shook her head, glanced at her watch. "Almost seven. I really do need to get home and practice. But your idea for a benefit is intriguing, Zander. I'll think about it."

"Perhaps you would at least consider coming to East Hampton. Have dinner with your old godfather, see the house again, the grounds. I have a small stable, a conservatory, a beautiful, heated forty-foot pool. You could—"

She paled. "No swimming."

He touched her cheek with a gentle finger. "Still don't like the water?"

She squared her shoulders. "I'll think about what you said, and call you," she told him. "Thanks for the drink. And the invitation to Ocean House." She shook her head at him as she moved toward the elevators. He watched as she glanced once more toward the high, mirrored bar.

With his eyes on the closing elevator doors, Karas nodded. *She doesn't remember*, he assured himself. *And yet . . . something is off. I'll have to watch her, find a way to keep her close. Well*, he thought, *there are worse things than spending time with a beautiful woman.*

Much worse. He turned to stare toward the mirrored wall.

Had someone been watching them?

CHAPTER TEN

THE UPPER WEST SIDE, NYC
SUNDAY NIGHT

STILL UNABLE TO shake the feeling that she was being watched, Maggie locked the double bolts of the apartment door behind her. Kicking off her heels with a relieved sigh, she went down the hallway to the kitchen, found a bottled water, then wandered into the living room. The brownstone on West 65th belonged to a musician friend who was on tour with the National Symphony and had agreed to rent the space to her for several weeks.

It was after eight p.m. She clicked on a tall crystal lamp, and soft light flooded the room. Her friend had good taste. It was a large, beautiful space, open, contemporary, and sophisticated. Gas fireplace, a wall of glowing cherry bookcases, and a baby grand piano set in the bay window. White linen love seats faced each other across a round glass coffee table topped by stacked books and an eighteen-inch-high sculpture of a conductor, his arms thrown wide.

Her eyes locked on the sculpture, and an image of her father flashed into her brain. *Finn, his long hair wild and his open tuxedo jacket flapping, his right arm thrusting the baton high into the air, eyes closed in rapture as he conducted the crashing chords of Beethoven.*

A brilliant, egotistical, and charismatic conductor, her father had led the New York Symphony for a tumultuous decade. And then one night, in the middle of a passionate performance of Beethoven's

Eroica Symphony, he had simply stopped, walked off the stage, and disappeared from her life.

God. She blinked and turned away. Her father was the last person she wanted to think about tonight. But the too-brief, shocking obituary published six months earlier in Europe was scorched into her mind.

The International Times

Classical Conductor Finn Stewart dies at 72

Orchestral Conductor Finn Stewart, the American Maestro who blazed an electric path for classical music for decades, is reported to have died Tuesday at a hospital in Vienna, Austria, after a long illness. Maestro Stewart, a dominant figure in the international music world, made history in the early eighties when, midway through conducting Beethoven's *Eroica Symphony No. 3* in E-flat major with the New York Symphony, he flung his baton to the floorboards, strode off the stage, and vanished forever into the night. Because he disappeared just weeks after his wife, pianist Lily Stewart, drowned in the ocean off New York's Manhattan Beach, the Mystery of the Maestro has fascinated classical music lovers for years.

The terrible words spun in her head, making Maggie physically ill, and she breathed deeply. She hadn't known her father was sick, had always thought she would see him again. But all of a sudden, all the answers to her questions had died with him. Damn, damn, why hadn't she searched for him sooner?

Restless, Maggie slipped a CD into the player. *Not Beethoven tonight*, she thought with a shudder. The opening chords of

Tchaikovsky's beautiful *Piano Concerto No. 1*, played by her favorite pianist, Vladimir Horowitz, tumbled into the room. Tchaikovsky always gave her solace.

Wandering to the high windows, she gazed out at slender tree branches and arched lighted windows across the narrow street. Lincoln Center was just two blocks down to the right. You couldn't ask for a better location.

Except maybe a cabin in the Blue Ridge mountains? Her fingers trailed soundlessly across the piano keys. Where was Michael? Why hadn't he called?

Call him.

No. I can't.

Oh, good God. You are a confident, forty-eight-year-old grandmother. There is no "should" anymore. Call him or don't call him, just get on with it.

But . . . the truth was, she was afraid. There had to be a reason why he hadn't called her. What would she do if Michael Beckett suddenly disappeared from her life? Dangerous thoughts.

I could not bear any more loss.

Tucking her legs up under her, Maggie stared down at her cell phone, willing it to ring. Michael would want to know about the meeting with Zander, his unexpected suggestion that they work together.

Face it, Zander's idea for hosting a music benefit at Ocean House intrigued her.

She stared into the fire, listening to Horowitz's gorgeous melodic chords. *Just call Michael.* She dialed his cell and waited. Four rings, then his low voice, the professional voice, sounding too distant in her ear. "You've reached Mike Beckett. Leave a message."

"It's me. Where are you?" She hesitated. "Call me."

She dropped the cell to the coffee table. Something was wrong. She could feel it.

Imagination.

Maggie leaned back against the soft cushions, welcoming the solace. Beyond the tall brownstone windows, streetlamps glowed orange, autumn leaves skittered and blew against the purpled glass.

Safe. No more roses, no reason to be afraid . . .

Her cell phone trilled with Mozart's Elvira Madigan theme, and she reached for it quickly but did not recognize the number. Be Michael . . .

"Magdalena O'Shea."

A man's low voice sounded in her ear. *Not Michael.* "Mrs. O, it's Jimmy Cosantino, from the theater. I'm calling about those roses. I found something on the security tapes I think you should see."

"First thing tomorrow?"

"I'm not sure this can wait, Mrs. O."

She glanced at her watch. Just after eight thirty. "Would you like me to come to your office now? Or you're welcome to stop by here, I'm not far away. Sixty-fifth Street."

A murmur, as if he was speaking with someone else. Then, "Sure, I'll swing by on my way home. Shouldn't take long."

She gave him the address and disconnected. What had he found? For a moment, she pictured the rehearsal room, shimmering blood red with the light of some four hundred roses. *Who does that?*

Long day, and not over yet. Just time to take off this too-tight gown and get into jeans and a sweatshirt before Jimmy arrived. She stood and headed down the hall to the bedroom.

Clicking on the lamp, the first thing she saw was the deep crimson rose glowing on the cream pillow.

"Good God!" She pressed back against the wall, her heart hammering hard against her ribs. *Someone had been in the bedroom!* Fear sharp in her stomach, she searched the shadows. Taking a deep, shuddering breath, she forced herself to check the bathroom. The closet. Under the bed.

She was alone.

But the intimacy of the single rose on her pillow was even more terrifying than the hundreds of roses left in her rehearsal room. Reaching for the rose, she saw the note, white vellum beneath the petals. Shakespeare's words spun in front of her eyes.

"Women are as roses, whose fair flower, being once displayed, doth fall that very hour."

Dane.

* * *

The last brilliant notes of the concerto echoed, and then silence filled the room. Maggie sat stiffly on the sofa, eyes on the front door's double locks, holding her cell phone like a weapon in her hand. A sharp six-inch kitchen knife glinted on the coffee table, inches from her hand.

After nine. Where was Jimmy?

Be honest, she told herself. It wasn't the stage manager who spun in her thoughts. It was the colonel. She needed to tell him about the roses. About Dane.

She clicked on her phone.

The doorbell chimed. She glanced at her watch: nine fifteen.

Pop. Pop. Pop.

She gasped, knowing that sound, and ran to the door.

The sound of a motorcycle, speeding away. She checked the door's peephole, saw no one. Slipping off the chain, she undid the double lock and cracked the door with caution.

The night air was cool, scented with smoke, car exhaust, sharp autumn leaves, pumpkins, and . . . something coppery.

She looked down, and froze.

Jimmy Cosantino was sprawled across the steps, his face and chest covered in bright blood. The backpack on the ground next to him was open and empty.

CHAPTER ELEVEN

MCLEAN, VIRGINIA
SUNDAY NIGHT

THE MEDIC'S RADIO crackled.

"Yeah, the guy just lurched up and ran off into the woods. Something about a dog. We'll keep searching until . . . well, I'll be damned."

The dark form of a man emerged from the trees, staggering, carrying a large Golden Retriever across his shoulders.

The medic ran toward them, helped them both to the earth. "Jesus, buddy, are you okay? I've never seen anything like this."

The man eased the dog to the ground, ran a gentle hand over his fur from head to tail. "Check him over, will you? Is he hurt? Easy, boy, easy. This guy's a friend. There you go."

"I'm an EMT, buddy, not a vet, but I'll do my best to take care of him." The medic bent to the dog, examined him carefully. "No injuries I can see. Looks okay."

"You're sure?"

"Yeah." The medic shook his head, still stunned by the image of the injured man walking out of the darkness carrying the huge dog. "But you both should be checked out." He signaled the ambulance driver. "Let's get you both to the hospital."

The man blinked, focused, clamped a strong hand on the medic's arm.

"No hospital. No one can know I've survived."

The EMT stared him down. "I'm not letting you out of my sight until I get you and your dog inside my van and check your vitals, buddy. Then, we'll talk."

"And *then* you're going to call a guy in McLean. Here's the number."

* * *

"Sorry to be so late, Chief."

"What the hell happened to you, Beckett?"

"Car trouble."

"Funny. You ought to be at the damned hospital, not here practicing your stand-up comedy routine. *Barely* standing, I might add."

Beckett lowered himself gingerly into a chair. "Nothing a little bourbon won't fix."

In the wood-paneled home-office of the Deputy Attorney General, Beckett held the chief's eyes. Behind the desk, the round seal of the US Department of Justice glowed in the lamplight.

The chief reached into a deep desk draw and removed a half-full bottle of whiskey and set it on the desk. "Good idea. Helluva day."

Beckett glanced over at the Golden, now curled on the floor by the fireplace and watching him with a wary expression. "We're a couple of tough old dogs, right, fella? Just sliding down the razor blade of life."

The dog continued to stare at him, not amused.

"Okay, so maybe the day didn't end exactly the way we planned it." Beckett smiled grimly, gripped the leather chair's arms, and forced himself to ignore the pain as he leaned forward.

"Someone tried to make me toast, Chief. Literally." He tried to laugh, but it hurt too much. "But I'm not as bad as I look. The ER doc said the dog and I were good, free to go. So, why did you want to see me?"

The chief set three glasses next to the whiskey. "Your pal Sugarman asked me to call you. He should be here any minute. I know you're retired, Beckett, so this has to be under the radar. Something new is in the wind. There may be some action on a 'person of interest.' *Your* person of interest."

Beckett stiffened. "Dane?"

A tall figure blocked the doorway. "The one and only, pal," said Simon Sugarman, entering the room. An ex-Marine who described himself as "big, black, and bad," Sugar had been friends with Beckett since their days together in Iraq.

"Chief," Sugar acknowledged the man behind the desk with a touch of fingertips to his forehead. "Hey, Shiloh, how you doin'?" He bent to touch the Golden's head, but the Golden shied away. "That bad, huh?"

Sugarman turned to Beckett with a raised eyebrow and held out his hand. "Long time no see. How's La Maggie?"

Beckett sat up straight, heedless of the shooting pain in his side, and grasped Sugarman's hand. "Maggie's in New York, preparing for a concert." He pictured the haunted eyes. "Still healing. What's going on with Dane, Sugar? What do you know?"

"We got word from one of our agents in Italy. They seem to think our old friend might be on the move again. Five, six weeks ago a guy with Dane's description was spotted leaving a fishing boat in a village harbor by the Tyrrhenian Sea. Near Livorno. Tall, pale hair, mirrored glasses. Hat. Gloves."

"Mirrored glasses . . . and gloves." Beckett flashed on a moment months earlier in France when he had seriously burned Dane's hand with his butane lighter during a brutal confrontation.

"Yeah," said Sugarman. "And not long after that, there was a suspicious death in an isolated Tuscan village."

"Tuscany is only a few kilometers from Livorno. Who died?"

"A doctor. Guy was already on our radar because he did a bit of off-the-books plastic surgery now and then to earn some extra lira."

Beckett stiffened, tried to control the fierce rush of fury. "Plastic surgery . . . Son of a bitch. Dane. Has to be. Do we know what he looks like now?"

"Nada."

"His location, then?"

Sugarman smiled. "No. But we've got inquiries flying all over the Dark Net. Welcome to a whole new day in Europe, pal. The way I figure it, Dane worked for Victor Orsini, so he either has Orsini's looted art, or he's searching for it. His hunger for the art—and the power that goes with it—is his fatal flaw. Well, one of them . . . Find the art, we find him. And the underground art world chatter says that something big is going down in Rome."

"When? And how big?"

"End of the week, that's all we've got. My guess is a major power struggle for leadership in the European market for stolen art, now that Orsini's gone. Got our eyes on the top Italian black-market art guy. My team, working with Interpol, followed a transatlantic money trail to a small Roman art gallery in the Piazza Navona. Owner's name is Angelo Farnese. 'The Angel.' He specializes in old masters, seems to be the one loosely in control of the international trade of illicit art since Orsini's death."

Beckett leaned closer. "Loosely? So you think a new leader is vying for control?"

"Maybe more than one. It's a swanky, sweet business, Mike. A major network, a global empire worth hundreds of millions. Maybe billions." Sugarman turned to the chief. "I'm guessing a hush-hush meeting of the top guns in the stolen art market, maybe a vote, under the guise of an under-the-radar art auction. One of those quietly arranged, very private sales to very private collectors. All the main players gathered together."

Beckett leaned in. "If Dane wants to take Orsini's place, he needs leverage, needs to get hold of Orsini's art to take control. Best guess, he's searching for the art Orsini hid just before he died."

Sugarman scowled. "Aren't we all. Talk about a king's fortune."

"And Dane will do anything to get it," said Beckett. "He won't hesitate to kill anyone who stands in his way, Chief. He likes the intimacy of a knife, but he's a master of explosives and disguises as well. Whatever he's planning, innocent people are going to get hurt. Because Dane *will be at that meeting*."

"Agreed," interrupted the chief. "Agents are on their way to Tuscany, and our top team is already in place in Rome and ready to roll. My fault it's last minute—truth is, I argued with Sugar about including you."

"Why?"

"You're too close to this one, Beckett. But Sugar convinced me that we need you. Don't make me sorry."

Thoughts raced through Beckett's head, collided, coalesced. He leaned forward. "We can use this. My gut tells me it's all connected. What happened to me tonight, being run off the road—that was as real as it gets, not a warning. Someone wants me out of the way." He smiled grimly. "Only one person I can think of. Let him think I'm out of his hair, he won't be expecting me. The meeting in Rome is the best shot we've had at Dane since he went to ground in July."

"This plays outside the box, Beckett," said the chief.

"Let me do this, Chief. My way."

The chief stared at him for a long time. Then he poured two fingers of dark whiskey into each glass and handed one to each of the men. "Okay, Frank Sinatra," he said, raising the glass toward Beckett. "Your way. What do you have in mind?"

Beckett told him.

"I don't know if you're a brilliant son of a gun or crazy as a loon," murmured the chief when Beckett stopped speaking, "but I'll see if I can get what you need." He held up his empty glass. "Another?"

"Why not? I'm not driving."

The chief chuckled, poured, then leaned back in his leather chair. "It won't be easy. You'll have to fly out late Tuesday night."

"Welcome to our lives, right, Shiloh?" For the first time since the crash, Beckett smiled. "I have just one request."

"Just one?"

"The woman Sugar asked me about. She's a pianist, Magdalena O'Shea. We're—close. Dane will come after her, no question, he's already told me so. I want her protected while I'm gone. Until I can stop him."

The chief gazed toward the night-filled window. "Okay, we don't want her hurt. How do you want to handle her?"

"There's no 'handling' Maggie O'Shea, believe me. The woman's contrary as a cat."

Shiloh raised his head, suddenly interested. The chief set down his glass and stood up with a sigh. "You sure about this, Beckett?"

Beckett closed his eyes. Saw the blinding headlights coming closer.

"Go big or go home, right? They almost killed my dog tonight, Chief. I'm sure."

CHAPTER TWELVE

TUSCANY

ON THE HARD tiles in the farmhouse attic, Dane rolled over onto his stomach and began a series of push-ups. Pale dawn light stained the window beyond the bed.

He was getting stronger every day. Switching to one-armed push-ups, he checked his watch. In just a few more days, he would be in Rome. "The Angel" had dared to tell him he *wasn't welcome* to attend the meeting of the top black-market art dealers he'd summoned to Rome. The man was strengthening his hold, resisting Dane's demand to take over the leadership role. A mistake. They would not shut him out. It was time to send all the art dealers a message. *He* was taking over the mantle from Victor Orsini.

The king is dead, long live the king.

And after that?

If he was going to take control of the stolen art market, he *had* to locate the art collection Orsini had hidden just before he died. If he had just stayed with Orsini that night in France, he would have been trusted to help conceal the canvases and would have known exactly where those paintings were. But Magdalena O'Shea had ruined his plans. It was all her fault.

Now, only two people knew where Orsini had hidden his art. Someone he trusted from his old days at Yale. And one other person. Orsini's son, TJ. The kid literally had the key to his father's hiding place, and he had no idea what he was sitting on.

Damned brat. I should have killed you when I had the chance.

He exhaled deeply. Dispose of one problem before concentrating on the next.

As he shifted his weight to the left arm, he could feel the tight knot of tension pulsing in his chest. It was always like this, just before an operation. In Germany, at the very moment he'd looked into the detective's eyes and opened his hands, so that the body dropped like a screaming stone from the fifth-floor window. The woman in Paris, the Saudi minister. Ireland, then four months ago in Athens. And in two more nights, Rome.

He lived for the drama. It was this edge—this risk—that kept life exciting.

The same way he'd felt before he became caught up in the world of violence, standing in the wings of the old theaters in London. Icy cold, not breathing—waiting for his cue. The smothering costumes, the creak of a floorboard, the scent of curtains musty with age. Then the great rush flooding his body as he swept forward into a brighter world, his worn velvet cloak shining richly under the magic of the stage lights.

He had gravitated to the roles of Shakespeare's villains, played so many of them in London's theaters over the years. Iago, Claudius, Caliban, Lear, Macbeth. Richard III, a particularly nasty piece of work. He smiled. You could always trust the bard. He understood vengeance, lust, betrayal. Rage.

Now the same cold expectancy was stirring in his loins.

I want a woman, he thought suddenly. He pictured Magdalena O'Shea, struggling beneath him on the dark wet sand, the long black ribbons of her hair blowing across her face as she fought him off. Bitch.

No. Don't think about that night on the beach in Cassis.

Control, he reminded himself. Always be the master of your fate. He had to have control, over his emotions, his missions, his enemies. His lovers . . .

His father had taught him well. Without control, you couldn't be safe.

I have to be safe.

Dane stood up and draped a towel across his sweating shoulder muscles. His one unbandaged eye sought his reflection in the dawn-streaked window. His hair was longer, lighter, spilling beneath the white bandages. Today, the bandages would come off.

What would his face look like?

His mouth twisted in a mocking smile. "You are one of those that will not serve God if the devil bid you," he said to the single wolf-like eye glittering back at him in the new day's sun.

* * *

"So how is La Maggie *really* doing, Mike?" Simon Sugarman's SUV sped south, too fast, on Virginia's George Washington Parkway. "She went through a helluva time in France."

Beckett stared out at the dark shapes of trees rushing by the window. "She's doing better, working to bring back her music. Not easy for a pianist who hasn't played in almost a year."

"She's a tough lady. But I'm guessing she still has the dreams. I sure do."

"The nightmares are there, all right. The sleeplessness, that sudden shine of tears. Emotional recovery can be just as tough as physical, but . . ." He hesitated. "But there's something more, Sugar, something she can't—or won't—talk about. It's like a cold black stone she's carrying around inside her heart."

"Give her time, Mike. She's worth it."

"Yeah, she had me at 'Who the hell are you?'" Beckett grinned. "I walked into a French cemetery as one man and came out as another. When I took an aggressive step toward her—she's the only woman I ever met who didn't back away. Stepped closer, in fact, chin up."

He shook his head. "But she's still grieving for her husband. It's only been a year."

"I know about fighting the ghosts, pal, so do you. No surprise she's still hung up on hers. Just keep trying."

"I am, because I want her to know I'm all in. Filed my divorce papers when we got back from France."

Sugarman's eyes widened as he gave a whistle. "You really are in. Your wife okay with it?"

"Yes, thank Christ. I didn't want to hurt her. Hell, Maggie didn't want to hurt her. But Jeannie's in a good place right now—hasn't had a drink in months."

"Good for her. And she knows you'll always be there for her."

"I loved her, Sugar. Still do, in my fashion."

"So, you're free to move on, too. Lucky bastard."

Beckett turned to Sugar with a surprised look. "You're as free as I am, Sugar. More."

"Not in my cards, pal. No 'love at first sight across a crowded room' for guys like me."

Beckett turned to the Golden, curled in the back seat, and threw him a famous-last-words look.

"Maggie's good for you. Got that brainy intensity thing going on, you know? And, damn, she sure stops traffic."

"Yes, the woman is drop-dead fine to look at, even on her worst day." Beckett smiled. "Funny, although she doesn't know it. Radiates intelligence, crazy talented. Loves *fireflies*." He shook his head. "She looks fragile as blown glass, but she is strong and fierce and brave as hell. Whiskey in a teacup."

"Sounds like she's the one who can keep you from walking the dark streets."

"There's just something about her. Something about me when I'm with her. I like myself more."

"I gotta say, Mike, sure sounds like you're in love with her."

Beckett's breath caught. "She's complex. Enormously challenging. And she surprises me. How could I *not* be in love with her?"

Sugar glanced over at him. "So tell her."

"Can't quite say the words."

"What's the problem, lover boy?"

"I'm closer in age to her father than to her," scowled Beckett, looking down at his cane. "I have *hats* older than she is. So what the devil is she doing with a battered old guy like me?"

"Not buyin' it. She's your safe place."

He stared at his friend. "Hadn't thought about it that way, but—yes. She lights up the dark places. Only—"

"You want to be a safe place for her as well."

Beckett let out his breath. "Don't you just hate irony? Because my life is all about violence. She wants me done with the darkness. But now I'm making the same call again. I'm going back into the dark."

"Yeah, well. There *is* that . . ." Sugarman's hands drummed on the wheel as he slowed to take the exit for the Key Bridge. "Maggie's sure not going to like that you're going to Rome with me, Mike."

"Maggie isn't gonna know." Beckett blew out a breath. "At least not until I get back."

Sugarman glanced into the back seat and spoke to the Golden. "Better file that one under 'upcoming disasters.'"

"Since when did you grow a conscience?" muttered Beckett. "Look, I know you can't always reconcile hurting someone you love in this business. There's always a personal cost. But I've got to know if Dane is back in the game, Sugar. He threatened Maggie—he *meant* it, damn him. I'm going *because* of her. I've got to find him."

"Hear that, Shiloh?" said Sugarman. "A man will do anything to protect the woman he loves when she's threatened."

Shiloh kept his opinion to himself.

Beckett ran a hand through his silvering hair. "You think it was Dane who tried to run me off the road? Why *now*? And if it wasn't Dane—then who the hell else wants me dead?"

Sugarman chuckled. "You really want me to answer that?"

Beckett scowled. "We don't even know that Dane will be in Rome. It could be a setup, Sugar."

"We have forty-eight hours to figure it all out, pal. Yeah, Rome could be a fool's errand."

"Then I guess you've found the right guy, Sugar."

Sugarman pulled up in front of the Key Bridge Holiday Inn and stopped. They looked at each other in the sudden quiet.

"You know you guys can bunk with me tonight, right?"

"I've seen your place, Sugar." Beckett smiled wearily. "Thanks for the lift. Shiloh and I will be just fine."

In the back seat, the Golden gave a slight growl, as if he knew better.

The two men grinned at each other. "Dang dog knows you better than you know yourself," said Sugarman. "Okay, then. Our flight for Rome leaves midnight Tuesday, from Andrews. Dane won't know what hit him."

Beckett shook his head. "When I'm done with Dane," he said, "I'll be done with *all* of it. For good. I just have to get Maggie to believe it."

Sugarman turned his dark eyes on Beckett. "*You're* the one who has to believe it, Mike."

His tires screeched as he sped off into the darkness.

CHAPTER THIRTEEN

ARLINGTON, VIRGINIA
SUNDAY NIGHT

In the impersonal Holiday Inn hotel room overlooking the Potomac River, the small clock was just striking midnight as Beckett lay in the too-soft bed staring at the shadowed ceiling. He closed his eyes, knowing he was headed back into the unforgiving darkness.

The Golden was sitting by the window, his eyes reflecting the lights along the river. Refusing to come to the bed. "Come here, boy, don't be alone tonight." He waited. Shiloh continued to gaze into the night, at something only he could see.

Taking a ragged breath, Beckett tried to find a quiet place to go to in his mind. A place without a sinister, knife-wielding killer, without blinding headlamps in a rearview mirror. A place without blood-soaked dust and the still and broken bodies of children in the hot Afghan sunlight.

A quiet place.

Maggie.

The image slipped softly into his mind, as if she knew he needed her. Standing as he had first seen her, less than four months earlier, in a Paris cemetery. Wild dark hair caught up, her slender frame vibrating in anger, huge soulful eyes flashing at him.

He stared at the shifting shadows on the ceiling, trying to imagine what his life would be without her. Couldn't do it.

His cell phone was on the bedside table. *Call her.* But what could he say to her?

As if sensing his conflict, Shiloh lifted his head and gave a soft bark.

"Okay. I know I shouldn't call her. But she's gotten so deep into my head."

I need to hear her voice tonight.

"Don't I get one more chance just to be happy?" Shiloh's eyes glistened at him from across the room.

"I'll take that as a 'yes.'" He reached for his cell, punched in the numbers.

Her voice, low and musical. Like a bass guitar.

"Hello?"

God, he missed her. That voice, stirring something so deep inside. The scent of her skin. The feel of her hair running through his fingers. Her face. Those damned beautiful edges . . .

He wanted to hold her.

"It's me," was all he said.

"Michael. Thank God. Where are you?"

"Can't tell you, ma'am."

"When will I see you?"

"Not sure."

A moment's silence. He could hear her breath, quick and sharp as a cold mountain breeze. "Why?" she whispered. "What's wrong?"

"I—nothing's wrong, Maggie. I just wanted to hear your voice." *Before I leave for Rome.*

"Shiloh! Is it Shiloh?"

He gazed over at the Golden. Two dark sad eyes stared at him from the window seat. "No change. Still got that mournful thing going on. I think he misses you."

"Tell him I miss him, too. But you need to tell me you're okay, damn you. CNN reported that there was a terrible car accident in Washington tonight, near the CIA. And, earlier, I felt so cold all of a sudden, as if—"

Accident. He pictured the gorgeous Beamer, engulfed in flames.

"Would I be talking to you, Maggie, if something had happened to me?"

"I just had this awful feeling . . ."

She was too damned intuitive. "When most people hear hoof beats, they think horses. *You* think zebras!"

"You're saying I'm overreacting?" He heard the smile in her voice.

"Like Bush in Iraq, ma'am. You think too much."

"I know a horse from a zebra, and I know when something is wrong."

Something was off. He heard the tension in her voice, became aware of other sounds in the background. "Where the devil are you?"

Silence. Then, "At the hospital. But I—"

Christ. He felt his heart constrict, gripped the phone tighter. "What's happened, Maggie?"

"It's *not me*, Michael. It's my stage manager, Jimmy. He was hurt in a mugging. But the doctors say he's going to be fine. I was just leaving."

He heard her cover the phone, speak to someone, her voice muffled. Then, "Let me call you when I get home."

Not gonna happen, he thought. What was going on?

"Listen to me, Maggie, don't hang up, we need to talk. I need to say I'm sorry."

"Sorry? You don't need to apologize for anything, Michael."

"I do. When you received your husband's mail at the cabin, I told you to stop loving a ghost. I was way out of line, I had no right to say that. I know grief has no timetable. Time never obeys our commands, does it? I have no idea how long it will take. But I'll wait for you, Maggie. I'll wait."

He heard her deep, shuddering breath. "Can you come to New York tonight? I need to be with you. *Want* to be with you."

He felt as if he'd been punched. "Nothing I'd rather do, darlin', but I'm going out of town for a few days."

"And you can't tell me where?"

"It's work, Maggie, I have to go. It's better if you don't know where I am."

"Why?"

"It's the truth. No questions for once. Please."

"Have you met me, Colonel? That won't fly."

"There are just things I can't tell you. Don't ask me to."

"And yet, here I am, asking."

He closed his eyes in frustration. "It's for your safety."

"I know that what you do is dangerous, I've seen it. But it's what you *don't* talk about that scares me the most."

"Maybe I don't use words, Maggie, but there's a place I go when the darkness gets bad. I'll take you there, if you want, when I get back."

"I want."

"Okay. I'll be back in a few days. And then I'll be on your doorstep in New York." *Kissing you.*

A soft breath. Was she imagining the kiss, too?

"Maggie?"

"I'm here."

"Just a few more days," he said softly.

"I can't picture where my life will be tomorrow, let alone a few days from now."

He smiled. "If you don't know where you're going, you'll end up somewhere else."

"Winston Churchill?"

"Yogi Berra. Where are you now?"

"Walking to the elevator."

He didn't want to let her go. "Just talk to me, darlin'."

"Without you and Shiloh to distract me, I'm all about music now. But I did run three miles this morning."

"I tried running once, but I kept spilling my drink."

That won a laugh.

"I like thinking of you playing the piano. Even if I don't know what a rhapsody is." He smiled, remembering the day in Paris when she had described a concerto to him in a way that made him want to kiss her.

Her voice softened. "Oh, no you don't, not again. A rhapsody is a one-movement work, with episodes, or variations. Free flowing in structure, with highly contrasted moods, colors, and tonality. There is a sense of improvisation, room to express great emotion."

"You've got the emotion locked, darlin'. But I still don't get the upside-down part."

"Upside down . . . you've *listened* to the *Rhapsody*?" He could hear the pleased surprise in her voice.

"It's your music, Maggie. Of course, I listened. Read about it, too."

"Rachmaninoff composed Variation 18 by inverting Paganini's original chords, his melody. That's your 'upside down.'"

"Sounds crazy hard."

"It is. But—" He heard the shuddery intake of breath, as if she was about to take a leap into the unknown. "My mother played it in Carnegie Hall. So it seems full circle, somehow."

Her mother. "Lily, right? You never talk about her, Maggie. What I know about your family would fit on Shiloh's collar."

Silence. One more deep, hurting breath. "It's too painful, Michael. I was just thirteen when she died. I have no memory of that night. I don't want to remember."

"Okay, darlin', you'll talk to me when you're ready." Her voice was fading in and out. "You'll take care of yourself, promise me?"

A low exhalation.

"Maggie? You'll do as I ask? For once?"

"I'll do it for *you*," she whispered in his ear.

"That was too easy. What's going on?"

Another hesitation. Too long. And then, "I'm at the elevator, Michael."

He shook his head, felt the pain shoot through his temples. "Just promise me you'll be careful while I'm gone—just a few days. Then I'll come home to you."

She took a breath, lowered her voice. He heard the elevator door ping in the background. "I can do as you ask, as long as I know . . ."

"*You know*, Maggie."

"Just don't get yourself shot, damn you."

She was gone.

CHAPTER FOURTEEN

NEW YORK CITY
JUST BEFORE MIDNIGHT, SUNDAY

You know.

Too tense to sleep, Maggie laid back against the pillows and looked up at the ceiling. Did she *know*? Michael was smart, challenging. Older, battered, with rainy eyes you could fall into forever. He'd played the guitar for her, sung to her in a voice soft as a caress. Told her legends of the mountains. Loved his rowboat. Loved his dog. Loved a wife and young son once, a long time ago, before the son died and the wife left him.

Since then, he was all about work. A loner.

She'd known him for almost four months, but—how well did she know him, really?

They lived hundreds of miles apart. Their work would keep them separated most of the time. And his work—God, would she ever get used to his world, so dangerous and filled with terror and violence?

And yet.

She pictured him at the cabin, sitting in front of the fire, the Golden's head resting so trustingly in his lap. Her heart tripped in her chest. *You know what's important*, she told herself. *He's a good man. Honest. A rescuer.*

You know . . .

But something was wrong. She knew it, felt it deep in her bones. She'd heard it in his voice. He hadn't told her the truth. Something big was weighing on him, something he couldn't talk about.

Okay, she hadn't exactly been honest either. Maybe she should have told him about the roses, about her suspicions that Dane had sent them. But he'd have jumped on his white horse and come charging in, determined to save her. Wanting to protect, as always. No, she'd deal with her problems herself, give him the space to deal with his. Maybe it was just as well, since now she was in New York and he was God knows where.

And she *was* handling things. The doors and windows were locked, the alarm set. At the hospital, she had told the detectives everything she knew—about the roses left at the theater and in her bedroom, and the security video stolen from Jimmy's backpack. He had been hit from behind with a blunt weapon. No gun, thank God. The popping sound she'd heard had come from the motorbike. The important thing was that Jimmy was going to be fine. But the sickening feeling of fear, of violation, was still with her.

Damn, why did everything have to be so complicated?

And what was troubling Michael?

She was the only woman he'd ever brought to his cabin in the mountains. Or so he'd told her. But she'd believed him.

The way he'd made her feel, just by looking at her. Singing John Legend's song to her, against her skin. His breath warm against her mouth. Even tonight, on the phone, she felt as if she'd been kissed. And, God, the man could kiss.

I just want to see him, she thought. *I just want to know he's okay.*

She touched her lips with her fingertips, then snapped off the light, slipped down under the thick cream quilt, closed her eyes.

Opened them.

You know.

* * *

The girl is curled on the edge of the low sofa, close to the piano.

If she reaches out, she can touch the pedals, or her mother's bare narrow foot. But she stays very still, listening to the music. The chords are haunting, dark with sorrow. She can hear her mother crying.

Just beyond the piano, French doors swing open to reveal a hidden garden. Shallow stone steps lead down to a long pool filled with shimmering blue water. Night is coming, and dark shadows spill across the pool in wavering indigo stripes. The very air is blue. She cannot tell where the water ends and the night sky begins.

Someone bangs on the door, shouting.

"Hide!" her mother warns her. "Hide now!"

She slips into the closet behind the piano, where her mother keeps her gowns. The closet is dark and warm and smells of Shalimar, her mother's perfume. She presses back into a deep blue velvet gown and watches through a crack in the door.

A man enters the room and strides toward the piano. Only his back is visible. She sees a white shirt, dark narrow jeans with frayed hems, black sneakers.

A low murmur. There is something about the voice . . .

Suddenly afraid, the girl shrinks back behind her mother's gowns, her hands clasped tightly over her mouth so that she will not make a sound.

The music stops without warning. The words are sharp now. Angry. She cannot understand what the man is saying.

Her mother cries out. A crystal vase filled with deep red roses topples to the floor and shatters, scattering shards of glass and petals like drops of blood onto the carpet. The scent of the roses fills her head.

Her mother runs out through the French doors. The man follows.

The girl cannot see his face.

All she can see is blue. The long blue pool beyond the open doors.

Then fog, a deeper blue, swirling toward her like water. The pool disappears.

The French doors slam shut.

Maggie cried out. Opening her eyes, she looked wildly around the dim room. No chilling blue fog. Just the antique writing desk, yellow reading chair in the curve of the tall window, books, and framed photographs crowded on the round bedside table. The Brownstone bedroom on West 65th. No pool, no blood-red roses. No angry, faceless figure by the piano.

A nightmare.

But still the dream's music, in that most haunting of minor chords, drifted in her head. What was it?

Flowing and emotional, moody, full of dark colors. That sense of improvisation. A rhapsody. One she has only heard in her dreams.

Maggie sat up, hugging her knees to her chest and staring into the darkness. This time she had not dreamed of Dane, or her husband, Johnny.

The roses, the French doors, the chilling, opaque blue fog. And the dark, aching music. The nightmare from her childhood had returned.

For the first time in many years, she was dreaming again of the night her mother drowned.

PART II

"There is a rapture on the lonely shore . . .
By the deep sea, and music in its roar."

— Lord Byron

CHAPTER FIFTEEN

NEW YORK CITY
MONDAY, OCTOBER 20

THE SMALL GOLD plaque announced PH #1. Maggie stood in front of a wide, carved wooden door and pressed the polished bell. Chimes playing Bach echoed somewhere in the distance.

She glanced at the gold watch circling her wrist like a bracelet. Almost noon. Lord, it had been a long night. The nightmare—spilled roses, haunting music, the terrifying blue. But this was the first time she'd dreamed of a pool beyond the French doors. What had happened beyond those closed doors?

The pool, she was sure, was a real memory. Where was it? She knew only that she had seen that pool before. Somewhere. A very long time ago . . .

She had not dreamed of her mother's death in so long. Why now? The trigger had to have been the roses left at the concert hall, and then later on her pillow.

Maggie sighed. There was just no sense of *why*. Jimmy had been hurt, someone had broken into her apartment. Been in her *bedroom*. It was no wonder she was unsettled and scared. No wonder the nightmares were back.

Once more she glanced at the doorbell as she shifted the leather bag slung over her shoulder. What had she been thinking, to ask a classical music legend to give her a lesson? No one was answering. Thank God. Just turn around and leave before—

The door swung open and Gisela Giulietta Donati smiled at her, banishing the darkness. "Welcome, my dear. I'm so sorry you had to wait." The woman waved a beautiful lacquered cane in the air. "They say eighty-two is the new seventy-five, but you can't prove it by me!" A glissade of laughter. "Please come in."

Tall and regal, today the aging pianist was dressed in a deep magenta dress with long flowing sleeves, a bright silken scarf at her throat. Five-carat amethysts, the color of her eyes, dangled from her ears. She reminded Maggie of the British actor Dame Maggie Smith, a woman "of a certain age," dramatic and elegant.

Maggie stepped into the hallway and Madame Donati took her hand. "Your mother was a beautiful woman. You look so much like her that it feels like yesterday."

Maggie squeezed the gnarled hand gently. "Thank you, that means more to me than I can say. I'm hoping you will tell me more about her. There's so much I don't remember, so much I missed. So much I still don't know."

"I have wonderful memories of your mother, Maggie, and I will tell you all of them. Come." Madame Donati drew her down an art-filled hallway toward a huge front room filled with light. The faint scent of Chanel drifted behind her. "We all lost Lily far too soon. When I think of all the glorious music she would have given us, given to the world . . ."

She shook her head. "And then there's that damned father of yours. Another great loss to the music world." Her gaze was distant, remembering. "He was called 'the bad boy of the classical world,' did you know that? Parties, alcohol. He was devastatingly handsome, passionate, charismatic. He once stopped Mahler's Second Symphony to turn and throw a handful of cough drops at a man in the first row. My God, you could hear a pin drop in the audience after that!"

"Just like him."

"Well, of course, his first love was music. He was a decade younger than I, but that never stopped him from shouting at me. 'Give it all you've got, Gigi darling,' he would demand. 'And *then*—crescendo!'"

Maggie smiled in spite of herself. "He would come off the stage drenched in sweat. The stagehands had to help him remove his soaked tux. I remember . . ." Her voice faded, went silent.

Gigi touched Maggie's arm gently. "I know, child. Music was his drug. But he was crazy in love with your mother. And you. When he spoke of you, his voice changed." She leaned closer. "That's why his leaving never made any sense to me. To any of us. Did you ever find out why he left? Did you ever hear from him?"

Maggie stiffened. "Other than the occasional postcard from somewhere in Europe, and a glimpse in a crowd, once, at a stage door? No."

"Knowing Finn as I did, I believe your father must have had a very good reason for leaving you, child."

"Can there ever *be* a good reason to abandon your young daughter?"

"I wish you could have found your father, Maggie. I wish you could have talked to him before he died."

"I wish it, too, Madame Donati. More than you know." They came to the long, light-filled living room. "Oh." Maggie gasped. "How beautiful. It's like discovering a secret wing in the Museum of Modern Art."

"MoMa is a lovely compliment, thank you. My husband, Emmanuel, loved art—he collected these pieces over many years. And please, call me Gigi. Only my students call me Madame Donati." She gestured to a long, low tuxedo sofa. "Shall we sit?"

"In a moment, please." Maggie did a slow pirouette, gazing around the room. The eighth-floor penthouse apartment, in a prewar building facing Fifth Avenue and Central Park, was like stepping back into the elegance of turn-of-the-century Paris. A velvet sofa in peacock blue on a huge Aubusson carpet, tall tasseled lamps, a low antique table set with an ornate silver tea service and small iced cakes. Every available wall space was covered by photographs and oil paintings in thick gilt-leafed frames—beautiful, glowing pieces that seemed alive. Beyond a wall of floor-to-ceiling windows, the cloudless sky was the color of lapis, the treetops shivered with gold and russet leaves.

And there—in its place of honor in front of the windows—a gleaming Bösendorfer concert grand piano. Drawn as if by a huge magnet, she approached the Bösendorfer. "May I?"

"Of course."

"Hello, beautiful," whispered Maggie, touching the shining wood, depressing the Middle C. The tone was perfect, filling the room with the long true note.

"My God, Gigi . . ."

The older woman appeared at her shoulder. "I know what you are feeling. This is an Imperial, with ninety-seven keys rather than the usual eighty-eight. The spruce comes from the same Austrian forest that Stradivari chose for his violins." Gigi's slender, age-spotted hand caressed the keys. "My lady here has a crystalline clarity, a singing sustain, and the most majestic, dark rich sound. As you will see . . ."

A crystal vase on a small table next to the piano held a dozen bright yellow roses, their scent spicy sweet in the morning air, stirring old memories. Maggie touched a velvet petal, trying to ignore the images of the scattered rose petals in her dream.

"Your father always gave your mother roses," said Gigi. "Scarlet roses. Do you remember? She would set them by her piano."

A Waterford vase, glowing crimson petals. Was that part of the dream real? Maggie turned to Gigi with a startled look. "I remember roses near a piano. My father gave them to her?"

"He wrote her love letters all the time, too, she told me once."

Maggie's gaze flew to Gigi's face. "I had no idea! Do you know what happened to them?"

Gigi shook her head. "One more of your mother's secrets," she said softly.

An attractive young Latina woman dressed in soft colors entered the room carrying a silver tray. "Ah, Graciela." Gigi smiled. "This is my friend, the pianist Magdalena O'Shea. I think Madame O'Shea would much prefer to try out our Bösendorfer now, before we have our tea." She turned sparkling eyes, filled with humor, on Maggie. "Yes?"

"Absolutely, yes." Maggie settled herself on the piano bench and drew the Rachmaninoff score from the large shoulder purse she carried. Dropping it to the parquet floor, she set her music on the piano and tried to calm her racing heart. "I've never played a Bösendorfer."

"What are you working on?"

"Rachmaninoff's *Rhapsody*."

"Oh *ho*, my girl, you do surprise me. His Theme of Paganini . . . Your mother's first performance at Carnegie, yes? A bold choice. Graciela, in honor of Rachmaninoff, we shall need a bottle of crème de menthe and two glasses." She planted her cane, then set her hip on a low stool just to the right of the keyboard. "Ah, Sergei Rachmaninoff. One of the finest pianists and composers of all time. He composed this rhapsody in the 1930s, at an estate he built near Lake Lucerne called Villa Senar. The 'se' and the 'na' combined his name, Sergei, and his wife, Natalia. Another great romance." She shook her head. "I hear that fool Putin wants to buy Senar now. I hope the heirs tell him to take a hike!"

She frowned, then stamped her cane hard on the parquet floor as if to banish her angry thoughts.

"So. We will begin by giving you a chance to warm up with the Allegro Vivace, then Variation 1 and the Tema, yes? Rachmaninoff had the temerity to take the theme from the very last of Paganini's twenty-four caprices—even though the eighteenth is by far the most beautiful, as you well know." A graceful wave of slender, gnarled fingers. "Begin."

One more stamp of the cane on the parquet floor, softer this time but no less commanding.

Maggie heard the shimmer of laughter in the lovely pianist's voice. *Just shoot me now*, she thought. Taking a deep breath, she raised her hands above the keys and began to play.

CHAPTER SIXTEEN

WASHINGTON, DC
MONDAY

BECKETT PULLED UP to a high iron gate and flashed his badge at the soldier on guard. The gate swung open and gravel crunched beneath the tires as he eased his rented jeep into a parking space under the trees. It was raining hard, and the parking lot, lit by lamps casting deep black shadows across glistening puddles, was almost empty.

"I come here whenever I'm in DC," he said to the Golden, who sat very still on the passenger seat staring out at the rain. "It's not easy, just something I've got to do." He touched the dog gently. "I'm glad you're with me."

Gripping his cane, he eased from the car, brushed off the stiff shoulders of his dress uniform, and flipped open a large black umbrella. "I know you don't like the rain," he said to the dog. "You can stay in the car if you want to."

The Golden eyed him for a moment, then looked at the slashing rain. Very slowly, he rose from the seat and lumbered out of the car.

Beckett moved the umbrella over the dog. "Thanks, fella," he whispered.

Together they made their way down the winding path of Arlington National Cemetery to Section 60. This was the section, Beckett knew only too well, where over seven hundred veterans from Iraq and Afghanistan were buried.

At the end of a row of simple white headstones, Beckett stopped and stood at attention in the hard rain as he gazed down at the soaked earth.

"Hey, E-Z, it's me. Beckett. And this is my friend Shiloh."

The words were carved into the pure white stone. *Ezra Berger*. But everyone had called him E-Z. *Easy*.

His gaze took in the rows upon rows of perfectly aligned white headstones, now silvered by tears of rain, as far as he could see. How many men and women had he known? Too damned many. *Christ*. In just two months, some 40,000 volunteers would descend on the cemetery, to lay Christmas wreathes on more than 240,000 graves. He'd done it himself, last year. It was a heartbreaking, soul-rending sight.

In Kabul, just last spring, E-Z had told him that he had a Christmas birthday. He was going to be twenty-two on December 25. *I'll come back at Christmas, E-Z. I'll come back with a wreath for you*.

No, there was no solace here today. What he needed was a double Jack Daniel's—but he wasn't sure that would help, either.

Beckett sat down on the cold wet grass, ran a hand over the grave. "Damn it, E-Z, why? I carried you into that medic's tent. You told me you wanted to go home. You could've come *home*, dammit. *Alive*. Why'd you go back?"

Whiskey Tango Foxtrot. He knew why. The same reasons he'd returned to Afghanistan for three tours. But he'd done it to protect all those young lives. Every man has to make his own choices, he thought.

He looked down at the new grave. "You weren't supposed to come home this way."

Shiloh whined mournfully beside him, brushing his single front paw against Beckett's leg.

"You know, don't you, boy? What it's like to suffer loss? What it's like to be the only survivor?" His hand found the warm damp fur, stroked the long, jagged lightning scars crossing the dog's shoulder. "To be caught in the darkness that seeps into your soul."

The Golden edged closer, somehow feeling his pain. Did Shiloh, too, remember running across that dusty Afghani square after his young friend Farzad? Did he remember the whine of automatic weapons, the crush of pain as the bullets slammed into his beautiful golden body to turn it into a mangled mess of red?

Afghanistan.

Just an ocean full of memories and pain. And loss. All those green kids. All those innocent lives, just beginning. His own son, if he had lived, would have been just about E-Z's age . . .

Beckett leaned back against the cold hard stone where his young friend was buried.

So many young ones lost. Beckett's breath came out in a long sigh. "I'm sorry, man," he whispered. "I feel as if I let you down."

Too many ways to lose the war after the guns go silent. Black pain engulfed him. Shiloh circled, then settled with his head and front paw on Beckett's thigh with a mournful, knowing expression.

After a long time, Beckett touched the Golden's head, rose stiffly to his feet. Because E-Z was Jewish, he found a small stone and left it on top of the memorial. Standing at attention, he gave his friend a final soldier's salute.

"That even in our sleep," he quoted softly, "pain that cannot forget falls drop by drop upon the heart." He looked down at his dog. "I wonder if maybe I left the best part of myself back there in Afghanistan," he said into the rain.

Then he and the Golden limped slowly down the dark path, away from the silent headstones.

* * *

Maggie's fingers raced over the keyboard in a final crescendo of chords. One last, sustained chord, and then her hands stilled. The notes echoed in the sun-filled room. Afraid to look at Madame Donati, she bent her head, closed her eyes, and tried to catch her breath.

"Almost as good as your mother. *Almost*."

Again, humor shimmered in the gentle voice. Maggie opened her eyes and smiled with relief. "Thank God."

"Don't thank him yet! You haven't touched the keys for almost a year, my girl, and it shows. Technically, well, you have work to do, of course. You want to be better than your mother, yes? You will come tomorrow at the same time. And this time we will *really* work. Tonight you must concentrate on the first movement, Variations two through ten. Four hours at least. I want . . . well, molto badass."

Maggie laughed. "A challenge I've never been given before."

"And I have no doubt you will rise to the occasion."

"I have so much to learn from you, Gigi. You have so much energy and spirit. What is your secret?"

"Keep busy, and you won't have time to die."

They exchanged an understanding smile. "All I can say," said Maggie, "is thank you."

"Bosh! All I can teach you is what tempo might work better, how to finger a difficult passage, what to leave out. Let me worry about those ambiguous accent marks. *You* will do all the real work, my girl. Your father always said a score should not be the endpoint, but a *departure*. Your job is to go beyond the score and create something new. So. Now we have earned our tea and our crème de menthe. And perhaps two stiff brandies as well? Graciela! We are ready, if you please."

The two women moved to the peacock-blue sofa and settled into the down cushions. Once again Madame Donati took both of Maggie's hands in her own and gazed down at them. "Your hands are made for the piano, Maggie. You don't have the hand span of men like Horowitz or Van Cliburn, but you have the touch. The technique will come back, my dear. But artistically—it is the heart of the piece, the magic, that counts. You have the feeling, Maggie, that rare ability to *transport* the listener. You are, quite simply . . ." She smiled. "Transcendent."

Gigi looked down at the thick, misshapen knobs on the spotted knuckles of her own hands. "Arthritis and age may have claimed my talent," she whispered, "but it cannot take away the music that still lives inside me. Or the way it makes me feel."

She leaned closer. "Your godfather, Zander, told me about the death of your husband," she said in a quiet, gentle voice. "I am so sorry. He was much too young to die." She looked away. "I lost my husband, Emmanuel, just a few months ago. We were married for almost fifty years."

"Gigi . . ." Maggie reached out to express her sorrow, but Madame Donati stopped her. "It was his time, Maggie. A person does not get to be my age without experiencing loss. Suffering grief."

"It's been a year since I lost Johnny," said Maggie softly. "But sometimes it seems like yesterday. I still love my husband, still miss him." She gazed into the sympathetic eyes of Gigi Donati. "Sometimes I can't breathe with the hurt."

Maggie rose from the sofa and moved to stand before a large, dark oil painting of a woman in a long blue gown, staring out at a ship foundering in a turbulent sea. "I feel like the woman in this painting. My husband drowned in a storm at sea."

"This is called *Miranda in The Tempest*," said Gigi. She waved a hand toward the painting. "A dear friend of mine compares grief to a shipwreck. He says at first it comes in waves one hundred feet high, crashing over you without mercy or warning. All you can do is hang on to the wreckage and try to stay alive."

"Yes," whispered Maggie. "That's exactly what it's felt like. Waves of grief. I've been drowning, too, for months . . . just like my husband . . ."

"But after a time, the waves come farther apart, yes? Not quite so high. And between the waves, there is life." Madame Donati touched Maggie's shoulder gently. "There is no closure when you lose someone you love. The waves never stop coming, I'm afraid. But then, I'm not sure we want them to. Memory is both the curse and solace of grief."

Maggie raised her eyes to the older woman. "You're right, I don't want to lose the good memories. I can move on when I'm between waves."

"I look at life like that beautiful instrument," said Gigi, waving her hand at the piano by the window. "The white keys represent happiness, the black—sadness. But the black keys *also make music*, Maggie. That is what matters. Music gives us something to cling to when we are lost. And after the music I heard you make today, I know you are coming back to life."

"Yes. I'm finding my music again. And—there is another man in my life now, someone noble and fierce, who is helping me to move on." Maggie pictured the colonel and smiled. "He makes me feel alive again."

"Noble and fierce." Light stirred in Gigi's old eyes. "Feeling alive. It sounds like the beginning of a grand romance."

"In opera and Shakespeare," muttered Maggie, "all the great romances end in tragedy."

Gigi chuckled. "Nonsense. I'm sure that being loved again is what your husband would have wanted for you. Just remember, Maggie. It's not the note you play. It's the note you play *next*."

"I keep asking myself, who am I now, after he is gone? What is my new identity without him?"

"You may not have all the answers, but you are asking the important questions. Terrible things happen to all of us, Maggie. The only control we have is how to survive—hopefully with humor and courage. You have learned how to behave with grace in the face of death." Gigi gazed at Maggie thoughtfully. "I think perhaps you might be the one to help me move on as well, my dear."

Maggie looked at her in surprise. "You? I cannot imagine how, Gigi, but I will do whatever I can."

"Come, then." Gigi took Maggie's hand, drawing her slowly across the salon and turning a corner to reveal a hidden alcove. A five-foot-high impressionist oil hung alone on the wall. It was a painting of a woman in shadows, seated by a window filled with a night sky, playing a cello.

"I am going to trust you with a huge and terrible secret, Maggie. Come closer. What do you think of this work?"

A huge and terrible secret... A dark sense of foreboding whispered against Maggie's skin as she moved to stand beside Gigi. Gazing at the beautiful cellist in the painting, she felt something stir in her chest. The tiniest spark of memory. What was it?

The swirling brushstrokes on the woman's sapphire dress, the shimmering richness of the scarlet draperies behind her. The night sky beyond the tall window pulsing with deep blue, the light streaming from a candle on the table touching the woman's face with flickering gold and shadow.

"It's"—Maggie searched for the perfect word—"*saturated* with color. Lit from within. This painting looks as if it belongs at the Met. I know very little about art, but the colors and brushstrokes are so deep and beautiful. The cello is glowing, vibrating, as if you can *hear* the music. And the expression on the woman's face as she strokes the bow . . . I *feel* something when I look at her, Gigi. I'd swear it is an original."

Madame Donati turned to her. "And you would be right—you have a good eye. It is an original Matisse. He called it *Dark Rhapsody*."

"*Dark Rhapsody . . .*" Again Maggie felt the thrum of a memory wash over her skin, like the haunting melody in her dream.

"This glorious Matisse is beautiful," said Gigi softly, "but it has a dark history. And it is not mine."

"I don't understand," said Maggie. "Did someone give it to you?"

"The truth is, my dear, I am a liar and a thief." Tears glittered in the old pianist's eyes as she waved her hands toward the Matisse. "You do not remember it? I gave this piece to your parents soon after I met them. This *Dark Rhapsody* hung above your mother's grand piano when you were a child."

CHAPTER SEVENTEEN

NEW YORK CITY
MONDAY

"I WAS BORN in a small Austrian mountain village near an Alpine lake," said Gigi Donati. "I was only ten years old in 1945, when the war ended. The Nazis were hiding their looted treasures all over Europe, including deep beneath Austria's lakes. Late one night, they came to my village, and I stole a small chest from a Nazi truck. I was hoping to find gold, of course, but the chest held only a violin, some candlesticks, some musical scores, and three rolled canvases of art from a gallery in Florence. I hid it all in my aunt's barn."

Gigi's words fell like stones into the quiet room. Afternoon sun flowed through the tall windows, suffusing her face with radiance. She stood by the grand piano, lost in memory, like a woman standing alone on a stage in a cone of light.

Listening with her whole body, Maggie could barely breathe.

"My best friend, Johann, found me. The next morning, when we went back to retrieve the chest, my aunt and cousin were just—gone. They had run away, I found out later. I was terrified, of course, for my family. I swore Johann to secrecy. He helped me hide the chest and kept my secret all these years."

Maggie stepped closer, laid a gentle hand on Gigi's arm. "This Matisse—this *Dark Rhapsody*—is one of the paintings you found?"

Gigi Donati nodded, unable to speak.

"I don't understand. How did it end up in my parents' home?"

Gigi drew a deep, shuddering breath. "The trunk was hidden in Johann's attic for many years. There were many Nazis, German sympathizers, and collaborators in our village, of course. We did not know whom we could trust, even after the war was over."

Gigi turned away to gaze blindly out the window over the treetops of Central Park. "It is so difficult to understand now—the fear, the hiding, who were the sympathizers? My mother had hidden a Jewish family for almost a year in our cellar. If I called attention to my family . . . Well, who knows? Fear is no excuse, of course, but that part, at least, is the truth."

"I believe you." Very gently Maggie took the old pianist's arm, brittle and shaking beneath her fingers, and led her to a chair. "Sit down, Gigi. May I get you some water? I'm not judging you, I only want to help."

"No water, I just need to say all the words . . ."

"I'm listening."

"We kept the art hidden for four years. Then, the day Johann turned sixteen, he went to Florence and searched for the art gallery stamped on the back of the canvases—the Felix Hoffman Gallery—so we could return his property. But there was nothing left, only a destroyed shell of a building. Shattered windows, bare walls, garbage, rats . . . Oh, God."

Maggie realized with sickening clarity what had happened. "The family was Jewish," she whispered. "They were taken by the Nazis?"

"Yes. The neighbors told Johann that Hitler's thugs had come for them in the dead of night. They looted everything from the gallery and took Hoffman and his wife, and their little girl and boy, with them. The family never returned."

"I don't know what to say," said Maggie. "I cannot imagine such horror."

"No one can. When Johann told me that we could not return the art to the rightful owners, we talked all night and finally decided to keep the secret and go on with our lives." She waved her hands in the air. "Oh, I know that is the coward's way out. Being young is no excuse, it is simply what we did. I went on with my piano studies, and Johann went to school in Vienna to study art."

"And the chest of art . . ."

"Stayed right where it was. His parents died not knowing that a king's fortune was hidden in their attic, just above their heads." Gigi stood slowly, moved to stand in front of the Matisse. "When I had a chance to study music in America, Johann sold some of the chest's contents on the black market to finance my expenses. And he gave me this Matisse, my favorite, to bring with me to New York." She shook her head. "As if I would ever sell it!"

"Thank God you didn't. But how did it end up with my parents?"

"A musician friend introduced me to Finn and Lily. I was a decade older than your parents, of course, but we had such a love of music in common. I told you that I taught your mother after she graduated from Yale. That is true. Both of your parents became very dear to me. It was your father who introduced my first concert at Lincoln Center. I played Liszt's *Piano Sonata in B minor*. Your father insisted it needed four hands to play, but I managed it."

She smiled faintly. "Then I married my husband, Emmanuel. He was Jewish. I could not bear to have the *Rhapsody* in his home. It seemed like a betrayal. And so, one night I told your father the truth about the Matisse, and gave *Dark Rhapsody* to him for safekeeping."

"My God. Finn knew?"

"I did not tell him everything. But, yes, I think he knew."

Maggie drew a deep breath. "How can I help you?"

Gigi stood straight, her chin high, and gazed at Maggie. "Look at me, Maggie. I am an old woman. I am running out of time. I need to make things right. I should have done it long ago. I want to return *Dark Rhapsody* to the family of Felix Hoffman, if there are any descendants still alive. If not, it should be in a museum. I am only sorry I waited so long."

"I know someone who may be able to help you," said Maggie. "Do you know where the other two paintings are hidden?"

Gigi shook her silver head. "I imagine they are still with Johann."

"He is still alive?"

"He was just a few months ago. I called him, asked his help to track down any of Felix Hoffman's descendants. He sent me an envelope after my husband died. I'm sure Johann's been feeling his mortality, just as I am. And, just as I do, he wants to right an old wrong before he no longer can."

"What was in the envelope?"

"Information that I hope will lead to the location of the other pieces—and perhaps to an heir. I've kept it in my safe deposit box. No note, he just sent two theater programs and a photograph of a woman."

"Will you get them for me?"

"Tomorrow." Gigi hesitated. Then, "There is just one more thing you should know."

Maggie looked into the amethyst eyes, now darkened by . . . concern? Guilt? Fear?

Gigi Donati took a deep breath. "I don't know for sure, but I've always believed that your father's disappearance from the stage so long ago had something to do with the *Dark Rhapsody*."

CHAPTER EIGHTEEN

NEW YORK CITY
TUESDAY, OCTOBER 21

JUSTICE AGENT SIMON Sugarman stood in Giulietta Donati's living room admiring an oil painting of several pastel ballerinas, glowing in the late morning light.

Damned if those dancers didn't look like they'd been painted by Degas. He shook his head wearily. *You need to get out more*, he told himself. *Get a life.*

Somewhere down the hall, a clock chimed the eleven a.m. hour. Light heels sounded across the marble floor behind him, and he turned.

Maggie O'Shea walked toward him, graceful, confident, hair still wild and black as a Cairo night.

He smiled down at her. "Doctor O'Shea, I presume?"

"Simon! It's been too long. I've missed you."

She moved in, allowed herself to be swallowed by his linebacker arms.

Sugarman kissed the top of her head, then held her away from him. Slender and glowing as the dancers in that painting behind her. Wicked smart, sure, a given. And those eyes . . . She would see right through him if he wasn't careful.

He gave a low laugh as he read the words on her narrow black t-shirt—*The Bach Stops Here*. "Oh, yeah. I've missed you, too, Maggie O'Shea. You're a sight for sore eyes, Doc."

He'd given her the nickname on a blistering day last July when they'd first met in her music shop in Boston, after he'd noticed the two framed PhDs in musicology on the wall. Now Maggie smiled into his eyes and shook her head. "Come and sit down, Simon. So much has been happening. I'm glad you're here. I need your help."

"I was just asking Beckett how you're doing."

Her eyes widened with surprise. "You were with Michael? Where?"

Uh-oh. "Just taking care of some old business. Nothing to worry about."

"Now *that* worries me."

He grinned at her. "Okay, so maybe sometimes Mike does the wrong thing . . . but it's always for the right reasons, Maggie. I'm the street fighter, remember? He's the knight."

Ignoring the disbelief in her expression, Sugarman wandered around the room, stopping by the grand piano. "Heard you'll be playing at Carnegie Hall. Good for you. I'll expect a comp ticket. Now maybe you can help me with this morning's *Times* crossword. It's about music, and I need an eight-letter word for the site where Carnegie Hall was built in 1891."

"Easy one. Goat Hill. Andrew Carnegie built the hall on the northern frontier of Manhattan—it was still a grazing area, not another building nearby."

He laughed, coming toward her. "Sheesh! Talk about a visionary. And now 57th Street is the most expensive real estate in Manhattan. Okay, so here's a piano clue, big shot. "Who was the Pole who provided his piano magic that same year, 1891? Ten letters."

"Does Paderewski have ten letters?"

"You're good." He sank back into the peacock velvet sofa with a sigh of approval. "This place is gorgeous. What'd you do? Vegas jackpot? Rob a bank? Long-lost uncle?"

"I've had more than enough drama in my life, Simon." Maggie waved an arm around the light-filled room. "Yes, it's beautiful, but not mine. Belongs to an old friend of my family, the international concert pianist Giulietta Donati. She had an appointment, but asked that I fill you in until she gets here. *She's* the reason that I called you."

Sugarman waved a finger at her. "You said on the phone that this had to do with missing art. You have got my attention, Doc. Tell me."

* * *

Maggie leaned forward, her eyes on Simon Sugarman.

In his midfifties, Sugarman was tall and lean as a granite spire, with close-cropped hair the color of coal, skin as black as asphalt, and a sheen of silvery whiskers around a hard jaw. Today, in his dark, well-cut business suit, white shirt, and quiet tie, he almost fit her image of a government agent. Almost. Until you noticed the bright spark of the diamond in his left ear and the dark blue Adidas running shoes beneath the cuffs of the fine wool slacks.

He caught her look, grinned as he touched the diamond in his ear. "A little bling never hurts, right?"

She smiled. "You haven't changed. I called you because I hope you are still doing your 'Monuments Men' thing."

"Yeah. Still alone, still doing crosswords, still at Justice searching for all that lost 'Cultural Property.' You'd be surprised how much illegal trafficking there is—every black market wants stolen antiquities, sculptures, art. Best lucrative investment there is. And now, because of you, I've added rare instruments and missing musical scores to my list. Who knew music was worth so much?"

"An autographed copy of Rachmaninoff's *Symphony No. 2*, lost for decades after the premiere, was found not long ago and sold for two million dollars."

He gazed at her with a choirboy expression. "Would you believe that last week I found a Rembrandt and a Stradivarius in an attic? But I had to leave them behind. Stradivarius was a terrible artist and Rembrandt made lousy violins. Ba da boom!"

She laughed. "Don't give up your day job."

"So, Doc, what's all this about? Looking for any more long-lost concertos?"

"I wish. But I didn't ask you here because of music. Are you still looking for Victor Orsini's missing art collection, Simon?"

The last time she had been with Sugarman, in the South of France, the agent was searching for a very wealthy art collector last seen in Paris. A man named Victor Orsini, who was suspected of selling priceless stolen art to private collectors so he could finance acts of terror against the US.

Sugarman leaned toward her. "Bingo. Turns out Orsini's father was a collaborator during the war. Helped the Nazis loot art from all over Germany, France, and Italy—and kept several pieces for himself as payment. Old Masters, Impressionists, the Moderns. Rubens, Rembrandt, da Vinci. Degas, Monet, Van Gogh. Matisse, Picasso, Klee. A king's fortune." He snapped his fingers. "Vanished into thin air the day Orsini died."

Pop! Pop! Pop! The terrifying sounds crashed into her head and she winced, because she'd been there that day. Heard the gunshots. Watched in horror as Orsini fell to the earth. But she only said, "That collection has to be worth millions of dollars."

"Could be billions. Tracking stolen art is a real challenge, Doc, because there's one hell of a black market for private collectors. And they know they've bought illegal items, so they ain't talkin'."

He grinned, waving a hand toward the art on Gigi's walls. "Great works of stolen art are rarely on view like this. They are hidden away, inside a cottage, a mansion, a palace, a basement, an attic, a secret room. Tiffany windows were found in a garage. The German collector Cornelius Gurlitt hid a collection worth millions in a nondescript walk-up in a Munich suburb." He shook his head. "As much as one-fifth of the world's art treasures was looted by the Nazis, Doc, valued at thirty *billion* dollars! Most of that art is gone forever. The recovery rate is only ten percent."

He turned to gaze at a fluid landscape. "My gut says Orsini's looted art is probably hanging somewhere in a private collection just like . . ." His voice trailed off and he turned to her, his dark eyes flashing with realization.

"Why are you looking at me that way, Simon?"

"Just months ago, in France, Orsini disappeared the night you found your godson. Two days later, Orsini was dead. He only had forty-eight hours to hide that damned art. Where did he stash dozens of canvases, how did he do it so quickly? It's been driving me crazy. But now, standing here looking at you—you were the last person to see him alive, Maggie."

"He didn't mention the art, Simon."

"Okay. But what *did* he talk about? It's important, Doc."

She closed her eyes, wanting to resist the memories. But they swirled into her head, insistent. "My husband," she said finally. "I accused Orsini of Johnny's death. He denied it. And—" Her eyes flew to his. "Oh, God. He wanted to know where his son, Tommy, was. The only person in the world he still loved. My godson."

Sugarman nodded slowly. "I'm putting myself in Orsini's head now, bear with me. You have this priceless collection of stolen art, you live a dangerous life. You have to plan ahead, find a hiding place. Just in case. You've got to leave the art to someone. Someone you trust, someone you love. What do you do? You go to that person you trust, ask him to help you find a safe place to store the collection. You keep it secret. Only two people, besides yourself, know the location. The one you've called on to help you over the years. And the one you love most in the world."

"TJ?" she whispered. "But Tommy is so young."

"Your godson knows where the art is, Maggie. Trust me."

"But that means . . ."

"That TJ is in danger. Yeah."

CHAPTER NINETEEN

TUSCANY
TUESDAY, OCTOBER 21

DANE PACED BACK and forth in the small attic room, his gaze on the setting sun beyond the window, his thoughts on a little boy with too many secrets.

He'd fallen asleep an hour earlier, and dreamed of a skinny, frightened young boy with too-long hair hiding his eyes, forced to watch a cruel father abuse his mother night after endless night. A boy who felt helpless, trapped, who would run off by himself to hide.

And now the kid had the key to finding his father's hidden treasure.

How would his life have been different if his father had been kind, gentle? Loving?

"Our wills and fates do so contrary run," he murmured. Hamlet understood.

Enough. Time to go to the vineyard, question the boy.

Dane needed that art. It was time to take action.

Beyond the window, the sky was turning purple with twilight.

Dane closed his eyes, inexplicably uneasy. *Was I really dreaming about Tommy Orsini?* he wondered.

Or was the little boy in the dream . . . me.

* * *

"Yes, of course I love Harry Potter. And Hermione, too. London is one of my very favorite cities." Maggie smiled, listening to her godson's flutelike voice. His face on her iPhone was happy and excited, so different from the way he had been just months earlier. The tousled curls and huge dark eyes brought back so many memories. "Yes, I remember my promise. We're going to celebrate your seventh birthday together, I wouldn't miss it. Have fun at your football game, we'll talk soon. Oh, sweetheart, I love you more!"

Maggie blew a kiss and disconnected with a sigh of relief and turned to Simon Sugarman. "You heard. He's in London on a school trip until the weekend. Thank God. He should be safe there."

"For now. We've bought a few days, maybe, that's all. I'll call Zach," said Simon, referring to TJ's guardian, "and make sure he knows the score."

"Do you really think TJ could be in danger?"

"If Dane hasn't made the connection to TJ yet, he will. Let's just say I think that the best way to keep your godson safe is to find that art—the sooner the better."

"Then I'll fly to France as soon as TJ gets home. If I ask him—"

"No! Absolutely not, Doc. He'll be safer if you're not there with him, trust me. Leave his protection to me. Can you do that?"

She locked eyes with his, her shoulders rigid with resistance. "I will think about it," she said finally. "Isn't there anything else we can do? Did Orsini leave a will? A letter, anything at all?"

"I suspect he had an inventory, but we've found zero. So let's talk about why I'm here."

"I remembered that you found a painting left behind when Orsini disappeared."

Sugarman nodded. "A small Cezanne—a landscape titled, *Auvers on the River Oise*, excuse my French. Last seen before that in the Stassfurt salt mills art repository near Magdeburg, Germany.

Believed to have been stolen from a Jewish banker in Florence, Italy, in 1942."

"Florence. Yes. That's the story that stayed with me."

He leaned closer, intrigued. "Thousands of pieces are still missing from World War II, in spite of the success of the Monuments Men. But I've been narrowing my search down over the last months. Florence is key. Turns out that Orsini's mother lived there during the war. I've been trying to walk back the cat, so to speak, find out what pieces her husband looted, try to track them down."

"But Florence was occupied," said Maggie. "Those records had to be lost or destroyed."

"That's what most people think. But the Nazis kept excellent records. So did the gallery owners and wealthy families, if they survived. The inventories are a place to start. One more path to follow."

Sugarman fell silent, gazing at a framed charcoal of a voluptuous nude, as if wondering how much to tell her. Finally he said, "As I said earlier, a guy like Orsini had to have help. In the early eighties, when Orsini finally found the art his father had stolen, he called on two people he trusted. Knew them both from Yale—they all were members of one of those secret societies. Skull and Bones, ever heard of it? One of them was older than Orsini, but 'once a Bonesman, always a Bonesman,' I'm told. That guy is in a tight security prison now, not talking until his appeal."

"And the other?"

"Another fellow Yalie, that's all I know."

She shook her head. "You always have more than one agenda, Simon. I'm guessing you know my parents met at Yale. Did Beckett tell you?"

"He might have mentioned it. Thing is, I went to Yale, too, small world. Your father was a legend, although I never connected him with you. But Yale is where I met Orsini, in the late seventies—before we went our separate ways. On Tapping Day, when Skull and Bones recruited the Juniors, he joined. I didn't."

"Light and dark?" she asked with a smile.

"Dark and darker."

"Sorry to disappoint you, Simon, but I only know three things about Yale. My parents studied music there. Yale has one of the best music schools in the US. And, they have a wonderful orchestra, the YSO—Yale Symphony Orchestra. It's celebrating its fiftieth anniversary this year."

The dark eyes on her flashed with interest. "Your folks were there, when, in the midsixties?"

"Yes. My godfather was there as well. They were all best friends."

"Holy smokes. Any way I could talk with them?"

"My mother died when I was young, my father just before I met you. But I'm sure my godfather, Alexander Karas, would talk with you."

Sugarman's eyes widened. "*The* Alexander Karas? Judge Karas, on the Supremes short list? He's your *godfather*?"

She smiled. "God help us if there's more than one of them." She stopped, said, "That second call Orsini made to someone at Yale . . . That's your Yale connection, why you want to talk with Zander. You've always insisted that there's a bad guy still out there."

"Still do. And I'm thinking there's a new leader in town now, a guy who knows where Orsini's art is hidden, a guy who wants to step into Orsini's shoes and take over the show. He'd have to be well connected to diplomats, global businessmen, government leaders . . ."

"As most Yale graduates are. So, Yale is one more common thread."

"So are you, Doc. Oh, yeah, I'd appreciate anything Alexander Karas could tell me about his good old Yalie days. You never know what seemingly innocent information will break a case."

"I'll call him, set it up."

"Okay, then. Now it's time to tell me why you asked me here."

She looked into Sugarman's eyes. Yes, Michael was right. Simon was one of the good guys. "Let me show you something. I think I might be able to help you."

She stood and led him across the room to the small alcove, stopping in front of the glimmering oil painting of a woman playing the cello.

Sugarman followed her, stopping just behind her shoulder to whistle. "Damn, but that's beautiful. Hits you right in the gut, doesn't it? If I didn't know better I'd swear it was a Matisse, but . . ." His eyes widened as he saw the expression on her face. "No! Giulietta Donati has an original Matisse?"

"It's called *Dark Rhapsody*."

Sugarman spun in a slow circle. "Those gorgeous dancers, the charcoal . . . Holy Mama. Of course. You are telling me that all of these are effing *originals*?"

She laughed. "Gigi says they are. All the other pieces are part of her husband's collection. But this piece is hers. At least, it has been in her care. But the artist is not the real reason I asked you here. This is." She gestured at the Matisse. "Help me lift this down."

Sugarman looked over his shoulder as if expecting to be arrested. "You're kidding, right?"

"Dead serious. Gigi Donati wants you to see this."

With a shrug of muscled shoulders, he lifted the heavy frame off the wall as if it weighed no more than a child's drawing and set it carefully on the floor.

Maggie tilted the canvas toward her and pointed to the faint writing on the back, close to the bottom of the frame. "It's easy to miss."

Once more Sugarman bent closer, then uttered a shocked oath. "Florence!"

"*Proprieta di Felix Hoffman Galleria, Firenze, 1943*," she read. "This painting appears to have come from an art gallery in Florence during the war. Gigi Donati wants to return it to the rightful heirs. She's hoping you will help her."

"Dead guys sure cast a long shadow, don't they?"

CHAPTER TWENTY

NEW YORK CITY
TUESDAY

"HARP."

In the light-filled penthouse, Simon Sugarman stood quietly for a long time, gazing at Matisse's extraordinary *Dark Rhapsody.*

"Harp?" Maggie stared at him. "That's a cello you're looking at, Simon. I'm afraid you've lost me."

He grinned at her. "HARP, as in H. A. R. P. The Holocaust Art Restitution Project. It's based in DC. I have a pal who works there. Their focus is on the historical research needed to verify art believed to be looted by the Nazis, in conjunction with HARP-Europe, for identification and restitution. Another Matisse, an *Odalisque*, was returned to a French family, the Rosenbergs, not too long ago. You've probably heard of Paul Rosenberg? Wealthy as King Croesus. Hundreds of artworks were looted from their Paris home during the war."

She nodded slowly. "Do you think HARP could help us with this Matisse?"

"I know they can. You did the right thing, calling me, Doc."

"It was 1945 when Gigi took this canvas from an SS truck in Austria, Simon, so it can't have any connection to the art stolen in 1943 by Orsini."

"Sure it can. If this Matisse came from Hoffman's gallery in Florence, Maggie, then there is some connection to the art looted by Victor Orsini's father. So start talking, Doc. I want to hear the whole of Gigi Donati's story. From the beginning."

"I will tell you myself, Agent Sugarman," said Gigi Donati from the gilt-edged doorway. She walked slowly toward Maggie, her silver cane tapping silently on the Aubusson carpet, and handed her an 8 x 10 manila envelope. "I have been to my deposit box. Here is the information Johann Vogl sent me." Turning back to Sugarman, she smiled, her eyes shining as she held out a jeweled hand. "And now perhaps this handsome gentleman will escort me to lunch?"

* * *

Maggie sat at the grand piano in her friend's Upper West Side town house, playing the last lingering notes of Rachmaninoff's Variation 9. As her fingers and breathing stilled, she realized that almost two hours had flown by.

Sugarman was probably still with Gigi Donati. The tall black agent and the gracious aging pianist had hit it off right away, and had gone off to have a fashionably late lunch together at Le Bernardin.

Maggie shook her head, wishing she could have joined them. But the Rachmaninoff rehearsals would not wait—as Gigi had taken great pleasure in reminding her.

She stood and stretched, arms high above her head, opening and closing her cramped fingers. The first Variations were coming together, slowly but surely. God, it felt *good.* Not transcendent yet—she smiled—but good.

And now she could turn her thoughts without guilt to the Felix Hoffman Gallery in Florence during World War II and any descendants he might have had. Her eyes went to the manila envelope Gigi had given her, still unopened on the coffee table where she'd left it. She had found only a brief mention of a Felix Hoffman on the

Internet. Hoffman was an Austrian Jew who brought his wife and young daughter, Rebekah, to Florence just before the war started. He had opened an art gallery that specialized in 19th- and early 20th-century art and rare music on the edge of the city. He and his family had disappeared in 1943, the gallery looted so completely that nothing remained.

Curling into the corner of the sofa, Maggie kicked off her Nikes and lifted the envelope. It was postmarked Vienna, Austria. She shook it, then opened it carefully and withdrew two performance programs. The first, smaller booklet was a program for a performance of *Tosca* at the Staatsoper in Vienna. The Vienna State Opera . . . Her husband had surprised her once with box seats in that beautiful theater for her favorite opera, *La Bohéme*.

Maggie shook her head and focused on the second program. Featuring a beautiful white stallion on the cover, it was for a performance of the Lipizzaner Stallions at the Spanish Riding School in Vienna. A telephone number was scribbled across the bottom, beginning with the international dialing code.

On impulse, she reached for her cell and dialed.

Four rings, five. Six.

"*Stallburg.*" A man's voice, low and gutteral. "*Spanische Hofreitschule.*"

Stallburg? "English, *bitte*," said Maggie. "Who is this?"

"The stables," said the heavily accented voice, louder. A rush of German words. Then, in English, "The Spanish Riding School."

Stables? "This is Magdalena O'Shea. I am calling on behalf of Gigi Donati about a man named—"

"We are closed." A sharp disconnect, a buzzing dial tone in her ear.

The Austrian Spanish Riding School. "All roads lead to Vienna," murmured Maggie.

Something else was in the envelope. She slipped out a glossy 5 x 7 photograph, lifting it to catch the light from the window.

Maggie gazed down into the face of a woman in her early- to mid-forties, with deep cobalt-blue eyes and a mass of thick black curls. It was a biblical face, a face of ageless beauty that could have been found in the old Jewish quarter of Jerusalem, some two thousand years ago. She was standing in front of a beautiful Renaissance building. A theater? It was so familiar. The Vienna State Opera.

She turned the photo over, squinting down at the faint, spidery words written across the bottom. *Hannah.*

Reaching for her cell phone, Maggie pressed a series of buttons. "Simon? Maggie. Have you finished lunch? I have something to show you." She listened, smiled. "Where are you now? Sixty-eighth and Fifth? Do you know Literary Walk in Central Park? Good, meet me there, beneath the statue of Sir Walter Scott. Thirty minutes. I'll bring coffee."

Disconnecting, she gazed once more at the arresting face.

"Who are you?" she asked softly.

* * *

"This place is like a cathedral," murmured Simon Sugarman.

He stood next to Maggie, gazing up at the canopy of giant American Elms, their leaves glowing deep amber in the shifting afternoon light.

She handed him a Starbucks.

"I figured you for a double espresso, no sugar, kind of guy," she told him. "Not this 'tall pumpkin-latte-extra-whipped' stuff."

He laughed and drank deeply from the Starbuck's container and wiped cream from his upper lip as he gestured at the huge elm trees surrounding them. "I love Literary Walk. All these busts of poets . . . I used to come here sometimes, after school."

"You grew up in New York?" She gazed at him thoughtfully. "I guess we've never really had time to share our early lives."

"Too busy dodging the bad guys. But I grew up in a housing project in Harlem." He grinned. "Another world in those days." Glancing at his watch, he shook his head with reluctance and took her elbow, drawing her along the wide, leaf-strewn pathway past a bust of Robert Burns. "Tick tock, tick tock," he said. "What do you have for me?"

"Gigi gave me these." She handed him the envelope with the theater programs and photograph.

He stopped on the path, extracted the contents, and raised a dark eyebrow.

"I called the number written on the Lipizzaner program," said Maggie. "It was for the stables."

"At the Spanish Riding School in Vienna? I'm intrigued." He reached for the photograph. Gazing down at the woman's face, he gave a low whistle. "Whoa. Who is she?"

"Check the back, her name is written there. Hannah. Now look at the State Opera program, the second page, where it lists all the musicians in the orchestra. There is a cellist named Hannah Hoffman. I'm wondering if she could be the granddaughter of Felix Hoffman. And if she *is* Hoffman's granddaughter, Gigi's Matisse could belong to her."

"A cellist . . ." Sugarman was gazing down at the beautiful face in the photograph.

"You have to find her, Simon."

Sugarman grinned. "*We* have to find her. Can't wait to see Beckett's face when I tell him that you and I are going to Austria together."

"Me?" She stopped on the path to stare up at him. "Oh, no. No, no, no. I have a rhapsody to prepare. I can't just run off and—"

"Sure you can. They have pianos in Vienna, Doc. And Gigi wants you to be part of this search, told me so herself. Not sure she trusts me quite yet, even though I turned up the old Sugar charm." He looked down at her face. "I've got business in Europe this week, I could meet you. You could check out the Spanish Riding School stables, and I could try to find this cellist. And then—"

"Don't even think about it, Simon! I let you talk me into going to France last summer. I was stalked, attacked, I almost drowned. I wouldn't go to the corner grocery store with you now." She turned away. "The last place I want to be is Vienna," she muttered.

"We've got a race on our hands, Doc. I want the art, Dane wants the art, somebody else out there knows where it is and wants to keep it away from the rest of us."

He touched her shoulder. "There's the exit to Fifth Avenue. Duty calls, gotta blow. Just think about it. What do a stable of classical dressage horses, the Vienna State Opera, and a beautiful cellist have in common? C'mon, you want to know as much as I do. Let's see if we can find out who this Hannah is, and go from there."

"I don't want to go to Vienna."

"Why not?"

The words of her father's obituary flew into her head. *Died in a hospital in Vienna*. She locked eyes with Sugarman and repeated, "I am not going to Vienna."

"It's the city of music, Doc. Of course you are."

CHAPTER TWENTY-ONE

NEW YORK CITY
TUESDAY NIGHT

MAGGIE LIT A candle in a small red glass in front of the statue of the Blessed Virgin and sat down in the first row pew to wait. It was almost eight p.m., and the small chapel was in deep shadow, lit only by the candles, the glowing altar light, and a graceful, swaying chandelier high above the nave. She was alone.

She gazed around the chapel where her old friend Robbie had suggested they meet. St. Malachy's Roman Catholic Church was known affectionately to New Yorkers as The Actor's Chapel. A small, narrow church set back between prewar apartment buildings on West 49th, between Eighth Avenue and Broadway, the chapel had a unique history. Even for Manhattan.

She gazed at the beautiful white altarpiece, backed by high stained-glass windows. She'd read that St. Malachy's had once been a traditional church. But then, in the 1920s, the New York theater district had taken over Times Square, and suddenly actors, musicians, and dancers were filling the pews.

The neighborhood had been very dangerous for a time. But now . . . still edgy, maybe, but revitalized. And safer. Thanks to Robbie.

She glanced at her watch and saw that it was after eight. Well, Robbie was never on time. But the next Mass was not until eleven p.m. when the post-theater performers would arrive. So there would be time to talk. To confess?

She closed her eyes and concentrated on steady breathing. Too much had happened over the last few days. Robbie's calm presence, his thoughts, always gave her perspective.

The sound of a door opening, the swish of heavy robes. Robbie—His Eminence, Robert Cardinal Brennan, the new Archbishop of New York City—walked toward her.

Maggie shook her head at him. Standing in the flickering candlelight, he was tall and slender, with long, tapered fingers. He always reminded her of the actor Richard Chamberlin with his medieval, Medici face, silvery gray eyes, and hair that was long and wispy as wheat. Tonight he wore a priest's simple black cassock.

Maggie rose and held out her hands. Robbie grasped her fingers, pulling her close to enfold her against his chest. His heavy jeweled crucifix pressed sharply against her breast. For a heartbeat, they stayed that way. Then he pulled back, strong hands still gripping her shoulders, to gaze down at her.

She saw the question in the light eyes but ignored it. "Look at you," she said fondly. "His Eminence."

"But still an unholy man." He smiled. "Still Robbie, from the Lower East Side. If God can work through me, he can work through anyone."

Robbie Brennan grinned as he gestured around the chapel. "Welcome to St. Malachy's. Graced over the years by Spencer Tracy, Roz Russell, Bob Hope, Irene Dunne. The greats. Douglas Fairbanks married Joan Crawford right on that altar. On Broadway opening nights this chapel is lit by thousands of candles."

"It's wonderful. Now I know why you suggested that we meet here."

His eyes swept the small flickering chapel. "New York's cathedrals are soaring, magnificent. My official residence is a three-story, fifteen-thousand-square-foot neo-Gothic mansion on Madison Avenue, worth somewhere upwards of thirty million. Gilt and red carpets, tapestries and priceless antiques. Lifestyles of the rich and religious."

He laughed softly. "And yet—I prefer to spend my private time in the carriage house on the mansion grounds, reading my books and listening to Schubert and Bach. I say Mass here whenever I can. I like to think I am like St. Francis, a revolutionary who rejected material wealth. I am most at home in a simple place."

"There always has been a bit of the actor in you, Robbie."

He fingered the heavy jewel-encrusted cross on his chest. "Enough to fool the Roman Catholic hierarchy, it appears." He chuckled. "But you did not come here to talk about me," he murmured. "You've had a grandson since I last saw you. I am so happy for you, but I cannot believe you are a grandmother, Maggs."

She smiled. "Ben is bright-eyed, funny, smart, and sweet-natured, like my son. They're all spending the month in California. I miss them, of course, but I'm grateful."

"And your godson in France. He is doing well now?"

"He's a remarkable child. But I'm concerned for his safety. I thought everything was behind us, but . . ." She pictured Dane's face, the single rose left on her pillow. "I'm afraid it's not over."

Shock flashed in the gray eyes. "A child should never be in danger. That explains why you are so pale. You looked beautiful the other night, as always. But not at peace. You lost your husband in such a cruel and terrible way. You lost your father not long ago. You almost lost your life in France. And now you fear for your godson. That's a lot to deal with. It's no wonder you are not okay."

Okay? Not even close, Robbie.

"I'm so damned angry at God," she whispered.

"God can take it, Maggie."

He leaned toward her. "But it's something more, isn't it? I could see it in your eyes at the Morgan. Sit. Talk to me."

"I didn't come here to confess my sins, Robbie. Nothing so liturgical."

"It's me, Maggs. Talk."

She sank to the wooden bench, gazed into the shifting shadows. "So many things," she said honestly. "I'm not sure where to begin."

"Plato said that 'the beginning is the most important part of the work.'"

"Talk about pressure," she muttered. Her eyes fastened on the flickering red candles and she shook her head. "Last summer a brutal terrorist held a six-inch silver dagger to my heart and tried to kill me—a man who looks like a wolf, whose eyes haunt my dreams. He threatened to break my fingers one by one, Robbie!" She shuddered. "I don't scare easily, but *that* . . . And now he may be back in my life. So, yes, I'm having nightmares. Flashbacks. I don't feel safe, can't seem to catch my breath. I'm not hungry, not sleeping, don't want to close my eyes at night. I'm a grown woman, Robbie, who is afraid to sleep without the lights on."

He shook his head. "I see a woman struggling to move on. To do what's right. You are stronger than you know, Maggs."

She looked into his eyes. "I don't know who I am anymore. The man I loved for so long is dead. The other great loves of my life, my son and my grandson, my godson, are all so far away." She shook her head. "Now there is a new man in my life, and I'm fighting to bring my music back. But . . ."

"But conflict rears."

"Conflict is an understatement."

She took a deep breath and the sharp, lingering scent of incense filled her head. "What would you say if I told you that I almost killed a man in France? That I wanted to."

His light eyes fixed on hers. "I would say . . . that you must have believed he deserved it. Sometimes death can right a terrible wrong. Is that what happened?"

"Yes." She looked down at the fingers gripped whitely in her lap. "And no."

"Tell me about the 'no.'" He waited silently.

"Someone else's bullet took his life," she whispered. "But I wanted him dead."

"Okay, then."

She stared at him. "Okay? I just told you that I tried to kill a man, and that's all you have to say?"

He looked at her expression and stood up. "Of course, there is more to say. Come with me, Maggs. St. Malachy's was my first parish, and the pastor is a friend of mine. He knows how much I like being here so he's given me an old desk in his office. We both could use a drink, and we will talk about this man you wanted dead."

* * *

The pastor's office, located off a hallway behind the altar, was long and narrow. At the far end, set beneath a simple wooden cross, was a scarred antique desk. The only items on its surface were a reading lamp, a well-worn paperback of the writings of St. Francis, and a small framed photograph of horses in dappled light, grazing near an ancient stone wall.

"This is for healing," said Robbie from behind her shoulder. "When I saw it I thought of you." He held out a silver gift bag.

She parted the tissue and withdrew a black t-shirt imprinted with the words, *Honor Thy Music*. "Oh, Robbie."

He handed her a crystal glass engraved with the words *Lux et Veritas*, filled with two fingers of scotch. "To you," he toasted. "To finding your way back to music, and to life." He gestured to the straight-backed chair and leaned back against the desk. "Now. Tell me about this man who deserved to die."

Maggie sat down and closed her eyes, pictured Victor Orsini standing in a convent garden in St. Remy. Pointing a gun at her. The sudden flash of light, the sharp *pop* of sound, the blossom of red on his chest, his slow-motion fall to the earth.

"His name was Victor Orsini. He was a brilliant and very cruel man, married to my best friend. Their son is my godson, Tommy. I blamed him for my husband's death." She swallowed the scotch, felt the burn. "But there's more."

"There always is, with you. You are a complicated woman, Maggie. Have been since I met you." He motioned for her to continue. "I'm listening."

"A priceless collection of art was confiscated from a Jewish art gallery owner named Felix Hoffman during World War II. In the chaos of war, the collection was dispersed—most of the art went to the Nazis' treasure chests, but other pieces just disappeared. My friend Simon Sugarman, an agent from the Justice Department, has been searching for Hoffman's collection for years. He believes that Victor Orsini inherited dozens of Hoffman's canvases, and hid them. Now Simon thinks he finally might have a way to find them. With my help."

"How is that possible?" Robbie Brennan tapped his fingers together thoughtfully. "Ah, of course. Did Orsini tell you the location of the art before he died?"

Maggie gazed at him with surprise. "Simon asked me the exact same question. The answer is no. But Victor did talk about his love for his son. Simon is convinced that Tommy Orsini could know where the art is hidden."

"He would want to leave the collection to the person he loved the most."

"Yes. But if Tommy knows, then he could be in danger. Finding the art is the best way to ensure Tommy's safety. And I may have found a way to help. Gigi Donati has a Matisse, discovered at the end of World War II, from the same collection. It's called *Dark Rhapsody*. One of the most beautiful paintings I've ever seen. Simon says it's the jewel of the Hoffman collection."

The light eyes flashed. "Now I'm intrigued. Do you think Gigi would let me see it?"

Maggie shook her head. "She wants to return it to the rightful heir. She's asked me to go to Vienna to help with the search."

"Ah, Vienna. I was there a very long time ago, with a friend from the Divinity School. The city of music. And you think it's possible Hoffman's heir could know more about the other missing art as well?"

Maggie lifted her shoulders. "Simon thinks so."

A long, low organ chord sounded in the church, reverberating throughout the office. A moment of silence, and then the notes of Bach tumbled like rain around them. Maggie lifted her face as if needing to be touched by the music.

Robbie leaned closer. "I know that look, Maggie. You're going to take all this head-on. Even if it's dangerous."

"I won't give in to fear, Robbie," she said quietly. "But I have no idea what to do. That's why I'm here."

"I was afraid of that," he muttered. "Okay. Start by doing what is necessary. Then do what is possible. And suddenly you are doing the impossible."

She smiled into his eyes. "I love it when you go all 'Thomas Aquinas-y' on me."

"Not Tommy. Francis of Assisi."

"Oh. Well, I was in the right century." She pushed her hair back from her face. "No one is going to scare me from helping the people I love."

"The things that we love tell us who we are," said Robbie.

"St. Francis?"

Laughter sparked. "Thomas Aquinas."

Maggie stood, reached out to place a gentle hand on his arm. "Ah, Robbie. I do love you."

As the unseen organist raced toward Bach's triumphant conclusion, the new Cardinal of the Archdiocese of New York gazed down at her. "The Lord can give," he said softly, "and the Lord can taketh away. I might be herding sheep next year."

"Aha! Now that *has* to be Thomas Aquinas."

His Eminence Robert Cardinal Brennan grinned down at her. "Elvis."

CHAPTER TWENTY-TWO

A VILLAGE IN TUSCANY

THE WOMAN WAS dressed in mourning.

The long black skirt swung about her ankles, white lilies were clutched against her breast, crystal rosary beads spilled like tears from her fingers. A dark shawl, draped like a veil over her hair, hid her face.

Pink dawn lit the sky and tiled rooftops of the remote hilltop village that hung so precariously over the deep gorge. Hidden in the shadows of the cemetery chapel on a grassy hill above the village, the old village priest stood silently, watching.

The woman made her way past dark passageways and ancient doorways, their coats-of-arms stained green with lichen. In the quiet piazza, a lone farmer set out cheeses and fresh rabbit for the morning's market.

At last the woman passed through a medieval archway and emerged from the shadows into the brightening light. A steep path wound up through the parasol pines, where the priest waited, out of sight, in the white-walled *Cimitero Comunale.*

When she pushed the rusted gate aside, the priest stepped deeper behind stone columns. The long chain of the onyx rosary beads tied to his belt clicked against his thigh and he gripped them close to keep them silent. As a young child, the girl had played with the smooth, glittering jet beads while sitting on his lap in the chapel. *God's black diamonds*, she would whisper.

Passing just yards from him, the young woman took a path crowded with aging headstones and weathered photographs. The grave she sought was new. There, in the north corner. The shadow from a high stone cross touched her face as she angled across the grass.

She stopped before a fresh mound of earth still crowned with flowers now brown and wilted in the Tuscan heat, the scent of their rotting petals sickly sweet in the morning air. Sweeping the wreathes aside, she gently set down the fresh lilies. Tears spilled from her eyes as she sank to her knees, touching the words so newly carved into the stone.

The old priest bowed his head, knowing the inscription. *Guiseppe Falconi, Il Dottore. Incipit Vita Nova.* The new life begins.

He had buried her father just yesterday—the village doctor, only fifty-two years old. Much too young to die. *I want to comfort you, Beatrice,* the priest told the daughter of his old friend silently. But still he remained hidden.

Closing his eyes, the priest heard once more the shriek of brakes as the doctor's ancient Ford descended the steep, treacherous mountain road just after midnight three nights earlier. A sound like thunder, then a pillar of fire rising like a red banner from the gorge. The empty bottle of strong local wine discovered, the next morning, on his bedroom floor.

In the ancient cemetery, the stillness was disturbed only by the distant rush of the River Serchio and the repetitive words of the prayers that tumbled from the young woman's lips.

The priest glanced toward the rising sun. Later today, he knew, Beatrice would be free to return to her father's house, and to the patient hidden in the cramped attic room. Today, his bandages would come off.

The patient . . .

He had learned of the patient from Beatrice herself, just hours before her father's death. He had been sitting, half asleep, in the dark, closet-like chapel confessional. The only sound was the click-click of his jet beads, shifting through his fingers. Then the heavy curtains to his left had rustled, and he'd heard the sounds of someone kneeling, breathing, beyond the wooden wall.

A tiny light winked on, and he slid back the small slatted panel. Through the grate he saw the top of a woman's dark head, bowed in the shadows. Then the whisper of a soft, familiar voice.

Bless me, Father, for I have sinned.

Tell me, my child.

And she had told him of a night six weeks earlier, when a tall stranger had appeared at the back door of their cottage just after midnight. A brimmed hat pulled low over his forehead, silvered opaque glasses hiding his eyes, a scarf wound above his chin to hide the lower half of his face. Her father and the man had talked behind closed doors until dawn.

And the next morning, her father had performed the first of several complicated facial surgeries in the back room of their cottage.

I have been nursing him, Father, through the long pain-filled nights. His body is strong, hard, deeply scarred. Not young, not old. He speaks fluent Italian, but he is not one of us. In the night, when the nightmares strike him, he shouts out in Greek, in German, in French. When he is awake, he calls me Mon Ange. His angel. He quotes Shakespeare to me. His hair, above the bandages, is the color of summer corn . . .

The patient had made only three requests of her, soon after he regained consciousness: for a book of Shakespeare's tragedies; a pair of gloves to protect the terrible, blistered burn scars on his right hand; and a player for the CDs he kept in his only possession, a worn canvas duffel bag.

He plays his CDs for me, Father. Such beautiful music. And he reads to me, from Shakespeare. When I told him my name was Beatrice, he said, "Then I shall be your Dante. And perhaps you will save me from my circles of hell." A soft breath. *"And I have called him Dante ever since."*

"But what is your sin, my child?" the priest had asked her.

And she had whispered the answer into the shadows.

Church bells sounding high above his head broke the silence of the cemetery, and drew the old priest back to the shaded chapel alcove. He watched as Beatrice stood, her hands moving in the sign of the cross. One last time, she looked down at the grave of her father. Then she turned away.

The priest waited silently until she descended the steps and took the turn for the clinic where she worked. Then he lifted his eyes. Her home sat alone on a small rise above the river, surrounded by slender cypresses.

It was time to confront the patient.

The old priest moved slowly toward the tall iron gate. Now the only sounds were the high cry of the crows and the click of rosary beads swinging against his robes.

CHAPTER TWENTY-THREE

NEW YORK CITY
TUESDAY NIGHT

MAGGIE SAT AT the grand piano in the borrowed town house on the West Side, a pencil clamped tightly between her lips, leaning forward to study the tumbling notes of Rachmaninoff's ninety-page score. The dog-eared pages were now covered by her handwritten notes, sharp exclamation points, scribbled stars and arrows.

She had reached the slower movements of the middle section, Variations 11 through 18. The transition to love, the great range of moods, from intimacy to heroism to tenderness. The time for the pianist's own improvisations. *Like my life*, she thought.

But Variation 17 was giving her trouble. The darkness, just before the light of the gorgeous 18th. She played a passage again, slowly, listening with her whole being. Gigi had suggested she try changing the tempo. "Bring in the pensive, the emotion," she had said. "Envision a woman dropping a flower on a man's grave." Yes. Maggie wrote across the page of notes, sat back, played the same measures with a building, trembling intensity. Okay, better. Now if only she could—

A quick, loud knock at the front door.

She glanced up. The shine of rain on the window, glistening against blackness. Rain? And when had it gotten so dark? She checked her watch. Good Lord. Eleven p.m. already. Who on earth could be knocking on her door at this hour?

The knock again, louder. She thought she heard someone call her name. She glanced around in panic. Where was a hammer when you needed one?

She reached for the heavy bronze sculpture of the conductor and moved to the front door. *Please, no more roses.*

"Who's there?"

"Open the damned door, Maggie. It's me. Zander!"

"Zander? Hold on." She set down the sculpture with relief—wouldn't do to shatter such an expensive piece of art—and fumbled with the dead bolts.

Alexander Karas, her godfather, stood on the front steps in a soaked raincoat, water glistening on his forehead, scowling down at her.

She couldn't stop the sudden bubble of laughter as she pulled him into the room. "Come in, I'm so sorry."

Rain dripped from his cap as he brushed by her. She reached for his coat, still smiling. "What on earth are you doing here at this hour?"

"Don't look so amused, dammit. Another interminable dinner party, just down the street. I saw your lights on."

She slipped off her glasses, rubbed her eyes. "Rachmaninoff is keeping me sleepless."

He snapped his umbrella shut and slipped out of his raincoat and hat, hanging everything on a wooden coat tree by the door. Then he turned to her.

"Do you have any scotch?"

"Good idea." She moved to an oak sideboard and held up a bottle of Spanish red wine. "Will a Rioja do?"

"It will have to." He came to stand behind her, took the bottle from her hand, and poured the wine into two glasses. "I've been thinking about your father."

She shook her head, gesturing Zander toward the facing sofas. "You should have called and saved yourself a trip in the rain."

Zander Karas sank into the white linen, held up his glass in a perfunctory toast, and drank deeply. "I wanted to see you. We didn't finish talking about Finn."

Her thoughts flew to Simon Sugarman and his questions. "Apparently everyone is interested in my father all of a sudden."

Zander leaned toward her, his gaze surprised and intense. "Who is everyone?"

"My friend Simon Sugarman, for one, an agent for the Justice Department in DC. He's searching for a missing art collection, questioning people who attended Yale some years back, especially those who might have been members of a secret society—Skull and Bones." She eyed her godfather over the edge of her wineglass. "He asked to meet you as well."

Karas' face became a mask. "Did he, now? And why is that?"

She shrugged. "You'd have to ask him."

"I will. Set up a meeting."

"Were you a member of Skull and Bones at Yale, Zander? Was my father?"

He drank again. "The thing about secret societies, Maggie, is—they're *secret*."

She looked out at the rain. "Not the denial I was expecting. Surely you can tell your only goddaughter something?"

He drained his glass and looked at her. "I can tell you what I do know about Skull and Bones. It's Yale's most elite society, almost two hundred years old. They choose some fifteen members every year—based on leadership, influence, and breeding, I suspect, and the chosen become lifetime members of the ultimate club, most going on to positions of great power. I'm told there are almost seven hundred living Bones alumni, so there have to be quite a few elderly members as well. They meet in a windowless mausoleum on the Yale campus called 'The Tomb.'"

Maggie leaned in to refill his wineglass. "Simon Sugarman went to Yale in the early eighties. He told me that there has always been a strong relationship between Yale and the Intelligence community."

Karas shrugged. "It's a known fact that the Bones members include titans of industry, politicians, theologians, filmmakers, authors, statesmen—and spies. John Kerry, James Angleton of the CIA, Rockefeller. Three presidents that I know of, including the Bushes senior and junior. Some of the most powerful men of the twentieth century are Bonesmen, Maggie, and their children as well. It's a vast social, political, and powerful network."

"With everyone committed to each other . . ."

Zander lifted his wine and looked at her with speculation over the edge of the crystal. "It would seem so. They work for the success of each other in the post-college world. Eventually they wield tremendous influence in US and world affairs. It's said that they don't do time in jail, only at the White House."

Maggie raised an eyebrow. "You seem to know quite a bit about this secret society, Zander."

"It's public record, Maggie. Several books have been written about Skull and Bones."

"Does the membership include musicians, by any chance? Or Supreme Court Justices?"

Her godfather just smiled at her and shook his head. He drank his wine, then said, "It bothers me that you didn't have a chance to see your father before he died. Did you know he was in Vienna?"

She stared at him. "No. Why would I? He chose to leave, to leave me behind, a lifetime ago. I've been done with his explanations, his justifications, for a long time." Maggie shook her head, moved away from Zander to stand by the piano. Closing her eyes, she trailed her fingers slowly over the smooth keys and pictured her father.

The last time she had seen Finn Stewart, just a month before her husband died, she had glimpsed his face in the crowd at the stage door in Milan, late at night after an exhausting performance. Tall and reed thin, he'd been standing on the edge of the well-wishers, gripping a huge bouquet of roses. *Red.* He'd been in shadows, but she would have known that face anywhere. The shock of long white hair, the brows like a wild bird's wings above the bright-blue eyes.

She had stopped to sign a program for a fan. When she'd looked up, he was gone. She'd found the roses later, left on the steps near the stage door. There had been no note. And then, just days later, the blindsiding obituary in the newspaper. Had he been saying good-bye?

She shook her head to dispel the stab of pain.

"Something's wrong," said Zander. "I see it in your eyes. What's going on, Maggie?"

She turned away as the images flew into her head like arpeggios flying across piano keys. Hundreds of blood-red roses, a shadowed face in an empty, darkened theater. A threat whispered in a silky voice on a rain-swept French beach.

I will come for you.

But Dane was long gone. He had to be.

Suddenly apprehensive, she set her wineglass on a table and moved to the window. Rain thrummed and clattered, running in silver ribbons down the windowpane.

"Maggie?" Zander came to stand behind her. Caught her eyes in the rain-streaked glass. "I'm your godfather. If something is wrong, I want to help you."

"Someone is stalking me. Sending me roses. Hundreds of roses. I found one on my pillow . . ."

"Good God. That settles it. You are coming to stay with me at Ocean House. You'll be safe there. And there is a Steinway grand piano, Maggie. Please. *Come to Ocean House.*"

* * *

Her godfather had been gone for an hour.

Unable to sleep, Maggie stood at the window gazing at her ghostly reflection wavering in the rain-swept glass. A sudden lash of rain blurred the image. Watching her face vanish into the watery darkness, she thought of Finn Stewart, disappearing into the night. All the years of unasked questions. All the years of hurt. Of loss.

Why did he disappear so long ago, when she'd needed him so much? Was Gigi right? Had he had a good reason for leaving? And what had her father known about her mother's death?

Too late now. And yet. One very deep, secret part of her wished that she had been able to see him one more time.

What was the matter with her? She turned away, saw the week's mail, once again forwarded from Boston, on the desk. Anything to distract her thoughts. She began to shift through the pile. Please, no more mail for her husband. Okay, safe. A BSO magazine, sheet music for sale, two bills for the rental apartment. Electric was so high here in Manhattan and—a postcard fell from the pages of the magazine.

She froze.

Postmarked just days earlier from Salzburg, Austria, it was a colorful photograph of several narrow shops lining a cobbled, twisting alley in the old town. At the end of the street, a clock tower glowed against a bright blue sky. Ornate, medieval iron guild signs hung above the shops. One sign, high over a blue doorway, said, "*Musik. Instrumente.*" A music shop.

She turned the card over. On the back, just two words, written in her father's spidery hand. *Ghost Light.*

CHAPTER TWENTY-FOUR

THE BLUE RIDGE MOUNTAINS
TUESDAY NIGHT

"Come on, Shiloh. You're acting like a turkey on Thanksgiving morning. I'll only be gone for a couple of days. Three at the most. And you like the Traymoors. They're good people, good neighbors, you'll be safe with them."

In the mountain cabin kitchen, Beckett squatted down, peering under the old farm table. The Golden, hunched as far back as possible under the wide oak table, looked mournfully up at him, then turned his face to the wall.

"You're killing me, big guy. Okay, so I know I promised we would stay together. We're a team, you and me, I get that. It's what I want, too. And when I get back, we have that appointment with Dr. Gallagher for your prosthesis fitting."

Shiloh ignored him.

"I know, one thing at a time. Right now I've got to get to Rome. I've got to find Dane. The two of us, we've got to take care of Maggie, don't we?"

He bent lower, reaching a reassuring hand under the table. "Come on, boy. This is a tough one, a needle-in-the-haystack trip. Sugar and I don't even know where Dane is going to be. I can't be worrying about you, too. We're too old for separation anxiety. I need you here, to hold down the fort. Just in case."

His computer dinged with an alert signal. Beckett raised his head in surprise, whacking the table hard. "Christ! Damn!" With a last look at the dog, he rose slowly to his feet. "We're not finished. And just so you know, Jill Traymoor bought those crunchy biscuits you like."

The words on his MacBook screen flickered in the shadows. Hours earlier he'd punched in key words for a very specific search. Rome, the dates for the end of the week, public events scheduled. The art dealer Angelo Farnese and his gallery. Nothing unexpected, nothing raising any alarms. He had added Maggie's name. Again nothing, thank Christ.

Think outside the box. Okay.

Sugar was looking at the art scene in Rome. So he would begin from the other direction. Start with a Tuscan village in the middle of nowhere. With a suddenly dead under-the-radar plastic surgeon named Guiseppe Falconi.

Once more he typed key words into his Mac.

"Ka-ching!" he murmured. Then, to Shiloh, "You're looking at the master, big guy. Seems Doc Farnese had a daughter named Beatrice. One more thread to follow."

Shiloh glared at him from under the table.

Reaching for his duffel bag, Beckett said, "Okay, we'll share a steak before I leave. But then it's time for me to find Dane. Time to jump into the deep end of the crazy pool."

Shiloh snorted with skepticism.

* * *

Standing at the brownstone window, Maggie's eyes followed the raindrops that slid in wavering ribbons down the glass. Shining in the lamplight like silver tears. Her own tears threatened and she took a shuddering breath.

Only her father knew he'd told her the story of the ghost light, so long ago.

What am I going to do?

You are going to Vienna, she told herself. *You are going to help Gigi find the true owner of* Dark Rhapsody. *And maybe, just maybe, if you can find the courage, while you are there, you will try to find your father.*

Because he is still alive . . .

She shook her head, squared her shoulders, and went into the bedroom. The midnight-blue suitcase was in the back of the closet where she'd left it. Lifting it to the bed, she unzipped the case and searched the side pockets. There—the small yellow satin jewelry case that traveled with her wherever she went, the bag that had belonged to her mother.

Maggie sat down on the bed, opened the case, and tipped the contents into her lap. An old black-and-white photo of Zander and her parents, standing, arms linked, in front of the Yale School of Music's Sprague Hall. Her slight mother, Lily, in the middle, a cloud of dark hair framing her beautiful face, smiling up at Maggie's father. Finn, serious and long-haired even then, looking down into Lily's eyes. And Zander, gazing at Finn over the crown of her mother's head.

Maggie touched the photo to her heart, then lifted the second item in her lap—a delicate necklace with a golden treble clef charm. She held it up, watched it sway like a pendulum in the lamplight. She remembered the necklace sparkling against her mother's throat, spinning tiny points of light into the shadows. It was one of the special memories she had of her mother.

She always told herself that someday, if she ever had the answers she sought, she would wear the necklace. But not yet.

Was her father alive in Austria? Had he faked his death? Why? Because he was in trouble?

With a shake of her head, Maggie slipped the items back into her mother's jewelry case and zipped it closed. Too much to think about tonight.

A faint ping from her cell phone. *Oh, no, did I miss a message?*

Maggie found the phone in the living room, just where she'd left it on the sofa.

Damn. Michael had called her. Damn, damn, *damn*!

She clicked on the phone and held it to her ear. Beckett's voice, low and easy, as if he were lying close to her in the cabin's big bed.

I just wanted to hear your voice, darlin'. I'll be out of touch for a few days. Don't worry about me, or Shiloh. He'll be with the Traymoors down the road—they spoil him rotten. And I'll be coming back to you as soon as I can.

A breath. Then . . .

Sunday. Me and Shiloh, we'll come to New York and find our way to Carnegie Hall. Five p.m. Sunday, at the stage door, okay? Like that movie where Cary Grant promises to meet Deborah Kerr at the top of the Empire State Building? I'll be there, Maggie. Carnegie's stage door. Wait for me. I will always show up for you.

A click. Dial tone.

"Oh, Michael," Maggie whispered, thinking of *An Affair to Remember*. "Deborah Kerr gets hit by a bus and never shows up to meet him."

I will always show up for you. She closed her eyes and tried to breathe, because she knew in her bones what Michael was planning.

He was going after Dane. Because of her. *She had made him vulnerable.*

CHAPTER TWENTY-FIVE

A VILLAGE IN TUSCANY

THE SUN WAS setting beyond the village wall, turning the Tuscan hills to ochre and deep gold, when Beatrice climbed the steep attic steps. She could hear the CD whirring on the ancient player, filling the small room with the beckoning chords of Mozart.

She stopped in the doorway, watching the patient as he stood alone at the arched window. For hours every day, he played classical music while staring out over the hills. She wondered what he was remembering. She had asked. But he never answered.

Today, unable to bear the waiting, she had hurried home, still dressed in her nursing uniform. Now she pulled the starched white cap from her head and shook her hair free as he turned to look at her.

White bandages completely swathed his head after his last surgery, the only openings for nostrils, mouth, and eyes. A strange golden iris, like a cat's eye, stared back at her. The other was still purple and swollen shut.

"*Mon Ange*. *Bella* Beatrice."

He had always called her that, in private, after the first time. And she had called him by the name he'd chosen for himself. Dante.

She smiled shyly at him as she moved to the table, stepping over a faint, reddish stain on the stone floor. "Did you spill your wine?" she asked him.

He shook his head. Sharp scissors glinted in his hand.

She hesitated for an instant, unsure, then reached for the scissors.

He sat down in the straight-backed chair. As she bent toward him, she saw the empty CD case on the table next to the player. "Piano concertos today," she murmured. Curious, she lifted the small case with the pianist's photograph on the cover. The eyes of a beautiful, dark-haired woman seated at a grand piano stared back at her. "She plays so beautifully. Who is she?"

The room was suddenly quiet as he pressed the eject button on the player. Very gently, he took the case from her hand and slipped the piano CD inside. "Someone I know," he said softly. "A woman with hair the color of night. She—" He stopped abruptly.

She took a step back, inexplicably frightened by the blaze of hatred that flamed in his eye. "What is it, Dante? What is wrong?"

"Betrayal," he murmured. "It is the worst sin of all. Your poet Dante understood. He composed a whole circle of hell for those who betray us. That was *his* vengeance. As for my own—" He turned away, and his voice shifted. "This moment calls for Schubert, I think."

The patient dropped a CD of the *Unfinished Symphony* into the machine. He smiled, and turned up the volume. The symphony began, very loud in the tiny room. He held out his hand to her.

"Beautiful Beatrice," he murmured. "In thy breast are the stars of thy fate."

"And yours," she whispered. Very slowly, she began to remove the bandages.

When the last bandage fell to the floor, he raised his head. Dusky light fell in bands through the narrow window to stripe his face with light and shadow.

She caught her breath and willed herself not to step back. Raising her hand, she touched his scarred cheek gently. "Father could have done so much more, if only he had had more time . . ."

The patient turned away from her to stare into the cracked mirror above the washbasin. "I am unfinished," he said softly. "Like this symphony."

She clasped his shoulder. "No, Dante."

"Do not trouble yourself, *Bella*. I was a handsome man once, but not a happy one. This face will do."

He smiled strangely and led her out onto a small balcony into the dying light.

She looked out over the umber valley, leaning back against him with a shuddering sigh as his fingers began to unbutton the white uniform. His right palm had been badly burned, and she could feel the ridged scars like sandpaper against her skin.

The chords of the symphony filled her head and she closed her eyes, giving herself over to the sensations in her body.

He tangled his hands in the black silk of her hair, pulling her head back, as the final notes of the symphony crashed around them.

His hands moved to her neck. Powerful fingers closed in a lover's caress around her pulsing skin.

"*Mon ange*," he whispered. "This is the last time we will be together. It is time for me to leave you." His thumb brushed her pulse.

"You're leaving? But—why?"

"I have unfinished business. I must go to Rome."

"No, no. You cannot leave me. Not now." She shook her head back and forth.

"Someone has taken something from me. I need to get it back. I need justice. I need vengeance." Very slowly, almost imperceptibly, his fingers began to tighten.

Suddenly wary, she tried to pull away from him. And at that moment saw the familiar onyx rosary beads, broken from their chain, scattered across the tiles.

God's black diamonds.

Fear gripped her. Her eyes flew to his face. "What have you done?"

He smiled. "I broke my rosary beads, *Bella*. A simple accident."

She twisted, trying to run, but his hands were locked on her neck. *Tightening*.

She clawed at his hands, forcing the words from her lips. "You cannot hurt me," she gasped. "I am with child."

His fingers froze on her throat as the symphony ended.

PART III

"When the cello enters . . ."

— Mstislav Rostropovich

CHAPTER TWENTY-SIX

ROME
THURSDAY

THE MAN WANDERED past the outdoor cafés that lined the centuries-old piazza, his wooden cane tapping on the cobblestones. He looked as if he wanted nothing more than a quiet aperitif in the soft Roman twilight. Only his eyes gave him away—they were alert and watchful, constantly moving. Cold as river stones.

He paused by the splashing Fountain of the Four Rivers to rest and admire Bernini's bronze statues, glowing in the dusk. The huge Piazza Navona, built on the remains of Domitian's Circus, was bathed in light and shadows. He felt, suddenly, that if he closed his eyes he would hear the echo of horses' hooves coming from the narrow alleys. What had Rome been like when chariots spun across the ancient stones and women filled tall urns with water from the fountains?

A black Vespa roared close, forcing him back to the present.

Colonel Michael Beckett watched the dark-eyed Roman girl thread her way through a flock of shrieking pigeons as he turned his attention back to the bustling square.

It all seemed so normal.

He shifted the strap of the black leather satchel slung over his left shoulder, easing the weight, as his eyes scanned the spired church and surrounding balconied buildings that glimmered red in the last of the light. Just past the church, the glass windows of *La Galleria dalla Chiesa*—the Gallery by the Church—reflected the busy square like a Roman painting.

At this time of day, the long rectangular piazza was filled with camera-laden tourists and mothers with baby strollers, street performers, and hunched old women with their small dogs. A pair of solemn, black-robed priests, their heads bowed, were deep in conversation.

One by one, his eyes found the members of his team.

Sugar stood in an arched doorway, Chicago Cubs cap pulled low over dark eyes, his cigarette a blazing arc in the shadows. And the others. A tired Midwesterner and his souvenir-laden wife; the Italian cleric holding out a hand to the fortune-teller in her bright robes; the movie-star-handsome waiter in his tight black vest serving the crowded café tables at Tre Scalini's; the young woman on the roaring Vespa. All alert, waiting for his signal. Waiting for the first sign of danger.

Beckett checked his watch, then turned slowly, searching the cafés, apartments, and shops. Bakery, gelato shop, leather boutique. His eyes were drawn once more to his destination—the art gallery in the heart of the piazza. Green door, large plate glass window showcasing a single religious painting. *La Galleria dalla Chiesa.*

He'd spent hours with Sugar learning every doorway, every balcony, every alley close to *La Galleria.*

Beckett was convinced that the guests inside the gallery would be fine. It was all about modern-day terrorism now, *protecting the perimeter*. Best outcome? He and his team would stop Dane well before he reached the gallery.

At least that was the plan. But with Dane, you never knew . . .

How is it going to happen?

Music lovers were climbing the centuries-old church steps next door for an evening concert. Sugar stepped into the crowd and moved toward the gallery's green door, disappearing into the ebb and flow of the crowd. Two members of the team, he knew, were already inside the art gallery, enjoying the current exhibit. Another team member was at the rear entrance, off a narrow alley. But Dane would choose the bright green front door, he was sure of it.

Where are you?

Beckett checked his watch once more. Almost showtime. Several well-dressed men and women already had entered the gallery, only to disappear, one by one, into the back room for their very private meeting with the gallery's owner, the man everyone in the underground art world called The Angel. The young woman on the Vespa parked, dismounted, and sauntered through the green doors.

He patted the leather satchel against his hip, hoping the excellent forgery of a small Caravaggio self-portrait would assure his entrance to the meeting—enough to get him in the door, anyway. That, and the new identity papers the chief had supplied, introducing him as a very wealthy American collector who didn't question an oil painting's provenance. Sugar had told him that pieces by the revolutionary late-16th-century Italian Baroque painter had been sold for over one hundred million dollars. No wonder looted art was big business. Who *has* that kind of money, he wondered, tightening his grip on the satchel.

Would he find Dane in the gallery? Or was he already here, somewhere in the square?

Beckett's eyes flickered over a strolling violinist, a vendor with a precariously laden flower cart shouting into a cell phone, a couple sitting arguing by the fountain—the woman in a purple scarf, the man's brimmed hat hiding their faces. On the edge of his vision, an old woman pushed a bright blue baby stroller across the square toward him. A nonna with her grandchild . . .

An image of Maggie flashed in his mind, pushing her new grandson in a bright blue stroller.

He shook his head. Not now.

Streetlamps blinked on above the piazza just as the church bells began to toll. Seven o'clock. Ignoring the pain that throbbed in his bad leg, Beckett moved closer. Time to head into the gallery.

But still no Dane.

Where are you? What is your plan? Dammit, what am I missing?

He was having second thoughts. *Something isn't right.*

The old woman crossing the square with the baby stroller came closer. Some part of the colonel registered the couple by the fountain standing, parting—the woman disappearing into the crowd, the man in the brimmed hat twisting away. Toward the art gallery! Something small, dark in his raised hand. A phone?

Christ! A detonator.

Too near the baby carriage. Beckett's eyes locked on the stroller. *Not the baby!*

"Bomb!" shouted Beckett, lunging toward the baby stroller. "*Una bomba! A terra!* Everybody down!"

The man with the detonator spun, raced to the left. The baby's grandmother screamed as Beckett rocketed into her, lifting her off her feet with one arm as he reached for the stroller handle. Somehow he wrestled both behind a low stone wall, pushed the woman down, and flung his body like a shield over the shrieking infant.

A blinding flash! The gallery's green door exploded with a searing roar. A great whoosh as the shock waves crashed against his back. Bright light and pulsing dark, screams tearing the air. A thunderclap of crushing, rushing air. A rain of sharp slivers of glass. Hot pain and the sickening coppery smell of blood.

A horrible moment of utter stillness, then the terrible ringing in his ears, the disorienting feeling that he was underwater. Beckett eased off the child, helped the frantic grandmother to stand. His hands ran over her, finding no injuries, no blood. "Are you okay?" he asked quickly in Italian. "*Il Bambino?*"

She was bent over her grandchild, her mouth moving, but he could not hear her voice. But the baby reaching for his nonna, tiny mouth open in a silent scream, looked unhurt.

Beckett stood, disoriented, dizzy and deafened, rescuing his cane from beneath the stroller as he turned to search the crowd. The square was in chaos. Small fires bursting into the darkness. He could not hear, and smoke was swirling over everything like a thick gray curtain.

Then, through the smoke, he saw the man who'd held the detonator, a black ski mask now shielding his face. Close, but turning to lose himself in the crowd. Beckett flung himself toward the bomber, swinging his heavy cane like a club. The man staggered, grasped the cane. Beckett felt the spine-jarring jolt as they both tumbled to the stones. Arms locked, they rolled together in a macabre lover's embrace, their faces only inches apart. Then they slammed into a wall, and Beckett reached for the black mask. Through the slits of the mask he looked into a dark glowing eye.

"Dane?" His hand, slippery with blood, searched for his gun.

The assassin smiled, unafraid, his hard body pinning Beckett's arm against the stones. Then his lips moved. Beckett could not hear the words, drowned by the wild roaring in his head. But the meaning was clear. *I am coming for her*.

"I'll see you in hell first." Beckett's fist shot forward.

Dane dodged, raised his arm. A punching weight. Beckett felt himself spinning down into blackness. Into silence.

The last image Beckett saw was the face of a woman with hair the color of night.

CHAPTER TWENTY-SEVEN

THE SPANISH RIDING SCHOOL, VIENNA, AUSTRIA
FRIDAY

"*Achtung! Bleib zurück!*"

There was no mistaking the command to stand aside. Clutching her special VIP tour pass, Maggie stopped with the other tourists in the outdoor covered walkway behind the Imperial Palace. From the left, the jingle of bridles, the thunder of hooves beating on ancient stones. She watched in awe as several enormous, beautiful stallions cantered past her, their pure white coats shining in the midday sunlight.

Her eyes followed the horses and their handlers into the "stallburg," the huge grassy courtyard of Vienna's famed Spanish Riding School stables, where each stallion was carefully guided into his stall.

Once inside, the horses turned so that their sleek, muscled necks and massive heads stretched through the half-open stall doors into the courtyard, their dark eyes curious and gleaming with intelligence. *Beautiful*, thought Maggie again, watching the trainers and grooms stay to share an apple or an affectionate rub. The scents of hay, liniment, and leather surrounded her. Watching the grooms move easily among the horses, she felt as if she had stepped inside a painting.

A movement to her left caught her eye. The sun was going down, and in the slanted shadows, she saw a man on the far side of the courtyard, seated on a low round bench in front of an easel. A small wagon by his side was filled with palettes, brushes, knives, and bottles. Bright tubes of paint were scattered on the grass around his boots. An artist. Intrigued, she lingered under the covered walkway waiting for the rest of the tour to move on. When the last tourist disappeared, she hurried toward the artist.

Stopping just steps behind the man, she peered over a paint-stained shoulder at the large 3' x 4' canvas. Against a bright cerulean sky, the outline of a noble horse's head stared back at her, silver-gray forelock long and silky, huge dark eyes still indistinct, unfinished.

Sensing her presence, the artist's neck muscles bunched, his head tilted. Without turning around, he spoke in German, his voice low.

Maggie stepped closer. "I'm American," she told him. "Do you speak English?"

His right hand kept moving. In spite of the palsy in his arm, his brushstrokes were firm and sure against the canvas. "Come around where I can see you."

She moved to his right and stood looking down at the canvas. "You've captured the horse's nobility, his intelligence, as well as his beauty." She smiled. "I'm Maggie O'Shea."

Did she imagine the sudden stiffening of his shoulders? A moment passed, and then he raised his head, adjusted wire-rimmed glasses, and stared at her. Smears of bright paint covered his veined hands and shirt. She guessed his age to be at least eighty—his hair was as white as the horse he painted, his leathery skin lined as old parchment. But it was his eyes that surprised her the most. Bright blue, as blue and clear as an Austrian lake at sunrise.

"And this fellow"—he gestured to the painting, and then to the stall behind her—"is *Conversano Bonavoia*."

She arched a brow as she smiled at him. "Quite a mouthful for such a beautiful creature."

"The colts are named immediately after birth, always double-barreled. The sire's line, and the dam's name." He grinned up at her, his teeth yellowed as old piano keys. "It's all about ancestry in Europe, isn't it? My personal favorite is *Maestoso Cattinara*."

Her gaze swept the stables. "These are the stallions who perform classical dressage?"

"*Ja*. The levade, pas de deux, the quadrille. All in perfect harmony."

"I've read about their 'Airs above the Ground.'"

"'Schools Above the Ground,' we call them. Flying changes, pirouettes, piaffe, passage, courbette. And of course the most famous movement of all, the *Kapriole*, where the horse leaps with all four legs into the air and kicks out with his hind legs. Astonishing."

"I've seen the photographs. But to be standing here, in Vienna, to see these elegant horses in person . . ." She shook her head in awe.

"Welcome to the Spanish Riding School. You are in the presence of the most noble and graceful horses in all the world, in my humble opinion. The Lipizzaners."

Maggie spun slowly, in a small circle, to gaze at the stallions in their stalls.

"You are looking at over four hundred years of breeding," said the artist, "thanks to Hapsburg Archduke Charles II. It takes six to eight years of training to become a School Stallion. Their trainers stay with them all that time." He waved his brush toward the stallions with a sweeping gesture. "*Pluto Bellornata, Neapolitano Madar, Favory Biserka*. All magnificent. I've spent the last year painting their portraits, to hang in the Winter Riding School."

She leaned toward the almost finished canvas. "Your work is beautiful."

He tilted his head toward her. "But you are not here to talk about my work. Or my Lipizzaners."

"No. I'm looking for someone. An old friend of Gisela Giulietta Donati."

The man paled, then set his brush too carefully on the easel and stood to face her. Questions shimmered in the old eyes. "I knew Gisela a very long time ago. Has something happened to her? Did she send you here?"

Was he telling the truth? Maggie couldn't be sure. She reached out to touch his arm with reassurance. "She is fine. She asked me to come. Is there a private place where we can talk?"

He shook off her hand, bent to gather his paints. "I have a small office behind the tack rooms. Will you come with me?"

"Of course."

He folded his easel, covered the canvas, and secured it on the wagon. Then he turned to her.

"I've loved Gisela since we were children," he said in a voice still shaking with disbelief. "My name is Johann Vogl."

* * *

"Stop, stop. Pay attention to the phrases, ladies and gentlemen. Again, please. From the Andante section . . ."

On the Vienna State Opera stage, the young, long-haired conductor, dressed in torn jeans and a faded gray t-shirt, raised his baton. A moment of silence. Then his arm arced in the air, plunged in a sharp descent, and once more the theater filled with beautiful, echoing music.

Simon Sugarman stood in the towering wings of the Staatsoper, the Vienna State Opera, searching the faces of the orchestra's musicians. Today they were rehearsing on the stage, not in the darkened orchestra pit, surrounded by the set of Tosca's Act I—a darkened chapel with a large portrait of Mary Magdalene against one wall.

There had to be—what? Eighty or ninety musicians in this orchestra. He counted five cellists. Two men and three women, all angled toward the conductor. He could see only one of the women's faces. But she had blue helmet hair and granny glasses—clearly too old. He pictured the photo he'd seen, but the other two female cellists had their backs to him, dark heads bent and bodies swaying, lovely muscled arms moving up and down, back and forth. Which one was Hannah Hoffman? His money was on the tall woman with the tossing jet-black ponytail and the great shoulders.

His eyes dropped to a sleek silver greyhound sleeping on the floor between the chairs. A dog at the opera? The Viennese sure loved their dogs. But come to think of it, why couldn't dogs like music, too? He shrugged. Just as long as it was someone else's dog.

The greyhound made Sugarman think of Shiloh and Beckett. He'd spent the morning with Beckett at the Rome American Hospital before flying into Vienna. The colonel had a concussion, brutal bruises. But otherwise mostly superficial injuries. Thanks to him, no one had died. Gotta love a guy brave as the Lone Ranger, right? But he sure looked like hell. Beckett's hearing had come back some time in the night, and now he was driving the nurses crazy. Sugarman grinned. Beckett was no fool; he surely knew the best way to speed up his release. Although with a concussion, he'd be kept on for a day or two.

Damn but the man was stubborn. Threatening Sugarman with a long and painful death if he breathed even a word of the Rome operation to Maggie. But La Maggie was no fool, either. "Good luck with that," he muttered.

Too bad about Dane, though. Not a damn trace. Epic fail there. God, he hoped to hell that Dane had no idea Maggie was in Europe.

The crash of cymbals scattered his thoughts, and he squinted at his watch. Rehearsal was scheduled to end in twenty minutes. The usher had been very helpful, guiding him through the beautiful old red-velvet-lined theater to the backstage area.

"It is the *Tosca* closing tomorrow night, Herr Sugarman. Puccini's great tragedy. They are rehearsing the finale of Act II, when Tosca stabs Scarpia. *Ach*, the orchestra is in such turmoil . . ." Then she had pointed a sharp, threatening finger at him. "Stay right here, Herr Sugarman. Do not move, and do not make a sound."

His thoughts returned to the woman he was here to find. Hannah Hoffman. Described as brilliant by the *Washington Post*, the cellist had been a featured soloist since age seventeen, performing with many of the greats—the Philadelphia Orchestra, the Seattle Symphony, the Tokyo Philharmonic, London . . . on and on. A real powerhouse. The reviewers called her "stunningly gifted, ferocious, passionate, and intensely poignant." Quite the package.

The music crashed around him as he gazed out at the empty theater. And speaking of stunning women musicians—where the hell was Maggie O'Shea?

She'd flown to Vienna last night, should have been here by now. He frowned, looked down at his watch once more. Time to get this show on the road.

But something just didn't feel right—JDFR.

He checked his cell for messages, then texted her. *Where r u?*

CHAPTER TWENTY-EIGHT

VIENNA
FRIDAY

THE SUN WAS just beginning to set over the Spanish Riding School in Vienna.

Maggie stood in Johann Vogl's small white-walled office behind the stables. Crowded with stacked canvases and photographs of Lipizzaners taped to the walls, it smelled of turpentine, paint—and horse. Dust motes danced in the beams of coppery light that fell in bars through a paned window onto a large oil painting of an arrestingly beautiful young girl with fair braided hair and shining amethyst eyes.

Lighting a green-shaded lamp on the cluttered desk, the artist gestured her toward the room's only stuffed chair, set next to an easel by the north window. Maggie watched him open a cabinet, take out a whiskey bottle and two glasses, and pour two stiff drinks. He handed one to her, then drained his glass and poured one more for himself. Hooking a wooden chair with his boot, he pulled it close and settled on it, whiskey in hand. Raising his glass toward her, he whispered, "To Gisela."

"To Gisela." Maggie swallowed the burning whiskey, then gestured toward the painting on the wall above his desk, now glowing in the setting sun. "You really are a good artist, Herr Vogl. Did you paint this young woman as well?"

He looked over at the portrait and smiled sadly. "You do not recognize her? That is Gisela, when she was a girl. When we first knew each other, before—" He stopped, his voice shaking, and put a hand to his throat.

"She was very beautiful."

"I've seen her perform, seen the more recent photographs. She still is."

Maggie leaned toward him and took a deep breath. "Gigi told me that you found her that night by the barn, that you helped her hide the contents of the Nazi chest."

His glass froze halfway to his lips. The bright blue eyes locked on hers over the rim of the glass, shadowed and unreadable.

"Is that what she told you?"

Something is off, thought Maggie, like the out-of-tune keys on an old piano. One of them—Gigi or Johann Vogl—was holding something back. She said, "Yes, that is the story Gigi told me. And that you've kept her secret all these years."

His breath came out, and he swallowed the rest of the whiskey. "*Ja*," he said finally. "That is true."

"Gigi still has Matisse's *Dark Rhapsody*. She never sold it. She said she'd found three paintings. Can you tell me where the other two canvases are? The ones you kept when she left Austria?"

He stiffened, shot her a wary look. "Gigi sent you here to ask me these questions?"

He stood, began to pace back and forth in the small room. The only sound was the scuff of his boots on the wooden floor and the distant, high whinny of a stallion somewhere in the courtyard behind them.

Finally Vogl stopped and turned to her.

"Are you one of those modern-day Monuments Men, searching for Hitler's looted art? Are you here to arrest me?"

"*Arrest* you? Good God, no. I told you the truth, I'm a concert pianist. Like Gigi."

"Museum experts, art scholars, educators, curators—you've all been searching for stolen treasures since the war. Hounding innocent Austrians night and day."

Maggie stood to face him. "My mission here today is personal. On Gigi's behalf, I'm trying to find any descendants of Felix Hoffman, who owned an art gallery in Florence in 1943—and Gigi's Matisse. You sent her the envelope with the opera house program and a photograph of a woman called Hannah—is she one of Hoffman's descendants?"

He watched her silently, his blue eyes fogged with distrust.

She held out her hands. "Gigi would like to return *Dark Rhapsody* to the rightful owner. She is looking for justice, Herr Vogl, not punishment."

Johann Vogl's breath came out slowly as he swiped at his eyes.

"Yes, I believe that the cellist Hannah Hoffman is the heir to the Matisse. I knew how troubled Gigi was by keeping *Dark Rhapsody*, and so I have been searching all these years. I found out about Ms. Hoffman quite by accident, when she came to Vienna to join the orchestra."

"Please, won't you tell me your story?"

"I loved Gisela when I was a boy," he said simply. "I never stopped. She was the love of my life. But, of course, she was too young . . ."

Maggie looked at the veined, age-spotted hands that gripped the empty glass. "You would have been twelve at the end of the war?"

"I don't like to talk about the war." Vogl turned away to gaze out the window, his eyes on several of the Lipizzaners grazing in the courtyard.

"The war changed so many lives," he murmured in a low voice. "Not all Austrians supported Hitler. I remember taking three of my Jewish neighbors' horses and hiding them in the forest."

"Did they survive?"

"The horses, yes. Not my neighbors."

He waved a paint-stained hand toward the stable yard. "The war was bad for all of us—and for horses, the Lipizzaners, as well. All the mares and foals, many of the stallions, the whole Lipizzaner line, were taken by the Germans to a Wehrmacht-controlled stud farm in Czechoslovakia. In the last days of the war, when General Patton knew that the Red Army was closing in, he knew what they would do to the horses. He said that no highly developed art should perish."

Vogl turned to her. "He understood. An American Colonel named Reed and his men were given just hours to herd the horses through the forests to Bavaria. So much risk, bravery, sacrifice. But they did it. Two hundred and forty-four Lipizzaners were returned to Austria. *Operation Cowboy*, they called it." He smiled faintly. "Reed said later that he was tired of so much death and destruction. He wanted to save something beautiful. And . . ." He shook his head and stopped, unable to continue.

"And you and Gigi wanted to save something beautiful as well."

The blue eyes locked on hers shined like lapis. "Gisela and I lived in a village in the Alps above Innsbruck, the Tyrol. I was almost a teenager in 1945, she had just turned ten. We would meet in her aunt's loft, not far from the lake, late at night. We would talk, plan our adventures. I would sketch her beautiful face." He gestured toward the portrait on the wall. "Until that one night . . ."

"What happened?"

"The Nazis happened. A convoy came, very late, to the alpine lake where her aunt lived. They were sinking chests—boxes of looted treasure—in the lake. Gisela was there, she saw them. Hid from them." He ran a hand through his hair. "What she told you was true. When I got there, she was terrified. She had stolen one of the smaller chests, hidden it in the far corner of the barn. The Nazis were coming back up the track. We ran."

There it was again. That look of guilt, as if he were holding something back. What wasn't he saying?

Vogl's eyes were closed, lost in his memories. "The next day, we went back for the chest. The house was empty. Her aunt and cousin had left by the back door and run to neighbors in the village the moment the SS took the cart to the lake. A good thing, yes? The SS would not have allowed them to live."

"Because they knew about the chests hidden in the lake."

"*Ja*. The Nazis took the horses, but the chest was still in the barn, where Gisela had hidden it. We carried it to my home, stashed it in a corner of the attic under a pile of blankets. Gisela was terrified that the chest would be discovered. We swore to each other that we would never tell anyone what we had found." His eyes found hers. "What we had done."

"You've kept your secret all these years?"

Again the hesitation, the quick glance away from her. Finally he spoke. "So many years . . . I turned eighty-four last week. But mistakes come back to haunt us. I never did tell anyone, but . . . I began to search once more for Hoffman's descendants. One night I went to the symphony and I found Hannah Hoffman, the cellist. I think she may be his granddaughter. It's why I sent the program and photo to Gigi. So she could make things right."

Maggie nodded, then leaned closer. "Where are the other paintings that were in that chest, Herr Vogl?"

* * *

"Thank you, ladies and gentlemen. You are as ready to say farewell to *Tosca* as you will ever be. And believe me when I say she is just as ready to say farewell to all of you. We will give her the send-off she deserves, yes? Perhaps the horns will not come in too early for a change? Do not forget that this is a special performance beginning at five p.m. So, I will see you tomorrow at four. Please be on time."

Outside the opera house, the sky was just beginning to fill with dusky color when the conductor lowered his baton and stepped down from his podium. The last chords of Puccini's *Tosca* lingered in the air.

Finally, thought Sugarman, watching the musicians rise, stretch, murmur to each other as they gathered scores and packed up their instruments. He shifted with impatience against the heavy red velvet curtain, searching the faces that came toward him. The tall, ponytailed cellist zipped her cello into a black case and hefted it on to her back like a backpack. Then she turned toward the exit. He stepped forward.

"Ms. Hoffman? Hannah Hoffman?"

The woman stared at him for a moment. Not the face in the photograph. Then she shook her head and cocked her chin over her shoulder before moving past him.

Sugarman turned. Only the greyhound, and one cellist, remained. She was petite, not more than five foot one, slim, with a mass of unruly black curls hiding her face. Had to be her. He watched as she zipped her cello—damn, almost taller than she was—into a bright red leather bag. Then she, too, hefted the instrument to her back, slipped oversized sunglasses over her eyes, murmured to the dog, and turned toward him.

Sugarman stepped forward, holding out his hand, but she ignored him as she and the greyhound walked right past him, heading toward the backstage door. What the devil?

It was then that he noticed how she held on to the dog's tether. Not the usual leash. A service dog? Nah, he had to be missing something.

"Ms. Hoffman?" he called after her.

She and the dog stopped, turned as one toward his voice. "Yes?" Lifting the dark glasses to the top of her head, she gazed toward him and smiled. "I'm Hannah Hoffman," she said softly. "And who wants to know?"

Sugarman looked down at her. "Holy moly, Batman," he murmured.

The eyes looking up at him were gorgeous. Huge, deep blue, brilliant. And unmistakably blind.

CHAPTER TWENTY-NINE

VIENNA

IN THE DUSKY backstage light, Simon Sugarman gazed down at the lovely blind cellist and shook his head mutely.

"Did you want to speak to me?" Hannah Hoffman asked.

"I . . . You . . . Geez, I'm never at a loss for words," he murmured.

She smiled. "Just begin with something easy. Your name?"

"Sugarman. Agent Simon W. Sugarman, United States Department of Justice."

"There. That wasn't so hard, was it?"

He grinned. Then heard himself say, "I'm grinning."

"Thank goodness."

Jesus, Sugar, you are a class-one idiot. "Sorry, I didn't mean . . . I meant to say . . . Well, damn."

This time she laughed, a sonorous sound that reminded him of the temple bells in Cambodia. "Please don't be uncomfortable, Agent. I'm just teasing you. I knew you were smiling by the sound of your voice. What I don't know is—"

"Why I'm here." He held out his badge, then stopped, reached for her hand, and set the badge against her palm. Her pale slender hand disappeared beneath his.

Her fingers explored the badge, then handed it back and shifted the cello off her shoulders to rest on the floor beside her. The greyhound stayed close, pressed against her thigh. "An agent coming to see me all the way from Washington. Should I be concerned?"

"No, on the contrary, we need your help. I believe my colleague Dr. Maggie O'Shea contacted you about a meeting?"

"Ah, mystery solved. I've been expecting her." She glanced around. "Is she here in the theater?"

"Just heard from her, she's running an hour or so late. I'm sorry. She's been held up at another meeting here in Vienna, at the Riding School."

"A beautiful place to spend time. And not far at all. Not a problem for us, is it, Jac?" She laid a gentle hand on the greyhound's smooth silver head, her voice softening. "This is Jac, Agent Sugarman. We have been together for a very long time."

She pronounced the J soft, "jeh," in the French way. "Nice dog," he said, eyeing the greyhound but keeping his distance. "Is he named for Jack Nicholson? Jack Kennedy? Jack be nimble?"

"Jacqueline du Pre, the cellist."

"*She*. Should have known by her pearl collar." He chuckled. "I have a pal at Justice who has a rescue Golden named Shiloh, but—"

She smiled up at him. "But I take it from the sound of your voice that you're not a dog person?"

"Prefer them to cats, if that counts. But I just have a small condo in DC, and I'm always on the move. Got no patience for all that 'hail fellow well met' stuff."

She looked down at her greyhound. "Not exactly a ringing endorsement, is it, Jac? Maybe you'll find a way to change his mind." She turned back to Sugarman. "I'm not sure I can be of help to you, Agent Sugarman. Dr. O'Shea told me she had questions about my family, but the truth is, I no longer have any family."

"Me either," he told her, surprising himself once more. "But we've come to ask about your grandparents. So what do you say to letting me buy you a Viennese coffee across the square in Café Mozart and I'll tell you what I know."

"My grandparents?" She closed her eyes for a moment, as if in prayer. Then she looked up, the sudden flash of bright blue astonishing. "It's Friday and almost sundown, Agent Sugarman. So how about we pass on coffee and instead you come home with me for a glass of wine and the Shabbat blessing? Dr. O'Shea can meet us there."

Shabbat? He hesitated, unsure. What the hell was the matter with him?

"You don't know me," he said, offering her a way out.

"You'd be surprised at what I can *see*, Agent. And—I have a 2010 Barolo."

He reached for her cello. "An offer a man can't refuse. Lead the way, Ms. Hoffman."

* * *

Not far from Hannah Hoffman's apartment in the old town, Johann Vogl was pacing back and forth in his small stable office. He had not spoken in several minutes.

Maggie had resettled in the chair by the window, sipping her whiskey and giving him time to collect his thoughts. Her eyes kept returning to the young girl in the portrait above his desk.

She told herself to focus on the old man standing in front of her. A man who had once been young and in love.

"You said that Gisela was the love of your life," she said gently, and waited.

Vogl shrugged. "I thought I was in love, yes, as only the very young can be. But after she found the chest—well, she was never the same. The guilt, the fear. The secrets. She found solace in her music. And then she left for America."

"Can you tell me what was in the chest?"

A distant high whinny somewhere in the courtyard. Vogl gazed out the window and let out his breath in a long, hurtful sigh. "I do not have much time left on this earth," he said softly. "The truth can no longer hurt my Gisela. And—like your American Colonel Reed—I do not want something beautiful to be lost."

He lowered himself slowly, as if in pain, to sit on the arm of the chair across from her. "Gigi and I looked at the contents of the chest together in my attic, that first night. A pair of silver candlesticks, a Russian icon. A beautiful violin in a velvet-lined case—a Stradivarius, I think."

"My God, a strad?"

He smiled. "*Ja.* And music manuscripts—scores by Mendelssohn, Tchaikovsky."

"Music . . ." Dear God. Maggie put a hand to her heart, suddenly unable to catch her breath. "Do you know"—she had to force the words out—"what the pieces were?"

He gazed into her eyes. "The Mendelssohn was, I think, a score for *A Midsummer Night's Dream*. As for the Tchaikovsky—it was a violin concerto."

"God, God," murmured Maggie. "I may be a pianist, but I think Tchaikovsky's *Violin Concerto in D major* is one of the most beautiful pieces of music ever written. And he wasn't even a violinist!" She shook her head in wonder. "He wrote it while suffering from depression, and that piece never fails to bring me to tears. He only wrote that one violin concerto. If he wrote another concerto like that . . ." She closed her eyes, overwhelmed.

Vogl nodded. "I was too young," he whispered to himself. "I did not understand."

"What happened to those scores, Johann?"

He looked away. "The war was cruel to all of us, Madame O'Shea. Gisela and I kept the chest's contents hidden for a long time. Eventually, I gave the violin to my father. He had no idea what it was worth. And—I sold the icon and the music manuscripts to a dealer on the black market."

"The black market." Maggie felt her heart clutch in disappointment.

Vogl gave her a thin, mirthless smile. "Starving artists are called such for a reason. I had to survive, and take care of my parents. As for the rest . . ."

"Gigi's *Dark Rhapsody* . . ."

"*Ja*. There were three rolled canvases. Oil paintings. The most beautiful I had ever seen."

"What happened to them, Herr Vogl?"

He locked his eyes on her, blue and shimmering as the twilight sky beyond the window. "We didn't know what to do with them. There was a gallery name stamped on the back of each item, the Felix Hoffman Gallery in Florence. Of course we had heard the rumors. The looting, the destruction of priceless art across Europe. There was a telephone in the village bakery. I called the number. But it was disconnected. The war . . ." He shrugged. "Well, we all were disconnected in one way or another, weren't we? You cannot imagine how it was."

"No, I can't. And I honestly don't know what I would have done in your situation."

"Thank you for that. I'm sure you would have tried to find the owners as well. But when I could not find the gallery owner in Florence, we did the only thing we could think of, to keep the secret. And I—well, as you have seen, I am an artist of sorts. I moved the canvases to the loft of my uncle's barn. I covered them with an old tarp, hoping that one day we would be able to tell the truth. But the secret was too terrible for Gisela. She went to Salzburg to study her music, and after her schooling she decided to move to New

York. I gave her the Matisse, the *Dark Rhapsody*, the day before she left. I never saw her again."

"I'm so sorry, Herr Vogl. It was not the life you had planned."

"No. I was a thief, was I not? The years rolled on. Every day I would read about owners suing for their looted art. Millions, billions stolen. There is even a movie about that now—have you seen it? *Woman in Gold*. A looted Klimt, hanging for years right here in Vienna at the Belvedere Gallery. *Ja*, I could have gone to prison for the rest of my life. Gisela as well. She would call me, sometimes, late at night, in a panic. I had to protect her."

What we do for love, thought Maggie.

"So," she said, "you just kept the other two paintings hidden, all these years?"

He looked at her for a long moment. Then, in a voice she could barely hear, he said, "That is what I told Gisela."

"My God," said Maggie. "You *sold* them?"

"I sold *one*, five years ago, to an Italian collector I found through the European black market. An art gallery in Rome handled the private sale. *La Galleria dalla Chiesa*, I think it was, in the Piazza Navona. The Gallery by the Church."

"And the painting?"

"It was called *Madonna with Child*. The signature was Bellini."

"Bellini," breathed Maggie, closing her eyes. Could it be true? "And the other?"

"Ah, the other . . ." He shook his head. "I am a traditionalist. I did not like it. Too modern. A naked woman on a beach, I think. All geometric shapes, an eye here, a hand there . . . now, I think the artist could have been Picasso. I painted over it and hid it." His gaze shifted to the portrait hanging above the desk.

Picasso? She followed his gaze and felt as if a stone had exploded in her chest.

"No! Gisela?" She crossed the room to look closely at his brushwork. "Oh, my God, Johann, *you painted a portrait of Gigi over a Picasso*?" Her fingers brushed lightly, reverently, over the oil. "It must be worth millions."

"You might say that. Just a few years ago a Picasso sold at Christie's for just over one hundred million dollars." Vogl came to stand behind her, gazing up at the portrait. "It's never been about the money," he said softly. "My Gisela has kept me company all these years."

CHAPTER THIRTY

ROME
FRIDAY, OCTOBER 24

"THERE WAS A woman," said Michael Beckett into the shadows. "What happened to the woman?"

The young charge nurse had just entered his hospital room and now hurried toward him. "There is no woman here, *il mio Colonnello*, other than myself. And you are not supposed to be out of your bed!"

Each breath took immense effort. Beckett leaned his forehead against the window, trying to ignore the pounding in his head. The sky was turning purple above the trees. "No, no, not a woman here in the hospital. Well, damn, maybe she is." He shook his head, trying to clear his thoughts, and groaned as the pain shot across his temples.

The muscled nurse stepped closer, laying a cool palm on his forehead. "You keep asking to go home," she reminded him. "But first you need to be better, *si*? Your hearing is back, the rest will come. *If* you stop fighting me."

"I'll go back to bed if you'll find me some crutches. Deal?"

She stared at him. "The feeling in your legs is returning?"

"Yes," he lied. Well, tingling. That counted, right?

The nurse frowned at him, reached for the arms of the wheelchair, and steered him back to the bed. Then she grasped him under the arms—none too gently, he thought—and hefted him back onto the low bed, settling his legs and then firmly pressing him back down to the pillows. Smoothing the white sheets with a brisk hand, she murmured, "*Prego*."

Beckett closed his eyes, now so sensitive to light, and tried to shut out the throbbing beep of the machines by the bed. *Think*. "There was a woman—a grandmother with a child—near the fountain in the Piazza Navona. Just before the bombing. I knocked them to the stones. Christ, I thought they were okay, but there was so much smoke. What if . . ."

"A nonna and her bambino?" The nurse cocked her head in thought. "I was on duty, and I do not remember them. But I will check for you." She handed him two white pills and a cup of water. "If you promise to stay in your bed."

He smiled as he swallowed the meds, gave her a feeble salute. "Sure, sure. *Va bene*." He grinned, tried to look cocky. Yeah, bring on the old Beckett charm.

The door closed softly, and he was alone with the endlessly chirping machines and his spinning thoughts. What happened to the woman?

He reached for Shiloh, needing comfort. His hand swept the air. No dog! He suffered a jolt of panic, then remembered that Shiloh was home. Safe.

Okay. I'm coming home to you, boy, just as soon as I can. Home to you and Maggie. Maybe tomorrow . . .

If the feeling in his legs would just come back.

He felt himself sinking. The meds were taking effect. Maybe tonight he would sleep, maybe he wouldn't see Dane's yellow eyes glittering at him through the slits of a black ski mask. Laughing at him. Threatening Maggie.

Damn it, man, you let him get away. Again.

Once more the image of a woman flickered on the edge of his thoughts. Beautiful, young. Not Maggie, but a stranger. And not the baby's grandmother . . . *What woman?*

He turned his head toward the window, but very slowly this time. Even an old dog could learn a new trick now and then, right? He gazed at the sky, his mind trying to remember the scene in the piazza.

The sky was turning deep purple beyond the glass. Purple. A woman in a long coat and a purple scarf had been sitting next to Dane at the fountain, just before he set off the bomb. He had been arguing with her, passionately.

Who was that woman?

Had to mean something. *Call Sugar.* He tried to reach for his phone, but the meds were taking him down, down. His phone disappeared as the darkness reached for him.

Who was Dane's woman?

* * *

The young woman wrapped the purple scarf more tightly around her neck, drew the long coat closer to her body. It was growing cold here in the stable yard, and she was nervous around the horses. Such huge beasts, so close she could smell them, hear their heavy hooves pawing at the earth.

Why had Dane sent her here?

Laughter to her right. She drew back into the shadowed alcove and remained still. Two grooms passed without seeing her, deep in conversation, and disappeared through a doorway into the long stable buildings.

She glanced up at the sky. Soon the sun would set. Lights were coming on around the yard, casting small pools of gold across the grass. Once more she focused on the tall windows of the stable office behind her. Two shadows moved back and forth across the glass. One tall and bone-thin, the other small, delicate. Graceful.

She watched them come together and then move apart, as if they were dancing. Then she reached for her cell phone and clicked it on.

Why was Dane so interested in this woman?

* * *

In the quiet stable office, standing in front of Gigi's portrait, Maggie shook her head in disbelief and turned to look up at the old artist. "I feel there is more that you are not saying, Herr Vogl."

Vogl straightened his thin, bony shoulders, his expression resolute, as if coming to a decision. Crossing the room, he bent to an old trunk and spoke over his shoulder as he reached for the hasp. "Debts always have a way of coming due, do they not? Before that happens, I have something I would like to give you."

Opening the ancient steamer trunk, he removed an oversized shoebox and held it out to Maggie. Setting the heavy box on the table, Maggie lifted the lid. Very carefully, she unwrapped a gray suede cloth, exposing two beautiful, very old silver candlesticks that glinted in the twilight.

Maggie caught her breath. "These are the candlesticks from Felix Hoffman's gallery? The ones you and Gisela found in the Nazi chest?"

"*Ja*. If Hannah Hoffman is the granddaughter, then these candlesticks would belong to her. Take them, please. Gigi would want the family to have them."

"I will get them to Ms. Hoffman tonight, Herr Vogl." She glanced over at Gigi's portrait and thought of Simon Sugarman. "And I will notify the proper authorities about the Picasso."

The old blue eyes filled with tears. "If it truly is a Picasso. Then I will begin to remove Gisela's portrait, so that the painting can be restored to all its glory. I want to put those days behind me, once and for all. I do not have much time left on this earth, Madame O'Shea. I would like to die in peace."

"That is what Gigi said."

"If that is true, then you must ask her again about that night by the lake."

"But—you found her there, and you both ran. Your stories are the same."

The old blue eyes blinked at her. "I found her, yes. But Gigi did not tell you the rest. *The Nazi captain found her first.* When I got to Gisela she was in shock, covered in blood. She'd killed him with an old rusted kitchen knife."

CHAPTER THIRTY-ONE

VIENNA
FRIDAY, OCTOBER 24

DANE PACED BACK and forth across the floorboards of the small fourth-floor hotel room he'd found in the warren of alleys behind St. Stephen's cathedral, the *Stephansdom*. The ornate Gothic spires of the church had shadowed his narrow windows in darkness for most of the day, while the toll of the great bells broke into his dreams. But the bed was adequate and no one knew him here. He could lose himself, if he had to, in the centuries-old tangle of crooked, dimly lit lanes.

Dane poured himself a second glass of Absolut and drank.

So the colonel had survived. No surprise there. But perhaps it was too soon for him to die. Now, the colonel, too, would suffer.

Dane winced as he touched the purple bruise on his jaw. The colonel was decades older, but strong. A trained soldier. He looked down at the jagged scar on his hand, remembering their violent fight just months earlier in the South of France. A worthy opponent.

You will pay, *Mon Colonel*, he thought. I will take from you what you love the most.

He reached for a plastic CD case on the table next to his iPad and gazed down at Magdalena O'Shea's face. She was close, just a few kilometers away. He just needed to be patient—she would lead him to the art. *His* art. And then . . .

He'd tossed the inventory on the table. Now he lifted it to the light. *L'Inventario*, folded and unfolded countless times, was gray and worn, the edges frayed, the scribbled words no longer distinct. The list he had stolen from Victor Orsini just before his death. *L'Inventario* of the Felix Hoffman Galleria in Florence, Italy, in 1943. Dane knew the canvases by heart.

Degas' *Five Dancing Women*.

Raphael's *Portrait of a Youth*.

Pissarro's *Boulevard Montmartre at Twilight*.

A small Cezanne, lost to him now. Left behind by Orsini, it had been found by Agent Simon Sugarman—and set Sugarman on his relentless search to find the rest of Hoffman's collection.

The inventory went on and on. An early Picasso. Monet, Klimt, Canaletto, Renoir, Goya, Bellini. And, according to Orsini and the experts, the most magnificent jewel in the collection's crown, Matisse's *Dark Rhapsody*.

The Hoffman Collection, of course, had been dispersed the night the family disappeared. Orsini's father had stolen several major Impressionist and Post-Impressionist pieces, including the Degas and the Cezanne, and hidden them away at his villa for his son, Victor. But the Nazis had looted the rest. Victor Orsini did not have the Picasso, the Bellini, or the Matisse. He had searched for them for years, especially Matisse's *Dark Rhapsody*. He had coveted it, obsessed over it. A Matisse, a missing piece from his window series . . . it had to be worth many, many millions. But it had disappeared along with the others into the Nazi tunnels or trains or warehouses or lakes. Unless . . .

Rumors had flooded the Dark Net for years. That the *Dark Rhapsody* had survived. Was discovered by an Austrian who survived WWII, then sent to a musician somewhere in the US. And now the rumors had surfaced once again. Did Agent Simon Sugarman have a lead on the *Rhapsody*? He had come to Vienna to search for missing art with Magdalena O'Shea—a US musician—by Christ, was it possible?

Dane closed his eyes, concentrating, ordering his thoughts. Magdalena O'Shea was a pianist—she had known Victor Orsini for years. His son TJ was her godson. She had blamed Orsini for the drowning death of her husband. That ill-fated connection to Orsini had led to her collision with Dane.

But the O'Shea woman also shared an intriguing Yale connection with Orsini, although her parents were decades older. Dane took a deep swallow of Absolut. Someone from Yale had helped Orsini hide his art . . .

Had she—or her parents—known about Victor's obsession with the *Dark Rhapsody*? Had she somehow found it, kept it from him?

Dane had followed her here, to Vienna, to find out. Let Magdalena O'Shea lead him to the art. And then—he would no longer need her. He smiled.

"If you poison us, do we not die?" he said into the silence of the room. "And if you wrong us shall we not revenge?"

Yes. Shylock, in *The Merchant of Venice*. One of his favorite roles. And so appropriate this night. Soon, he would know what Magdalena had found.

Dane lifted the iPad, needing release. *Kiss*? *Def Leppard*? No. He pressed a key and the raw battle cry of Metallica's *Seek and Destroy* filled the room. Turning up the volume, he closed his eyes and thought of Magdalena O'Shea.

As if he had conjured it, his cell phone buzzed.

CHAPTER THIRTY-TWO

VIENNA
FRIDAY, OCTOBER 24

"PLEASE MAKE YOURSELF at home, Agent Sugarman. The wine-glasses should be on the shelf over the bookcase."

In the old apartment in Vienna's Jewish Quarter, Hannah Hoffman gestured toward a row of glassware as she moved without hesitation toward a cabinet in the dining area. Reaching for a bottle of wine, she held it out to him. "The Barolo?"

He smiled, gazing at the label and then at the rows of wine bottles set in a small rack behind her. "How did you do that?"

"There are four other senses, remember? And I've developed a good memory. Barolo, bottom rack, second from the left." Reaching for an opener, she began to uncork the wine. "I have some light perception, I can see some shadows. I'm comfortable in my skin. But tonight I'll let you pour, since I don't always have a steady hand and I'm guessing you don't want red wine all over your shirt." She smiled back at him.

He took the bottle from her and poured two glasses of wine. "Somehow I doubt that would ever happen. You really know your way around this place." His gaze took in the deep-blue sofa, polished cherry dining table. The cello, now freed from its casing, sat in a stand by the bookcase. Tall windows along one wall, letting in soft purple twilight, and the small open kitchen. "Really a nice apartment. Comfortable, interesting. And pretty." *Like you.*

"Thank you. I wanted to live in this neighborhood, the inner city, near the Judenplatz. This town square was the center of Jewish life in the Middle Ages. It's hard to believe that I would have been refused residence here in the thirties and forties. Somehow I have felt more a Jewess, living here in Vienna. Now the rental is almost up, but it has suited us, hasn't it, Jac?" She turned toward the sleek greyhound, stretched on a long floor pillow beneath the bookcase. "The trick is to know where everything is, and to leave nothing on the floor. I've taken my share of spills and crashed into countless doors, I promise you. Learned the hard way. So, time for a toast?" She held out a graceful hand for her wine goblet.

He stepped closer, carefully set the glass in her hand, and clinked.

"*L'Chaim*," she said in her low musical voice.

"To you, Ms. Hoffman."

"We are enjoying a glass of wine together, Agent. Surely we have moved to first names. My name is Hannah."

"And mine is Simon. Although friends call me Sugar."

"I like Simon. It's a strong name." She moved to the bookcase and slipped a CD into the player. Soft music filled the room.

"Is that Bach?"

"Yes." She cocked her head, surprised that he recognized the piece. "*The Brandenburg Concertos*. Some of my favorite music."

"My mama loved them. She used to play them at night after work, while she cooked dinner in our fourth-floor walk-up. The sixth was her favorite. She said it was full of joy and made her think of forests and lakes on a summer day."

"Your mother was a wise woman. Do you know that the Brandenburg manuscripts were nearly lost in World War II? They were being transported for safekeeping to Prussia by train in the care of a librarian when the train came under aerial bombardment. The librarian escaped the train to the nearby forest, with the scores hidden under his coat."

"What a loss that would have been for my mother. For all of us."

She came to stand in front of him. Close, looking up at his face. "When I touch something, or someone," she began, "I'm able to draw it in, for all my other senses. I know you are very tall, and that you have a strong grip and a deep bass voice." She smiled. "And I don't need sight to know that you are a gentle man."

"Gentle?" He laughed. "No one has ever called me gentle, Hannah," he murmured. "*Ever.*" He took her hand, held it to his rough-whiskered cheek. "My pals back home describe me as 'big, black, and bad.'"

She stepped closer. "I've heard worse. And Jac seems to like you. She's a good judge of character." She hesitated, then added, "May I?"

When he remained silent, slender fingers brushed his eyelids and nose, feather soft. She smiled when she felt the diamond in his ear, then moved on to his closely shaved head.

Her hand fell from his face and she stepped away. Pushing the heavy black hair away from her brow, she said, "You're wondering how I can play the cello if I cannot see the music."

"You are full of surprises, Hannah Hoffman," he said. "Sure, I'm a big fan of Ray Charles, Stevie Wonder, and Ronnie Millsap. But they play jazz and blues for piano and guitar. Classical music seems so much more—" he thought of Maggie O'Shea—"well, complicated. Impossible."

"It is true that I tend to be a soloist, as it is extremely difficult for a blind musician to work with the demands of orchestra rehearsals. But I already knew the *Tosca* score and was able to step in."

A tiny "ping" on her watch caught her attention. "Almost sunset. It's time to light the Shabbat candles," she told him, moving to the dining room table. "Perhaps there will be another time for this conversation."

Two brass candlesticks, highly polished, stood on the dining table next to a silver cup. The only other item was a loaf of bread, *Challah*, on a cutting board, covered by a soft square of linen.

Hannah slipped a white lace veil over her hair and lifted a small book of matches. "I take it you are not Jewish, Simon?"

He shook his head, then realized she needed to hear his answer. "My mama took me to church every Sunday in Harlem when I was a kid. But in my business, Hannah, you see a lot of bad stuff. Really bad stuff. Takes away your belief in the good after a while. God and I—well, we don't always see eye to eye when it comes to his choices."

"Then we will just concentrate on the 'good' tonight. Shabbat has meant a day of rest, of harmony, for over three thousand years. We don't even pick a flower, we just enjoy the peace." She glanced at the greyhound, stretched on the carpet by her feet. "Even Jac must rest."

"Shabbat begins with the lighting of two candles—the opposites of light and dark, of work and rest. We begin at sundown because the world began in darkness." The match flared and, using her fingertips to feel the wicks, she lit both candles. "The woman of the home kindles the lights to welcome the Sabbath. I remember seeing the candlelight reflected in my husband's eyes, just before I lost my sight . . ."

She was married?

The candles flickered to life. Hannah extended her hands over the flames, drawing her palms inward three times in a graceful, circular motion. She covered her eyes and began to recite the blessing. "*Barukh atah Adonai, Eloheinu . . .*"

He was unexpectedly moved by her words, by the beauty of her carved face beneath the veil, her narrow hands as they circled the firelight in the shadows, drawing the light into her eyes. Eyes that could not see. It was one of the most beautiful moments he could remember. He felt as if he had just stepped back in time, into a home in ancient Jerusalem. He glanced at the front door, half expecting Moses to enter the room in long flowing robes.

The prayer was brief, low, and musical. Then she opened her eyes and said, "Good Shabbos, Simon."

"Good Shabbos, Hannah Hoffman."

"I love the candles," Hannah said into the silence. "They symbolize family, warmth, and dreams. Prayer. Wherever you are, the candles make it *home*."

"For me," he said, "firelight takes away the darkness."

She fixed her eyes on him, like blue flames under water. "For me as well. My world is mostly dark," she told him. "But sometimes I perceive light. Flickering. Shadows." She turned away. "I am a woman in shadows."

"We have more in common than I realized," he said. *But all I see is light when I look at you.* His eyes touched on the cello behind her, and he heard himself say, "While we wait for Maggie, will you play something for me?"

"Of course. I promised you only good this evening, did I not? I think . . . yes, you will enjoy Dvorak's *Cello Concerto*. Dvorak always said that the finale should end gradually, 'like a breath.' Listen for it."

"You can play music on Shabbat?"

She smiled. "Every no allows a yes. Reading and music give us peace." She slipped off her veil, dropped it on the table, and moved unerringly toward the cello. Grasping the long neck, she sat in a straight-backed chair and settled the instrument between her knees.

As if it were a signal, Jac rose and came to settle at her feet, her smooth narrow head close to Hannah's thigh. Hannah lifted the bow with a soft sigh. And then, in a moment so intimate and intense that Sugarman caught his breath, she simply wrapped her body around the cello.

Dark Rhapsody, thought Sugarman, *come to life*.

For a heartbeat of silence, there was only this beautiful woman, dark head bowed, lit by the flicker of candlelight. Then, with a slight nod and a dip of her shoulder, she stroked the bow across the strings and began to play.

* * *

Not far away, in the Spanish Riding School's small stable office, Maggie raised shocked eyes to Johann Vogl.

"What did you just say?"

"Gisela killed the Nazi who found her that night. She stabbed him with an old knife she'd found in the barn loft."

"But that is—impossible."

Vogl shook his head. "My Gisela was strong, and strong willed. You would be surprised by what fear will make you do."

Pop. Pop. Pop.

Maggie heard the gunshots in her head, felt again the small pistol recoil in her hand as—just months earlier—she had aimed at the heart of a man dressed as a monk and pulled the trigger.

"No," she said to Vogl. "I know what fear can make you do. And rage."

He stared at her. "*Ja*, I think maybe you do." He poured another finger of whiskey into her glass, and one for himself, then turned to gaze out at the darkening sky.

"When I got to the barn that night, it was very dark, too quiet. Then I heard a keening sound, very soft, like an injured animal. I climbed the loft ladder and found Gisela curled in the corner, covered in blood . . ." Vogl stopped, as if the memory was too terrible to revisit. He turned to Maggie. "She was not hurt, not physically. But her eyes were wide and staring, her skin so cold, she was shaking and in shock. I just held her for a very long time, until finally she was able to tell me about the trucks, the soldiers, the chests. She had been running for her bike when one of the troopers stopped her."

"Horrible," whispered Maggie. "She must have been terrified."

"*Ja.* The Nazi grabbed her, spun her around. She just reacted out of pure fear, like any of us would. She had the knife in her belt, and then it was in her hand." His breath came out. "His hands closed around her neck and—she stabbed him in the chest."

"Good God. Was he dead?"

"She thought so. Somehow her panic gave her the strength to drag him behind the bushes. She did not remember what happened after that."

"But the soldiers—they must have discovered one of their own was missing?"

He shrugged, the bony shoulder blades sharp in the waning light. "It was very dark, very chaotic. When I came up the road, the trucks were just leaving. I hid in the forest until I could no longer hear them. And then I found Gisela."

Maggie moved to stand next to him, laid her hand on his arm. "You helped her hide the body," she said softly.

"I buried him, God help me. Behind a boulder, deep in the woods, along with Gisela's bloody coat. And then we got the chest, and I took her home."

"And kept the secret all these years."

"*Ja.*"

"What happened to her aunt? Surely the Nazis would not leave any witnesses behind."

"You are right, of course. But as soon as the cart left for the lake, Gisela's aunt and cousin fled by the rear door and ran to the village to hide with friends. I do not know what those SS planned. But the war was over, you see. Everyone knew it. The Reich was in flames and German soldiers were deserting, running for their lives. It was total chaos all over Europe. Every man for himself. In the end, I think that is what saved Gisela and her family. But we will never know."

CHAPTER THIRTY-THREE

VIENNA
FRIDAY, OCTOBER 24

THE LAST NOTES of Hannah Hoffman's cello shimmered in the dusky room as Maggie entered.

"Like a breath . . ." murmured Sugarman, as he drew her toward the slender cellist. "Maggie O'Shea, meet Hannah Hoffman. Hannah, this is my friend Maggie. The two most beautiful musicians I know."

"The *only* musicians he knows," murmured Maggie with a smile as she reached for Hannah's outreached hand. "I'm so happy to meet you, Hannah. Thank you for agreeing to speak with us." She flashed a surprised look at Sugarman as she realized Hannah could not see. He just shrugged back at her, shaking his head.

"The pleasure is mine," said Hannah. She made a sign with her hand and her greyhound was immediately at her side. "And this is my beautiful Jac."

Maggie kept her hands still, knowing not to touch or distract a service dog. "Hi, gorgeous," she said. "Another music lover, I see. I'm guessing Jacqueline du Pre is your namesake?"

The greyhound gazed at Maggie but stayed by Hannah's side. Hannah smiled as she leaned down to give the dog a hug. "My biggest fan. Please, sit down, Maggie. I have been playing for Simon while we waited for you. Simon, will you please offer Maggie a glass of wine?"

Again, Maggie flashed him a look, this time with a raised brow. What had she missed? Simon's expression was enigmatic as he rose to fill her glass.

Maggie leaned toward Hannah. "I've heard your stunning recording of the Dvorak. And the Bach Suites as well. But my favorite is your Saint-Saëns. It's as beautiful and elegant as you are."

"Ah, *The Swan*. I love playing that piece, it's the first I performed in concert. We always remember that terror, don't we?"

"I *still* suffer paralyzing stage fright."

Hannah smiled with understanding, reaching to smooth a hand over the glowing wood of her cello. "I was telling Simon that the cello is the closest instrument to the human voice—the masculine tenor. But—"

"But when you play, it's in *your* voice."

"Of course you would understand. I've been listening to your recordings as well, Maggie. Your piano sings, and makes me cry. Your Grieg Concerto is . . ." She held out two slender hands and smiled. "Well. I don't know how you do it."

"Grief," said Maggie quietly. "Music tells our stories."

"We have that in common, then. Perhaps you and I could play together one day."

"Okay, you two. Enough. You're forgetting that I'm here, an impatient and hungry man." Sugarman began to set dishes of fruit, bread, and cheese on the table. "Time for dinner. And then Hannah will tell us her story."

* * *

"My grandparents disappeared in the war."

Hannah Hoffman's words fell like cold stones into the quiet room. On the table beside her, the candles burned low. Two lamps cast soft shadows and wavering pools of light across her gaunt face.

Grief shimmered in her eyes as she leaned forward, seated in a velvet wing chair across from the sofa where Maggie and Sugarman listened in silence.

Maggie reached out to touch Hannah's arm in gentle sympathy. "Can you tell us about them?"

Hannah's hand made a graceful arc through the air. "My grandparents were Austrian Jews. Just months before the war began, they fled Vienna and opened an art gallery near the Duomo in Florence, believing they would be safe. Grandfather named it The Felix Hoffman Gallery. He was so proud. The gallery specialized in nineteenth- and early twentieth-century paintings and rare musical scores and instruments.

"My grandmother played the violin, quite beautifully according to my mother, and gave music lessons to the wealthy families nearby. Their young daughter, Rebekah—my mother—had a tiny violin of her own. They were very happy, my mother told me, in spite of life under Mussolini. But then Hitler invaded Italy, and within six months, my grandparents' lives ended in Poland."

Hannah's deep blue eyes glistened with tears and sorrow as she turned away.

Sugarman cleared his throat and shifted his chair closer to the trembling cellist. "But your mother, Rebekah, survived . . ."

A faint smile. "Yes." Hannah brushed away the tears as she rose and went to the bookcase. Her fingers counted the shelves and moved unerringly across the book spines, feeling the surfaces, textures, and shapes. Then she drew a small tooled-leather book from the shelf and removed a white vellum envelope from its pages. "I have my mother's last letter to me; I always keep it close. Would you like to hear my mother's story in her own words?"

Sugarman took the letter from her and began to read in his low-timbral voice.

* * *

My dearest Hannah,

From the time you could first speak, like any child, you would ask me to tell you the stories of my childhood. I would tell you only of the happy times, about the years when I still lived in Florence with my parents, because you were too young to know the terrible truth. Now you are nine—still too young to understand—but this morning my doctors told me that I am very ill. I can feel the pain in your heart when you read these words. I don't want to leave you, my darling, my own heart is breaking into a thousand pieces. Now, for the first time, I understand how it must have been for my parents.

Your Grandfather Felix was a renowned art gallery owner who loved music and beauty and telling stories. Your Grandmother Ella loved to sing and dance and play the violin. And she loved to read. They gave me and my baby brother a safe and happy home. You deserve to know their story, my dearest child, because we must remember. We cannot forget what happened to us. To all of us.

Here is how it happened, on my eleventh birthday in 1943, when my parents, my baby brother, and I were taken from our apartment in the middle of the night and sent away to die.

That day is still so clear in my mind, as if it were yesterday. May 3, 1943. I wanted the hours to fly by, because that night we were to have chocolate cake from the pastry shop on the corner. We lived just off the Piazza San Lorenzo, in rooms above Papa's gallery, and he had promised to close the shop early so that he could come upstairs for a special dinner. Mama had said that she would play 'happy birthday' for me on her violin while I blew out the candles . . .

Finally, it was time. I was wearing a new white dress with tiny butterflies on it. When there was a loud knock at the door, I thought it was the first party guests. But it was Signor Bartolomeo, another gallery owner, who rushed in, shouting for my father.

Then everything happened at once, like in a nightmare. I remember that my mother's eyes were red and swollen from crying, Papa's dear face so white that I did not recognize him. Then suddenly the crash of breaking glass, the terrifying sound of heavy boots on the stairs.

The SS troopers and local police stormed in, screaming "Sie müssen mit uns kommen!" You must come with us.

I can still see the shine of my mother's silver Shabbat candlesticks, knocked over on the dining table. The punctured balloons, the smashed cake. My baby brother clutching his teddy bear to his heart. Beethoven's Emperor Concerto was being broadcast on the radio as we rushed to gather a few precious belongings. I still hear that music in my dreams.

Down the stairs, with our small suitcases. My mother sobbing because her mother's candlesticks were too heavy to take with us. As we were pushed into the alley, I looked back and saw the gallery's smashed windows, huge yellow swastikas painted on walls now bare of paintings. My father's safe, broken and empty. My father's face, broken and empty as well.

We traveled by train for three days, packed in like animals. No food, very little water. My beautiful white birthday dress, torn and filthy. They told us we were going south, but the sun through the broken wooden slats told us the truth. We were going north. We were not human, just numbers in a transport headed to Poland. And then we arrived at Auschwitz.

They put us in lines. Right away, my father was separated from us. The last moment I saw him, he was smiling so brightly at my mother. She was gripping my brother so tightly that he cried. The soldiers were taking all the younger children from their mothers. So much screaming. They took my brother, pulled him from my mother's arms. His bear fell to the earth, a soldier laughed and kicked it away. I never will forget the agony on my mother's face.

Children under fourteen were always sent immediately to the gas. But I was tall for my age, and strong. My mother lied, she saved me from the crematorium by telling them I was older and could play the violin. The Kommandant liked music, and so he let me stay with her.

We were given those filthy striped pajamas, and then we were tattooed. Ours all began with the number one. After that we were taken to Birkenau, where the women and children were kept. My God, the smell, the sounds . . . But I was one of the lucky ones. My work detail was in the kitchens, the laundry. The stables, if I was lucky. There was a Kommandant who would let me play my violin late at night in his quarters. For 'favors' no eleven-year-old girl should ever have experienced. The next morning, I could not bear to look at my mother. She must have known, but—her eyes were blank.

She lost so much weight, she would not talk. Except once. Her last words were not for me, but for the woman in the bunk next to ours. Another musician, younger and stronger than my mother, named Helen.

"Take her," said my mother, pushing me toward Helen. "I cannot bear for another child to die in my arms."

The next morning she stumbled in the work line. They beat her. I tried to lift her, to carry her, but one of the soldiers saw me and held a small pistol to my heart. Then he moved it slowly, so slowly, down my body to my thigh, and smiled as he pulled the trigger. Of course, they did not get me any medical treatment. If one of the women in our barracks hadn't been a nurse, I would have bled to death.

The Nazi pigs left my mother to die on the cold hard ground. The women said she was the lucky one.

It was a lawless universe, unthinkable. Unimaginable. The SS had swimming pools and tennis courts at the camps, while we lived in hell. What I have told you, my darling Hannah, does not begin to describe what happened to us. If I told you everything, you would not be able to sleep for years.

But somehow I survived, to give birth to you—my joy. I stayed with Helen until the Americans liberated the camp. We found our way to England, and then it took us months to reach the United States. We found an apartment in Brooklyn, and after a very long time, I settled quietly into my new life. I studied, I worked, I learned English, I read and listened to music and played the violin and kept to myself. Like my mother before me, I gave music lessons to the neighborhood children to help pay our bills. You know that I met your father late in life, and that you were our miracle.

What you do not know, what I found out from my mother's friend Helen only after I was a grown woman, is that my father thought that he paid for my freedom with his art. Our neighbor, Bartolomeo Orsini, was another gallery owner—but not as successful as my father. His gallery was struggling. He was an angry man. But he became friendly with the German soldiers who occupied Florence . . .

Simon Sugarman stopped reading. His eyes, filled with shock and anger, found Maggie's.

"Simon?" said Hannah. "What is it?"

"Something in your mother's letter, Hannah. I'll finish reading and then I'll tell you what I know about Orsini. Deal?"

"Deal," said Hannah Hoffman. "I trust you."

Sugarman flashed pained eyes at Maggie and once more lifted Rebekah's letter to the light.

Those were terrifying days for Jews in Florence. Every night, families disappeared. One night Orsini discovered that the Nazis were planning to go to my father's gallery within hours, to confiscate his art and music. They had a list of the treasures they wanted. Orsini went to my father, told him that he would try to get me out of Italy—for a price.

The price was for the best pieces in my father's collection. My father agreed.

Now you know the rest of the story. I believe that my parents thought they would have time to escape as well, that they would find a way to meet me in America. But that was not to be. The Nazis came too soon.

What I want you to know, to hold on to, is that my parents sacrificed their lives for my life. And without knowing it, for yours.

When I think of your grandparents now, my dear one, I remember the happier times. My mother playing such beautiful music after dinner, my father busy in his gallery. I would join him after my lessons, and he would tell me about his paintings. His stories were better than any fairytale.

My favorite painting was the one he always said he was saving for me. A beautiful woman with dark hair, playing the cello, the night sky glowing through the window behind her. Papa called it Dark Rhapsody. He said it was the jewel of his collection. I don't know whatever happened to it. Perhaps the Nazis stole it, perhaps that collaborator Orsini. My only hope is that, somehow, it survived.

Because in the end, hope is what matters. I will always love you, my dearest child. Always remember the courage of your grandparents, who gave their lives for ours.

Your loving Mother

* * *

In the dimness of the old town apartment, Hannah turned toward Maggie, swiping at the tears on her cheeks. "I think I chose the cello because of my mother's story about that painting," she said softly.

Maggie blinked back hot tears of her own. "You are Felix Hoffman's granddaughter," she murmured, rising to fold Hannah in her arms. Then she stood, retrieved the shoebox from the hall table where she had left it, and gave it to Hannah. "This afternoon I met an elderly man who was a boy during the war. He found these items in a chest in the Austrian Tyrol, when the Nazis were hiding their looted treasures in Alpine lakes. The candlesticks were in a chest containing items stolen from your grandfather's gallery in Florence. Now they belong to you."

She heard Sugarman's sharp intake of breath as he stepped closer.

As if caught in a dream, Hannah held out her hands with disbelief. Very slowly, she opened the box, unwrapped the suede from the heavy silver candlesticks, and ran her fingers over every inch of the tall tapers. The blue eyes widened with shocked understanding. "My grandparents' Shabbat candlesticks?" she murmured. "Dear God, their *candlesticks*!" Tears ran like rain down her face. "How can I ever thank you?"

Maggie exchanged a look with Sugarman. "We have an even better gift for you, Hannah," said Maggie. "We believe we've found your grandfather's *Dark Rhapsody*."

CHAPTER THIRTY-FOUR

VIENNA
FRIDAY, OCTOBER 24

"Hot damn. Quite a night for both of us, hey, Doc?"

Sugarman maneuvered the rented black Fiat though the narrow, ancient street that twisted its way toward their hotel. Maggie had just finished telling him about her conversation with Johann Vogl.

"I'll meet with him first thing tomorrow to examine the Gigi portrait and to discuss the best way to authenticate the painting underneath. No way we'll let him touch it. Christ, he really thinks it might be a Picasso?" His breath came out in a shocked whistle. "You can bet your grand piano I'll be asking him about those black market contacts as well. Vogl may know or remember something important. Some *one*. Maybe luck will be on our side."

"I should have asked him," said Maggie.

"Not your job, Doc. Mine." He smiled in the shadows as he eased into the brightly lit square. "You did good."

She returned his smile. "The look on Hannah's face when she touched those candlesticks . . ."

"Yeah, that was a moment. The whole night for me was . . . well . . ."

"I was there, Simon. I saw the look in your eyes." She flashed an amused grin. "I suspect you may be going to the opera tomorrow afternoon. I think Hannah wants to see you again."

"You smokin' something? Hannah Hoffman is the last complication I need in my life right now. Hell, Maggie, she's—" He slowed as they came to a roundabout.

"Blind? I can't imagine that would scare you away, Simon."

He choked with laughter. "*Scare* me? Have you met me, Doc? It would take more than a blind cellist to scare me off! But she has that hound always by her side."

"You're calling Jac a *hound*? Seriously?"

"I have nothing in common with Hannah Hoffman," Sugarman protested. "Okay, so she plays the cello like a dream, but . . ." They swung by the Vienna State Opera, shining with golden lights, and approached their hotel on Führichgasse.

Maggie said, "But you don't need any more complications in your life. Understood. Will you call me as soon as you've seen Johann Vogl? He mentioned selling musical scores as well—ask him about those. Good Lord, he remembered a Tchaikovsky and a Felix Mendelssohn."

"Music to your ears."

"Yes. But, Simon, one thing is still troubling me."

"Only one?"

She ignored him. "Felix Hoffman's art and music collection disappeared in 1943, when he and his family were sent to Poland. You believe Victor Orsini's father stole pieces from that collection. And those paintings were hidden in a villa in Florence, right? But Gigi and Johann Vogl found Hoffman's pieces in a chest the Nazis were hiding in an Austrian lake. In 1945."

Sugarman pulled to a stop in the courtyard in front of their hotel. "Here's what I think happened. Hoffman's collection was broken up, like so many others during the war. Orsini's father stole several pieces from Hoffman, just before the SS arrived at the gallery that night. The rest of Hoffman's collection was looted, sent on to Germany for the Führer. Then the Americans and Russians showed up, and there was a mad dash to hide the treasures. Alpine lakes, underground vaults and mines, Swiss banks, private chateaus, and Bavarian castles. Some documented, others not. Some of the art fell into the hands of Allied troops, some went to art dealers, many were destroyed in the bombings or on purpose. Countless treasures will never be found, Doc. But I'm gonna keep looking."

"Because we have to save what is beautiful," she said softly, quoting Johann Vogl.

"Yeah. So. Up for a nightcap?" He handed the keys to the valet as they stepped from the car into the cold lamp-lit night.

"I wish. But there is a grand piano with my name on it in one of the small public rooms, courtesy of the concierge. I have hours to go before I sleep." She thought of Gigi's impossible rehearsal demands. "*Many* hours. And I'm meeting Hannah for early coffee."

"You two really hit it off."

"I feel such a strong connection to her. I don't know if it's music, or loss, or just something inexplicable. But I feel as if I've known her forever."

"I know the feeling. Okay, then. I'll call you in the morning, as soon as I leave Vogl."

She reached out to touch his arm. "Wait. Have you heard from Michael?"

A heartbeat of silence. "Geez, Doc, I'm not on his speed dial."

"I saw a report about last night's bombing in Rome. Innocent people were hurt, Simon!" He looked away and her breath choked in her throat. "Just tell me he wasn't there, tell me he's okay—"

"He'll call you, Maggie. Trust me. Trust *him*." Simon set a hand on her shoulder. "When do you leave for the airport?"

Maggie looked up into Sugarman's eyes. "Actually, I'm not going home. I'm driving to Salzburg."

"Salzburg? What the heck is in Salzburg?"

"Not what. Who. I'm going to find my father."

* * *

"What's happening, pal?"

Beckett scowled as he held the cell phone to his ear. "I'm in a hospital and it's after midnight, Sugar. Every time I cough I see stars. What the devil do you *think* is happening?"

Sugarman chuckled. "Sorry, lost track of time. They ready to release you yet?"

"I'll find out in the morning."

"Going home should make you happy."

Beckett gazed toward the crutches propped against the wall, then down at his unmoving legs. "I'm still way short of happy," he muttered. "You sure no one died, Sugar?"

"No bodies. I'm sure. Your warning saved lives, Mike."

"Thank Christ. Okay, I've remembered something. Dane was with a woman in the square, just before the bombing. Narrow coat, thick purple scarf, long dark hair. Looked young, had a pretty profile. They were having quite an argument."

"You have my attention. Height?"

"They were sitting on the edge of the fountain. But she got up and ran into the crowd just before—" He squinted, trying to picture the moment he saw the woman turn and disappear into the crowd. "Right, she was five three, maybe five four."

"You think they knew each other?"

"Oh yeah."

"The woman fits, Mike, good work. Because when my agents got to that Tuscan village, they found the body of the town priest. And there was no sign of the plastic surgeon's daughter you told me about."

"Beatrice . . . Don't tell me. Young, pretty. Maybe five foot four, with long dark hair."

"Bingo."

Beckett smiled grimly. "Any word on Dane?"

"Hasn't surfaced. But you and I both know he will."

"If I hadn't run toward that grandmother . . ."

"Then you wouldn't be the man you are. Don't beat yourself up over this one, pal. Just get your butt back to DC. And in the meantime, I'll see if I can find out anything about your mystery woman."

"Speaking of mystery women, how did it go with Hannah Hoffman? Is she the granddaughter?"

"That, and a whole lot more. She's like no woman I've ever met."

Beckett chuckled. "I'm thinking that's a good thing, Sugar."

"Well, it isn't. Okay, so it's hard to ignore a beautiful, ethereal five-foot woman lugging a cello around. I need to put a continent between us, pronto. But her opera is closing later today, so she could be returning to the States for her Matisse."

Beckett grinned. "Beautiful? *Ethereal?*"

Sugarman ignored him. "And speaking of missing art, I may have a solid lead on Felix Hoffman's collection, thanks to La Maggie. I'm following up in the morning, then heading back to DC."

"How *is* Maggie?"

A breath. Then, "Fine, fine."

Why the hesitation? "Sugar . . ."

"She's okay, Mike, really. More than okay. But she heard about the bombing in Rome, who hasn't? She's no fool, she knows you're neck deep into something bad. You've got to call her, pal, let her know you're okay."

"I will. Is she on her way home?"

"Not exactly. What do you know about her father?"

Beckett felt his stomach fall. "She never talks about him. Or her mother, for that matter. Her father died some months before I met her. Why, what's going on?"

"She told me in New York that dear old pops is Finn Stewart."

"Finn . . . Sounds like that actor in Star Wars."

Sugarman made a losing-buzzer sound. "This Finn is a Maestro, a well-known orchestral conductor. Make that *was*—I got the feeling that he's been off the grid for a long time. There was some big mystery about his disappearance, way back when. He was one of those flamboyant, over-the-top brilliant musicians, like Bernstein. But the doc closed that door on me pretty fast, pal, I think his leaving must have hurt her. Badly."

Beckett closed his eyes. Why hadn't she told him? "I'm guessing she was just a kid. So why her interest in her father all of a sudden?"

"Maybe because I asked her about him when I was with her, after she told me that her parents and godfather all went to Yale."

"Yale. So you still think there's a connection between Hoffman's missing art and someone who went to Yale years ago?"

"I know there is. Orsini called *two* people from his secret society when he needed help hiding that art collection. And those Skull and Bones connections of his went way back. All for one and one for all. The first guy he called went to Yale in the fifties. So . . ."

"Okay, the Yale connection can go way back. You think Maggie's parents knew something?"

"Maybe they did. My gut says it's all inextricably linked somehow. They were at Yale in the sixties. Musical legends, even I heard about them, years later. Something just feels off, you know? Maggie's father knew about *Dark Rhapsody*; he has been missing for decades. Why?"

"Is that why you're asking me about Finn Stewart?"

"I'm asking because now, suddenly, Maggie thinks he's alive, in Salzburg. After all this time. And she's determined to find him."

"Damned woman thinks she can steer the river," muttered Beckett. He reached for the crutches by the bed. *Not gonna end well*, he thought.

* * *

Aggravated, Maggie listened to the busy message on her cell phone. Who was Michael talking to at this hour? He hadn't answered her text, either.

Dropping the phone to the bed, she lay back, pulled the quilt over her head, closed her eyes. Tomorrow could be a big day. She might find out if her father was really alive. But deep in her heart, she had to ask herself—did she want to see him again?

The darkness took her.

The French doors open slowly.

The girl steps into the deep blue shadows. Giant leaves the color of ink close around her.

Where is she?

She emerges suddenly from the shadows into startling blue light. Half blinded, all she can see is a hunched stone creature with an evil smile, standing guard over a hidden garden.

She slips uneasily past the creature into the garden. The sunken pool before her is very long and narrow, fringed by a tangled wall of huge red roses. The water is the color of a deep ocean, shimmering like a mirror.

A woman swims alone in the pool. Her narrow arms reach and pull, strong long legs kick rhythmically as bubbles flashing with blue light swirl up and over her naked body. Her hair is long and spins out behind her in fluid ebony ropes.

Somewhere music is playing, the melody haunting and dark with sorrow. The woman swims in time to the tempo, graceful as a dancer through the blue water.

The music grows louder as black clouds spin across the sun. The huge roses begin to twist in the wind, their crimson petals blowing like drops of blood into the water.

A sound. Breathing.

The girl looks toward the tangle of giant leaves.

The blurred outline of a man's face appears, distorted with anger, half hidden behind the roses.

Turning in the pool, the woman flings out her hand, reaching toward the girl. Then she spirals away, down into the deep blueness.

The music reaches a crescendo. The girl watches in horror as the water slowly turns to a terrifying cobalt blue, watches until only a gossamer shadow drifts far beneath the depths . . .

Someone was screaming. With a frightened cry, Maggie sat bolt upright in the bed. The woman was drowning! Panicked, she flung out a hand, sure she would feel the pool's cold water against her skin.

No. Sheets, smooth and silken-soft beneath her fingertips. *Where am I?*

Vienna. Her hotel room in Vienna. In the early morning shadows, Maggie hugged her knees to her chest, breathing in deep gulps of air, trying to calm her pounding heart. The nightmare had changed. This time the girl had left safety behind, ventured out through the doors into the terrifying garden. Watched the woman swim through the blue, spin down into the depths . . . What else?

The chords of haunting music spun in her head.

The man's face.

She had seen a man's angry blurred face peering out from huge dark leaves.

Dear God. Was it the face of her father?

CHAPTER THIRTY-FIVE

SALZBURG, AUSTRIA
SATURDAY MORNING

SOMEHOW MAGGIE MANEUVERED the rented Citroën into a too-small parking space in the crowded square, barely missing the flower cart perched on the cobblestones just inches from her bumper.

It's been too long, she thought, turning off the engine and gazing at the bright colors of the vibrant, busy Saturday morning market. Melons, garlands of onions, fragrant basil, peonies the color of rubies. *Too long since I've been in this beautiful city.*

She'd risen early. Trying not to think about the nightmare, she had focused on her music, become lost in the Rachmaninoff for several hours. Then, after awakening Gigi with a very-early-in-New-York call, she'd had coffee with Hannah, invited her to New York, settled her bill, and headed west. And now here she was, once again back in Mozart's extraordinary birthplace.

Just ahead of her stretched the Baroque Mirabell Gardens, shining emerald in the soft sunlight. Somewhere, a band was playing. Mozart, of course. She smiled, remembering, suddenly, the dancing scene from *The Sound of Music*. She turned in a circle, breathing deeply. The air was cool and crisp, with just a hint of apples. And there, just across the River Salzach, was the Hohensalzburg, the fairy-tale fort-like castle on the hill. She had performed there during the Salzburg Festival several summers ago, playing Mozart's gorgeous *Sonata in C minor* in the palace's Golden Chamber.

Since Mozart's favorite instrument was the piano, that summer she had played several of his Concerti—the No. 20, highlighted in the film *Amadeus*, and the No. 21, with its gorgeous Elvira Madigan theme—in the impressive and beautifully lit Festspielhaus, Salzburg's main concert hall.

But the best moment had been her performance of her favorite Mozart work, his *Concerto No. 23*, in the intimate, open courtyard of the Residenhof. Losing herself in his sheer musical genius, the bright tumbling joy of the notes. Until the totally unexpected heavy rain had pelted down . . . She shook her head, remembering the chaos—for the audience and musicians as well. All those suddenly unfolding umbrellas and people scattering for cover. She'd continued to play until the rain made it impossible. Now they had a roof for inclement weather. But she had loved playing beneath the stars.

Okay. The memories were lovely, but it was time to focus. Because across the River Salzach, in the shadow of the fort, was the *Altstadt*—the old town of Salzburg. Mozart's birthplace. And hiding somewhere in that warren of medieval spires, narrow alleys, cupolas, and small squares was her father.

She hoped. Maggie slipped the postcard from her pocket, addressed in her father's old-fashioned spidery script, with the two-word message only she would have understood. *Ghost Light.* The photograph showed an ancient twisting passageway with dozens of medieval wrought-iron guild signs hanging above the shops. At the end of the alley, framed against the bright postcard-blue sky, was the clock tower of the old city hall.

Is that the street where you've been hiding, Finn?

Maggie opened her map of the old town, slipped the postcard in her pocket, and headed toward the bridge.

* * *

A high whinny broke the air as Simon Sugarman crossed the stallburg toward the small office where Johann Vogl worked. Too bad he didn't have time to check out the Lipizzaners. They were gorgeous.

He stopped before a high wooden door and reached out to knock. "Herr Vogl? It's Agent Simon Sugarman. We have an appointment."

The unlatched door swung open silently. *Uh-oh.*

The smell hit him first. Metallic, sweet, coppery. Damn. He pushed through the door.

"Shit!" Morning sun fell in shimmering bars through a tall window, lighting the old white-haired man who lay sprawled facedown on the floor, one hand reaching toward the far wall. Dark red blood stained the back of his shirt, formed a thick black pool beneath him.

Sugarman bent quickly to the man and felt for a pulse, knowing by the color of the blood, and by the absolute stillness of the body, that he was too late. "Sorry, pal," he murmured. Death had occurred hours earlier, probably not long after Maggie O'Shea had left.

Maggie. *The killer had been following Maggie.*

Sick with the knowledge, he raised his eyes toward the far wall, searching for the portrait of Gisela.

A large rectangular gilt frame hung on the wall. It was empty.

* * *

It was almost five p.m. Maggie had drawn a three-block circle around the old clock tower on her map, and for the past several hours, she had explored the old streets one by one. Now the sun was going down and she was tired and losing hope.

"Talk about a wild goose chase," she muttered, stopping to finish the last of her water bottle. "Damn it, what the hell am I doing?" Let her father stay lost. Stay dead.

It would be dark soon. Time to call it a day, return to the hotel she'd booked near Mozart's home, maybe go for a long run along the river. Then tackle Rachmaninoff's rhapsody for several hours before soup and an early night. Her flight left at eight a.m. tomorrow, so she had to be up before dawn. Welcome to the glamorous life of the concert pianist. She smiled, shook her head with a wry twist, and turned the corner.

The sign on the side of the centuries-old wall said "*Getreidegasse.*" Why was it so familiar? Ah, she thought. Number 9. The yellow building where Mozart was born. The popular shopping street was busy, filled with early evening strollers. Not the quiet street she was searching for. She came to a small alley, turned right, then left, deeper into the maze of narrow cobblestoned passageways that were now shadowed with dusk.

She suddenly became aware of the quiet. Glancing behind her, she realized that she was alone in the small lane. Shops on either side of the street were closed or boarded up. Windows were black. Darkness filled the narrow, deserted street, just a single streetlamp blinking on some thirty feet ahead of her.

Just keep moving. Time to head home.

The sound of tires on stone, out of sight, but slowly following. She turned to search the lane. Nothing. But the ominous sound drew closer. The small knot of fear. What if . . . She reached for her phone.

A sudden low roar behind her. Panic flared as a motorbike skidded around the corner and sped across the stones toward her. A bright headlamp—aimed directly at her! She cried out and pressed into a doorway. The Vespa shot by her, hot air rushing against her face, a gloved hand grabbing for her shoulder.

She stumbled. The driver, dressed all in black, with a dark-glassed helmet covering his face, stared directly at her as he shot past.

"God in heaven." Maggie ran out into the lane, straining to see a license plate, but it was too dark. At the end of the street, the bike skidded to a halt, began to turn back toward her.

Maggie turned and ran.

The roar of the bike grew louder behind her.

There, a passageway just beyond the row of tangled bicycles. She ran faster, turned the corner. Cobblestones bending right, then left. The thunder of the bike filled her head.

Keep going!

Another turn, another. A narrow alley. *Quick, before he sees you!* She ran into the alley, sank down into the shadows behind a large trash container, and held her breath.

Sudden silence. Darkness.

Was he out there, waiting? Had he found her?

No lights, no sound. Only the faint mew of a cat. And her heart banging in her ears. Damned thief, trying to steal her shoulder bag. Nerves taut as piano wire, she clutched her purse against her chest, pressed back into the shadows, and counted to sixty.

Okay, she'd lost him. Very slowly, she stood, tried to see down the alleyway. Empty. *Just get out of here, get back to the hotel.*

She turned the corner. And saw the clock tower in the last of the twilight, framed at the end of the tiny street. Above all the crooked shops hung the large ornate guild signs, festooning the narrow passage like lanterns.

She fumbled in her purse, found the postcard, checked the shops. A guild sign showing a boot, another with a duck. *Yes!* She turned and hurried down the passageway.

The street was empty, filled with dark cobalt shadows. She walked slowly past the ancient, decorated facades of the shops, her eyes lifted to the wrought-iron signs swinging above her head. *Kaffee.* Antique Jewelry. *Die Uhr . . .* clocks?

Soft footsteps on the cobblestones behind her. Heart clutching, she spun around. No one.

Keeping a wary watch over her shoulder, she hurried on. Halfway down the passageway, she found the shop she sought. The iron sign above her, in the shape of a violin with the words, *Musik Instrumente*, was exactly as pictured on the postcard. And beneath the sign, painted on the shop's mullioned window, the words, *Das Geschaft Des Geigenbauer.*

Maggie checked the small translation section of her guidebook just to be sure. Yes. The Violin Maker's Shop. She peered through the small panes of the dusty glass window. Dark, quiet. Nothing but shapes and shadows. The heavy oaken door was closed.

God, God. Would she find her father in the shop? So many months since she had glimpsed him in the crowd near the stage door. And then—the obituary. Was he really alive?

Why on earth had she come? Did she even *want* to find the man who had abandoned her so many years ago? What if it was her father's face in her nightmare?

She felt the panic building in her chest. Was she ready for the answers? Not even close. But face it, the child deep inside her still longed for her father. And if Finn was in trouble . . .

What if, what if. You're here. This is what you wanted, what you told Gigi . . . one more chance to talk to him. Just do it.

With a final glance over her shoulder at the empty alley, Maggie took a deep hitching breath. Then, knowing she could be wrenching a door open onto the past, she reached for the worn brass handle.

* * *

A small bell over the door announced her arrival. The interior of the shop was shadowed, smelling of polish, old wood, and—a vaguely familiar scent that made her think of tall fir trees and winter forests. Dust motes spun in an angled bar of light that spilled through the mullioned window. Maggie stood very still. Quiet. Only the ticking of a grandfather clock, somewhere in the darkness. And, almost inaudible, the low distant notes of Chopin's *Heroic Polonaise*, played by Horowitz. The owner had good taste.

"Hello?" Softly.

No answer. Louder now, "Hello? Is anyone here?"

Trying to ignore her feeling of relief, she wandered deeper into the small room, which was crowded with string instruments of every size and make. Cellos, violins, violas . . . scattered on tables, displayed on shelves and walls, swinging gently from hooks on old oaken rafters. A Schimmel grand piano stood in solitary splendor near the window, glowing in the last of the twilight. Maggie's breath came out in a soft woosh of appreciation as she ran a palm over smooth, warm wood.

Stacks of decades-old 78 rpm records, their cardboard jackets faded and stained, were scattered on a table next to an antique phonograph. An image of a large grooved record spinning on a turntable flashed into her head. A Mozart concerto . . . Did her parents have such a collection when she was a child?

Several stringed instruments rested on a shelf nearby. Reaching for a deep red violin, Maggie plucked a string and smiled as she heard the pure pitch of the A note trembling in the silent room.

"*Berühren Sie nicht die instrumente, bitte*. Do not touch the instruments, please."

The low, bass-like voice came from behind her, across the room. A voice she hadn't heard in a very long time. She spun around.

The black outline of a man emerged from the deeply shadowed doorway. He was tall and thin, with a wild mane of long silver hair and a face like a falcon. He moved toward her with an edgy, aggressive energy, a loping, elegant gait she'd never forget. Maggie found herself looking into eyes that were fierce and blue as an October sky.

"Hello, Father."

CHAPTER THIRTY-SIX

SALZBURG
SATURDAY NIGHT

IN THE VIOLIN Maker's Shop in Salzburg, a lamp clicked on, spilling a small circle of light over a graceful cello. Finn Stewart whipped his glasses off, peered toward her. "Come into the light where I can see you."

Trying to breathe, Maggie squared her shoulders and stepped into the gold pool of lamplight.

"My God. *Maggiegirl.*" Finn Stewart's shocked eyes locked on hers. The ghost of an old smile played across his lined face as he leaned toward her. "You have your mother's eyes."

The voice so familiar, like a bass echoing on an empty stage. Tall, craggy, and still too thin, with new, deep furrows on his pale face, he was dressed in faded jeans and a white open-collared shirt with the sleeves rolled up. His once dark hair was longer, almost to his shoulders, now pure white shot with streaks of silver. Age had drained him of color, but the brows still spiked above those intense blue eyes.

He was longing and childhood, sorcery and music. *Don't be taken in by it*, she cautioned herself, and stood very still, suddenly apprehensive and unsure.

"You're alive . . ." she murmured.

"I know how you must be feeling, but—"

A wave of blinding anger washed over her. "You don't know anything about me, Finn."

He stiffened. "Cold as a British beach in winter . . ." Then stepped closer as understanding sparked. "That damned postcard. That's how you found me."

Wordlessly, she held out the postcard and waved it in the air.

She saw his lined face turn ashen, watched the sudden lightning bolt of fear leap into his eyes. "What?" she whispered. "What is it?"

"I should never have sent it." Finn Stewart glanced at the window, moved quickly to lock the door. Pulling down the front shades, he turned to her. "Does anyone know you are here?"

"Why do you—?"

"Tell me, Maggie! It's important!"

"I told a friend I was coming to Salzburg, but . . . no. No one knows about this shop." At least that much was true.

She watched the muscles of his face relax and he forced a smile as he gestured toward a worn sofa along the far wall. "Come, sit. Do you want tea? Water, wine?"

"Not wine."

The long silver hair fell over his eyes as he shook his head. "Ah, of course, my reputation precedes me. But no wine for me, not anymore. I've been clean since I came to Salzburg." He tugged at a necklace hidden beneath his shirt and held a bronze disc to the light. "My sobriety medallion, two years and counting." His mouth lifted in wry amusement. "Although *no one* should be cold sober when those pompous music critics ask, 'Who created music?'"

Tucking the medal back inside his shirt, he took a step toward her. "I am glad to see you, Maggiegirl."

Maggiegirl.

The nickname conjured a fragment of memory. *It was snowing and very cold. She was walking with her father under trees festooned in icicles. He was holding her mittened hand and laughing down at her, telling her a story about a very lonely princess who lived in an ice castle and played a harp.*

Maggie closed her eyes. "You told me a story once, about a princess who played a harp sonata. The music fell around her like crystal tears. And you said—"

"Music tells our stories, Maggiegirl."

She gazed up at him. "Don't call me that, Finn."

He frowned. "Leonard Bernstein called his daughter Critter—would you prefer that? But you're right, of course. I gave up that right a long time ago. So why have you come?" He glanced toward the shaded window once more, as if expecting to see someone lurking in the dusky shadows. "You shouldn't be here, Maggie."

"Why?"

He just shook his head and drew her away from the window. "Are you all right?"

"I'm fine."

"You never could tell a lie, sprite. I'd win big playing poker with you." The faint smile didn't quite reach his eyes.

"It's been a difficult year for me," she admitted.

"I know you lost your husband," he said, "and I'm very sorry. I know what it feels like to lose the ones you love." His eyes grew distant. "Grief always stays with you, doesn't it? But hopefully not the raw lunacy of those early days."

Glancing at the grand piano, she gave a slight shrug of shoulders. "I'm finally playing music again. I'm finding my way."

"Carrie Fisher once said, 'Take your broken heart and make it into art.' That's what you're doing. Some of the best music comes out of the darkest places. You have music in your bones, Maggie."

"A gift given to me by you and my mother."

His smile, soft and gentle, finally reached the faded eyes. "Your mother insisted that you have music in your life. Not for the fame and glory, but so that you would have *humanity*. So that you would know beauty. So that your life would be rich with compassion and passion and love. Something far beyond this world."

Maggie brushed the sudden tears from her cheeks. "She was right. She gave me the greatest gift of all. And you had a gift to share as well, Maestro. Once upon a time."

"Another lifetime," murmured her father. "You know I haven't conducted in years." He frowned. "Decades."

"The Mystery of the Maestro," she quoted the *Times*, "who suddenly walked off the stage during a breathless performance of *Beethoven's Eroica Symphony* and disappeared forever into the night."

"I've never understood why orchestral conductors are the subject of such endless fascination," grumbled Finn. He swept the long wisps of silvery hair back from his face with frustration.

"Maybe because the great conductors tend to be larger than life—enigmatic, theatrical, passionate, seductive, charming yet solitary. Always on fire."

"Is that what you see when you look at me, Maggie?"

She stared at her father. Finally, she said, "I see pride. Loss. Loneliness. Music."

He reached out to her. "Maggie . . ."

She shook her head with warning and turned away to the table with the old 78 rpms. "You were a legend," she said softly. "At school I was 'Finn Stewart's daughter.' All the kids wanted to know what you were like. The world knew you, but I didn't. Not really . . ."

She lifted a jacketed album to the light. "Johann Strauss Waltzes," she said under her breath.

Her father came to stand behind her shoulder. "We had quite a collection of classical music albums back in the day. Your mother used to hide money and letters in the album covers." She could hear the amusement in his voice. "That was after she read a book about a World War II spy who used a French record shop for passing secrets in the album jackets."

She turned to find his eyes on her, unsettling in their intensity. "What?" she whispered.

"Sorry. I can't believe you're really here, can't seem to take my eyes off you. You look so damned much like your mother. My God, you just show up on my doorstep with so much of Lily in you that I—"

Maggie felt something stir in her chest. "Finn . . ."

But now it was her father who turned away, to lift an album with a painted portrait of a bearded Tchaikovsky on the cover. "Water stains in the lower corner," he muttered, "but still plays like a dream. Lily loved this piece." He placed the recording on the ancient turntable, set the needle arm in the outer groove, and clicked a button. A whirring sound, and then the opening chords of *Swan Lake* spilled into the room, surrounding them.

For several moments they listened in silence. Then her father said, "Adolf Hitler kept a vast record collection of 'forbidden' music by Jewish and Russian composers. The family of a World War II Russian officer finally disclosed that music banned under the Third Reich—including works by Mendelssohn, Offenbach, Rachmaninoff, and Tchaikovsky—were discovered in 1945 hidden in Hitler's bunker, with scratch marks indicating that these 78 rpm recordings, publicly labeled 'subhuman music,' had been played repeatedly, in secret."

Finn looked down at her. "Can you imagine never hearing Tchaikovsky, never taking your grandchildren to *Swan Lake* or the *Nutcracker*, because his glorious music was destroyed forever?"

Maggie thought of her new grandson. "No, I can't." She hesitated, then said, "You have a grandson named Brian, and a great-grandson now, named Ben." She smiled as she pictured his dear smiling face. "He was born in September. He has your eyes."

"I know about him. I've followed your life, your career, looked out for you in my fashion. I promised your mother I would." His breath caught, as if it hurt to breathe. "I know you are preparing the Rachmaninoff. And I know some of what happened to you in France."

Surprised, she searched the old, familiar eyes for answers. She settled on, "Where have you been all this time?"

"Amsterdam, Norway, southern Spain. Cornwall, the Outer Hebrides, Prague. And Germany. Do you know there is a house in Dresden called 'The Singing House'? Whenever it rains, the drainpipes and gutters make the most amazing music." He ran a hand over a scarred cello. "Now I rebuild music for others. Each instrument has its own history, its own story. How can people neglect . . ."

He stopped when he saw the expression on her face. "Why are you really here, Maggiegirl? Sorry. Maggie."

Maggie looked away. "So many reasons," she said softly. "I met Gigi Donati recently. She has very fond memories of her friendship with you and my mother."

A silver eyebrow spiked. "As I do of Gigi. Brilliant old girl, legendary talent. Getting on in years, but aren't we all? She is well?"

"Very well. She's been helping me with the Rachmaninoff. And—she told me about the painting."

Finn looked at her sharply. "What painting?"

"*Dark Rhapsody*."

"Gigi told you about *Dark Rhapsody*?" Shock shimmered in his voice.

"Yes. She said you knew its provenance, and that you'd kept it for her for many years."

"Your mother loved that painting. It was hung—"

"Over her piano."

"You remember."

"I remember. And now I'm in Europe because Gigi asked me to find *Dark Rhapsody*'s rightful heir."

"Ah. I've wondered about that. And did you?"

"Yes. A lovely cellist named Hannah Hoffman, playing in Vienna."

"The blind cellist? I've heard her play. Exquisite. But Vienna is not Salzburg."

"No. I came to Salzburg because I thought you were dead. And then the postcard arrived. Why did you let everyone think you were dead, Finn? Are you in trouble?"

Her father smiled tiredly. "They have been after me for a long time."

"Who's 'they'?"

"It no longer matters. You shouldn't be here, Maggie."

"Too late." Maggie stepped closer to her father. His scent bombarded her with memories. Tall pines and winter forests. Her breath hitched. "I think I would have come no matter what. The truth is, I need answers. The nightmares have come back."

"About your mother."

"Yes. I have so many questions, Finn." Her voice was barely audible. "About her. But also about you. Why you left your music. Why you left *me*. One minute I had a father, and the next minute I didn't. I was only thirteen, Finn. I needed you."

"I know I hurt you, Maggiegirl. I did everything wrong by you." He reached to touch a viola on a stand next to him, as if he could postpone his answer. "Do you know that 'sorry' comes from the word 'sorrow'? It breaks my heart that I caused you sorrow, Maggie."

She stared at him. "But you did. And sorry doesn't change the past."

"You said you remember seeing the *Dark Rhapsody* above your mother's Steinway. Are your memories of that time coming back?"

"No. Yes. Oh, God, I don't know. Just flashes. Tumbling shards, like a kaleidoscope."

He was very still. "What do you remember about that time?"

"You don't forget the day your father walks out of your life."

"I deserve that. Of course you have put up a wall between us. With good reason." His eyes were suddenly bright. "What else?"

"Fragments, in the nightmares. They might not even be real memories. I'm hiding in the closet behind the piano. There are angry voices, a man's legs. Roses scattered on the floor. I walk through a door . . . I remember a pool, a woman swimming, a blurred face in the vines. The air is pulsing with dark blue fog." She shook her head back and forth. "God, everything is *blue*! I can't see, I'm so afraid. And then I hear music. Impassioned, haunting music."

"A rhapsody . . ."

"Yes! A rhapsody. Do you know it?"

"Let it be, Maggie. There is a reason people repress memories. They can only hurt you."

"They can't hurt as much as not knowing! I have to know what happened when I walked through that door. Something is blocking the memory, and I don't know why."

"It was such a long time ago."

"Talk to me, Finn. I need to know the truth about what happened to my mother! I need to walk through that closed door. You owe me, Finn. You have answers. I know you do, damn you! And I'm not leaving until I get them."

"You're as stubborn as your mother was! I should never have sent you that damned postcard."

"But you did. And here I am."

He shook his head in exasperation and began to turn out the lights. “I’m taking you back to your hotel. There is a door at the rear of the shop; it leads to an alley no one uses. My rover is parked there.” He turned off the last lamp, and looked down at her in the sudden darkness. “We will talk tomorrow morning.”

His narrow face was pale in the light of the streetlamp that fell past the edge of the window shade, reminding her of the nightmare, and she took a wary step back.

“I have a flight home in the morning. Why not *now*, Finn?”

His gaze moved to the window. “Because it’s not safe for you here.”

CHAPTER THIRTY-SEVEN

VIENNA
SATURDAY NIGHT, OCTOBER 25

"SO, BECKETT, YOU been sprung from the hospital yet? Tomorrow? Good news. What time is your flight?"

In a dark corner booth of the Café Leopold Hawelka on Dorotheergasse, Simon Sugarman sat with his back to the wall, eyes locked on the café's front door while he drank his espresso. "I'm staying in Europe, things have taken an unexpected turn. Johann Vogl is a murder investigation now. And—I've got to get to Provence. Young TJ Orsini's room was searched last night. Torn apart. No idea if they found anything."

He listened, tapping his fingers on the table. "Kid's fine, no one was there, thank God. But this race has taken an ugly turn."

The small bell over the front door jingled, and he saw the silver greyhound, followed by Hannah Hoffman, enter the café. "Gotta boogie, Mike, my friend is here. I'll fill you in when I know more." He disconnected and rose to his feet, calling, "Over here, Hannah." Then he hurried across the room, guided her back to the booth, and helped her settle on the red-striped banquet.

"You chose the far corner booth," she said in her low voice.

"I'm like Wild Bill Hickok, always sit with my back to the wall." He grinned at her, hoping she would sense it, as he flagged a server in a stiff black jacket. "Coffee?"

"Please. An *Einspaenner*. Double espresso with whipped cream." She returned his smile.

"Make it two," he said to the waiter. And then, to her, "You had me at whipped cream. I like this place—it's dark and not touristy. Not even a menu."

"I thought you would like it. Jac and I come here often after a performance. It was an artist's haunt in the thirties. A good place to wind down." She touched Jac's smooth head and then said, "You enjoyed our *Tosca*?"

He loosened his sports coat. "Not sure 'enjoyed' is the right word when no one makes it out alive. That Scarpia's a helluva villain, isn't he? But the best part was listening to an amazing cellist."

She leaned toward him, pleased. "You said you wanted to talk."

"When are you flying to New York?"

"Tomorrow evening. Special arrangements are made for Jac as well. Gigi Donati has invited us to stay with her. She called me this morning. We had quite a long talk."

"You'll like Gigi, she's a class act. But—"

The coffees arrived. Hannah sat back, ran a narrow finger around the rim of her cup thoughtfully. A hesitation, and then, "But? There is something in your voice. I feel as if you want me to leave Vienna as soon as possible. Why is that?"

He raised his cup to his lips, drank. Buying time. Finally he said, "You're right. Something's happened, but I—"

"Tell me," she insisted. And then, with a spark of humor in her voice, "I don't like to be kept in the dark."

Sugarman shook his head. "You are something else, Hannah Hoffman. Okay. It's not good. The old guy I went to see this morning, the artist named Johann Vogl who sent us to you, was murdered sometime during the night."

Shock registered as her face drained of color. "Oh, dear Lord. The man who returned my grandparents' candlesticks? You found him?"

"Afraid so."

She closed her eyes and whispered a prayer in Hebrew. Then, "May he rest in peace. I wanted to thank him. What happened?"

"Someone wanted what he had. A painting, possibly a Picasso."

"And the painting was gone when you got there."

"Bingo."

She pushed the heavy black curls back from her face. "You think someone found your artist and his painting by following Maggie."

She surprised him. "That's exactly what I think. For someone who can't see, you sure see a lot. And that means . . ."

"That I could be in danger as well? Johann Vogl knew about me—so his murderer might know about me now." The dark eyes glistened with thought. "But I don't have the *Dark Rhapsody*, Simon."

"We don't know what the killer knows, Hannah. Or what he thinks. But we know he's looking for your grandfather's art. And we know he's capable of violence. Of murder."

She drank her coffee, then leaned toward him, disappointment and confusion glimmering like sudden rain in her eyes. "Is that why you came to the theater today? To *protect* me?"

"I came because I wanted to hear you play." *I wanted to see you again.*

She sat back. "All right then. What do you want me to do?"

He tried not to stare at the wisp of whipped cream on her lips. "If it's okay with you, I'll see you home, wait while you finish packing, and get you and Jacquie on the next plane to the States."

"I will think about it." She brushed the cream from her mouth. "But Jac and I are not leaving here until I finish my *Einspaenner*."

Sugarman leaned back against the red banquet. "Okay by me," he murmured.

She clasped the large white cup with both hands and stared at him over the rim. "So you will drop us at the airport and then go off to do . . . what, exactly?"

"You already know what I do, Hannah."

"You work on the side of the angels. Rescuing beauty for future generations. Protecting the world's treasures matters, Simon. Art reminds us of who we are as human beings. It makes me so angry—and so sad—that people will wantonly destroy precious art."

"You make me sound like a saint. The high road's not always my thing, Hannah. Sometimes I make up the rules after it's over."

She laughed. "I get that searching for lost art is only the tip of your iceberg." She held out an encouraging palm. "So . . ."

"Johann Vogl was murdered on my watch, so I'll be working with Interpol to find his killer—and trace the Picasso that was stolen from him."

"And then?"

He tilted his head at her. "Actually, first. I'm heading to Provence as soon as I leave you. Have to make sure that Maggie's godson is safe. He's got a bull's-eye on his back because he may know the location of more pieces stolen from your grandfather's collection. And the guy looking for the art—looking for TJ—is a real whack job. Likes to hurt people."

"I know about TJ. I saw Maggie again this morning. We talked for over an hour. There is just something about her. I feel very close to her. She told me what happened in France. We talked about losing our husbands." She closed her eyes, put a graceful hand to her heart. "And we talked about two little boys, about the same age, with dark curly hair and huge soulful eyes. Her godson, TJ, has been through more than any young child should have to endure."

Two little boys? Sugarman leaned closer. "TJ is a great kid, in spite of everything he went through. I'll do whatever I have to do to keep him safe."

"I don't doubt it. How did you ever become a rescuer?"

"A rescuer?" He shifted uncomfortably, took another long swallow of coffee. Finally, he shrugged and said, "I'm just a crossword-loving vet who enlisted in the Army the day I graduated high school in Harlem, shipped off to Nam, then earned my JD at Yale in the early eighties with the help of the GI bill. Had a housemate named Victor Orsini while I was at Yale. Turns out his father stole a warehouse full of priceless art—some of it your grandfather's—that eventually found its way into his son's arms."

She nodded slowly. The small lamp on the wall above her lit tendrils of her black curls, turning the fine strands to gold. He pictured her playing Dvorak on her cello the night before. One of the most beautiful moments he could remember . . .

Her low voice broke into his thoughts. "And that led you to *Dark Rhapsody*."

"Eventually. And to you."

She smiled in the shadows. "So I have my grandfather to thank. His shop in Florence was the link?"

"Roger that. Orsini stole some of your father's art, and music, too. The Nazis got the rest. All that art has disappeared. It's hidden somewhere, and I'm looking for it. Your grandfather, Felix Hoffman, is the connection."

"My mother's letter said that Matisse's *Dark Rhapsody* was the jewel of my grandfather's collection. Why is that?"

"Your grandfather had a collection of forty, maybe fifty pieces of art, some of them worth hundreds of thousands of dollars on today's market. But the Matisse is special because it's thought to be the most unusual of a series. Matisse loved brilliant colors and light-filled windows, and he painted many gorgeous window scenes—*Open Window at Collioure*, *The Blue Window*, *The Window at Tangier*, *Violinist by the Window*—but your *Dark Rhapsody* is one of his rare pieces, far as I know, with a dark night sky. All the rest are painted in sunlight, or dusk. And, well, he painted a cello and goldfish in front of a window once, but never a window with a beautiful cellist lit by candlelight. And just a few years ago, in Paris, a Matisse sold for forty million dollars."

"Oh. You are very good at what you do, aren't you?"

He scowled. "I'm really good at my job. At life, not so much."

"Jac and I don't agree. Anyone who can spell Aeschylus correctly is okay in our book."

"Aeschylus? How the devil do you know that I . . ." His gaze sharpened. "Well, well. As in, a nine-letter word for 'Ancient Greek Tragedian.' So you *were* listening. You do crossword puzzles, too?"

She nodded, smiling that he'd made the connection.

"What paper?"

"*New York Times*, Sunday."

"Ouch. Pencil or pen?"

"Seriously?" She smoothed the greyhound's head. "He has to ask?"

Sugarman laughed. "Should have known. You are one damned piece of work, Hannah Hoffman. Seriously."

"I'm going to take that as a compliment." And then, "Your parents raised an interesting man."

"They were the interesting ones." He leaned back against the banquet, folded his arms across his chest, and gazed at her. This woman was full of surprises. "My mama was a nightclub waitress, and a hellava cook. Pop was a redcap for the railroad. We lived under a soot-covered sky in a walk-up tenement on 125th Street in Harlem."

"Honest work."

"But hard. They sacrificed so much for me, told me to always have hope. During the day my mama cooked for the white ladies on the Upper East Side. My dad worked all day, then came home and drilled me in history. He taught me to use my head, not my fists. 'A black man can't show anger,' he said. He . . ." His voice fell away.

"Simon?"

His breath came out. "He always told me, 'You do what you gotta do.'"

"And do you?"

He grinned. "Let's just say I have a sliding scale when it comes to right and wrong." He glanced at his watch. "We have just a few more minutes. And you promised to tell me how you learned to play the cello."

She looked down at Jac. "Ah. He's still fixated on the blind thing." Her eyes, dark as opals, rose to his. "The simple truth is, I learned to play the cello as a child, when I could still see. So I'm one of the lucky ones. I told you that I have some light perception, I can see some shadows. But I already know colors, faces, birds, trees, and flowers. What a city looks like against a sky full of stars." She laid a gentle hand on her dog. "I know how beautiful a greyhound is. I'm comfortable in my skin, Simon."

"I can tell. And I'm glad you know what Jacquie looks like."

"Me, too." She hesitated, then took a decisive breath. "I lost my sight three years ago, in a car accident. By then playing the cello, finding those notes, all that exquisite music—it was part of me, like breathing."

"A car accident took your sight?"

"A truck came out of nowhere. It still plays in my head, over and over, in such horrible slow motion. In my dreams, I still have my sight. I can see those huge blinding headlights coming at us . . ." She shook her head, letting the words trail into silence.

She turned away, but not before he saw the black rain wash across those remarkable eyes. *Us?* Must have been bad. Really bad. Sensing there was so much more she wasn't ready to say, he reached across the small round table, touched her hand. "I have a pal—Mike Beckett, you'd like him—who says, 'Bad things happen fast, but we live through them slow.'"

She grasped his fingers, held on tightly. Her skin was warm, soft. But the delicate fingers were surprisingly strong. "Yes, that's exactly how it was. How it *is*."

"Except that you still can play your beautiful music," he said softly. "The universe left you a gift."

She pushed her half-finished coffee away and stood up. The greyhound immediately stood by her side, at attention. "Yes. But the price was too high, Simon."

He stared at her. "Hannah . . ."

"Not now, I can't. We have work to do." She bent to Jac. "Come, my beautiful."

My beautiful . . . But he said, "Work to do? I'm not going to like this, am I?"

"Probably not. Jac and I are not going to New York, not yet. We are going with you to Provence."

"Dammit, Hannah. I *have* to dive down that rabbit hole, you don't. No way I'm bringing you there with me."

"It's my choice, Simon. Somewhere out there is a man who wants to hurt Maggie and her godson. Perhaps Jac and I can help you with Tommy Orsini. It's the least I can do."

"But you don't even know TJ. Why would you try to protect a kid you don't know?"

"I lost my little boy along with my husband in that car accident, Simon. He would have been about TJ's age now. Losing a child—it is the most terrible, darkest thing that ever happened to me. Even my blindness doesn't come close. I couldn't help my son, but maybe I can help TJ. I will find a way."

"You don't pull any punches, do you?"

"Not when it comes to a child, no. You said it yourself, Simon. You do what you gotta do."

CHAPTER THIRTY-EIGHT

SALZBURG
SUNDAY MORNING.

It had rained sometime in the night, and now the high alpine meadow was blanketed in a soft opalescent light. The sky was early-morning blue, and the towers and cupolas of old Salzburg gleamed in the valley like a town in a fairy tale.

Maggie had postponed her flight, and now she sat on a weathered wooden bench, gazing down at the spires of Nonnberg Abbey just below her on the hillside. She could see the walled garden, with its winding paths and small trees and the crosses that lined the way. The abbey bells tolled and echoed over the hills, calling the faithful to Sunday prayer.

Like Leonard Bernstein's *A Quiet Place Suite*, she thought. Or, as someone had called the work, "a quiet, sweet place." She shifted on the bench. Her father sat very still beside her, his falcon profile enigmatic and etched sharp as the mountain's granite in the morning light. True to his word, Finn had appeared at her door just after seven a.m. with Starbucks and a Red Sox cap pulled low over his head and whisked her off in the dark, beaten-up Land Rover. Feeling her eyes on him now, he turned to her and waved his arms over the verdant, sheep-dotted hillside.

"Seem familiar?" he asked with a faint smile. "*The Sound of Music* was your first Broadway play. Your mother and I took you. It was your favorite movie for years."

She gazed down at the abbey, picturing the scene from the movie. "Still is. The hills *are* alive here, and filled with music. Is that why you brought me here?"

"We're here because it's a safe place to talk," he said quietly, looking down at his boots. "It's all about sight lines. We can see anyone coming for miles."

"I don't see anyone. So, let's talk."

"It's your agenda, Maggie."

She suddenly could not think of any words to begin. Finally she said, "I told you I've been having dreams about my mother. Do you have them, too?"

His face softened as he gazed up at the clouds. "About Lily? All the time. I dream that I am running through a huge, shadowed theater. Your mother is playing the piano somewhere behind me, dressed in a long white gown, waiting for me to find her. And you are curled beneath her Steinway with a book, the way you always were when you were just a wee girl. The music is so beautiful. Chopin, yes? His *Ballade No. 3*. It shimmers, echoes from the rafters. The three of us together. I don't want it to stop . . ."

Her father's head came up, his eyes meeting hers, bleak and lost. "But it is just a dream."

"I remember hiding under the piano when I was very young," she said. "I remember how Chopin made me feel. An aching, a longing for something I couldn't name . . ."

"Yes. Why is it that chords and rhythms combined in just the right way can make us feel so much? I'm glad you remember. You were so tiny, so precocious. So solemn and gifted. I can see you, sitting at the piano in your favorite flowered shirt. Your feet didn't even reach the pedals! All the years I was gone, I would think back to those moments. I can still see that little girl, her fingers flying over the keys in a blur." His expression softened. "Chopin was always your favorite. I was in the audience at the Royal Festival Hall in London, the night you played his *Ballade No. 1*. My God, that terrifying, complex coda. But you did it, and I was never so proud."

"You were there?" Something shifted inside her. "How have you lived so long without your music?"

He locked his eyes on hers. "But I still have music, Maggie. Just listen."

She tilted her head, closed her eyes. What did she hear? Birdsong. The soft echo of church bells and the faint whisper of the nuns' Gregorian chanting beyond the convent walls. Pines rustling in the soft mountain breeze. The low call of the sheep. A car horn, muffled by distance. She smiled.

Finn Stewart nodded at her. "Salzburg Morning Symphony," he murmured. Very slowly he stood up, raised his hands, and, with a sharp downbeat, began to conduct an orchestra only he could hear.

Maggie's heart twisted in her chest. She had watched him conduct so many times, from theater wings to balcony seats and front row center. Mesmerized by her father's frail arms carving so deftly through the air, she felt herself falling into the memory.

She is sitting in a chorister seat, behind and above the orchestra, facing the conductor. The tumultuous chords of Beethoven's Eroica Symphony *are falling all around her. She cannot take her eyes off her father. The baton arcs with a grand flourish. His gestures are powerful and angular, his body bending low and then rearing up like a stork. He beats the air with furious up and down movements, cuing the horns with a riveting spread of arms and fingers, gathering the violins with deep, floor-scraping, left-handed scoops, as if he is tearing the music from his body. A fierce backhand slash of the baton, then signaling the cymbals with a climactic thrust, his fingers spread like stars.*

His open tuxedo jacket flaps like raven wings behind him, black tie undone, his hair a wild white halo around his head, and his face—eyes closed, chin raised, his expression one of profound passion and—He opens his eyes. Looks right at her. His eyes widen with . . . incomprehension? Fury? Fear? Without warning, in the middle of the first movement, he throws down his baton, leaps from the podium, and runs off the stage into the darkened wings.

Maggie opened her eyes. Just like that, in the toss of a baton, he had disappeared from her life. She felt the tears hot on her cheeks as she stared at her father. "Oh, Finn," she whispered.

He heard her voice and froze, suddenly, the way he had so many years ago. But this time he turned to her, his shoulders slumping. "Of course, I miss the music," he said softly. "I would give anything if I could come home. If I could conduct again."

She could barely breathe. "Why can't you, Finn? I don't understand. You were made to conduct. What is going on with you?"

He ran a bony hand through his silvered hair. "I've grown old, Maggiegirl. I'm seventy-three, life has passed me by. I used to conduct for thousands. Now I sit alone and forgotten, playing Mozart in a dark, drafty music shop. And the irony is, *for the life of me, I cannot figure out how I got here.*" He gazed out over the mountainside. "Music is sound and rhythm . . . and silence. I miss the sound of people *listening.*"

Whatever she had expected, coming here, it was not this. She surely hadn't expected him to strike this deep chord within her. She wanted to say, "*Come home, to me and your family. Give us time to get to know each other again.*" But she said, "Come home, Finn. To music, to your life. Give me time to ask the questions I need to ask."

"First the tragedy, then the farce," he murmured. "I've made a train wreck of my personal life, and yours. Musicians are notorious for their own destruction, don't you know that? Beethoven, Schubert, Bach. Even Mozart! Schumann's failed suicide . . . Why do you think he wrote *Ghost Variations*?"

"Don't you dare give me that tortured genius crap! You are still a brilliant musician. It's time to make things right."

"I'm too old, sprite, it's been too long."

"Don't you remember what Leonard Bernstein said? 'To achieve great things, two things are needed—a plan, and *not quite enough time*.'"

The ghost of his old smile. "I wish it were that simple, Maggie. You don't know, you can't—"

"Then tell me! It's why I've come. I want to know—I *need* to know—how my mother died."

"Ah, sprite. It's so complicated. When we were first married, we were so damned happy. Life was more than we could have imagined. We had our music, our friends, our dreams. And then you came along and it was even better. God, you were such a beautiful child. Still are."

He swiped at his eyes. "I'm not sure when it started to go south. It was the sudden success, I guess, for both of us, taking us down different paths. Gigi was coaching your mother, and Lily was making quite a name for herself. She played like a goddess, you know it. Her Carnegie debut was astonishing. They made a recording of it—*Lily Stewart Plays Rachmaninoff at Carnegie Hall*." His gaze swept the roofs of the abbey. "Haven't seen that album in years. It's got to be in the shop somewhere. You need to hear it. She seemed happy, I thought she was . . ."

Finn stood up, began to pace, the words tumbling faster and faster. "Then I met Lenny Bernstein in New York. Larger than life. Took me under his wing, and the next thing I knew I was in the classical music stratosphere. I called Lenny 'LB.' Parties, expensive wine, late nights, adulation. Tours. Guest conducting. Always, first and foremost, the music. It was my drug, Maggie. I'm not proud of it. No excuses, right? But my world was spinning, it all went to my head. And somehow, your mother was left behind. It was my fault, *totally* my fault. I would be gone for days, then come home only to change my shirt and give you a trinket and a quick hug."

He shook his silver head. "Lily was not jealous. I want you to know that. She was *lonely.* The arguments with your mother came more frequently, became more bitter. Then, just after your thirteenth birthday, Lily finally asked for a divorce."

"A *divorce*!" The words hit Maggie with the force of an electric shock. "I had no idea."

Finn gave a humorless laugh. "Neither did I. By then I was a God, Maggie, a *Maestro*! I still sent your mother *love* letters, for God's sake! I couldn't understand why she would want to leave me. I was hurt. Furious."

She stared at him. "I hear the angry voices, in my nightmare. And—oh, God—I see a face, Finn. A face with no features. Is it *you*? Were you *there* when my mother died? She was such a strong swimmer. How could she drown?"

Before he could answer, her cell phone rang, as unexpected and out of place as a shot on the hillside. She glanced at the number. Simon Sugarman.

"Simon, this is not a good time . . ." She felt herself go pale as he spoke, his words quick and shocking. "What? He's *what*? Oh, God. What will we tell Gigi?" A heartbeat. She gripped the phone tighter. "No, please no. Which hospital? Yes, okay, I understand. Of course. The next plane."

She disconnected and turned to her father. "I have to get back to the States."

"What's happened?" said Finn.

She shook her head in disbelief. "The man I visited yesterday in Vienna has been murdered. Someone must have followed me there.

If I hadn't gone to see him . . . Oh, God, Finn, that lovely man is dead because of me!"

"I was afraid of this." Her father reached out, put a hand on her shoulder. "It's not your fault, Maggiegirl. His murderer is to blame, not you. But you are going to have to be very, very careful now."

His touch was so familiar, so reassuring, so . . . She forced herself to step away. "I can't do this now. I have to get to the airport. Gigi Donati was attacked in her home in New York. She's in intensive care."

CHAPTER THIRTY-NINE

LENOX HILL HOSPITAL, NEW YORK CITY
SUNDAY, OCTOBER 26

"HOW IS SHE?" The quiet words, and the hand on her shoulder, woke her. Maggie opened her eyes, saw Robbie Brennan's concerned face wavering above her. She blinked in the shadowed room, jet-lagged and disoriented, unsure for a moment where she was. She'd begun the day in Salzburg with her father . . .

Then Simon's call, the mad rush to the airport, the anxious nine-hour flight to New York. She shook her head, trying to clear her thoughts, and squinted at her watch. Only four p.m.? Why did it feel like ten or eleven? *But it's six hours earlier here in New York*, she reminded herself.

"Maggie," said Robbie. His voice penetrated the fog, and she heard the beeping sounds of the machines, saw the tiny blinking green lights, became aware of the sharp smell of alcohol and the warm, still skin beneath her hand. She realized she was sitting by a hospital bed, clasping Gigi's withered fingers. Raising her head, she saw that the window opposite the bed was gray with rain hurling against the glass.

"Robbie?" She stood, let herself be folded into his reassuring arms. "Oh, Robbie, she hasn't awakened yet."

"It will be okay," he said into her hair. "God has a plan for Gigi. And this isn't it."

She heard the swish of his black robes as he moved to the side of the bed and gazed down at the aging pianist. "Ouch," he murmured. "She's going to be royally pissed when she looks into the mirror."

"Those bastards hit her, Robbie! Look at her face, so bruised."

"What's the prognosis?"

"Guarded."

His breath came out in a relieved whoosh. "Could be worse. She's a tough old broad, Maggie."

"You're right about that." Very gently she laid Gigi's hand on the blanket and stood to face her friend. "What are you doing here?"

"I came to visit a parishioner and heard about Gigi."

"I'm glad you're here. I keep trying to pray, but it's been so long, I don't know what to say."

Robbie touched her shoulder. "'Please' and 'Thank you' are the two greatest prayers of mankind."

She remained silent, her eyes on the rain that slashed across the window.

"St. Augustine said, 'Faith is to believe what you do not see.'" He drew her away from the bed. "The detective by the door told me this happened two nights ago. She was home alone. Graciela found her in the morning."

"Why, Robbie? Why would anyone hurt such a remarkable woman?"

"For her art, Maggs. I'm told one of her paintings was stolen."

Dark Rhapsody? "Oh, no," whispered Maggie. "If they took her Matisse it will break her heart."

"I don't understand," said Robbie. "What do you—"

"Is that you, Robbie Brennan?" said an imperious voice from the bed. "If you are here to give me Last Rights, then they will be the last rights you ever give anyone, young man."

Robbie and Maggie turned as one to gaze into Gigi Donati's bright amethyst eyes.

"Then it's lucky for me you've awakened," said the Cardinal with a wink. "I'll go get your nurse." He turned to Maggie. "Prayer is the world's greatest wireless connection," he said as he disappeared through the door.

Maggie breathed a silent "thank you" and moved to Gigi's bedside. "We were so worried about you. How are you feeling?"

"Like a Steinway fell on me." Gigi moved her head very slowly toward the machines. "Good God. Where am I? What happened?"

Maggie leaned toward her. "Perhaps you should wait until the doctor comes."

"Tell me, Maggie. Now."

Don't tell her about Johann. Not here, not yet. "Someone attacked you in your penthouse. Did you see who it was?"

Gigi closed her eyes, trying to think. "No one attacked me. I fell." Her eyes flew open, bright with memory and outrage. "Is Graciela all right? Did they hurt her?"

"No, no, she's fine. She found you."

Gigi sighed with relief. "I had a ticket for Lincoln Center. But I was tired, so I gave my ticket to Graciela and went to bed. No one was supposed to be home. Then a sound woke me, footsteps, whispering. I opened my bedroom door. Lord, it was so dark. I saw two men, one very tall, dressed all in black. They were carrying—something. I ran toward them, of course, swinging my cane and shouting."

"Of course you did," murmured Maggie.

Gigi gave a faint chuckle. "Lost my damned balance, fell flat on my face." Her eyes flew to Maggie. "What did those bastards take?"

"Some of the art, I'm told. The detectives will—"

A nurse entered and bent over Gigi, taking her pulse with a quiet, "It's so good to see you awake, Madame Donati. Your doctor will be right in." Turning to Maggie, she said, "I'm sorry, but you'll have to leave."

"Come back after you have given Rachmaninoff his four hours," demanded Gigi. "And not a moment sooner!"

Maggie stood, not sure whether to laugh or pass out. Her watch told her it was now only five p.m., New York time. *No time for sleep yet*, her exhausted brain warned her. *You have to practice the rhapsody, get yourself to Carnegie Hall* and—Oh, God, Carnegie Hall. The stage door!

I'll be there, Maggie. Five p.m. on Sunday, at the Carnegie stage door . . .

She froze, turned to the nurse. "What day is it?"

Sunday . . .

* * *

The sliver of sky above the Seventh Avenue skyscrapers was metal gray with rain and dusk. Streetlamps and window lights shimmered in halos of fog as Michael Beckett, with the Golden by his side, rolled his wheelchair across the wet sidewalk toward the unobtrusive stage door on 56th St. behind Carnegie Hall. The small sign said, "Artist's Entrance." A uniformed guard seated at a desk just inside the glassed door rose and came forward.

"Evening, sir. Performance won't be over for several hours, at least. Long wait in this rain."

Beckett shifted in his seat, frustrated that he had to look up. "I'm here to see a pianist, Maggie O'Shea. Magdalena O'Shea." He touched the small bouquet of white lilacs resting in his lap. "We're supposed to meet here today, at five o'clock."

The guard shook his head, unconvinced. "She's not here, haven't seen her in several days. She's somewhere in Europe, I think. You sure it was for today?"

"I'm sure." Beckett looked down at the Golden. "You think she knows where I've been? You think she's pissed?"

The dog's eyes seemed to be saying, *I told you so.*

"Yeah, I hear you. But we're not giving up. Gonna find her, fella, and make it right." He turned to the guard. "Just in case she shows . . . tell her we were here."

Then he grasped the wheels of the chair and he and the Golden turned back into the rain.

Some forty-five minutes later, when Maggie O'Shea came running up 56th Street, no one was waiting at the stage door. But someone had left a small bouquet of white lilacs, now soaked by rain, on the pavement beside the door.

Just like her father had left his bouquet for her, so many months earlier.

She sank to the step in the cold hard rain and gathered the lilacs against her chest. Then her body folded and she wept.

CHAPTER FORTY

VIENNA
SUNDAY, OCTOBER 26

UNABLE TO SLEEP, Dane paced the small hotel room. He was naked, as was the woman in the rumpled bed behind him. He gazed at the graceful, sleeping figure draped by the white sheet, one slim leg exposed.

Why had she come? He had told her not to . . . he didn't want her here. She was nothing to him. *Meant* nothing to him.

And yet. Why did he want to reach out and shift the sheet over her leg so the cold would not wake her?

He stopped pacing with an angry sound and stood at the high window. Outside, the tiny, empty square behind the cathedral was sheathed in darkness, the thin bars of light from the streetlamps lost in deep shadows.

One shining eye gazed back at him, reflected in the tarnished window glass.

Spy my shadow in the sun, and descant on mine own deformity.

Shakespeare's words flew unbidden into his mind. He had played so many villains in his early days, but Richard III was surely the cruelest. The most innately evil. A monster. And yet . . .

Born with a deformed spine, Richard's deformity was greatly exaggerated by Shakespeare, who portrayed him as a frightening hunchback—as well as a soulless murderer who would kill anyone to become king.

Gazing at his own deformed face in the dark glass, Dane spoke into the shadows.

"What do I fear? Myself? There's none else by.

Is there a murderer here? No. Yes, I am."

No. Yes. His gaze returned once more to the young woman asleep in his bed. The woman who had chosen to be with him. *Bella Beatrice.* "Unloved," whispered Dane into the silence. "Unloved because of his deformity."

* * *

Maggie's aching fingers came down with a crash on the keyboard. A jarring, cacophonous echo—then silence.

"Damn, damn, damn," she whispered. Jet lag, exhaustion, finding her father, worry about Gigi, fear for Michael. Whatever the reason, the Rachmaninoff just wasn't coming together tonight. "You might as well blame it on the Bossa Nova," she murmured, angry with herself. *No excuses.*

Wasn't that what her father always had said?

Don't think about Finn. Don't think about all those still unanswered questions. All those unresolved feelings.

She stood up in frustration and moved away from the piano. On the coffee table, a vase held the soaked, wilting lilacs she'd rescued from the stage door steps. Her chest hurt with the knowledge that she hadn't been there in time. That Michael had been waiting for her alone in the rain.

No excuses.

She checked her cell phone. Still no messages. Where was he? If only—

A soft knock on the front door.

Dropping the phone to the desk, she hurried across the room, checked the peephole. No one in the hallway that she could see. "Hello? Is anyone there?"

"It's us." Muffled. Michael . . .

She unlocked the heavy door, swung it open. "Michael! Where have you—" She stopped in confusion, her eyes drawn down. Michael Beckett was seated below her, in a black wheelchair, looking up at her with a dark scowl on his bruised face, the Golden close to his side.

"We were at the theater," he said. "You weren't. We're here to find out why."

Willing herself not to show the shock she felt at his appearance, she stepped back and gestured them in. "Apparently someone has decided to hit you in the face. Again," she said lightly.

"Happens quite often," said Michael, rolling toward the sofa. "You'd think I'd have learned to duck by now."

"You'd think." She bent to kiss Shiloh on his smooth head. "I've missed you, sweet boy." She raised a brow toward Michael. "How is he doing?"

"Same. Vet had no answers." He held up a small take-out bag. "Turkey sandwiches for us, veggie for you. When is the last time you ate?"

"I have no idea," she said with surprise. Turning to the small bar in the corner, Maggie set a bowl of water on the floor for the Golden and added ice to a crystal glass. "But right now, I'm thinking you both need a drink."

"I need a lot of things, but a drink will do." He flashed that lopsided smile at her, the slow one that began deep in his eyes. "For now."

He eyed her t-shirt. "*Here Comes Treble*," he read aloud. Turning to Shiloh with a scowl, he muttered, "I think we're in for it, big guy."

The Golden seemed to agree and headed for the water bowl.

She handed him his bourbon, kicked off her shoes, and curled on the sofa. He rolled his chair closer to her, but did not touch her. For several moments, there was a tense silence between them. The only sounds in the room were the soft strains of Heifetz's violin on the radio, the slurp of Shiloh lapping his water, and the drum of hard rain on glass.

Finally, she said, "I ran all the way to the theater, but I was too late. You'd already gone."

"I will always show up for you," he said quietly.

She waved a hand toward the bouquet she'd set on the table. "I found the lilacs you left. They're beautiful."

"They're a peace offering. I'd rather take my chances smoking on the Hindenburg than telling you this, because you are going to be very, very pissed when you find out that I—"

"That you were in Rome," she interrupted. "Do you think I don't know you? You went after Dane, when you knew I didn't want you to go. What the *hell* were you thinking?" She leaned toward him until their faces were just inches apart. "Some part of me is so furious with you that I don't know what to do with all this anger burning inside me."

His face softened. "And the other part?"

A heartbeat. "It's easier to be angry than afraid," she whispered. "Not a lot scares me, but the thought of never seeing you again just makes me want to lock my arms around you and never let go. It's my fear I can't face, not yours."

"You don't need to be afraid, Maggie." He looked over at the Golden. "Hear that, Shiloh? Don't you love it when the bad guy wins? You owe me twenty big ones."

The dog glanced at Maggie as if she'd thrown him under the bus.

"Not so fast. Shiloh can keep his money, because the truth is—I'm afraid that life with me is not enough for you."

"Not *enough*?" Beckett's silver eyebrows danced. "You and me, we have a thing, Maggie."

"A 'thing'?"

"Don't you get it? I *want* to be with you. You showed up in my life, beautiful as a concerto, and messed up every plan I ever had. Now, there's always something missing when we're not together. I want you sitting at the piano in your crazy t-shirts. I want you watching the birds. I want you in my bed." He smiled, put his strong hands on her shoulders, pulled her toward him. "Some fights are not worth fighting even if you win," he said, "but other fights you have to fight even if you lose."

"Only you would say that."

"I don't know whether I'm showing you the darkest part of me, or the deepest part. Maybe they're the same."

Her eyes locked on his. "I cannot bear to lose you, Michael. I thought you knew that." Very slowly she rose, stood in front of him, and set her hands on his chest.

"Doc said no weight on the leg until tomorrow, Maggie. At the earliest . . ." He scowled. "I'll be standing first thing in the morning, you can count on it. But—"

"Who said anything about you standing? Close your eyes, Shiloh."

She lowered herself onto Beckett's lap, curled into him, wrapped her arms around his neck, and began to kiss him. He tangled his fingers in her hair, pulled her closer. His lips were hard and warm and he breathed words into her mouth, and she felt herself falling into him and then somehow the wheelchair began to spin, and they were spiraling slowly, slowly, around the shadowed room.

CHAPTER FORTY-ONE

NEW YORK CITY
SUNDAY, OCTOBER 26

THE ROOM WAS filled by a soft darkness, lit only by firelight that flickered from the hearth, lighting Shiloh's fur with streaks of copper as he slept close to the warmth. Maggie lay folded in Beckett's arms on the sofa.

He shifted to look down at her beautiful face. They had eaten the sandwiches. He had told her about Rome. And that Dane was alive. She had told him about the roses. About Hannah and Matisse's *Dark Rhapsody*. And, finally, Johann Vogl's death.

He tilted her chin to look at him. "You said your godfather wants you to come and stay at his estate in the Hamptons?"

"Yes. But I—"

"I think you should go, Maggie. Hannah, too, when she arrives. It's secure there, off the beaten path. You're in the center of the storm here, it will be safer for both of you. I'll take you. Stay for a day or two. We can leave for East Hampton in the morning."

A heartbeat. Then, "You're right."

He cocked a silver brow and gave her his slow smile. "Even a broken clock is right twice a day, ma'am." He glanced at Shiloh for a reaction, was rewarded with a "good one" look.

"This is serious, Michael. My Carnegie stage manager and Gigi Donati were attacked. My godson is being threatened, maybe Hannah Hoffman as well. And Johann Vogl is dead. People close to me are in very real danger. I don't want anyone else to get hurt. Especially because of me."

"They won't, Maggie, not on my watch. Count on it. Now how about Shiloh and I leave and you get some rest. Big day tomorrow."

"Not yet."

Something in her voice. He stilled. "Maggie?"

"I want to tell you about my father."

Go easy. "Sugar said you went to find him in Salzburg. But I thought he died several months before we met?"

"I thought so, too."

"You found him alive, I see it in your eyes. I know it's hard for you to talk about your parents, but . . ."

She was silent for a long time. Then she said, in a voice so low that he pulled her closer, "Something happened to me a long time ago. I never talk about this because it's a story about a young girl who watched her mother die."

"Christ, Maggie!"

"My mother was Lily Stewart, a beautiful and brilliant concert pianist. She loved to swim . . . but she drowned in the Atlantic Ocean when I was thirteen. I just withdrew. I turned to stone, stopped talking, shut myself off from the world. From *myself*!" She turned to him. "I felt so guilty, Michael. I was a teenager—moody, belligerent, always arguing with her. It never occurred to me that I would lose her. I never had the chance to make things right. And I've always felt, deep in my heart, that there was something I could have done to save her."

Maggie swiped at her eyes. "Not long after that, my father—the classical music conductor, Finn Stewart—vanished. I went to live with my grandmother in Boston. After that, only the occasional gift in the mail. It was decades before I saw him again."

"Your father just . . . left you?"

"In the middle of a Beethoven performance he looked right at me, stopped conducting, and just walked off the stage and out of my life."

"Your mother drowned, your father walked . . . No wonder you have nightmares of water, problems with trust. It's a wonder you can stand up at all. Your father was a fool, Maggie. Any man who abandons his kid is not worth it. There was something wrong with your father, not with you."

"When I was young, Michael, we were happy. I adored my father, and he loved me, I know he did. We were inseparable. But then—nothing."

"And yet you went to Salzburg to find him."

"It's hard to explain. Even to myself." She shook her head, smiling faintly. "If he faked his own death, he had to be in trouble. But, even more than that—I think I went to Salzburg because of the yearnings of a lonely child with too many terrible unanswered questions."

"Was he able to give you the answers you need?"

"Not enough. I had to leave, and too much was left unsaid." She pushed her hair away from her face. "Seeing him again reopened old wounds, deep hurts I thought had healed over decades ago. But also, there was something about him, something I didn't expect. The way he talked about my mother, the way he looked at me, his memories of our time together." She held out her hands palms up. "He was bigger than life once. Now, he's a shell of the giant he was. My reaction to his vulnerability—his sorrow—scared me. I felt walls coming down, after all this time. I felt *close* to him again. I came away wondering if everything I've believed all these years is wrong."

"Maybe you need to see him one more time, give yourself a chance to find out."

"I'm afraid, Michael. Afraid of the answers."

"You need to understand why your father left you."

"Yes. But mostly I need to ask him about my mother's death." She gripped her fingers together, the knuckles turning white. "Losing my mother was the defining moment of my life. She's been gone for almost forty years now, but it still feels as if every choice I've made since then was colored by that loss. I turned to music for solace. I distanced myself from friends, relationships, became independent to a fault. Music was my refuge, the only thing that helped with the grief, the only thing I could count on. I could curl up and hide behind the notes . . ."

There was such profound pain in her voice. "You were afraid everyone you loved would leave you."

"That's about what happened, isn't it? My first love, Zach. My husband, Johnny. But it's more complicated than that. *What if I am my father's daughter?* What if I can walk away so easily from someone I love?"

"You won't have a chance to find out." He hugged her tighter, closer. "I'm so sorry, darlin'. No child should have to watch her mother die."

"The truth is, I don't remember it. I don't know what happened. I just know I was *there*, because I see fragments, images, in my nightmares. I hear haunting music. More, these last weeks. I thought I had put it all behind me, but—" She shook her head helplessly. "When I try to remember, everything turns dark blue. Giant waves roll in, bringing fog the color of ink. It's like being underwater at night. I don't know if my memories are real—or dreams."

"Do you *want* to remember what happened, Maggie?"

She raised her eyes to his. "I don't know. What if I can't remember because the truth is so unspeakable?" She choked, fought desperately for breath. "I think my father knows what happened. I've asked him, but he won't tell me. And that terrifies me."

Michael cupped her face in his large hands. "Sometimes the conversation we're most afraid to have, darlin', is the one we need to have the most."

She leaned forward until their foreheads were touching, unable to answer.

"Okay, then," said Beckett. "Whatever you decide, whatever you remember, Shiloh and I will be here for you."

As if he understood, Shiloh rose slowly from his bed by the fire and lurched to Maggie's side, setting his chin on her thigh and looking up at her with his soulful, glistening eyes.

"Oh, Shiloh," she murmured.

"He'd never tell you he was awarded a medal for bravery in combat."

"Warriors come with many faces," she said, stroking the Golden's scars.

Beckett bent closer. "You said you don't remember much. You may never know exactly what happened. Can you tell us what you *do* remember, Maggie?"

"I remember very clearly that my parents had been arguing, fighting, for months. I didn't know it at the time, but my mother had asked Finn for a divorce. That night, I remember being in a room, I don't know where, with my mother. She was playing the piano—a rhapsody, I think—and suddenly there was a terrible banging on the door. 'Hide!' she whispered. I can still hear the fear in her voice."

Maggie put a palm to her chest, as if her heart was beating too fast. "I hid in a closet. I heard angry voices, shouting. I remember a shattered vase, roses strewn all over the floor. I saw a man in a white shirt, raising his arm. My mother cried out. *I was so afraid, I didn't go to help her, Michael.*"

"Easy, darlin'. You were a child. What happened next?"

"She ran through French doors into a garden, shouting that she was going to swim. The man ran after her. I followed them to the door. But all I could see was blue. The air was thick with swirling blue fog. Then I felt a sharp, terrible pain in my head and I lost consciousness. The next thing I remember is waking up in the doctor's office. My father was sitting on the bed. He said, 'Your mother is gone. She died last night.'"

He put his hand on her cheek. "Where did your mother die?"

"In the ocean, Manhattan Beach, not far from our apartment. She swam there all the time. But she went alone that night. Her body was never found. That's what my father, and all the newspapers, said. But . . ." She pressed her hands to her temples in confusion. "But in my dreams, I don't see the ocean. I see a pool surrounded by roses."

She looked at him, her eyes blinded by tears. "And in my dreams, I see—No. I can't say the words."

He took her hands in his. "Tell me, Maggie. You've got to let the words out. Trust me. *What did you see?*"

She grasped his hands tightly, holding his eyes, and breathed out. "Something I wasn't supposed to see. A face, half-hidden in the rose bushes. Watching."

"Whose face, darlin'?"

"I think it was my father."

CHAPTER FORTY-TWO

EAST HAMPTON, LONG ISLAND
MONDAY MORNING, OCTOBER 27

"I FEEL AS if I've fallen into a Winslow-Fricken-Homer painting."

Michael Beckett shook his head with disbelief as he maneuvered the SUV down the narrow, winding road. Maggie had offered to drive, but he had insisted that his right leg was good enough. So far so good.

She looked at his profile, so craggy and strong, and felt a sense of safety wash over her. After last night, it was one she welcomed. One she needed. They had talked for a long time in the darkness. And it had lightened her. Now, she felt stronger, ready to face the new day. Ready to face the answers. Whatever they were.

"Welcome to the Hamptons." Maggie turned to smile at the Golden, settled in the back seat next to Michael's wheelchair, crutches, and carved mahogany cane. "You, too, Shiloh. You're in Eastern Long Island now, only one hundred miles from Manhattan but truly another world."

Beyond the car windows, the morning air sparked with bright sunlight, the red cedars burned with the last fires of autumn. With each bend in the road, dramatic coastal scenes unfolded before them—shingled windmills, villages and tiny harbors crowded with boats, undulating dunes and, beyond, walls of wild grasses, glimpses of waves crashing against miles of windswept, desolate beach.

"We're strangers in a strange land," muttered Michael to the Golden as they passed a quaint fish market with bright buoys hanging from its windows.

Shiloh stared thoughtfully out the window but chose to reserve judgment.

Michael grinned. "Almost there. What should I know about your godfather?"

"Well, as you will see, Alexander Karas comes from old money. Law school at Yale, where he met my parents—and, I suspect, became a member of Yale's secret society, Skull and Bones. Went on to serve twelve years in both Republican and Democratic administrations. He was tireless in his quest for peace, described as a 'peace-process junkie' more than once by the *Times*. Zander is unflappable, can go for hours without sleep or food. One hell of a prosecutor, hates flying economy, favors jeans, not-quite-regulation haircuts, and fine whiskey. Oh, and did I mention he looks like Randolph Scott?"

"Christ. Does the guy walk on water in his spare time?"

"What spare time?" She grinned. "He is on the Metropolitan Museum of Art board. And Lincoln Center's Avery Fisher Hall as well . . ."

"Come up with one flaw. Just one."

"He tells awful jokes. Don't feel you have to laugh. Unless you want to live." She laughed, surprising herself.

"I'll keep that in mind. Ever married?"

"No, no wife or children. He says he's married to his work. But I always thought maybe there was 'the one who got away.' A secret love, like Beethoven's mysterious Immortal Beloved." She looked up from her map. "The turn is just ahead. There. Old Beach Lane."

Beckett turned left into a winding lane under a canopy of ancient elms and tall pines twisted by the wind. She'd seen these pines before . . . Maggie opened her window to breathe in the cold pine-scented air. And to calm her suddenly skittering nerves.

What was the matter with her?

You know, she told herself. Another mile, past horses grazing in white-fenced paddocks. One horse, a beautiful black mare, raised her great sleek head to watch them. Then the trees parted like a curtain and the road opened into a sweeping driveway. Michael slowed as crushed shells crunched beneath the tires.

The elegant Hamptons home was perched on the edge of a low seagrass-covered bluff overlooking the Atlantic. All stone and glass, it was two stories high, with a curving porch and great expanses of windows beneath gables and a gambrel roof. A hint of formal gardens and a slate terrace, and the glint of deep-blue waves cresting beyond the dunes.

"So this is how a Supreme Court nominee lives," muttered Michael as he turned off the engine.

"Short list," Maggie reminded him. "I think the President announces his nominee next week."

Michael opened the door, reached for his cane, and whistled to Shiloh. "Time to meet the godfather," he said.

"Not taking the crutches?" asked Maggie.

An ironic smile. "It's a man thing."

Maggie stepped out of the SUV and gazed up at the beautiful old house. The faint rustle of a breeze through dying leaves, the scent of chrysanthemums sharp and spicy in the air. Somewhere beyond the house, the soft whinny of a horse, and the distant thunder of waves crashing against a headland.

The silvering shingles and the cry of the mare stirred a fragment of memory, as if it came from a long-ago dream. *A rusted iron gate, a glimpse of a garden blooming with giant wild roses . . .*

A sense of uncertainty washed over her, as if she were about to play a dissonant chord on the piano. Inexplicably wary, but trusting her instincts, she turned to Michael. "I think maybe we should get back into the car and leave."

She felt his hand, strong and steady, on her elbow. "What is it, darlin'?"

"I told you that my mother drowned at Manhattan Beach, in New York. But—" she looked up into his eyes— "it was the Atlantic Ocean. No pool, no hidden garden. That's why my dreams have never made sense. But now—I have a bad feeling—I can't explain it—that Ocean House holds some of the answers to my mother's death."

"Okay. We'll just get back in the car and—" He raised his head. "Christ. Too late, Maggie."

She heard the great door open, turned to see her tall, handsome godfather coming toward them down the broad stone steps.

"Maggie! Colonel Beckett," said Judge Alexander Karas in his deep, familiar baritone.

"*Welcome to Ocean House.*"

Part IV

"If by your art, my dearest father, you have put the wild waters in this roar, allay them . . ."

— Shakespeare, *The Tempest*

CHAPTER FORTY-THREE

OCEAN HOUSE
MONDAY, OCTOBER 27

"THIS PLACE IS something else," murmured Michael as they entered the two-story, octagonal foyer. He set his cane firmly on the floor and did a slow turn, taking in the high stained-glass windows, the richly colored Persian carpets, the bouquet of lilies overflowing onto a round cherry table. A graceful, floating winged staircase curved right and left up to a distant, shadowed landing.

"And this is only the foyer," smiled Maggie, turning to Zander. "It's good to be here, thank you."

"The pleasure is all mine, Goddaughter. As I told you in New York, this old place needs voices, laughter, movement, life. And a dog." He chuckled as he bent to rub Shiloh's head.

The Golden shied away with a soft growl. Maggie caught Michael's quick concerned glance, shook her head at him. "Shiloh hasn't been himself lately," she said to Zander. "Will you show us around?"

"Of course." He turned to Michael with a sweeping gesture of his arms. "My father, Sebastian Karas, loved this old place. He was born here, as was I. But it fell into disrepair during the later years of his life. I've spent this last year, since he died, trying to bring back Ocean House's former glory. Two full work crews, inside and out, seven days a week. The East Wing is still a shambles, as well as the boat house, and much of the grounds."

"I'd say you are knocking it out of the park, Judge," said Michael, gazing up at the intricate pattern of the stair railings. "Only God could have done better."

"You think so? But the only difference between a judge and God, Colonel, is that God doesn't think he's a judge."

A beat of silence, and then Michael chuckled, too loudly. Both Maggie and Shiloh threw him a look.

"That bad, eh?" said Zander. "I owe you one, Colonel. The library is down the hall to the left, through those doors. We can meet in there tonight for a sixteen-year-old Black Maple Hill bourbon. I think the library is the most beautiful room in the house."

"You had me at Maple Hill, Judge," said Michael. "I'll look forward to it."

"But right now," said Zander, "a toast." Three flutes of French champagne bubbled on a small table, and he offered the glasses. "Welcome back, Maggie."

Michael raised his flute. "I could not live without champagne," he said. "In victory, I deserve it. In defeat, I need it."

"Can't argue with Churchill," said Maggie, taking a long sip. "Let's just hope we don't end up *needing* it while we're here," she said under her breath.

"Come, this is the room I want Maggie to see." Zander led them across the expanse of foyer toward two huge double doors and drew them open. They stepped into a high-ceilinged ballroom, surrounded on two sides by tall windows. At the far end, set in a curve of shining glass, stood a Steinway grand piano. Maggie caught her breath, and Michael moved to stand by her side.

"Maggie?"

"It's okay," she said in a whisper. But she moved closer to him.

Zander gazed fondly at the sweeping ballroom. "Maggie's parents and I used to have our Gatsby parties here in the old days, Colonel, just after we left Yale. They were newlyweds, and we all were beginning our lives in Manhattan, but we would drive here on weekends. We did it for years, although not nearly as often after I went to DC."

He turned his eyes on Maggie. "I told you that my father was especially fond of your mother. I think because she reminded him of his wife, my mother. She played the piano, too, did you know that? She had the look of your mom, with her long dark hair, and heart-shaped face. Both women died too soon." Zander's eyes clouded. "My father always said your mother gave him back a little bit of his wife, especially when she played the piano, and he encouraged Lily to come often. She brought you here almost every week when you were a young child." He hesitated. "Although less often when you were older . . . I thought you might remember this room."

Maggie gazed at the glowing, oyster-colored walls, the polished oak floor, the sun pouring in bright bars through the tall windows onto several Renaissance landscapes. And felt the faint stir of memory.

"Yes, I *remember*. There were chairs set up, in rows curving like arms, over there. And there. My mother sat at the piano, in a long beaded dress." She smiled and turned to Michael, who was watching her, his hand resting on Shiloh's head. "It's a happy, lovely memory. I used to sit up there"—she gestured toward a narrow, high balcony that ran along one side of the wall—"and listen to the music. My father would play the violin, I think."

"Yes!" Zander smiled. "And I would play host and pour the champagne. I couldn't play a note, Colonel. Still don't know why Maggie's parents gave me the time of day. But I'm glad they did." He smiled at Maggie. "And I'm glad you remember some of those times. I'm hoping this Wednesday's party will bring them back."

He turned to Michael. "I'm hosting a benefit here for the fiftieth anniversary of Yale's orchestra. And I'll be announcing the bequest of Ocean House to Yale for a new art museum. I hope you will stay to attend the gala, Colonel, with my goddaughter."

Beckett glanced at Maggie. "I'd be honored, Judge, thank you."

"Maggie," said Zander, "I've also invited Gigi, if she's well enough. And the Archbishop."

"Now *that's* a party," muttered Beckett to the Golden. "At least we won't be the oldest guys there."

Zander laughed as he gestured toward the piano. "I know you will need to practice for several hours every day while you're here, Maggie. Consider this room yours."

"I will, Zander. Starting this afternoon. Thank you."

"You're sure you won't consider playing for us all on Wednesday night? It would be—"

"A career ender!" Maggie held up her hands with a smile. "You do know the Carnegie folks are promoting the Rachmaninoff rhapsody as my *first* public return? I'm afraid they won't go for *second*. But Hannah Hoffman has agreed to help you out. She's transcendent—you won't be sorry."

"Can I help it if I'm your biggest fan? Now come this way. I want to show you the gardens, and you'll see how Ocean House got its name." Another set of double French doors led to a broad slate terrace. It was the perfect October day in the Hamptons, cool and crisp, with the sharp hint of apples and leaf smoke in the air. The surrounding woods swayed with bright spears of orange, crimson, and gold. In the distance, the low undulating dunes sparkled silver in the light. And echoing in the air, the muffled thunder of ocean waves crashing against the beach.

Maggie gripped Beckett's hand and caught her breath as they gazed out at the riot of chrysanthemums, asters, and goldenrod that spilled downhill, in manicured terraces, to a huge, shimmering infinity pool.

"Easy, darlin'," Beckett said softly, his eyes on the pool. "Anything?"

Her breath came out in a surprised, relieved whoosh. "No. No bad memories here."

Zander came up behind them and pointed to the west, toward the paddocks. "We have a stable here, to house some beautiful rescue mares. And there"—he gestured east—"down by the beach is an old boathouse, although the water is too rough to do much boating. I've kept my boat moored at the harbor for years. Over there, you can see the glass roof of the conservatory, through the trees. I've been filling it with orchids and other tropical plants."

"No roses?"

"Your mother loved them, didn't she? But no, the formal rose garden is long gone. Didn't do well in the salty air."

Okay, thought Maggie, *that's good. No roses.*

* * *

Almost four thousand miles to the east, Simon Sugarman stood with Hannah Hoffman and her greyhound on the terrace of a Provençal vineyard. Just months earlier, he had stood in this very place—although the dog on the terrace that day had been a brutal Doberman, not a gentle greyhound. He remembered, too, hiding in those woods at the edge of the property, keeping watch. The image of Maggie O'Shea as she strode bravely across the terrace and disappeared into the house was still so clear in his mind. Just before all hell broke loose.

The vineyard was much as Sugarman remembered it, almost unchanged since the summer. Rows of vines still climbed the undulating hillside behind the shuttered stone farmhouse, although now they were heavy with clusters of crystal-green and burgundy grapes. The blue stone terrace was the same as well—the small round table, the splashing fountain, the ochre pots of autumn geraniums drooping in the last of the late-day sun. Only noon back in the States, he thought, but here in Provence the sun would set within the hour.

"Come sit," he said, taking Hannah's elbow and guiding her to the old metal café chairs scattered under a shading arbor of purple vines. "I wish you could see this light—it's clear and kind of shimmery. Opalescent. Learned that in a crossword." He chuckled. "Never seen light like this anywhere else."

Jac followed them silently, wary and alert, her eyes on the pair of leashed Dobermans held close to the two muscular guards standing at the far end of the terrace.

"I don't blame you, Jacquie," he murmured. "I never trust a Doberman, myself."

"You said the dogs are leashed, Simon?" Hannah asked, sensing Jac's disquiet.

"Yeah. I just hope they know we come in peace."

She turned her smile on him, the wild black curls swinging like a cape around her shoulders. Huge tinted glasses shadowed her eyes. "I'm glad you're here, Hannah," he said, shifting his chair closer as he drew a narrow box from his jacket pocket and pressed it into her hands. "This reminded me of you."

He watched as she raised the long gossamer scarf to her cheek.

"It feels so beautiful. No one has given me such a gift in a very long time, Simon. What color is it?"

"Like the sky at twilight." *Like your eyes.*

She swirled the scarf around her neck and touched his arm. "The sky . . . How can I thank you?"

"Just remember your promise. If we discover anything about the location of the art, I go on *alone*. You're on the first plane to the States. *Capisce?*"

"Unless you ask me to stay."

Sugarman shook his head, unsettled by the way she kept him off balance. "You're going to love TJ," he said, moving away from the minefield of her words. "But this little boy has been through a helluva lot—more than any kid should have to suffer, so we need to be careful—"

"*Monsieur Sugar!*"

Small running footsteps on stone. The guards stepped closer as Thomas John Orsini—TJ—raced across the terrace and threw himself at Sugarman. A pretty young Frenchwoman, TJ's nanny, followed and settled herself in a chair on the far side of the terrace.

"Whoa, little pal!" Sugarman looked fondly down at the child. Soon to be seven, TJ was still thin as a hockey stick, with huge dark eyes and a mop of black curls tumbling in his eyes. "It's good to see you again, mophead. You've grown since July. You'll be as tall as I am soon. Slap me five."

"I have missed you and Maggie," said the boy in his flutelike voice, smiling as he hit Sugarman's huge palm with his own much smaller one. He glanced shyly at Hannah and the greyhound, then back to Sugarman. "Did you bring Shiloh with you?"

"No, little pal, not this time. But you're coming to New York soon, right?"

"*Oui*, I will see Maggie and Shiloh and *Mon Colonel* for my birthday. I am practicing the Bach, the way she taught me, to surprise her."

"My main man! And now I want you to meet another special lady. This is Hannah, and her dog, Jac. Hannah is a musician, like you and Maggie. But she plays the cello." He drew the child closer to Hannah's knees. "This is TJ, Hannah."

The boy stood in front of her, serious and formal, and made a small bow. "*Bonjour, Madmoiselle Hannah*. May I touch your dog? She is beautiful."

Hannah set a quieting hand on Jac's head. "I'm sure she would like that. Will you let her smell the back of your hand first? She's my friend, but she also is a service dog. Do you know what that is?"

TJ did as she asked, and then began to stroke Jac. "She is here to help you walk?"

"To help me see."

"Oh, okay," said TJ, as if it were the most natural thing in the world to meet a blind musician. "Give me your hand, *Madmoiselle*." He took her hand and held it to his face. "This is what I look like." And then, "I am still afraid of the dark. Do you get scared sometimes, too?"

Hannah glanced over at Sugarman. "Yes, I do. But Jac helps me. Playing my cello helps, too. And children. I had a little boy once, about your age."

The child looked around. "Where is he?"

A breath. "In heaven, with the angels."

"Oh. My papa is in heaven, too."

"Jac and I would like to hear more about your papa," said Hannah, taking the little boy's hand and drawing him closer.

CHAPTER FORTY-FOUR

OCEAN HOUSE.
MONDAY, OCTOBER 27

"PLAY FOR ME."

Late-morning light knifed into the ballroom through the open French doors, changing the Steinway's wood to a glowing copper. Michael stood by the piano, close to Maggie, as she prepared to tackle the Rachmaninoff. She set her music down and turned to him with a shake of her head. "You've heard me play many times, Colonel."

"But never Rachmaninoff's *Rhapsody*, ma'am. I know how important this is to you." He looked down at the Golden. "To us, too, right, fella?"

Shiloh yawned.

"An offer I cannot refuse." Maggie laughed. "Have a seat, then, gentlemen, and prepare to be dazzled by my favorite variation of Rachmaninoff's *Rhapsody*. I give you—the Variation Eighteen."

She settled on the bench, held her hands above the keys for a long moment. And then she began to play.

Just over three minutes later, Maggie opened her eyes as the final notes lingered in the air and turned to her audience. Shiloh was sound asleep, snoring. Michael was looking at her with a bemused expression on his face.

"What?" she whispered. "What is it?"

"That sounded like . . . the music from the movie *Somewhere in Time*. And . . . *Groundhog Day*?"

"Yes, you're right, it's in both movie soundtracks. What did you think?"

A moment of silence. Then, "I think that you were born to play this piece. You don't even seem to know it, but what you have, Maggie, it's like . . . sunlight. It just simply *happens*. You are made of music."

She stared at him. "You understand. Yes, this variation is so personal to me. You heard that, in the music. It's Paganini's A-minor theme, but inverted, turned upside down, to a major key. Rachmaninoff took something so dark and sad and aching and changed it into—"

"Something beautiful and transformative," said Beckett. "Like what has happened to *you* over the past year. Watching you play, watching your face, I can *see* the transformation. With every note you are finding your way. It's like this music is telling your story."

A sound at the French doors, heavy footsteps. Beckett stepped in front of Maggie as a long shadow fell across the piano.

"I am sorry to interrupt," said a low, accented voice, "but I heard the beautiful music." The stranger froze, a shimmer of shock on his wizened face. "Is it you, Miss Maggie?"

Sensing no threat, Maggie stepped from behind Beckett to gaze into the stranger's face. He was well into his seventies, dressed in stained work clothes and boots. "Yes, I'm Maggie," she said. "And you are . . ." She stepped closer. "Good Lord! Miguel?"

"*Si*. You were such a sweet child, Miss Maggie. You and I used to listen to your mama play her music. I thought I was dreaming just now, thought that I was hearing Miss Lily play again."

Maggie reached to touch his shoulder. "That's the best compliment I could be given. I remember you, Miguel. You let me help you in the garden."

"*Si*. We always chose the most beautiful roses for your mama."

"My godfather says the rose bushes are long gone now."

He looked at her with an odd expression. "The formal gardens, yes. But not the wild roses."

Maggie stiffened, suddenly anxious. Sensing, somehow, that another door to her past was about to open. "Wild roses? Where are they?"

"Still growing outside your mother's favorite place, of course, the small cottage, by the lap-pool in the woods. Do you remember it? She loved it so much that she made it her own private music room. She would disappear there for hours, to swim and play the piano and listen to her records. The Judge's father, Señor Karas, asked me to move his Rhapsody Grand Piano there for her."

The gardener's voice seemed to be coming from a great distance, as if through fog, and Maggie felt herself swaying. Then she felt Michael's strong body close to hers, and managed to find the words. "I can't remember, Miguel. Where is my mother's music room?"

"Hidden away, in the woods over there—" The old gardener gestured beyond the French doors. "There is a path, long overgrown by sea grape vines these last decades. No one has gone there in many years, including myself. But I will take you there, if you want to see it."

Another door, about to open.

"Yes, Miguel. I very much want to see my mother's music room."

* * *

Far to the east, in Provence, the sun dropped behind the vine-covered hillside and the air turned lavender with twilight. Sugarman sat listening to the woman and boy as they spoke of kites and basketball, swimming and music and his treasured coin collection. And, *bien sur*, all his *amies* at school. "But no *girls*, *Madmoiselle Hannah*, I am much too young."

Hannah laughed, and then, finally, she asked TJ if he remembered going to any special places with his father, before his papa went to heaven.

The child looked toward the vines, lost in memory. Then he said, in a voice so low that she had to bend forward to hear him, "My papa spent most of his time in his office. But every Sunday morning he would take me on a special outing."

Hannah grinned down at him, tousled his hair. "That sounds like fun. Where did you go?"

The boy pushed the dark curls from his eyes. "Sometimes fishing. Sometimes hiking. Sometimes to a museum. He loved to look at the pictures and tell me stories about them."

Sugarman chucked the boy's chin gently. "I like to go to museums, too, mophead. Anywhere else?"

TJ closed his eyes as he rubbed Jac's head. "To church. He liked the organ music. And once—to a church that wasn't a church."

Sugarman felt Hannah stiffen beside him. "A church that isn't a church?" she asked. "How is that possible?"

"My papa called it a . . . ruin, I think." He pronounced it "roo-een." "You know, very old, falling apart. No altar or organ or statues. No stained glass or roof. Just rocks and stones and tall grass. Some of the walls are still there, but they are broken. They let the sunlight in."

"It sounds beautiful to me," said Hannah. "I saw the ruins of an abbey in Wales, a long time ago, when I still had my sight. Tintern Abbey. Flowers grew through the stones, and you could see the sky through the walls, where the windows used to be. I remember how special it was. More like a church than a real church."

"*Oui*, that is what my papa said. That it was our special place. We had to hike to get there, but I didn't mind. It had a beautiful cross, taller than I am, and a windmill nearby. He gave me a key, and said I should go back there one day, when I grew older."

"A key?" Sugarman glanced at Hannah as he leaned toward the boy. "Did this special place have a name, TJ?"

The child squinted at the purpling sky, then turned a stricken face toward Sugarman. "I cannot remember it, *Monsieur Sugar*. I am sorry. Papa would be very angry with me."

"No, no, your papa would have understood. I'm thinking that maybe your papa wrote the name down for you, just in case?"

The boy's eyes brightened. "My coin! Yes, it is on one of my coins. I will show you."

He dashed across the terrace and disappeared into the farmhouse.

Sugarman turned to Hannah. "Are you thinking what I'm thinking?"

"The Provençal countryside is dotted with church ruins," she said softly. "And old abbeys and chapels have crypts."

Light, quick footsteps. "Here it is," cried TJ, holding out a long golden chain with a coin and a small silver key swinging from the central links. He thrust the necklace into Sugarman's hands. "I think it says the name on the back. It is in French, *Monsieur Sugar*."

Sugarman held the heavy, round gold coin in his hand. The front was decorated with a small cross made of three emblems—an anchor, a cross, and a heart. He turned it over.

Five words engraved on the metal.

La Chapelle du Santo Rosario.

CHAPTER FORTY-FIVE

VIENNA
MONDAY, OCTOBER 27

"Do you know where Magdalena O'Shea is, Dante?"

Beatrice sat on a chair by the window, staring down into the square. She was dressed in a long flowing blue robe, her hand resting with love on the new, slight curve of her abdomen. Staring at the enigmatic smile on her lips, Dane thought she looked like one of Orsini's Madonna paintings.

He scowled and shook his head. "No. She dropped out of sight in Salzburg."

"But you don't seem upset."

"Because I know how to find her. Thanks to you."

"Me?" The smile turned on him, the dark eyes lit with surprise. "What did I do?"

"You followed Magdalena O'Shea after she left the Lipizzaner stables. To the apartment of Hannah Hoffman, yes? The agent Simon Sugarman was there as well. He is the key player, the one searching for the art. He is in Europe for a reason, Bella. He knows Tommy Orsini; the boy trusts him. He is the one I will follow. The boy is well protected, so Sugarman will do the work for me. He will lead me to the paintings, and eventually he—or Hannah Hoffman—will lead me back to Magdalena O'Shea. Then everything will come full circle."

"But you are here with me, in Vienna. How will you know what Agent Sugarman learns?"

"Many of the men who worked for Victor now work for me. I have two teams keeping watch. One here in Europe and one in the US. My New York contact, Thanos, called while you were sleeping. Sugarman and Hannah Hoffman are at the vineyard in Provence, questioning the boy." He smiled. "There is a tracking device beneath his car now. And I have a truck, standing by."

Beatrice rose, walked across the room to stand before him. She set a hand lightly on his chest and looked up at him. "I'm glad I could help you. It makes me happy. I only wish . . ."

"What?"

"That my father was alive. To know I am happy. To meet the bambino."

Dane looked away. "Don't think about his accident, *mon ange*. Just believe that your father is in heaven and somehow knows your joy."

She took his huge, scarred hand and drew it, very gently, against her abdomen.

"I know you have done some terrible things in your life," she said after a while. "And terrible things have been done to you. Your mother left you when you were too young. Your father was violent, vicious. He started it all when he locked you in that closet so long ago. These things mark a child, leave many scars. But I have seen another side of you. I know you can be a decent and kind man. Worth loving."

He stared at her, unconvinced—and unnerved.

She raised a hand to stroke his scarred cheek. "You just don't believe there is something in you worth loving, Dante. Can't you try to feel our joy?"

"Bella Beatrice . . ." He felt the soft swell of her—of his child—beneath his burned fingertips. "For the first time in my life," he told her, "I think perhaps I do."

CHAPTER FORTY-SIX

OCEAN HOUSE
LATE DAY MONDAY, OCTOBER 27

EVERYTHING WAS GREEN, even the light. The path through Ocean House's woods was almost invisible, overgrown with high, ancient rhododendron bushes, dense with hemlock, birch, fallen limbs, and vines. Maggie had been following Miguel for at least ten minutes—alone, in spite of Michael's offer. Well, *offer* was not quite the word, she thought, picturing his dark expression.

Let me be there for you, Maggie. You don't have to face this alone.

But I do, Michael.

This was something she had to do on her own. Because now, deep inside her, she knew what she was going to find.

Up ahead, the pines and undergrowth thinned. Miguel stopped to part old, tangled branches. "We're here, Miss Maggie. Through these leaves. Do you want me to stay with you?"

For an instant, she hesitated. Then, "Thank you, no. You've been a good friend. But I have my cell, and I know I can find my way back when I'm ready."

He nodded without speaking and then handed her a flashlight and a small key. "For the cottage. I doubt there will be electricity. I hope you find what you are looking for, Miss Maggie." Then he disappeared into the forest.

Maggie stood very still, trying to breathe. She could hear the soft sounds of the woods—doves, the rustle of tiny animals, wind sighing through the leaves—but all as if from a great distance. Now her whole being was centered on the small cottage waiting for her beyond the leaves.

Okay, on the count of three. One, two . . . She stepped through the vines into the clearing.

The first thing she saw was the high, rusted iron gate. It creaked loudly as she swung it open, just as she remembered. She followed the curving stone path to the blue front door. The key felt hot, burning, in her palm. The lock resisted for a moment, then gave. She set her hand on the tarnished doorknob, very aware that she was once again opening a door to her past.

The door opens . . .

She knows this room!

She steps over the threshold into the dusky gloom.

The electric switch—here, on the wall. No light. The flashlight clicks on. Shadows waver around her. The glass lantern is still on the side table, the matches beside it. Light blooms.

She blinks. To her right, the tall oak bookcase, filled to overflowing with her mother's beloved 78 rpm vinyl records. Next to the lantern, the old turntable. She closes her eyes for a moment, hears the soft chords of Swan Lake, *like an echo in a long tunnel.*

To the right, the closet door. She shakes her head. Not yet.

A flowered shawl is tossed over a low sofa, as if her mother has just dropped it there for a moment.

Straight ahead is her mother's beautiful Steinway grand piano. She is drawn to it helplessly, as if she is a tidal pool drawn by a full moon. She touches the wood, gently presses a black key. The A sharp. Out of tune. But, oh, the piano is gorgeous.

Designed and built in a local workroom, it is a limited-edition Steinway & Sons "Rhapsody" grand piano, its colors all varying shades of deep blue. The word "Rhapsody" is painted in gilt script on the intricate music rack above the keyboard. Sophisticated, romantic, beautiful. Like her mother, Lily.

The wall opposite the piano is bare. There is a slight fading on the paint, as if a large oil painting once hung there. Long gone now. But in her mind, she sees a beautiful dark-haired woman playing a cello against a night sky. Dark Rhapsody.

Beyond the piano are the French doors she remembers. They are closed, covered by white curtains. She is afraid of what she will find when she opens those doors.

The music in her head crashes to a stop.

Hide! Her mother's voice, frightened.

Now a dark blue fog is seeping into the room, from beneath the French doors. She forces her body to move through the blue shadows, toward her mother's closet. She opens it slowly, is assaulted by the ageless scent of Shalimar. She staggers, steps back. Opens her eyes. There are the gowns, jewel-colored silks and satins, just as she remembers them.

I hid here. I didn't help her . . .

The door closes.

The sharp sound of the closing door behind her snapped Maggie back to the present. She spun around.

A tall, looming presence in the cobalt shadows, stepping toward her.

CHAPTER FORTY-SEVEN

PROVENCE
LATE DAY, MONDAY, OCTOBER 27

"STARS WERE THE last thing I ever saw," said Hannah into the silence of the car.

Stars . . . Sugarman took his eyes off the road to look at her. They were in the Audi he had rented, driving toward the Marseilles-Provence International Airport just northwest of Marseilles. He had arranged three seats for her on the flight to New York—for her, Jac, and the red-cased cello now stashed with the greyhound in the rear seat.

Unsure what to say, he remained silent, reaching across the seat to touch her arm.

"Are the stars out tonight?" she asked him.

"Yes, the sky is full of stars. You're thinking of the night of your accident?"

"I was in the car with my husband and son—around this time of day. We were headed for ice cream, after dinner. So simple, really. Just one of those lovely, small, unfurling everyday moments we take for granted. I remember gazing out the window, thinking about all the beautiful stars in the night sky. Searching for the Pleiades cluster, to show my son. And then the world exploded and disappeared forever."

"I can't imagine losing a child," said Sugarman into the darkness.

"That's because it truly is unimaginable. It was the worst thing that ever happened to me, Simon. I thought it would kill me. My blindness is nothing compared to that loss. When a child dies, the pain sends you into a deep black hole. Grief swallows you whole, crushes the soul out of you. That night, my son was wearing a blue woolen coat with silver buttons. My dreams are haunted by a little boy in a blue coat. I hear him crying . . ."

In the back seat, Jac whined softly. Sugarman wanted to pull the car over and take her in his arms. "What can I do, Hannah?"

"You are listening, Simon. Sometimes I am ambushed, and just need to say my son's name out loud to someone I trust. Max. His name was Max. When I play the cello, I am playing for him."

"Honestly, Hannah, I would never have handled loss the way you do, with so much grace. But I don't know what I would do. I've never had a child to lose. Or a wife. I've loved only one woman in my life, and she almost died because of me."

She touched his arm, somehow understanding. "How long have you been alone?"

"Seems like forever."

The lift of narrow shoulders in the shadows. "You seem like a man who would enjoy a wife, children."

"Maybe. But I'm a black man, Hannah. You can't understand it until you've been stopped and searched by the cops just because of how you look, until your hotel reservation mysteriously disappears, until a white woman crosses the street when she sees you coming. My brother is in prison, where nothing good can happen. I watched my father beaten in the rail yards. My first 'talk' wasn't about the birds and bees, it was about keeping my head down, not arguing or calling attention to myself. Now we tell our teenage boys, don't wear hoodies, don't fight back. Hell, I got on an elevator last week and a little white girl hid behind her mother's skirt. 'Is that man going to hurt me?' she cried."

"Oh, Simon, how those words must have hurt you."

"Oh, yeah. They cut. I'm a proud man, Hannah, but I live in a dark world. I carry around some pretty serious demons. Makes me wary of sharing my life, you know?"

"I do know. Everybody hurts. Bad things happen to all of us. We get knocked down. But what matters is getting up again, in spite of the demons. What is it that you say? 'We do what we gotta do.'"

She shook her head. "After I lost Max, I was a mess for a very long time. Maybe if it all had happened slow, I could have seen it coming, prepared somehow. But it happened fast. In the beginning, I hated being alone, being locked in the constant, terrifying dark. I hated not being able to look at photos of my husband, my son. I hated my cane, but I hated falling more. I hated spilling my food or losing my keys or phone, such simple things. Lord, I missed running across the grass in the park, driving my car—my damned independence. I even hated Jac when she first came to me. Can you imagine?"

"Nope, I guess she's kind of grown on me." He grinned, glancing into the back seat.

"My heart was so angry, Simon. One night I smashed my cello into a thousand pieces, crawled into a cave, and refused to come out." She shook her head with regret. "Maggie and I, we have that loss of music in common. But we both realized, finally, that it was our music that would save us. Now I thank God every day for my music. The cello has given me back my life."

"I've never heard anything as beautiful as you playing the Dvorak."

"I'm glad. Now I am able to focus on simple pleasures again—the smell of the woods after a rain, the feel of Jac's smooth head beneath my fingers, the sound of the ocean, sunlight on my face. Memories of Max. Crosswords in braille." She smiled. "The touch of a soft scarf around my neck. It took me a long time to come out of my cave, but here I am. I even bake cakes again." She laughed faintly. "And sometimes, when I play my cello, I am able to believe that life is not a tragedy."

CHAPTER FORTY-EIGHT

OCEAN HOUSE
LATE DAY, MONDAY, OCTOBER 27

THE MAN STANDING in the shadowed doorway of the Music Room stepped toward Maggie.

"Finn! Good Lord, you scared me half to death! What are you doing here?"

"Good to see you, too, sprite." The old, wry smile. He held out his hands to her. "Sorry, I didn't mean to frighten you. But after you left Salzburg with so much unfinished between us . . . damn it, Maggie, you're my daughter. I should have come home a long time ago. Let me make it right, after all these years."

"How did you know where to find me?"

He frowned. "You were closing in on the answers when you left me in Europe. It was only a matter of time." He waved a hand around the small cottage in the grand gesture of a Maestro. "Where else would you be?"

He ran long fingers through his wild white hair. "God, this place is exactly the same. I half expect your mother to walk through that door."

Finn sat down on the piano bench, stretched his long, jeans-clad legs out in front of him with a regretful sigh, and stared at his boots. "We hung the Matisse right over there, on the wall." He turned, gestured toward the wall by the piano, now faded and empty. "This can't be easy for you, Maggie."

"No. But at least now I know I'm not crazy." She took a deep breath. "My mother died *here*, didn't she, Finn? Not in the ocean off Manhattan Beach, as the reports said. Please. I feel it. It's not just a dream. *Tell me the truth!*"

A long moment of silence. Then, "Yes. She died here. In the pool beyond those doors."

She'd known it. But now she turned away from the doors to sink into the sofa. Wrapping her mother's flowered shawl around her, she breathed in the faint scent of Shalimar. Then, leaning toward her father, she said, "I don't know what's real and what isn't. I need to know what really happened that night."

"Yes, Maggie. You do." Finn Stewart gazed toward the curtained doors for a long time, as if seeing that night unroll in his head.

"I told you your mother was very unhappy, that she wanted a divorce. She began to take you to Ocean House every weekend. It became her safe place, her escape. She spent hours here, playing, composing. No one knew about it, except for you, me, Zander, and his dad." He gave a faint smile. "And my old friend Miguel. I just saw him, up at the house."

"He brought me here, to the cottage. I didn't remember it on my own."

Her father nodded, not surprised. "I didn't *want* you to remember it," he said. He stopped by the old vinyl records, ran a hand over them, his intense eyes lost in memory. "That night, I showed up here, unexpectedly, at the cottage. Lily was sitting at the piano, playing that damned rhapsody she'd composed. She was wearing a long green silk robe, and she looked so beautiful . . . I'd been drinking. I'd brought her roses. But I was angry, so damned angry with her. Of course, I didn't know you were hiding in the closet. If I had, everything would have ended so differently. Your mother would still be alive . . ." His eyes filled with blue rain. "But we fought. She flung the roses back at me, they crashed to the floor. She ran out of the room, into the garden, and I followed her."

Maggie could barely breathe, could not take her eyes off her father. "And then?"

Her father held out his hand to her. "Come with me, Maggiegirl. Come with me through those doors. You've come this far. It's time we both face the memories. It's why I've come home."

* * *

"I can't."

Maggie stood facing the curtained French doors, her hand on the silver knob. "I can't go out there, Finn."

"We can go back to the house, sprite. Or you can open the door. Let me be here for you."

You've waited so long. Just do it. She threw him a look, squared her shoulders, and opened the doors.

The first thing she saw was the twisted face of the stone creature she remembered, guarding the hidden garden.

Beyond it was the pool. *The pool in her dreams.*

Empty now, the lap-pool was almost fifty feet long, narrow and rectangular in shape, lined by dark blue tiles. Huge scattered leaves were caught in the pool's blue depths, swirling and spinning like water.

Maggie stepped through the doors.

It was the blue hour—*L'Heure Bleu*—that time of day when edges blurred and sounds muffled and the air shimmered with a deep blue light. Shallow stone steps led down to a small terrace. Surrounding the pool, just as she remembered, were the wild rose bushes, immense now, their dark green leaves and thorns tangled like Sleeping Beauty's castle.

Maggie stood very still. And the memories washed over her like waves from a storm-tossed ocean.

The scent of roses fills her head.

Voices, shouting.

Afraid for her mother, she opens the French doors.

Indigo shadows. The air is blue, chilling.

Her mother, spinning in a long, narrow pool.

Blue light swirling like fog over her naked body.

Somewhere music is playing, the melody haunting and dark with sorrow.

Her mother begins to spiral down into the depths, to disappear . . .

No!

The blurred outline of a man's face appears, pale and angry, half hidden behind the roses.

A face without features, but one she knows . . .

Maggie became aware of her father, standing just behind her. She spun around.

"It was you, Finn! You were there, when my mother died. I saw your face! The dream was real, it was a real memory! Oh, God—"

She clutched his shirt, looked up into his eyes, her grief accusing, inconsolable. "Tell me!" she cried.

Her father gazed down at her, eyes full of sorrow, regret, and terrible pain.

"Yes, Maggie. God help me, I was there, at the pool, the night when your mother died."

The terrible words hung in the air between them.

Her father stood silently, looking at her, unable to speak.

"Damn you, Finn!" Unable to face the pain, Maggie turned and ran from the pool, through the French doors, and out into the night.

* * *

The water in the shower was hot, stinging. Maggie lifted her face to the stream of water, letting it wash away the tears. But the tears wouldn't stop, mixing with the shower water to run down her face.

A sound behind her, the shower door opening. Knowing, unafraid, she turned.

Still in his shirt and jeans, Michael stepped into the shower and wrapped her in his arms. "Darlin'," he said against her hair, holding her close.

"Oh, Michael," she whispered. "It was my father . . ."

"Just breathe, Maggie. We'll take this on together."

"Hold me, Michael. Just hold me."

He wiped the tears from her eyes, pushed the heavy wet hair back from her face. "My pleasure, ma'am."

He held her for a long time, as the water poured over them in a hurling waterfall of heat and steam. Slowly, slowly, in the safety of his arms, the tears stopped.

She lifted her head and, without speaking, began to undo the buttons on his shirt. Loosened his belt. He smiled down into her eyes. His jeans fell to the tiles; he kicked them out of the shower. Very slowly, he put his hands around her back, and pulled her against him. The touch of his hands scorched her skin.

Her pulse quickened.

His hair brushing her face. Lips almost touching, just a breath of air, asking.

She slid her arms around his neck, drew his head down to hers.

He kissed her deeply. She felt the unfurling begin, murmured words into his mouth. "Love me," she whispered. "I want—I need—something good and true and beautiful."

"*You* are good and true and beautiful," he told her, pulling her closer to kiss the hollow of her neck.

He lifted her against him and she wrapped her legs around his waist. His profile was etched dark against the shadowed half-light, his silver eyes burning into hers.

The hot water cascaded over them, and she did not know where her body ended and his began. She closed her eyes and let herself fall with him.

Finally, when the storm was over, he folded her in a huge soft towel, lifted her against his chest, and carried her to the big bed.

"I've never kissed a woman like that in all my life," he whispered against her neck.

They were the last words she heard, just before the darkness took her.

CHAPTER FORTY-NINE

CARMARGUE, FRANCE
TUESDAY, OCTOBER 28

"WELL, TALK ABOUT another world!"

Simon Sugarman eased the rented Audi to a stop and gazed with astonishment through the windshield. He had left Hannah at the airport in Marseilles over an hour earlier and texted her flight plan to Beckett. Then he drove west to the northern edge of France's Carmargue region, just south of Arles—an isolated, surreal land of gypsies, marshes and ponds, wild white horses, bulls and flamingoes.

He stopped for directions to the chapel in the medieval, walled town of Aigues-Mortes—Dead Water, some name for a town. No one could—or would—help him. Then he remembered that TJ mentioned a windmill, and he stopped by the local gendarmes. A quick flash of his badge, and now here he was, driving down a twisting, rutted dirt path through a heavily wooded forest, so tangled and dense that he needed his headlamps to guide him through the shadows.

The forest opened up just as the road dead-ended at a crumbling stone wall. Sugarman eased from the car and looked across the low wall at the remains of an old windmill, its huge wheel wedged deep in a high, rushing stream. A medieval gristmill? And there, beyond the water, the centuries-old chapel ruin, set on a gentle rise in a field of lavender.

La Chapelle du Santo Rosario. The Chapel of the Holy Rosary. Bingo.

He fingered the necklace with the coin and key, tucked safely in his pocket. The unusual cross on the coin—a Carmargue cross—and the name of the chapel had led him to this peaceful, hidden glade. *Thank you, TJ.*

He took a deep breath, suddenly wishing Hannah was by his side. He pictured her smiling at him, the silken scarf glowing against her skin. First gift he'd given a woman in—well, forever. In another life, maybe . . .

But here he was, alone again, in the middle of a French forest staring at a centuries-old pile of rocks. But—admit it—the ruin was very beautiful, an old abbey of ancient stones, its roofless, vaulting arches and empty rose window frames now only a dark tracery against the bright blue sky.

Climbing over the wall, he hiked closer. Over the decades, nature had reclaimed what was hers, the 11th-century abbey now overgrown with dense foliage. The remnants of a lantern tower, its silver stones in a broken pile on the grass. Flowers spiked from niches in the walls, green vines climbed the stones and carpeted the area where the nave had once been. A cracked, lichen-covered tomb stood to one side, and there—the remains of a cloister, where an ancient, gnarled olive tree now bloomed.

His gaze searched the ruin as he moved with care among the stones. A crumbled door sat against rock. The remains of a transept. He stopped, gazing down at the toppled Carmargue cross with its three emblems of the region—the anchor, the cross, and the heart. He thought of TJ's coin. Right on the money, kid. Pun most definitely intended.

Now if only he could find—there! Beyond a centuries-old sarcophagus. Bushes and vines, crowded together. Hiding an entrance? He made his way across the rock-littered grass, pulled hard at the tangle of dried leaves. Yes. Stone steps, disappearing into the earth. The entrance to the crypt?

Be there, baby.

Sugarman pulled a flashlight from his jacket and descended into the gloom.

Fifteen steps below ground, the air musty with age and stone dust, he came to a door. A solid door, with a modern lock. Built within the last *years*, not centuries. And he knew without a doubt that someone had built a room here, beyond the door. He reached into his pocket and removed the chain TJ had given him. The gold coin caught the light from his lantern and flung bright sparks against the cold black walls, like diamonds in a mine.

The silver key was on the chain, next to the coin. He inserted the key into the lock and twisted. With a smooth, quiet click, the door opened.

The air inside was comfortable, climate controlled. Sugarman raised his flashlight and swept the interior of the room, the cone of light piercing the shadows like a sword. He judged the cubed room to be approximately twelve by twelve feet, with clean, gray-painted walls and a tiled floor. And on the floor—

Canvases.

Dozens of canvases, of every size, stacked and leaning face-in against the walls.

There had to be forty or fifty pieces.

He stepped inside, reached for the nearest canvas, and tilted it toward his light so that he could see the subject. Color! The colors struck him first, scarlet and cerulean blue, peacock and ochre, and deepest emerald, brilliant and glowing.

He bent closer. Five dancers—ballerinas—backstage. The movement. The luminosity of the pastels. The *intimacy*. Had to be—Degas?

Where had he read that the artist used to sit on the backstage stairs, trying to capture the very personal moments of the dancers. Christ. Degas.

He turned the next canvas, and the next, to the light. Okay, he was no expert, but he'd bet his mama's secret fried chicken recipe that he was looking at original works by Monet, Caravaggio, Pissarro, Goya . . .

Felix Hoffman's collection, stolen by Victor Orsini. Some pieces hidden here for over thirty years.

He'd found them.

Sugarman gazed at another painting, and then another, filled with an unfamiliar exultation. A feeling that he was experiencing a moment few men would ever know.

Finally, he blew out his breath, released his shoulders, turned to the door. Too late, he sensed the sudden dark presence, glimpsed the raised arm arcing toward him in the shadows.

A crushing pain.

Blackness.

CHAPTER FIFTY

OCEAN HOUSE
TUESDAY MORNING, OCTOBER 28

THE EARLY LIGHT was soft, pink, filtering through the high glass roof of the Ocean House conservatory. Somewhere, the slow music of water dripping in a fountain. The scent in the air was heavy, redolent with the lush tropical scents of lilies and jasmine, plumeria and gardenia.

Unable to think clearly, Maggie had fled from the bedroom, needing to run—somewhere, anywhere—away from the devastating image of the nightmare. Morning stars glimmering on the conservatory glass had drawn her across the wide lawns. Michael and the Golden had followed her, and then Michael had wrapped her shoulders in his jacket and gone to find her father. Now, more than ever, she needed answers. Needed Finn.

Clasping Michael's jacket tightly against her body, comforted by his scent, Maggie wandered down an aisle of bright, impossibly colored orchids, stopping to touch one, then another, with a gentle finger. Her eyes dropped to Shiloh, staying so close to her side, and her fingers twined in the comforting ruff of his neck. "I remember being here with my mother," she said in a soft voice, "so long ago, gathering bouquets of blooms to make fairy crowns."

"Sprite."

She turned. Her father stood very still, just down the aisle, looking at her. The new light touched his face with gold. "Your colonel said you needed me." He stepped closer, his eyes questioning.

"I know, Finn. I know what happened."

"Come here, Maggie." He took her hand, drew her to a small stone bench surrounded by clematis vines. "Talk to me. What do you think you know?"

"I need the rest of the truth, Finn. The *whole* truth, for once!" She locked her eyes on his.

His breath came out in a huge, shuddering sigh. "Maggiegirl. It was all such a damned big lie . . ."

"Such a *long* lie," she said.

"I told you your mother asked for a divorce. It was the last thing I wanted, and I refused. We had a huge argument. Lily was furious, she ran from me. Into the garden. I ran after her, grasped her arm. She pulled away from me, defiantly stripping off her clothes. She jumped into the pool, began to swim. I can still see her, her body so white and beautiful, slicing through the dark water."

His eyes found hers. "She was a good swimmer, Maggie, often swimming at night in the ocean. I thought she needed time to calm down, so I left. I went to the house, fixed myself a martini. But I knew we had to talk, knew I couldn't leave things that way between us. So I went back to apologize. I was almost there when I heard you screaming. My God! I ran through the roses, felt the thorns tear at my face. And I . . . I . . ."

"You saw me."

A heartbeat of silence. Then, "Yes. You were collapsed on the stones, soaking wet, at the edge of the pool. I didn't see your mother in the darkness of the pool, not then. Only you. I ran to you, gathered you up in my arms. I carried you into the music room, settled you on the sofa."

"I remember your arms around me, feeling safe," whispered Maggie. "And then you went back to the pool. You found my mother?"

"No, I didn't find her. Zander was there. *He'd* found her, laid her on the terrace, was giving her mouth to mouth. But . . ."

"But it was too late," said Maggie with horror. "My mother was dead."

"There's so much more to it."

"*Tell me*, then! Why did you hurt my mother, Finn? Why weren't you faithful to her? I thought you loved her!"

She saw the leap of shock in his eyes. He became very still. "You think I was unfaithful to your mother?"

She faltered. "Weren't you? All those stories over the years . . . Why else would she want a divorce?"

Finn's face was a mask. "I had many faults, but I loved your mother. I was angry, yes. But I would never have hurt her. I wasn't the unfaithful one, Maggie. *It was Lily*."

CHAPTER FIFTY-ONE

OCEAN HOUSE
TUESDAY, OCTOBER 28

MICHAEL BECKETT STOOD on the broad front lawn of Ocean House, drinking black coffee and watching Shiloh nose through the flowers while they waited for Hannah Hoffman to arrive. Sugar had texted him hours earlier. He was still in Provence, had a good lead on the missing art collection. He'd dropped Hannah at the Marseilles airport and would sleep a few hours before he headed west. Better to search in the light of day.

Beckett glanced at his watch, then his phone. No word since. Not like Sugar. Something wasn't right, especially since Sugar seemed eager to return to the US. Maggie had told him some time during the night about the blind cellist who was the heir to Gigi's Matisse. Her *stolen* Matisse. Hannah—and *Sugar*? One thing at a time, Beckett cautioned himself.

Shading his eyes, he searched the sloping lawn, tried to see any sign of life near the conservatory. All quiet. He hadn't seen Maggie since he'd left her there, earlier in the morning. He'd brought her father to her, and then gone back to the house. They'd needed time to talk alone.

But now the sun had been up for a while. And just moments ago, her fierce, crashing music had spilled through the ballroom's open doors. What had happened between them?

Worried, he flung a small stick high into the air. "Hey, Shiloh, get the stick, fella. Go for it." But Shiloh, sad-eyed and ears laid back, ignored him, moving as slowly as an old man along the bushes. His limp was more pronounced today. Beckett shook his head with concern. The dog he loved, and the woman he loved . . . how could he help them?

A sound, the crunch of tires on shells. He looked up, saw the low black sedan approaching, and whistled to Shiloh. "Here, boy. Watch out for the car. We're the welcoming committee."

Shiloh, resting in the boxwood bushes that lined the drive, struggled to stand.

The car stopped, the engine idled. The tall driver, his face concealed by the shadow of a capped hat, came around to open the door. Beckett stepped closer.

A silver cane and one lovely long leg, in a bright pink high-heeled sandal, appeared. *You're a goner, Sugar*, thought Beckett with satisfaction. Then Hannah Hoffman stood before him, thick dark curls caught back from her face and soft blue scarf knotted around her neck, looking fresh and beautiful in spite of the long flight. Beckett reached out, grasped her hand in his. "Ms. Hoffman? I'm Mike Beckett, a friend of Maggie's. Welcome back to the States."

"Ah, the colonel. Of course. Both Maggie and Simon have told me all about you."

"Ouch. Don't believe everything you hear." Beckett smiled. The driver set a tall red case in the shape of a cello on the step as a sleek, elegant greyhound leaped gracefully from the car and came to stand beside Hannah.

"This is my friend Jac," said the cellist. "I don't go anywhere without her."

As Beckett grinned at the dog, he heard a sound behind him—a sound he'd never heard before. Part gruff growl, part soft whine, part happy purr, as if . . . He turned.

Shiloh was standing tall and frozen, his liquid eyes shining and locked on the greyhound, as if he'd never seen anything quite so beautiful.

"Well, well," said Beckett. "This just got real interesting."

"It seems you have a best friend, too, Colonel?" asked Hannah with a light laugh.

"Hannah and Jac, meet my Golden, Shiloh. Shiloh saves me from murderous Girl Scouts, mailmen, marauding butterflies, and the dreaded FedEx truck." He glanced at the Golden, whose expression could only be described as thunderstruck. "Shiloh, this is Hannah and her greyhound, Jac."

The Golden remained still as a lawn statue. "Shiloh seems to be the strong silent type," murmured Hannah.

"I would say the more accurate word would be 'smitten,'" said Becket. He bent once more to the greyhound. "And I surely don't blame him. Hello, beautiful."

Hannah smiled, then turned toward the driver, who had placed her luggage in the driveway and was now preparing to leave. "Thank you, Thanos," she said. "You've been very kind."

Beckett watched as the driver, his face turned away, tipped his hat and roared off down the driveway. His instincts twanged. *What was there about that guy?* He leaned toward Hannah. "I'll just let Sugar know you're here." He typed a quick text. *Hannah here. Did you arrange for a guy named Thanos to meet her plane?*

Hannah's fingers, gentle on his arm. "Will you take me to Maggie? I've been worried about her."

Beckett raised his head, listening for the faint, pulsing music. He put his hand over Hannah's. "She's sparring with Rachmaninoff right now. But will you come with me? Your host, Alexander Karas, has gone to DC for the night. I can take you to your room, and then perhaps you'll join me for a cup of coffee. I think you and I have a lot to share with each other."

"I know we do. And coffee would be perfect."

Beckett's cell pinged. *Message not delivered.*

Christ. What was going on with Sugar? He bent to Hannah, settled her hand in the crook of his arm and turned to whistle to Shiloh. "Well, will you look at that," he said softly.

Shiloh was edging slowly, shyly, closer to Jac. Impatient, she closed the gap in one long stride, until they were nose to nose. "Looks like our best friends are getting to know each other, Hannah," said Beckett. "Is that a problem for you? I know Jac is a service dog."

"I don't think it will be, Colonel. I trust her. And we need all the friends we can get, don't we?" She fluttered her fingers and immediately Jac was at her side.

For a brief moment, Shiloh looked as confused as a lone pine tree in a parking lot. Then he simply moved to Jac's free side and followed them into the house.

* * *

Still reeling from the pain of her father's words, Maggie's fingers tore across the keys, filling the Ocean House ballroom with the furious, rapid runs of Khachaturian's Toccata. She could not face Rachmaninoff today, not with so many terrible questions swirling in her head. For so long, she had blamed her father for her mother's death. Now, it seemed as if her whole life was a lie.

It made no sense. *She* made no sense.

With an oath, Maggie's fingers froze on the keys, and she swiped at the tears running down her face. She needed to express her pain, her confusion, her fear. She needed Beethoven. She closed her eyes. The blistering, searing opening notes of his *Piano Concerto No. 5*—the *Emperor Concerto*—spilled like her tears into the air.

Chords upon chords, her fingers flying feverishly over the keys. Profound, powerful, and passionate, she gave herself up to the complex and mammoth notes. Was consumed by them.

Faster and faster, gasping for breath.

And then someone was on the bench next to her, two arms around her, slender but powerful. Holding her tightly.

"Hush, my friend. You're going to be okay, Maggie."

Hannah's voice.

Maggie's slick fingers came to rest on the keys, her breathing slowed, and she opened her eyes, surprised by the tears coursing down her cheeks.

"Oh, Hannah," she whispered. "I really need a friend right now."

"We've shared so much in such a short time that I feel very close to you. Will I do?"

"I feel the closeness, too." Maggie gripped Hannah's fingers but kept her eyes on the piano keys. "I'm so scared."

"I know, Maggie. So am I."

"I want to be strong enough to run *toward*, into the heart of the fear, the way Michael does. But I'm hiding behind the music, behind the chords. I'm still running away . . ."

"Nonsense! You found your father. And now you're *here*, aren't you, ready to face your past. You are 'running toward' something, Maggie. You just haven't gotten there yet."

"I'm glad you're here."

"I don't need to see your face to know you need a friend. I wouldn't be anywhere else."

Maggie took a shuddering breath. "What if I was too scared to help my mother when she died? What if I've been wrong about my father? And, God help me, what if I've been *right*?"

Gentle fingers grasped Maggie's hands. "Your colonel told me some of it. And something *isn't* right, Maggie. It feels very wrong, in fact. We'll find the answers together. Is it too early for a glass of wine?"

* * *

The sound of water.

Simon Sugarman groaned, opened his eyes, tried to focus. Coughed.

It was dark, wet. Too *wet*. He coughed again, gagged, spit dirty water from his mouth. He was lying in water, several inches deep. Damned cold water. And rising.

What the hell? He heard the drip-drip-drip close by, the low creak of ancient, grinding machinery.

The windmill. He was in the windmill.

He tried to move his arm. Okay, then. *You bastards made a big mistake, not taking me out.* He took a breath, sucked in another mouthful of thick, muddy-tasting water. Shit. Time to blow this joint.

He shifted, found a pocket. No phone. Very slowly he sat up. No broken bones. Helluva headache, though. He reached up to his face. Was he feeling blood or water?

Dizzy, he pulled at his shirt cuff, squinted down at his wrist. *Bingo!* They'd missed his watch. His brand-new Apple Watch. His stainless-steel, Milanese-loop, GPS-set, *water-resistant* watch. Worth every bit of the six hundred bucks he'd shelled out. "Gotta love the toys," he murmured.

He pressed the switch; light glowed. Oh, yeah. The local gendarmes could be here in minutes, if his car was gone. But first, he had to get back to the art. He shook his head, fiercely angry with himself. Then groaned as the pain stabbed. "You goddamn fool," he whispered. Even a green agent knew not to lose sight of his surroundings. How could he have made such a rookie mistake? Flunking Agent 101—all because of the most beautiful art he'd ever seen.

I underestimated you, Dane. It won't happen again.

Sugarman lurched to his feet. Held up his wrist to light the darkness, find the door. Probably barricaded. Better get a move on. Cold river water swirled around his shins. Bastards had ruined his favorite pair of Valentinos.

He closed his eyes against the pain, tried to breathe through it. Thought of Hannah. Thank God she was on a plane, warm and dry, and not here with him. Jesus.

He found the old wooden door. Pushed. Daylight?

What the hell? Why hadn't they locked him in?

He staggered out onto the grass, headed back toward the ruin. Toward the art.

Art that, he knew deep in his gut, was once again gone.

CHAPTER FIFTY-TWO

VIENNA
TUESDAY, OCTOBER 28

IN THE SMALL hotel room in Vienna, Dane stood in front of the painting of the young girl named Gisela. The brushstrokes were strong, beautiful, the colors mesmerizing. The old man had been quite the artist. Too bad, really, that Johann Vogl had to die.

He reached out to touch the thick, swirling strokes of paint. Underneath the young woman's portrait, he was sure, was a long-missing Picasso. Worth millions. One more step in his quest to take over the black market in art. To having more wealth and power than he'd ever dreamed.

He glanced out the window, down into the square. Where was Beatrice? She'd gone to the corner market over an hour ago. Perhaps he should—

His cell phone buzzed. Checking the text from his man in Provence, he felt a fierce bolt of anger.

Team at ruin. Crypt empty. How do we proceed?

Empty? Impossible. Fucking impossible. Quickly he typed, *The art should be there. Search again. Find it!*

He waited, began to pace. What had happened? A ping.

No art found at ruin.

He was typing a furious reply when he heard her key in the lock.

Beatrice set a paper bag down on the table and moved toward him. "I bought your favorite tortes and then I—What is it? What's happened?"

"The art. The paintings are gone."

"What do you mean, gone?"

"When my men got to the ruin, the hidden room was empty."

"What about Agent Sugarman?"

"No sign of him. I suspect he's heading back to the States." He turned away from her, grasped his coffee cup, and hurled it across the room to shatter against the wall. "Either Sugarman has the art, or someone else got there first."

She bent, began to gather the shards of pottery. "Then we will follow Sugarman, and we will get the answers."

He took her arm, raised her gently to her feet. "Leave it, don't cut yourself. Pack your clothes. I've made arrangements. I have a plane ticket for you. I want you to go back to Italy, be with your cousins. Have the baby there. Be safe." *From me.*

"And you?"

"I am going to the US. To finish what was begun a very long time ago."

She dropped the shards to the table and put her arms around him. "We are going together, *Cuore Mio*."

"No. It's too dangerous." An image of her father flashed into his head, and he turned back to her. "I am not a good man, Bella. I've done very bad things. I've justified all of it because of my past, but you know that I—"

"You've reacted to pain. I don't blame you for it."

"You *should*! I tried to hurt you in Tuscany, Beatrice. I almost—" He held a hand to his eyes.

"You were cornered, you were afraid."

"No. I've made conscious choices, all along. I don't want my choices to affect you, Bella. Or the baby."

"We won't let that happen, Dante."

He ran a hand over his scarred face. "Now I am that man again, the same on the outside as I am on the inside. Broken, as ruined as my face. I cannot be fixed, *mon ange*. Not even by you."

"I don't believe you. I know you've done many bad things in your life—I awaken to your nightmares. But I believe our baby can transform you. We will stay together. We will find the art. And we will make a new life somewhere safe."

* * *

Maggie, Hannah, and Michael Beckett sat in deep burgundy velvet chairs before the fire in the Ocean House library, drinking a very old Bordeaux from Zander's collection. Both dogs were curled on the carpet in front of the flames, flanks touching, eyes half closed. Zander had been right about the room. Tall, diamond-paned windows flickered with firelight. Yale's blue and white banner—*Lux et Veritas*, Light and Truth—hung over a U-shaped desk. Floor-to-ceiling bookcases were filled with rare leather-bound volumes to create a truly beautiful space.

"At least two of us are contented," said Beckett, his eyes on the dogs. He set his wineglass down with impatience, stood up, and began to pace. "No word on the identity of Hannah's driver yet, but Sugar sent me a message that Thanos wasn't his guy. So, just in case Dane knows where we are now, I've ordered extra security here for the next several days. Until after the party." He turned to Maggie. "You haven't remembered anything more about the night your mother died?"

"No, and I wonder if I ever will. Dreams are confusing, never totally real. The last thing I *do* remember is a sharp, crushing pain.

Finn told me that I hit my head, hard, when I collapsed. The doctors said I had a serious concussion. When I finally woke up, my memory of that night was totally gone."

"Except for those dreams," said Hannah, taking a sip of wine. "But sometimes not remembering can be a blessing."

"I thought so, too, for a very long time," said Maggie. "But I'm ready now. If only I didn't have more and more questions."

"I think I can answer some of them," said Finn Stewart from the doorway.

All three heads turned as Maggie's father walked into the room. He nodded to Michael and his daughter but went directly to Hannah, bending to take her hand. Jac was by her side in an instant, a low warning sound in her throat. "It's okay, Jac," said Hannah quietly.

"I'm Maggie's father, Finn Stewart," he said. "And you, I'm told, are the heir to Gigi's Matisse. My wife, Lily, loved that painting. I've been following your career, Hannah. A rising star in the cello world. You'll be playing the Bach *Cello Suites* tomorrow night, for the Yale party? I wish I could have had a chance to conduct you."

"It's not too late to find your way back to the podium," said Hannah. "But the important thing now is that you're here for Maggie. Finally. That's a good beginning."

"Not good enough," said Michael, his voice stony and unforgiving. "We have questions. Too many things don't add up. So, pour a drink and take a seat, Finn."

Lifting a bottle of sparkling water from a glass tray, Finn settled into the chair next to Maggie. He started to reach for her hand, then thought better of it and gripped the rolled leather arm instead. He locked eyes with Michael. "I was drinking so much in those days, I couldn't say for sure what I saw. All I knew was that I had to protect my daughter from any more pain. I couldn't let her take the blame for something I caused. And I knew her grandmother would take good care of her."

"So you ran," said Michael.

* * *

"I was conducting Beethoven's *Eroica*," said Finn Stewart into the silence. "The irony, I see now, playing a piece that reaches so far into the past." He shook his head.

"We were sold out, they had filled the chorister seats—" he turned to Michael— "those seats for overflow guests, behind the orchestra, facing the audience—and I knew Maggie was up there somewhere, watching me. I was approaching the end of the first movement. God, I was on fire. The music was roaring with dissonance, the heroic struggle, those climactic *sforzando* chords! That damned third horn actually came in on the beat. And then . . ."

Now Finn was standing, gesturing wildly with his arms, overcome with memory. In the flickering firelight, Maggie thought he looked unworldly—like a God conducting a storm on Mt. Olympus.

"It was so beautiful," she whispered. "But then you looked up into the seats, you looked right at me. You just stopped conducting. And you ran off the stage." Maggie leaned toward him, her voice fierce, vibrating with remembered pain. "Why didn't you take me with you? You just disappeared into the night. You walked off the stage and left me behind. What did I do to make you leave me? Why did you *stop loving me*?"

Finn opened his eyes, found hers. "Christ, *is that what you thought*, all these years? No wonder you . . ." He shook his head with sorrow. "No, sprite," he said gently. "I wasn't looking at you. I was looking at the man sitting directly behind you. Someone I met a long time ago, at Yale. Victor Orsini."

CHAPTER FIFTY-THREE

NEW YORK CITY
TUESDAY NIGHT, OCTOBER 28

His Eminence Robert Cardinal Brennan opened the door. "Zander! What are you doing here at this hour? I thought you were in East Hampton with Maggie. I'm planning on joining you all there tomorrow for your gala."

Zander brushed by him, entered the Cardinal's New York office on Madison Avenue. "They all think I'm in DC for the night. But . . ."

Robbie gestured toward an easy chair. "But here you are. Have a seat, Zander. I'll get us a drink." He moved to a table, poured two stiff single malt whiskeys, and handed one to his guest. "I'm thinking you aren't here to discuss the Red Sox. Or Thomas Aquinas, for that matter."

Zander drank the whole two fingers of whiskey in one long swallow and held out his glass for a refill. "How far can a man ride his ambition? I'm finally so close to getting everything I ever wanted. The highest court in the land . . ."

"If you want to test a man's character, you give him power."

Zander stared at him and nodded slowly. "Now my sins are catching up with me, Robbie, and I don't know what to do."

"Sins against God, Zander? Or sins against man? Because God will forgive you, but I'm afraid men won't." He poured more whiskey into Zander's glass, sat across from him, and waited.

"Tomorrow I'm going to withdraw my name from the President's consideration for Supreme Court Justice."

"It's that bad?"

Zander took a deep breath. "Finn Stewart has come home. Maggie's missing father. He's in the Hamptons with her."

"I suspected the reports of his death were exaggerated. But why is this a problem for you? He was your good friend. And I would think you would be happy for your goddaughter. How is Finn connected to your court appointment?"

"I thought I'd put it all behind me," murmured Zander, staring down into his glass.

"But the devil is hard to cast out."

"*Impossible.* He's why I'm here. It's all going to come out now. Finn will know everything."

"A good man apologizes for the mistakes of the past, but a great man corrects them. Maybe it's time to right a wrong, Zander. What happened?"

Zander swirled his whiskey, shook his head. "I fell for Maggie's mother, Lily, years ago. She would come to Ocean House when Finn was gone, so beautiful and talented and lonely, and I was—well, I was lonely, too. She was married to my best friend, but . . ."

"The eternal struggle between two principles—right and wrong." Robbie gazed at him over the rim of his glass.

"I never expected to fall in love with her." Zander stopped at the window, pulled back the heavy drapes to gaze out at the winking lights of Madison Avenue. "One night, when Lily was at Ocean House, I found her crying by the music room pool. She told me she was divorcing Finn. I thought we could finally be together, but she refused to be with me. She still loved him, she said. She didn't love me.

"I was blinded by fury. I just wanted her to be with me. I was gripping her arm, shouting at her. She fought back, tried to wrench away from me. She screamed that she would never love me. I grabbed her, swung her around. And, God help me, I hit her. So hard . . ." He dropped his head in his hands.

"She was stunned, lost her balance, fell into the pool." He turned to Robbie. "I didn't know what to do, I just turned and ran."

"Good God!"

"I'm not proud of it. I panicked. But almost immediately I realized what I'd done and ran back to the pool."

"Ah. And you saw Maggie there."

"Yes. She was screaming, soaking wet. I think she'd jumped in to try to rescue her mother. And then *she looked up and saw me*."

He shook his head back and forth.

"She was hysterical. I moved toward her, but she fainted, just dropped to the stones. Must have hit her head when she fell. It all happened so fast. Finn showed up, came running. I shouted for him to take care of his daughter, and I jumped in to save Lily."

"But she was gone."

"Yes." Zander dropped his head into his hands. "My beautiful Lily was gone."

CHAPTER FIFTY-FOUR

THE HAMPTONS
WEDNESDAY, OCTOBER 29

THE BOAT, MOORED on a floating dock in the Three Mile Harbor Marina just north of East Hampton, was sleek and compact. Dane slipped the false passport back into his jacket pocket. The rental, in the name of Richard York, had gone well. No one questioned his name, borrowed from Shakespeare's Richard III of York. No one looked beyond the mirrored sunglasses, the cap pulled low over his forehead. No one questioned leather gloves on a cool autumn day. Just a quick swipe of a credit card. Welcome, Mr. and Mrs. York. Enjoy your two nights on the *Dream Weaver*.

Now Dane gazed out the porthole at the boats in the colorful, crowded marina.

For the first time in months, he felt at home. The strong scent of fish at low tide, the rhythmic lap of water against hulls, the bright blue afternoon sky, the clink of rope and metal against tall masts—all reminded him of the tiny harbor in Greece where he had gone to ground after Victor Orsini's death.

He would go back there as soon as he took his rightful place in the stolen art world. He would bring Beatrice and the baby with him.

His thoughts moved to Beatrice, jet-lagged and suffering from morning sickness, asleep in the wan sunlight on the deck above him. He hoped the boat's slight rocking would soothe her, not make her sicker.

His eyes slid over the narrow galley counter. All was in readiness. The nylon rope, the duct tape, the set of filled syringe needles, all ready to go. And his favorite knife, his *Laguiole*, sharpened and waiting for him. So much more intimate than a pistol.

He slipped the items into a strapped leather bag, then pulled the curtains across the portholes to darken the cabin. So. Everything was now ready for his special guest. He glanced at his watch. Another hour, and he would leave for Ocean House.

Finally, the last act was about to begin. Magdalena O'Shea would lead him to Victor's art. One way or another.

But first, he would wake Beatrice, settle her in their motel room down the road, suggest a well-deserved hot bath. Breathing deeply of the cold salty air, he reached for the still-unopened bottle of Absolut on the counter. Hesitated. Reached instead for the kettle.

Beatrice had told him that hot tea with sugar settled her stomach.

* * *

The ballroom glittered with candlelight and the notes of Schubert spun through the air.

Maggie stood at the doorway, gazing at the scene before her. The rows of gilt chairs, now filled with tuxedoed and bejeweled Yale alumni and guests, were set in a half circle facing the stage. A long table against one wall held platters of hors d'oeuvres and tall crystal glasses of Dom Perignon. On the low stage at the end of the room, beneath the tall windows, a popular string quartet from Yale was coming to the end of its performance.

Another chair was set to the side of the stage, with Hannah's cello on its stand beside it, ready for her solo. She was still upstairs, Maggie assumed, mentally preparing to play several of Maggie's favorite pieces—three of the profoundly moving Bach *Cello Suites*.

Beyond the French doors, the night was black and silver, the air a translucent wash of gray. *Fog*. The fog was rolling in, falling like a silver veil over the lawns and dunes and turning the world to silent, shimmering metal. Maggie shivered in spite of the warmth in the ballroom.

Strong hands slid around her waist, pulled her close. The scent of the mountains touched her cheek, and she leaned back against Michael's chest. "I've been waiting for you," she said softly. "Where have you been?"

He turned her around to face him, touched her face with the warm palm of his hand. "Texting with Sugar. He should be here any minute. And he is *not* a happy camper." He gave her his lopsided grin as his eyes moved over her shoulders, bared by an off-the-shoulder dress the color of plums. "You look astonishingly beautiful. Are you sure we can't skip this popsicle stand and head straight upstairs?"

God, she loved his hands. "We are staying for Hannah," she reminded him with a smile.

He drew her behind a wall of tall potted greenery. "As soon as she's finished, then, we have a date." He wagged his spiky eyebrows at her in the best tradition of an old vaudeville villain and pressed his lips to her shoulder. Holding her close, he whispered, "Dance with me. I want my arms around you."

His eyes were on her, burning with light. A thrilling shiver passed through her. "There's no music."

"Sure there is." He began to hum against her ear, then spun her around and caught her close, trapping her body against his, swaying slowly. Heat ignited, powerful and intense as a struck match.

"Later," she managed, locking her eyes on his. "Right now I have to mingle with Zander's guests."

"Not quite yet." He stopped a passing waiter, swiped two glittering flutes of champagne from the silver tray. Handing her a goblet, he raised his own to her as he leaned closer. "To intelligence and passion."

"To later tonight," she whispered.

Across the room, waiters began to close the French doors against the creeping fingers of fog. Suddenly anxious, she asked, "Where is Shiloh?"

"Hard to tear him away from Jac."

She nodded, unsurprised. "It's good to see him happy again. Simon has that same look in his eyes when he's near Hannah. I hope he gets here in time to hear her play." She saw the expression on his face. "What? What's happened to Simon?"

"He found Hannah's grandfather's art in a French chapel ruin, had a run-in with a gristmill, ended up with a bad headache and an empty crypt."

"Oh no," she whispered. "Poor Simon. Poor *Hannah*. I hope she doesn't—" The lights began to blink and Maggie gazed around the crowded ballroom. "It's time for Hannah's performance. I don't see her . . ."

The guests took their seats, the lights dimmed, Zander walked out onto the stage and stood in a cone of light. "Wayne Newton said, 'When I die, I'd like to come back as a cello.'" Rewarded with laughter, he smiled. "To me, there is no other sound like it. And no other cellist like our next guest. Hannah Hoffman will inspire you. She transcends technique, somehow finding the truths that give profound meaning to our world. Hannah's music embodies our Yale motto, *Lux et Veritas*. Light and Truth."

Zander looked to his right, toward an empty doorway. His shoulders lifted in a slight question as he continued. "Tonight, Hannah will play the first three Bach Suites for unaccompanied cello. For me, they are remarkable because they achieve the effect of three to four voices, even though there is only one." Zander held out his hand. "So, please give your warmest Yale welcome to our very special guest cellist, Hannah Hoffman."

A rustle of expectation in the audience as heads turned toward the doorway.

No one entered.

"Where is she?" whispered Maggie.

"Ms. Hoffman," Zander said again, his voice now slightly raised.

The cone of light by the entrance remained empty.

Maggie gripped Beckett's arm, hard. "Something's wrong," she whispered.

At that moment, the high, mournful howl of a dog filled the night air beyond the fog-filled windows.

"That's Shiloh," said Beckett, fear ripping his voice. Heedless of his bad leg, he ran through the French doors into the misted night. Maggie kicked off her heels and ran after him.

"Shiloh!" shouted Beckett, standing on the edge of the terrace. "Where are you, fella? I'm coming!"

Again, the terrible, agonized howl, beyond the dark woods, near the stables. Maggie grasped his arm. "I'm a runner, Michael. Get help and follow me. I'll find Shiloh." Before he could stop her, she hiked up her cocktail dress and took off across the lawn, her legs a white blur in the thick gray night.

Faster. Toward the stables. Unable to see through the curtain of mist, she followed Shiloh's anguished howls. For a moment, silence. Then sharp, frenzied barking filled the night. *Closer*. "Be okay, please be okay," she whispered.

Fifty yards. Twenty.

There!

A large, quivering shape in the blackness, shaggy head lifted in raw pain.

She ran faster.

Another shape, darker than the shadows, crumpled and still on the grass. *No, no. Please God, no,* she prayed.

She ran up to Shiloh, fell to her knees, and threw her arms around him. “I’m here, boy, I’m here. What’s happened to you?”

He struggled against her, sank to the earth. She looked down. His great golden head was resting on Jac’s inert body.

CHAPTER FIFTY-FIVE

OCEAN HOUSE
WEDNESDAY, OCTOBER 29

"OH, JAC . . ." Maggie bent to the greyhound, listened for breath. Tried to feel a heartbeat in the still, smooth curve of Jac's chest. In the distance, shouting. Flashlights, blurred and haloed by mist, coming toward her over the hill.

"Breathe, Jac, breathe," she whispered. Frantic, she ran her hands over the greyhound's motionless body, feeling for an injury, blood. There! The smallest rise of the chest. A shaky breath, another. A heartbeat. Weak, but undeniable. The faintest movement. Shiloh lifted his head, his eyes shining at her in the darkness, bewildered and frantic with pain.

"She's alive," whispered Maggie against the Golden's fur. "We'll get her help, we'll—" She stopped speaking, struck by the sudden and terrible realization that Jac should have been—would have been—with Hannah. She spun around, searching the darkness.

Where was Hannah?

* * *

"Over here! Maggie, is he all right?" Beckett's flashlight flew across the grass, scattering the silver shadows, and locked on Maggie.

"Shiloh is okay, Michael," she called out. "He's with me. Jac is here, too. Hurry. She needs a vet. I don't know what's wrong."

Beckett lunged across the last yard of grass toward the Golden and gathered him in his arms. Zander, Robbie, Finn, and several other guests ran up behind him, surrounding them. Zander was shouting orders into his phone. Robbie dropped to his knees, spread his jacket over the greyhound.

Maggie pulled Beckett's head toward her and said against his ear, "Hannah is missing. It has to be Dane. We have to find her."

A high, frightened whinny. A shout, from close by. *Inside the stables.*

Beckett stiffened, raised his head. "Search the stables!" he shouted. "Hannah Hoffman could be in there."

The men scattered, disappearing into the curtain of fog.

Maggie heard the nervous stamp of the horse's hooves, the high whinny from a distant stall. She bent to Robbie. "Can you stay with Jac until the vet comes?"

"Of course, I will. Just be careful."

"And you." Her eyes searched the low roof of the stables, indistinct in the black, wavering shadows. Two trucks were parked to one side, where a wall of high grasses created a thick, shifting gray curtain. So many places to hide.

Her father appeared from behind one of the trucks. "Anything?" she asked. He shook his head. She was walking toward him when a sudden movement caught her attention.

Shiloh lurched to his three legs, unsteady, his ears raised, listening. His nose fluttered with scent, pointed. For a brief moment, his eyes dropped to the silent greyhound and he hesitated, as if he couldn't bear to leave her. Then he barked twice, turned and, with his graceless, rocking gait, loped into the darkness.

"Get Michael!" cried Maggie to her father. Then she followed the Golden into the fog-laced dark.

* * *

The mist-bound night was ghostly, the roar of waves muffled by the smothering blanket of fog. The moon a shimmering penumbra against scudding black clouds. She heard the sound of the water before she saw it. The whispering susurration of the waves, rolling onto the rocky beach.

Maggie froze, raised her head to listen. Distant shouting beyond the hill. But here—only the sound of the ocean. And then she heard it, Shiloh's low growl. Somewhere ahead, in the shadowed mist. She moved cautiously forward, her bare feet quiet on the windswept dunes.

A black shape loomed, like a large hunched animal. The boat house. She moved toward it. "Shiloh?"

A fierce snarl. Shiloh took shape in the dark, standing motionless, the hair standing up on his back, his eyes locked on the old wooden door. It was ajar. Inside, through the slats of broken boards, impenetrable blackness.

She held her body still, staring at the door, trying not to think of a wolf watching, waiting for her in the fog. Where was Michael? Heart hammering against her ribs, she took a deep, painful breath. *Be strong*, she told herself. *Be strong for Hannah. And for Shiloh.*

"Dane," she called. "I know you're here. I've come for Hannah."

Silence. Fog the color of ash swirled like smoke around her. Then a movement, beyond the door.

Dane stepped from the mist. A silver pistol was aimed at her chest. Slipping off his amber aviator glasses, he met her eyes and smiled at her.

She tried not to flinch when she saw his distorted face, but no surgery could change those terrifying eyes. She knew he'd seen the flare of her shock. She felt the Golden tense to lunge, heard the low growl in his throat. Gripping his collar with all her strength, she said, "*No*, Shiloh. *Stay*."

Stepping in front of the dog, holding him firmly behind her, she faced Dane. "Where is Hannah Hoffman?"

Dane glanced over his shoulder, toward the churning ocean. "Are you still afraid of the water, my Juliet?" It was the name he had called her in France. His voice was as silky and terrifying as she remembered.

"The wild waters roar and heave," said Dane, waving the pistol toward her heart. "The brave vessel is dashed all to pieces. And all the helpless souls within her drowned."

"What do you want from me?" she whispered.

"I want the Matisse. The *Dark Rhapsody*."

She stared at him. The sound of running steps, coming closer in the pulsing haze. "Here!" she cried. "We're here!"

A shout in return, lost on the wind.

"Take care of your hands, my Juliet." His eyes slid toward the black ocean. "The tide is coming in."

Then he smiled at her once more and vanished into the cloak of fog.

Maggie willed herself not to follow. "Stay, Shiloh," she said again, holding him against her body.

What had he meant about the tide?

Something was wrong. She turned to face the beach, straining to see through the fog. The haze of moon edged behind a cloud and darkness spread like a mantle over the sand. Now she could hear the fearsome crash of the waves, see the faint line of phosphorescence where they foamed against the sand. And something else . . . Maggie felt the panic ice through her. She took a step into the dunes, searching the roaring shadows. *There.*

A small rowboat, on the very edge of the water. Slowly, inexorably being pulled by the tide out into the waves.

Breaking through the fog, the flutter of a blue silken scarf. *Hannah's scarf!*

Pure terror washed over her.

Not Hannah. Dane couldn't be that cruel.

"Shiloh! Get Michael!" She began to run.

Across the dunes, across the sand, through the spinning tendrils of mist. Toward the dinghy. Toward Hannah. Toward the water.

Not the water. Not again.

Without slowing down, she launched herself into the wall of black water racing toward her.

And dove into the watery heart of her fear.

The ocean was freezing, numbing. The high waves broke over her, knocking her to the bottom. Sucking at her. Her dress clung to her, heavy, pulling her down. Sand and salt water filled her mouth.

She struggled to the surface. "Hannah!" she cried.

God, God. My mother drowned, my husband drowned. You. Will. Not. Drown.

So dark, water in her eyes, stinging. The ocean frigid, heaving beneath her, thrusting her down. Where was the boat? *There.*

The dinghy was some ten feet ahead of her, just where the waves gathered strength, crested, ready to break.

Some deep part of her was aware that the last time she'd been in the sea, she'd been trying to get to shore. But tonight, she was swimming away from safety. *Into the depths of the ocean.*

She took a deep stinging breath and dove beneath the dark, roiling surface, swimming, fighting against the incoming waves toward the old dinghy. Wave upon fearsome wave plunging, pushing her back, pulling her down.

She opened her eyes. A halo of glimmering spray, caught in sudden moonlight.

Blinded, she swam, fought, reached, missed. Flung herself forward, felt the old wood beneath her fingers. Slipped away. *Reach, damn you! Yes.* Held on.

Wave after roaring wave broke over her. The dinghy was flung up, then crashed down. She held on for dear life, gasping, trying to pull herself up and over the edge of the small spinning boat.

Tired, she was so tired. Try one more time. Just once more. So cold . . .

A huge wave caught the dinghy, spun it toward the beach. She was losing her grasp, her hands cramping, freezing. *My hands*, she thought. And then, just hold on!

I can't . . .

She felt her fingers slipping off the boat. Bone-deep fear gripped her.

"I've got you, sprite."

Words against her ear, familiar. Strong arms. Safety. Was she dreaming?

"It's okay, Maggiegirl. I'm here." Cold hands gripping hers, helping her to hold on. Not Michael's hands.

"Where's . . . Michael?" She could only manage the two words.

"Couldn't find him in all the chaos. You're stuck with me, kiddo."

"Do it. Myself . . ."

"Sure you can. I'm just here to help. Almost there . . . *Hold on!*"

Another wave, a fierce crash of spray, flinging them high, higher, then down, churning, cascading forward, fast, faster.

The dinghy slammed onto the beach with a stunning crunch and broke apart.

Hannah!

Maggie and her father spilled to the sand. Seawater washed against their feet.

Somewhere close, the Golden barked.

Shuddering uncontrollably, Maggie staggered to her feet and stumbled toward the smashed boat.

Empty. Just a blue silk scarf—Hannah's scarf—soaked and torn, tied to the gunwale.

"Bastard. We'll find her, Maggie."

Maggie looked at her father. "Thank you."

Finn Stewart coughed and spit out water. "Didn't know I could run so fast," he chuckled. "Hell, didn't know I could still swim."

"Took you long enough." Her body would not stop shuddering, but somehow, she managed the smile.

"There's the Maggie I remember. Now let's get you someplace warm and dry."

"What the hell were you thinking, Finn?"

"That I've finally found you again and I'm damn well not going to lose you this time."

Frigid water swirled around their ankles. Together they stared down into the battered dinghy, now broken and wedged deep into the wet sand. "You braved the ocean to find her, Maggie," said Finn.

The moon edged from behind a cloud. Her father's face caught the misted light, pale with shock, the way he had looked in her dream that night by the pool, staring at her from among the roses. The night her mother drowned.

Something's not right.

She blinked, looked down, became aware of her soaked clothing, and was transported back to the night her mother died. Memory crashed in like the black ocean waves against the sand.

"I remember," she said, turning to her father. "I remember all of it."

CHAPTER FIFTY-SIX

OCEAN HOUSE
WEDNESDAY, OCTOBER 29

"It wasn't your face I saw that night," said Maggie to her father. "It was Zander's face. *He* was the faceless man at the pool. The man in my dreams."

"Yes," said Finn. "It was Zander. He was there. Zander was your mother's lover."

Maggie's chair was drawn close to the fire in the Ocean House library, her eyes riveted on the flames. Michael sat beside her, his strong hand on her knee and his eyes on her father. Shiloh was curled at her feet, and she rubbed her bare foot against the warmth of his fur. With an uncontrollable shudder, Maggie gathered the thick white robe closer and cupped her hands around a steaming mug of tea laced with brandy.

She turned to her father. "Why didn't you tell me? Why did you let me think it was you?"

"I was in shock. Your mother was dead. I didn't know what had happened. I'd gotten there too late. I heard you screaming and then found you collapsed on the stones. Zander blamed *you*, Maggie."

"Me?" She felt as if she'd been struck.

"He said you and your mother were fighting, and you pushed her. He said it was an accident—but how could I let you live with that?"

Her father stood and began to pace, his face all sharp planes in the firelight. "Zander and I, we knew we had to protect you. He took your mother to his boat . . . brought her to the ocean off Manhattan

Beach. I stayed with you. Everything I did that night, Maggie, every decision I made, was to protect you."

Maggie stood, went to her father, gazed up into his eyes.

"But *I didn't hurt my mother*. I jumped into the pool that night. I jumped in to *save* my mother. I'd heard the shouting, ran to help her. I saw Zander hit her, I saw my mother fall into the water." She flinched as if struck by a fist.

Finn cupped her face in his hands. "Zander lied to me. He was protecting himself. I know that now, Maggiegirl."

"That's why my clothes were soaked," said Maggie. She swiped at the tears filling her eyes. "But I couldn't find her. The pool lights were out. The water was too dark, too opaque. Too *blue*. I remember climbing out, shouting for help. And then I felt a terrible pain in my head." She looked at her father. "Somehow you were carrying me, running . . . It's the last thing I remember before I woke up in the hospital."

"All I could think about was getting help for you," said Finn. He took her cold hands in his and held them against his heart. "It's going to be okay, Maggie. We're going to be okay."

The grandfather clock began to chime, eleven p.m. Maggie raised her eyes to Michael. "It's late. We should have heard something by now. You're sure Jac is going to be okay?"

Michael dropped another log onto the fire, watched the red sparks spiral upward in the shadows before answering. "You ran straight *into* the Atlantic Ocean, at night, and you're worried about a dog." He shook his head. "Yes, Jac will be fine. One more crime Dane will pay for. Right, Shiloh?"

The Golden gave a low, fierce growl, his eyes shining like black stones in the firelight.

Michael touched Maggie's shoulder. "We've got to go. I told Sugar I'd help with the search for Hannah as soon as I was sure you were okay."

"Hannah can't *see*! She must be so frightened, so alone."

"We'll find her, Maggie, count on it."

Maggie pushed the robe aside. "I'm coming. I've got to *do* something!"

"You almost drowned just an hour ago, Maggie. In freezing water. Your lips are still blue, dammit. *Stay put*. Hannah can't be far. She's Dane's bargaining chip. He can't risk hurting her." Beckett paused and looked at his phone. "Sugar just texted. There's a good lead. A couple rented a boat in Three Mile Harbor Boat Yard. Just north of here. There's a fingerprint . . . Let's go, big fella."

Shiloh lurched to his feet, impatient, sensing action.

Maggie hugged Michael tightly. "Find Hannah for me," she whispered. "And don't get shot!"

Michael glanced at Finn. "She always says that." A hesitation. Then, "You believed that staying in Maggie's life put her in real danger. I get that. You did what you did to keep her safe. And you were there for her tonight." And then he and the Golden were gone.

Finn turned to Maggie. "He's right, you know. I would have given anything to stay, to be part of my girl's life."

"I loved you so madly," she whispered.

"I won't blow a second chance, sprite." Finn leaned forward, his face a mask of concern in the flickering firelight. "But right now it's all about Hannah. Dane told you he wants the Matisse, Maggie. The *Dark Rhapsody*. How the *hell* are we going to get Hannah back if we don't find that damned painting? It could be anywhere." He shook his head back and forth. "If only Lily were here. She loved that painting, she'd stare at it for hours. She knew its secrets. I can still see her, curled on the sofa in her music room, playing those old classical records of hers as she gazed at that painting."

"That's it!" Maggie set her teacup down with a sharp crack. "I know where my mother hid the answers. You told me yourself, when we talked in Vienna, what my mom would always do. I just need to get my coat. Then we're going to her music room."

* * *

"Mom knew something, Finn. About *Dark Rhapsody*. We just have to find it."

Maggie sat on the soft red-patterned carpet in her mother's music room, in front of the tall, overflowing bookcase. Piled in front of her were dozens of dusty, old vinyl record albums—78 rpms—albums that had been stored in the room since before her mother's death. She reached for the top one, withdrew the record, and peered inside the twelve-inch square cardboard sleeve.

"Nothing but the record," she murmured, setting it aside and reaching for the next one.

Finn Stewart sat on the sofa, a frown curving his mouth. "What the hell is going on, Maggie?"

"You told me that Mom read a book about a World War II spy who used a French record shop for passing secrets in the album jackets." She reached for another album. "And that she would hide money, letters . . ."

"We could be wasting our time, sprite," said Finn, waving one more album cover at her.

"Ha!" cried Maggie. "O ye of little faith." She held up a one-hundred-dollar bill.

"Good God. Here's a letter I wrote to her," said her father in an odd voice. His fingers shook as he opened it, a sudden, faraway expression on his lined face. "My darling Lily," he read aloud. He fell silent as he scanned the first paragraph and the shine of tears filled the old blue eyes. "God," he whispered. "We were so young. I loved her so much." He leaned toward Maggie. "But old love letters won't help us."

"Just read," said Maggie. "Here's another one. There's got to be a message, a clue, in here somewhere."

Forty-five minutes later, they'd found and read several of Finn's love letters. But they'd found no mention of *Dark Rhapsody*.

"One more pile to go," said Maggie. "I've been looking for . . . here it is!"

She held out an album cover that showed a beautiful woman in her twenties, seated at a grand piano. Dressed in a long emerald gown, her long, wild black hair caught back from her face, her green eyes gazed at the photographer. The title was *Lily Stewart at Carnegie Hall. Rhapsody on a Theme of Paganini, Op. 43. Sergei Rachmaninoff.*

"By God. I remember that night," said Finn softly. "The first time she ever played at Carnegie Hall."

"It's why I chose it for my own performance there. Tell us your secrets, Mom." She held her breath, removed the vinyl record, and reached into the sleeve. Caught her breath as she withdrew several pages of an unfinished, penciled musical score.

She studied the music, humming the notes softly, her hands shaking so hard that the notes and chords blurred before her eyes. The music washed over her, passionate and haunting, bringing memories in waves.

"It's the music from my dream," she whispered. "The rhapsody my mother was composing when she died. Her *Dark Rhapsody*." She turned, held the pages out to her father.

And then a pink envelope, caught behind the score, fell to the carpet.

CHAPTER FIFTY-SEVEN

OCEAN HOUSE
WEDNESDAY, OCTOBER 29

THE LETTER, ON pale pink paper, was written in her mother's scrawling, loping handwriting. The date was 1982.

My dearest one,

What would I do without you? I was so blessed to meet you when I did, to become your friend. And for you to become my confidante, for all these years. Yale changed my life. It gave me so many gifts—my music, Finn, my beautiful Maggie. And you.

I am sitting on the sofa in my music room at Ocean House. The rain is smashing into the pool outside the door, stirring the dark water, and the ghosts are swirling in my head tonight. I'm thinking about the people I've loved, the bad choices I've made, the people I've hurt. The people who have hurt me.

I'm going to ask Finn for a divorce tonight. He is so gifted, so brilliant. But too dazzled by the glittering world of the Maestro. It is his destiny, but not mine. What looks so glamorous from the outside can also be very lonely. You know the feeling, you understand. My eyes are finally open, and I know what I am going to do. I'm going to start over, somewhere far from here, and make a new life for myself and my daughter.

I've tried to put everything I've been feeling, all the chords of joy and sorrow, into a rhapsody I'm composing. Music tells our stories, that's what Finn always says. This Dark Rhapsody will be mine.

I've always believed that we remember the moment we meet the people we will love, the people who will matter most in our lives. I remember the moment I met Finn, standing in the rain in front of Woolsey hall. The first moment I held my beautiful infant Maggie in my arms. And I remember the first time I saw you, standing so tall and straight, in the Marquand Chapel Quad. You were—what?—all of twenty? Twenty-one? And I was, well, let's just be kind and say a bit older than that.

The Divinity School was hosting an afternoon of sacred music. Mozart's Requiem, Bach's Mass in B minor, Schubert. I was playing Schubert's Piano Sonata, and you were on the edge of the crowd, listening. Really listening. I can still see the look on your face. As if you saw God. You always did love Schubert. And Bach.

You came up to me after the program was over, asked me to coffee. I was so late for an appointment, but there was just something about you. Like a medieval prince, I thought, with the kindest eyes I'd ever seen. I never made it to that appointment, did I? And I was never sorry.

That was the beginning of our friendship. I think you were the best friend I ever had, my dear one.

And then, in 1980, we met Victor Orsini and all our lives changed forever.

It was Yale's reunion weekend, remember? Yale again, always the thread entangling all of us together. It was your Fifth Reunion, our Twelfth, I think. You and Finn were members of Skull and Bones—of course I knew, how could I not?—and they hosted a very private cocktail party in an art gallery on Chapel Street for their current and past members and spouses. It was there that we met Victor Orsini. Such a scholar, such a lover of religious art. But a man without a soul. He took quite the shine to you, didn't he? To all of us, I think. Maybe he knew, in some deep part of his heart, that he would need us one day. And that we all would have our price.

That proved to be the case. Victor found a fortune in looted art from World War II hidden in his mother's villa in Italy. He called Finn, one of the Yale friends he trusted the most, for help. He needed to find new, safe places to hide the art, far away from Florence. Finn refused, of course. But I, well, I will confess that I overheard Finn's conversation with Victor. Late that night, after Finn was sleeping, I called Victor back, told him that Finn and I would help him. I told him that I knew a place, a wonderful safe place, to hide his art. Finn never knew what I'd done.

And then I called you. You found a hiding place for him in southern France, an abandoned chapel, through your contacts. I loved Gigi's Matisse, the Dark Rhapsody, so much. And so I told Victor that my price was three of the paintings from his collection. I know you are keeping them safe for me.

It is very late. I do not know if I will mail this letter, or leave it hidden here, in the music room. I do not know if Finn will ever

That was all. Her mother's letter stopped in mid-sentence. Maggie searched the album once more for one last forgotten sheet of paper, but it was empty.

Finn put a hand on her shoulder, locked his eyes on hers.

"I never knew, Maggie. Never knew that your mother called Victor Orsini and told him we would hide that damned art. My God . . ." He ran his fingers through his hair, shocked, trying to absorb his wife's words. "But it finally explains why Victor was threatening me after Lily died."

"What do you mean?"

"In Salzburg, I told you that you weren't safe, that someone was after me. When your mother died, Victor contacted me, demanding back the art he'd given her. When I told him I had no idea where any art was hidden, he didn't believe me. Then the threats began.

Against my colleagues, my friends—my life. I didn't believe he actually would hurt me, but then—"

"Then he appeared behind me at the theater, and you knew his threats were real. That I was in danger."

"Yes. All I knew was that I had to protect you. I needed time to figure everything out. It's why I disappeared. But, sprite, if I wasn't the one who helped your mother hide the art, then who did? Who was supposed to receive this letter?"

Maggie sat back on her heels and closed her eyes. The answers were in her mother's words. She let the words spin into her head.

They are my favorite composers—Schubert and Bach. Who had said that to her?

I am at home in this simple place. It suits me.

And there it was. Maggie stood up, folded her mother's letter carefully, lovingly, and handed it to her father.

"I know who has the answers," she said into the silence of the room. "And I think he will have Matisse's *Dark Rhapsody* as well."

CHAPTER FIFTY-EIGHT

THE HAMPTONS
DAWN, THURSDAY, OCTOBER 30

HANNAH WOKE WITH a start. Where was she?

She reached out. "Jac?" she whispered. "Jac?"

Silence. She knew, suddenly, that she was alone. On a strange, narrow bed. Fear for her greyhound skittered down her spine, clutched her heart.

Oh, God, where was Jac? Where was *she*? What had happened to her? She couldn't remember. Her braille watch told her it was four o'clock. But a.m. or p.m.? She had no sense if it was day or night, no way to tell in the blackness of her world.

Think, think.

Use all your senses. You know how to do this, how to take care of yourself. Focus. Listen. Smell. Touch. Feel . . .

Her mouth was dry, she felt heavy, exhausted, dizzy, nauseated. Headache. She'd been drugged. She tried to remember the last thing she did, the last thing she knew. She had been sitting in her bedroom at Ocean House, preparing for the concert. She was ready, dressed in the new, cobalt blue sheathe. She'd bought it because the saleswoman said it matched the silk scarf Simon had given her.

Her hand flew to her neck. Bare. No scarf. Okay. No time for tears, no time to feel sorry for herself. At least she was dressed, could feel the clothing against her body. Her hand smoothed down her chest, over the narrow belt, over her hip. Yes, the silk felt the same. She was still wearing the new dress. Had to be a good sign, right?

Her feet were bare, spiked heels God knew where. Too bad, they would have been excellent weapons. But bare feet would be soundless, she thought. And better for running.

She moved her arms, her legs. No pain, nothing broken. Another good sign. Best of all, she wasn't tied up. Whoever had taken her had overestimated the strength of the drug. And *underestimated* her. She felt a split second of pride before the fear returned, full force.

Don't give in to it.

Keep going. What did she remember?

Being alone . . . The housekeeper had taken Jac to the kitchen for some supper. She'd known the way downstairs to the ballroom, had been gathering her music. And then—

A sound. A presence, *behind her*! A man's scent.

A strong arm, grabbing her around the neck. A sharp sting.

Oh God. She closed her eyes, sickened. *Jac, my beautiful Jac, where are you? Where are* you, *Simon? I need you both.*

She took a deep, steadying breath. *You can do this. They are looking for you. Help them out.*

Phone? No, she would never bring her cell to the performance. So it had to be still in her room at Ocean House. What, then?

Figure out where you are.

She sat up with great care, using her hands and feet to feel her way. She was on some kind of hard bed, or cot. A bunk? She felt dizzy, her body rocking back and forth.

She took another deep breath. Became aware of the scents around her. Salt water, oil, that unmistakable scent of shells at low tide. And then she heard the shriek of the gulls.

Gulls. She raised her head to listen. The clang of a distant buoy, the rhythmic clink of metal on masts, the high cry of the gulls. Somewhere, a foghorn. She was by the water.

She forced herself to be still, became aware of a faint rocking beneath her. Not her body, then. A boat. She was on a boat!

No throbbing sound of engines, thank God. And no voices. Was she still in the Hamptons? The harbor?

She stood, gingerly. When she felt steady, she slid her foot forward. Holding out her hands in front of her, and using the bunk bed as her guide, she began to pace out her space. Count her footsteps. To the left, to the right, straight ahead. Bow to stern. Okay, a small bathroom, a narrow galley, *steps*!

"Ouch! Damn!" Her hand hit something hard, and she barely managed to keep her voice low. She froze, listening. No one.

Okay, start over. *Just don't hurt your fingers!*

Should she scream? No, if there was a guard outside . . . *Don't think about that.*

What did Audrey Hepburn do, in that movie *Wait Until Dark*? She'd played a blind woman in danger. Did she have a weapon? *Damn, damn, why can't I remember?* Something about a doll—no help there. Light bulbs! Audrey broke the light bulbs.

But I don't know where all the lights are.

What else? A weapon was a good idea. Back to the tiny kitchen, then. Her hands felt over the countertop. Two bottles. Wine? She reached under the sink, felt a small can of—she sniffed. Lysol. Perfect. She slipped it into the pocket of her sheathe. Careful not to make a sound, she began to open and search the drawers. *I need a knife, I need a knife.* Empty. She remembered the bottle of wine, kept searching. *Yes!* She gripped the corkscrew in her hand. Touched its tip. Sharp. Could she use it? Yes. For Jac.

She tucked the wine opener through her belt and turned toward the steps.

Stopped.

The faint scent of cigarette smoke drifted down into the cabin.

* * *

The renovated, 1890s coach house was beautiful. Maggie stood on the quiet, stone-paved drive where horses and carriages had once tread, gazing at the ancient red bricks and the ten-foot-high arched door. It was still not quite light, the air dusky with soft gold. The sharp autumn scent of dahlias and chrysanthemums surrounded her in the cold morning air.

An image of Michael's face slipped into her mind, and she suddenly felt very alone, wishing he was beside her. But he was still with Simon. Hopefully they had found Hannah by now.

She glanced down at her cell. Still no news.

And so, she had left Ocean House alone, before dawn, arriving in Midtown Manhattan just over two hours later. Found a parking space not far from Madison Avenue and 53rd, and made her way to the imposing three-story mansion facing the avenue. Then down the curving alley to the rear of the mansion grounds, where the coach house was half-hidden in a copse of golden oaks. Surprisingly, no one had stopped her.

With a last glance behind her, Maggie rang the bell. Chimes rang beyond the old stone walls, a light came on in an upper window. Moments passed. Another light, just inside the glassed front door. The sound of a key, turning in a lock. The huge arched door swung open.

A tall figure in a long black cassock, the heavy jeweled cross on the chain around his neck blinking in the new morning light. "Maggs?"

His Eminence, the Cardinal of New York City, stood in the doorway.

CHAPTER FIFTY-NINE

EAST HAMPTON, NY
THURSDAY, OCTOBER 30

ONE STEP AT a time. Careful, careful. *Feel* the step, listen for a telltale creak. How many steps? Hannah tried to picture a small boat—had she ever gone below decks? Surely there couldn't be that many steps.

Cold air on her cheek. She lifted her face to listen, felt the touch of mist on her skin. Gulls, the slap of water against a wooden hull, the faint tap of rope against a mast. A sound above her, to the left. And then, once more, the drift of cigarette smoke. Yes, to the left.

Of course, Dane had left one of his men to stand guard.

Please let it be night. Please let me be invisible.

She took the final step.

A rasp of breath, a large hand gripping her wrist painfully. "What have we here?" The voice unknown, threatening.

She grasped the can of Lysol and aimed in the direction of the voice.

The guard screamed, dropped her wrist.

She wrenched away. "That's for Jac," she whispered. And then she began to shout.

Distant barking. Jac? Oh God, too far. Get away! Get off the boat!

She slid her feet forward, hands outstretched. Cracked into a bench, or something hard. She fell to her knees, raised her voice. "Here!" she screamed. "I'm here! I need help!"

Men shouting, running footsteps.

She managed to stand, turned toward the voices, two more steps. Three. Four.

A railing!

She grasped, held, gasped for air. Jump overboard? No, no. Climb to the dock. Were there steps? A rope?

She held on, moving along the railing. Touching, feeling, reaching . . .

Stairs!

Sobbing, she stepped up.

A hand around her ankle!

She fell backward, hitting the deck hard.

The man knelt on top of her, slapped her.

Hannah felt his fingers on her neck. She wrenched the corkscrew from her belt and plunged it deep into his back.

"And *that's* for stealing my scarf!"

The steel fingers tightened. She couldn't breathe! *Be brave, please be brave.*

A desperate growl. A whoosh of air as a large animal hit the body still on top of her, sent the man sprawling to the deck. *Jac!* Another dog, another deep growl, filled with fury.

"Hannah! Christ, Christ—Hannah! She's here, Mike!"

Simon's voice. Footsteps. She felt herself gathered against his chest, felt his lips pressed against her hair. Felt herself falling into him. She reached out, touched Jac's smooth head pushing against her cheek.

"I've been waiting for you two," she whispered. "Is my cello okay?"

And then, nothing at all.

CHAPTER SIXTY

NEW YORK CITY
THURSDAY, OCTOBER 30

MAGGIE GAZED AT her friend's shocked face. Robbie Brennan—her mother's dear friend, her confidant. Just hours earlier, after reading her mother's letter, all the small hints and pieces finally had coalesced. It had all been there, in front of her, in his church office at St. Malachy's. His voice still echoed in her head.

I visited Vienna when I was a divinity student. It had been *Yale's* Divinity School.

When I listen to Shubert and Bach, I feel closer to God. Her mother's words, in her letter.

And then there were the whiskey glasses—engraved with the words *Lux et Veritas*—in the church office at St. Malachy's. Light and Truth, Yale's motto. She'd seen the same motto on a banner above Zander's desk. Robbie had gone to Yale as well. *He* was Sugarman's missing "Yale connection."

She pictured the framed photograph on his office wall—wild horses by an abandoned, overgrown chapel in a lavender field. Orsini's final hiding place for art in France—found, too late, by Simon Sugarman. The sale of the ruin arranged via the Vatican by none other than the Archbishop of New York City himself.

I am at home in this simple place. He'd been describing the carriage house behind the Archbishop's mansion.

"Maggie? What's wrong? Why are you here so early?"

Robbie's words scattered her thoughts. "May I come in?"

Robbie stepped aside, held the door open. "Of course." He was watching her face, raised a concerned silver brow. "I drove home late last night. Has there been news of Hannah Hoffman? How can I help?"

He led her down a shadowed hallway, through more brick archways, into an open sitting room with soaring ceilings, reclaimed hickory floors, and a white, tiled kitchen on one end. A modern steel staircase led to a high, railed loft. The living space was quite bare, the few pieces of furniture very simple, austere. But several large abstract paintings graced the walls and a gorgeous sculpture of a horse was set on a wooden table crowded with books.

"Please, have a seat," said Robbie. "I'll get us some coffee and we can—"

"Robbie. I found the letter my mother wrote to you."

"A letter from Lily?" He shook his head in confusion. "What are you talking about, Maggs?"

She held it out to him. "She never sent it. It was hidden in her music room at Ocean House. But she names herself—and, I think, you—as the two people who helped Victor Orsini hide Felix Hoffman's art collection."

He paled. Wordlessly, he opened the envelope, adjusted his glasses, and began to read her mother's words. For several moments, the only sound was the tick of a grandfather clock in the hallway. Then he folded the letter and set his gaze on Maggie.

"My dear Lily," he murmured, sinking into the closest chair. "I've truly loved very few people in my life. Your mother was one of them." His head came up. "As a friend, of course, a very dear one. And you were another. Still are."

"You and I . . . we did not meet by chance, then?"

He shook his head. "No. I sought you out, because you were your mother's daughter. She wanted her relationship with me to stay private. But she asked me to watch out for you. After she died and your father disappeared, I felt an obligation to watch over my dear Lily's daughter. She never stopped loving your father, you know."

"I'm beginning to understand that."

"You are what you allow," he said as if the words explained everything.

"I saw the photograph of the ruins in your St. Malachy office," said Maggie. "You found the chapel in France. Arranged for the Vatican to sell the property to Orsini?"

"It was more complicated than that, but . . . yes."

"And then my mother—my *mother*—helped you arrange for several of the Hoffman paintings to be shipped here, to you."

"Two dozen of them, yes. Shipped out of Genoa, hidden among pieces of art legally owned by the Vatican, on loan to museums and churches."

"And one of the churches was yours," said Maggie.

The Archbishop nodded. "It turns out it was easier for me to abandon my principles than I thought it would be. No moral ambiguity for me! I was pastor of St. Malachy's back then. And there was a very convenient attic in the old rectory." He gazed at the abstract painting hung on the far wall. "It's a Lamar Briggs," he murmured. "I will miss it." And then, "Is your colonel on his way here to arrest me?"

Maggie shook her head, surprised. "That's for Simon Sugarman to decide. I'm here because—" She stopped, moved closer to him. "My God. Simon told Michael that the art hidden in southern France disappeared before he got to it. We all thought it was taken by Dane, but—"

Robbie Brennan gave her an innocent, choirboy smile. "My French friends may have gotten there first."

"Because of me. You knew—"

"Yes, I knew. That night you came to see me at St. Malachy's, you told me about your upcoming trip to Vienna. About Simon

Sugarman's search for the art. I realized it was only a matter of time before your agent friend tracked down the ruin. So I arranged to have the art removed. Unfortunately, the timing was a bit tight."

"Did your men hurt Simon?"

"Nothing serious. They had their instructions. He was only out of commission for a short time."

"Where are those paintings?"

"One thing at a time, Maggs. I may need a bargaining chip when Simon Sugarman comes for me." He shook his head. "But that's not why you're here—"

"I think you can help us find Hannah Hoffman."

"What can I do?"

"The man who has Hannah wants the Matisse. *Dark Rhapsody*. I told you about Gigi's *Dark Rhapsody* that night at the church. I trusted you. But you stole it, didn't you? You have the Matisse."

Robbie Brennan's eyes shined with sudden pain. "Gigi was *hurt*, Robbie! How could you condone that? She was your *friend*," she said, her voice too quiet.

Robbie's head came up. "She wasn't supposed to be home, Maggs! The men I sent . . . they thought they were alone. It was an accident, you have to know that."

"I do. Gigi told me so herself. But she would never have been hurt if you had not stolen the Matisse. A painting that belongs to Hannah Hoffman, not to you."

He remained motionless, staring down at his clasped hands. "Too many people have been hurt because of me."

"Talk to me, Robbie. I know you are a good man. How did this happen?"

"I am a man of God, yes, Maggie. But the operative word is 'man.' I am not divine. I am fallible, *I am human*. I have no family, I am alone. I have no need for material things, except for art. A reminder that there is still great beauty in this world. *Goodness*. The art makes me feel closer to God."

He shook his head, gazing out the window toward the mansion on Madison Avenue. "But how can a man who claims to have a special connection with God break God's laws? Is it hypocrisy, or faith?"

She remained silent.

He stood up, moved to stand before the abstract oil, gazing at the bold slashes of color as if they held the answers he sought. "Very few of us have faith without doubt, Maggie. Even in the priesthood. I have always struggled. Of course, I want to be madly in love with my God, but is yearning enough? Or did God make me this way because he *wanted* me to have ambition, to have pride? To wield great power in his church? To help so many in need over the years? I always have believed that I had good reasons for my choices, my actions. But . . ."

He turned back to her, his light eyes seeking hers. "Perhaps by challenging my faith—by *daring* my God—I have been convincing myself that I am right? And that I will be forgiven? Or is hubris my fatal flaw, my mortal sin? Have I twisted my religion to suit my needs? I have no answers. Only that I suspect I am past redemption."

"I don't believe that. Neither do you. You can return the Matisse, Robbie. Just tell me where it is. For my mother. For Hannah."

He looked at her for a long moment, then rose slowly from the chair and turned toward the stairs. "Come with me."

Together they climbed some twenty steps to the high, shadowed loft. At the top of the stairs, he clicked a switch.

Maggie caught her breath. The room was very long, with no furniture. Only the paintings. Framed, unframed, large, small. Caravaggio, Degas, Monet, Pissarro, Raphael, Cezanne—lining the walls in all their glory. And at the very end of the room, alone on a wall in a circle of light, a painted woman sat against a window filled with night, playing her cello in the candlelight.

"Oh, Robbie . . ."

A sound on the stairs behind them. They turned as one.

Dane stood on the landing, his pistol trained on Robbie.

"Act III begins," he said. "Death Comes to the Archbishop."

CHAPTER SIXTY-ONE

NEW YORK CITY
THURSDAY, OCTOBER 30

DANE STEPPED INTO the loft. For a moment, his expression flared as he took in the dozens of glowing paintings hanging on the walls. "Well done, Your Eminence. I hope you have enjoyed them. Because I'm afraid the time has come to commend you to your God."

"Who the hell are you?" asked Robbie Brennan.

Maggie stepped in front of Robbie as she turned to face Dane. "This man's name is Dane. He's a brutal, twisted man who has terrorized me, stalked me, held a knife to my throat. I told you about him, at St. Malachy's. And now he is here because he wants Felix Hoffman's collection. He's willing to kill to get it, Robbie."

Dane turned his wolf's smile on Maggie. "Did you enjoy the roses I sent you, Magdalena? I want to thank you for leading me to Orsini's treasures."

"How did you find us?"

"You are quite a good driver, Magdalena, but you don't use your rearview mirror nearly often enough."

"You should have died on that beach in France," she whispered. "I would have walked away without a backward glance."

The pistol circled in the air. Came to rest on the Cardinal's chest. "Ay, but to die, and go we know not where."

"Robbie is a man of God. He's done nothing to you. Just take the art and be damned."

"It's not enough, my Juliet. You ruined my life. Now it's my turn to ruin yours. Think therefore on revenge and cease to weep." His hand shot out, fast as a striking snake, and gripped her right hand. "I haven't forgotten my promise," he told her, his words silky and menacing. "Your fingers. You will never play music again."

He pulled her toward him, his hold tightening.

Crushing.

God, God. The pain in her fingers was excruciating.

His hands were like a steel vise.

Please God, not my hands.

Maggie kicked out, fighting to pull away, and fell to her knees. Robbie lunged toward Dane, and the pistol swung around to train on his heart.

"No!" cried Maggie. "Don't shoot him, Dane!"

A soft voice, at the top of the steps. "Dane? She called you Dane. What is going on, Dante?"

Clasping her injured hand to her breast, Maggie looked toward the stairs. A young, dark-haired woman stood on the landing, her hand protectively on her abdomen. Confusion shimmered in the dark eyes.

Without turning, Dane spoke. "I told you to stay downstairs. Go to the truck, Bella. Tell them—"

"I don't take orders. I repeat, what is going on, Dante?"

Staring at the young woman, Maggie heard the echo of Michael's voice in her head. *There was a woman—the doctor's daughter. Beatrice.* Sudden understanding flashed, and she stood slowly, holding out her hands. "My name is Magdalena O'Shea."

"Magdalena . . ." A jolt of recognition lit the woman's face. She turned to Dane. "The woman who was at the stables? The pianist?"

"I know about you, too," said Maggie slowly. "Beatrice, yes? You lived in a village in Tuscany? Your father was the doctor who performed Dane's surgery."

The woman's eyes flew to Dane, suddenly wary. "I don't understand."

Dane moved toward her. "Don't listen to her, Bella. Just go downstairs and wait outside."

Out of the corner of her eye, Maggie saw Robbie take advantage of the distraction to lift the heavy cross and chain from his neck. A glint of gold as his hand disappeared into the deep pocket of his vestments.

"Tell me now, Dante." Panic trembled in the woman's voice. "What does she know about my father?"

"Nothing, she knows nothing."

"His name is Dane, not Dante," said Maggie. "I don't know what he told you, Beatrice, but the Tuscan authorities believe he murdered your father."

The young woman's face turned translucent as water. She took a step back. "No, no it's not true. My father died in a car accident."

"The police in your village have proof. The car was tampered with. I'm sorry."

"Bella, let me—" said Dane.

"He murdered your priest as well," said Maggie.

"God's black diamonds . . ." Beatrice shook her head back and forth with pained disbelief. "The black rosary beads, scattered on the attic floor. You told me they were *your* beads! You lied?" Her eyes filled with horror. "*Liar!* You lied to me about my father. Dear God,was *everything* a lie between us?"

"No, Bella, please . . ."

She ran at him, her fists beating at his chest. "How could you do this to me, Dante? To our baby? I despise you, I hope you rot in hell."

It all happened at once.

Robbie lunged toward Dane, swinging the long-linked chain with its heavy golden cross like a medieval weapon.

Pop Pop Pop!

Dane's pistol flashed in the shadows just as the chain caught him across the temple. Blood blossomed over his eyes. As he spun away, his shoulder caught Beatrice. Stunned, she fell backward against the low loft railing with a cry.

Maggie ran toward the young woman. Watched in horror as Beatrice's legs hit the low wall and her shoulders slid back, out over the void.

Beatrice screamed.

For a split second Dane was frozen as the mother of his child teetered on the edge of the railing. Then, with an agonized shout, he threw himself toward Beatrice, his strong arms reaching, grasping her shirt just as she was about to tumble over the edge.

His body jerked sideways, lifting her away from the railing to safety. But his momentum propelled him forward.

With an astonished gasp, he hit the steel rail with the full force of his body.

Robbie burst from the shadows, arms outstretched, lunging toward Dane. "Hold on!"

Dane reached for him, clutched his arm. For a split second, their eyes locked as both men rocked over the railing. Then the steel gave way with a roaring crash, and they plunged together over the edge.

"No! *Robbie!*" Maggie flung herself toward the loft's edge.

A terrible smashing sound, loud as the crescendo of a symphony.

Then silence.

Robbie . . . She had to get to him. Overwhelmed by horror, blinded by tears, she twisted toward the stairs.

The young woman lay in front of her, so still on the loft floor, her arms locked across her abdomen. *What had she said about a baby? I've got to help her and the baby.*

She dropped to her knees. "Beatrice? Beatrice, it's Maggie. Where are you hurt? Is it the baby?"

Dear God. The young woman was covered in blood. Maggie reached out to check her pulse. "Talk to me."

Beatrice opened her eyes. "*Il mio bambino?*"

"I'm calling 911. Your pulse is strong. Hold on."

Maggie fumbled for her cell phone, dialed with shaking, slippery fingers. Then she pulled off her jacket, spread it across the woman's chest.

Beatrice clutched her arm, the single word barely a whisper. "Dante?"

"I don't know." Maggie staggered to her feet. Dizzy. *Don't pass out*, she told herself. "Help is coming."

She made it to the stairs. Slipped, fell. Her heart was thundering, sharp pain knifing across her breast. Somehow, she got to her feet. Gripping the bannister, she slid down the last few steps.

"Robbie!"

He was next to Dane, lying on his back. His eyes were closed, legs bent at an unnatural angle, like a broken puppet.

"Robbie, talk to me. Please!"

She smoothed the hair back from his brow. His skin was white, a sudden stain of blood smeared across his forehead. She heard the sobs, realized they were coming from her throat.

His face began to spin. She squeezed her eyes shut and bent her head to his mouth, listening for a breath. "Breathe, Robbie, breathe!"

Yes!

He coughed, light eyes opening slowly. Trying to focus on her.

"Maggs?"

"I'm here, Robbie." Sirens in the distance. "The ambulance is on its way. Don't move."

He moved his head, smiling faintly at her. "Justice and irony shaking hands . . . God is just balancing the scales. Don't be afraid, Maggie. It seems I am madly in love with my God, after all."

"Don't leave me, Robbie."

"See to Dane."

"No."

She touched his cheek with gentle fingers. "You didn't have to fall. You tried to *save* him. Why?"

"Blame your friend Thomas Aquinas." He winced in pain, gripped her hand. "God himself would not permit evil in this world if good did not come of it, Maggs."

She swiped at her tears, suddenly sickened by the smell of blood on her hands. "No fair playing the Tommy card," she whispered, turning to Dane.

Dane had fallen on his back, and he lay in a pool of bright red blood, his eyes open, glazed and staring. He was so still, she thought he was dead. She touched his neck, and he looked right at her.

She flinched, trapped by the glittering golden irises. Very slowly, he reached for her, pulled her toward his mouth.

She tried to pull away, but her body felt like water.

"Beatrice?" he gasped against her cheek. His lips were cold, hard. "The baby?"

She wanted to tell him that Beatrice was dead, wanted to watch his pain drown those terrifying eyes. But she said, "They are safe. She asked for you."

For a brief moment, the cruel face softened. He nodded, racked by violent coughing. Red drops of blood ran in ribbons across his face.

"Sin, death, and hell have set their marks on him. Bloody thou art, bloody will be thy end." His grip on her arm loosened. The room was hot, spinning. She couldn't catch her breath. She thought she was going to be sick.

She became aware of the sticky warmth streaming down her arm.

"Fly away, fly away, breath," whispered Dane, his eyes on something only he could see. "I am slain by . . ."

His breath rasped once, then stopped.

Shouts. A door opening. Running footsteps.

She stared down at Dane's frozen, disfigured face, at the bright drops of blood on his white, still lips.

Dripping *onto* his face?

She blinked with shock, suddenly aware of a terrible stinging, burning in her chest. It was so . . . Hard. To. Breathe. What was happening? She looked down.

Oh, no.

For a heart-stopping moment, she stared at the pulsing crimson stain on her sweater.

"Michael . . ." she whispered. Then the notes of the Rachmaninoff began to spin before her eyes. Faster and faster. She tried to move her fingers.

So heavy.

So cold.

Her sweater now soaked with blood.

Not Dane's blood. *Her own.*

* * *

"Sprite! Maggiegirl! Can you hear me?"

She was swimming in a dark blue fog. Somewhere, a voice. Beeping sounds. Pain. The fog was growing darker . . .

"Maggie! It's Finn. It's *Dad*! Please, squeeze my hand, talk to me."

Dad? Fingers hurting so much. She tried to focus, tried to think. Tried not to sink into the blue.

"Your colonel is on his way. You're in the hospital. Hold on. Hold on for him. For me."

Michael. She tried to open her eyes. *Too heavy. Stones on her lids. On her chest. Try to move your fingers. Can't. Please no. Not my hands. Don't take my music. Not again.* The cobalt fog pulled her down.

An echo of a man's scream shattered the fog. The loft! She forced the word to her lips. "Robbie?"

"He's alive, Maggie. And the mother and her baby are fine. But Dane didn't make it. That's all I know."

A large, warm hand, stroking her forehead. Comfort, safety. Like when she was a little girl. Sleep.

A woman's voice, murmuring. Mother? No. Gigi. Humming music close to her ear. Rachmaninoff. She struggled to open her eyes. *I'm afraid, Gigi.*

Swimming down, down into the deep blue fog.

Flashes of light. She could not breathe.

"Dammit, Nurse! Nurse!"

From a great distance, an alarm bell.

The sound of running boots, the sudden scent of the mountains enveloping her. Michael's voice, against her ear. "I'm here! Stay with me, Maggie."

I want to . . . for always.

The chords of a rhapsody, so beautiful, lifting her, folding her into the notes.

Music tells our stories . . .

"Hold on, Maggie! Don't leave me!"

I don't want to leave you . . .

Want to stay.

Stay . . .

She fell spiraling into the blue.

CHAPTER SIXTY-TWO

HUME, VIRGINIA
FIVE WEEKS LATER

"CAN I OPEN my eyes yet?"

"Patience, ma'am. All will be revealed." She could tell by the sound of his voice that he'd turned to the Golden. "Woman thinks just because she got shot she should get special treatment."

Keeping her eyes closed—trusting—Maggie smiled.

"Do you need to stop? Rest?" Michael's arm was around her waist, holding her close, as they walked slowly over a carpet of soft grass. He'd awakened her in the cabin before dawn, handed her a thermos of hot coffee, and hustled her and Shiloh into the car. They had driven for about half an hour in the gray predawn light when he'd turned into an unmarked dirt lane, parked in a copse of trees, and told her to close her eyes.

"My chest is healing, Michael, so are my fingers. Being with you and Shiloh is exactly where I want to be."

He drew to a stop. "Okay," he said against her ear. "*Now.*"

Very slowly, Maggie opened her eyes.

The sun was just rising over the trees, touching her cheek with warmth and dusting the bare November branches with new gold. They were standing on a small rise, overlooking a valley filling slowly with light—as if liquid sun were being poured into a shallow green bowl. Below her, farms, horses, fields of purple vines. The undulating hills spilled in ever brightening waves toward the distant Blue Ridge Mountains.

"Oh, Michael . . ."

"Shiloh and I have been planning this surprise since you got out of the hospital."

"It's beautiful. Beautiful and peaceful and perfect."

"I was hoping you would say that." He spread out a blanket, steadied her arm as she sank to the grass, and settled beside her. Taking her hand, he raised the still-bruised fingers to his lips, his breath warm and real against her fingertips. "Welcome to Hume, Virginia, in the foothills of my Blue Ridge Mountains."

His eyes swept the autumn landscape. "When I was a boy," he said slowly, "I wanted to own a ranch in the mountains just like this. But somewhere along the line, Afghanistan got in the way . . ." He gestured toward a small herd of horses grazing in the meadow. "'There's something about the outside of a horse that's good for the inside of a man.' Old man Winston sure knew what he was talking about."

"*This* is your place," she said, with sudden understanding.

He nodded, his eyes sparkling like granite in the morning light. "One night before you were shot, you asked me how I dealt with the darkness. And I told you I had a special place where I go, when I can't breathe." He looked out, his eyes distant, toward the mountains. "Been here quite a lot lately."

"You said you'd take me one day." Her eyes left his to sweep the brightening hills. "There's nowhere else I would rather be."

"Shiloh and I, we come here when we need to feel that there is peace somewhere in our world. Light, to banish the darkness." He gestured down the gentle slope to the right, where the horses grazed and new sun lit the roof of an old barn, turning it to bright copper. "See that ranch? It's been there for well over a century. Think of the history . . ."

Her gaze found the ranch, low red buildings the color of old brick, surrounded by acres of wooded hills and fenced pastures. "I can't imagine a more peaceful place."

"I'm glad. Because as of yesterday, it's ours. Mine and Shiloh's. Right, big fella? We're partners. Signed the papers just before dinner."

Shiloh's tail thumped on the grass in his version of a happy dance.

"Oh, Michael." She cocked her head at him. "Are you going to live here?"

"Nope. Love the cabin too much. We're going to *work* here."

Maggie turned to stare at him. "I'm almost afraid to ask . . ."

He flashed the crooked grin she loved. "Don't be. When I was in Afghanistan, Maggie, every night I'd look up at a vast black sky filled with stars and wonder if I still had a soul. I have the answer now. Shiloh and me, we've found a new purpose in our lives. We're starting our own business. A 'Shelter to Service' program. Dogs working with vets. We'll hire war veterans and their dogs, teach them how to help other vets. We'll train rescue dogs, similar to Jac. But our dogs will help the wounded warriors."

He touched his finger to her cheek. "Dane is gone, Maggie. It's time to start over. Leave the darkness."

"And does this new place of yours have a name?"

A spike of silver brows. "Sunrise Ranch."

She smiled and lifted her coffee cup. "To you and Shiloh."

Shiloh gave a happy woof and hopped off. She watched the Golden nose with interest through some low bushes, his gait uneven as ever, but his gaze now eager and strong.

"He gets his prosthesis next week," said Beckett.

Maggie nodded. "But he's already like a new dog. Bless Jac's heart." They exchanged a quick smile. "Has Hannah told you she's moving to DC, to be a cellist with the National Symphony?"

He grinned. "Jac will be closer to Shiloh, and Sugar will be closer to Hannah. Everybody wins. And speaking of romance . . ." He turned. "Shiloh! Come, fella. You're part of this, too."

The Golden hopped over and sat, straight and tall, next to Michael.

"Part of what?" said Maggie with a raised brow. "What's going on, you two?"

Michael looked at the words on her t-shirt—*Don't shoot the piano player*—and shook his head at her. "I still can't believe we almost lost you." He rubbed a hand across his eyes. "You had us all scared to death. Sitting in that hospital, night after night, I made a deal with God."

"You—and *God*? And no lightning struck you down?"

"I think he enjoyed having the upper hand for a change." His voice was gruff, vibrating with long-held-in emotion. "I told him that if he let you live, I'd tell you the truth. The truth about how I feel."

"Now I'm scared."

Something whispered across his eyes. Michael took both her hands in his, pulled her close enough so that they could feel each other's breaths. "Magdalena O'Shea. Maggie. Looking at you is like staring into the sun. You burn off the darkness, blind me with your light. *I love you*. You've gotten so deep in my head, in my heart—I am so deep in love with you that I can't breathe."

He shook his head back and forth, and she leaned in close to put a hand over his heart.

"You and Shiloh," he said softly, "remind me what it's like to feel elementally alive. That it's the simple things I've been fighting for, dreaming of, all my life. A woman, a man, standing together in the sunlight. A dog, braver than hell. A ranch in the mountains. Peace.

"Shiloh and I, we want to be a family with you. We want to come home every night to your music. Your light. We want to spend our lives with you. So—*I'm in if you are*." His silver eyes were locked on hers, waiting. "Feel free to tell me when you know, ma'am."

She felt the sharp rush of love and raised her palm to his face. "I can't think of anything *else*. I've wanted to say the words for so long. I *feel* them. But for me, it's never been a question of love. It's about trust. About fear of losing you. Because once I say the words, there is no going back."

"We all have to decide, ma'am, if this is the life we want to live. The person we want to love. The choice is *yours*, Maggie. Just trust me. Say the words."

"You actually make me believe that I can trust again. Believe in the future." Maggie's eyes met his, and she said the words out loud for the first time. "I love you, Colonel Michael Jefferson Beckett."

He wrapped her in his arms and held her close, his breath against her lips. "Say it again, darlin'."

"I love you."

FINAL CURTAIN

CARNEGIE HALL
LATE DECEMBER

THE AIR WAS electric.

Maggie stood in the darkened wings, waiting, gazing out at the theater. Carnegie Hall had never looked more beautiful. The faces of the audience were a pale blur in the flickering shadows. The circle of lights glowed above red velvet tiers that curved toward her like enveloping arms from all those who had been here before, welcoming her home.

The musicians were in place. The Steinway grand piano silent, expectant, waiting for her.

She raised her hands, shook her head at her trembling fingers. Stage fright. *Deal with it. You'll be fine. Just breathe.*

She searched the boxes above her. Her son and his wife, home from California with her new grandchild.

Sugar and Hannah, heads bent together, whispering. She smiled. The Matisse *Dark Rhapsody*, the oil painting that had brought all of them together tonight, had a place of honor in Hannah's new apartment in Foggy Bottom.

Her eyes found Robbie, black-robed and solemn, now forever bound to a wheelchair. Next to him, Gigi, resplendent in amethyst velvet.

And there—Michael Beckett, her Colonel, craggy as his beloved mountains, his silver eyes gazing right at her with that crooked smile. "I am so in love with you, too," she whispered.

The oboe played its long, tuning A note. Almost time. Her pulse began to race. No sound like it in the world, she thought.

A bright rustle of expectant sound, and her gaze flew to the stage. Finn. Her father, just taking the podium. Tall and gaunt, his proud falcon face carved and serious, his hair like shining threads in the spotlight. What was he thinking? They had talked in his dressing room, just hours earlier.

Tonight, you will meet your grandson, and your great-grandson, she'd said.

I can't, sprite. I don't want them to know what I did.

They need to know how much you sacrificed for love, how much you have always loved them. And your great grandson has your blue eyes. You can't miss out on that.

The clapping began, bringing her back to the present. Growing louder and louder, until the air vibrated with applause. A quick bow, a deprecating smile. *Welcome home, Dad.*

Any minute now.

Once more her gaze swept the audience. All those classical music lovers, whispering, expectant, waiting for the lights to dim. Waiting for Rachmaninoff. Waiting for her. Her father's words, shared so long ago, spun into her head. *Some night, Maggiegirl, someone will hear you play. Someone broken, someone hurting, someone lost or afraid. Your music could change that life.*

It's why you do it, she told herself. *Because you can pass on something beautiful. And someone will be listening.*

She smoothed the long, midnight-blue silk over her hip, adjusted the shoulder. Shook her tingling fingers. One more deep breath. Her mother's necklace, with its golden treble clef charm, was warm against her skin. She pictured her mother, Lily, seated at her grand piano, playing the Rachmaninoff so many years ago. *Music tells our stories*, she thought.

This Rhapsody is for you.

The lights dimmed.

The audience fell quiet. It was the sound of people *listening* . . .

Her father looked toward her, gave a slight nod.

Holding her head high, Maggie strode out onto the stage.

AUTHOR'S NOTE

Thank you for joining me in Maggie's world.

More than anything, I wanted to tell a good story, create characters with depth, and paint pictures with words. And, whenever possible, make the reader *feel*.

I never planned to write a sequel to *The Lost Concerto*, but everyone, myself included, wanted to know what happened next to Maggie, her Colonel, and Shiloh. Also, for me, I wanted to explore Maggie's past. And so *Dark Rhapsody* was born.

I learned the legend of the "Ghost Light" during a backstage tour of Sarasota's beautiful Opera House and knew it had to be part of Maggie's story. But while many theaters have Ghost Lights, Carnegie Hall does not—except in my imagination. All other aspects of Carnegie Hall, including its history, are as accurate as I could make them.

In the interest of accuracy, the Yale Symphony Orchestra (YSO) was founded in 1965 and celebrated its 50th Anniversary several months before Maggie and her godfather do.

As for the settings and locations, there are some places that just speak to you—

Tintern Abbey in Wales became the inspiration for a climactic scene in southern France.

In New York City, I have loved walking the High Line with my family. I remember discovering the Morgan Library on Madison

Avenue, with its beautiful Chopin score in a glass case, and *knowing* I had to set a scene with Maggie there. I felt the same way sitting in St. Malachy's Actor's Chapel. Robbie Cardinal Brennan came to life for me in that tiny church.

Cemeteries, for me, are a source of deep emotion and remembrance. I wrote two of my most moving scenes after visiting Arlington National Cemetery in Virginia and discovering a tiny Tuscan cemetery on a hillside near the village of Montepulciano in Italy.

Two years ago I visited Vienna for the first time. Touring the Vienna State Opera, I saw—in my imagination—Simon Sugarman standing in the darkened wings, waiting for a musician. Who was it? Hannah Hoffman was born at that moment. Likewise, when I learned the story of the Lipizzaner stallions, and stood near the Spanish Riding School stables as those gorgeous stallions thundered past, I knew where Johann Vogl would share his secrets from the war.

Many years ago I visited Salzburg with my family and was fascinated by Nonnberg Abbey. I can see Finn, conducting his imagined orchestra on the hillside above the abbey.

Over the centuries, thousands of priceless pieces of art, musical scores, and valuable instruments have been documented as stolen, destroyed accidentally or purposely, or simply disappeared. Henri Matisse's *Seated Woman*, looted by the Nazis almost seventy-five years ago, was recently found in a Munich, Germany, apartment. Almost every piece of art I list in "The Hoffman Collection" did exist at one time, and is still documented as missing, looted or destroyed during the World War II years. But the Hoffman Collection itself, and Matisse's *Dark Rhapsody*, exist only in my imagination.

You may be interested to know that, like *Firebird* and *The Lost Concerto*, net proceeds from *Dark Rhapsody* will go to nonprofit organizations that benefit our most vulnerable women, children, and families. Royalties will support inner-city food banks, education, health, shelter, child protection, the arts and economic development, with an emphasis on programs that promote dignity, independence and safety, and combat poverty, hunger, sickness, and homelessness. A list of these organizations is included on my website, HelaineMario.com.

If you are interested in learning more about PTSD and animals helping veterans, here are several websites for more information:

https://www.ptsd.va.gov/public/ptsd-overview/basics/what-is-ptsd.asp
K9s for Warriors: www.k9sforwarriors.org
Paws for Vererans: www.pawsforveterans.com
Battle Buddy Foundation: www.tbbf.org

And finally—the music.

As many of my readers know, my son, Sean, was the inspiration for Maggie's vocation and her beloved classical music pieces. I'm listing below several of "Maggie's favorites," many newly included in *Dark Rhapsody*, for those of you who love classical music.

Bach—*Cello Suites* (Yo Yo Ma)
Beethoven—*Moonlight Sonata*
Beethoven—*Piano Concerto # 1 in C major*
Beethoven—*Piano Concerto # 5 in E flat* (The Emperor)
Beethoven—*Concerto in D major for Violin*
Beethoven—*Symphony No. 3 in E-flat major* (The Eroica)
Chopin—*Piano Concerto No. 2 in F minor*
Chopin—*Ballades, Nos. 1–4*
Chopin—*Heroic Polonaise*
Dvorak—*Cello Concerto in B minor*
Grieg—*Piano Concerto in A minor*

Khachaturian—*Toccata in E-Flat minor*
Liszt—*Hungarian Rhapsody # 2, C-Sharp minor*
Mozart—*Piano Concerto # 19 in F major*
Mozart—*Piano Concerto # 21 in C* (associated with Elvira Madigan)
Rachmaninoff—*Rhapsody on a Theme of Paganini*
Rachmaninoff—*Piano Concerto # 2 in C minor*
Tchaikovsky—*Piano Concerto #1 in B-Flat minor*
Tchaikovsky—*Concerto in D major for Violin*
Vivaldi—*The Four Seasons*

And finally—I thought Maggie's story was finished. But now a new character has come into my head, surprising even me with a shocking secret that will change Maggie's world. To be continued . . .

CPSIA information can be obtained
at www.ICGtesting.com
Printed in the USA
BVHW081933250419
546577BV00001B/5/P

9 781608 093519